MW00355401

BATTLE OF THE BULLIES

Fenyx Blue

Author, mentor, coach and teacher Fenyx Blue has always been an advocate for bullying prevention. Fenyx is a bold, loving, unapologetic and evolving voice who refuses to be silenced. Ms. Blue is a soldier in the anti-bullying movement encouraging every phoenix in the world to rise up. Blue has witnessed physical and cyber bullying first hand so she knows that everyday people can stand up and make a difference to combat bullying if they only learn to use their voice or to act immediately. Fenyx hopes that targets of bullying will read her books and choose to follow their dreams no matter how difficult life seems. She wants to inspire students to support other students so that hurt people can no longer hurt other people. She created Team Bully-Free Forever so that young people can educate, entertain, and persuade their peers. In the battle against bullying, Fenyx remains at the front lines fighting for peace, tolerance, and self-love.

All rights reserved. No part of this publication may be reproduced, distributed, or transmitted in any form by any means, including photocopying, recording, or other electronic methods without the prior written permission of the author, except in the case of brief quotations embodied in reviews and certain other noncommercial uses permitted by copyright law. For permission requests, write to the author at the address below.

Fenyx Blue
fenyxblueink@gmail.com

ISBN 978-1-7353734-0-9

Printed in the United States of America

First Printing, 2020

To my favorite upstanders, Legacy, Khadijah, and Latarius Washington. You are everyday heroes.

CONTENTS

ACKNOWLEDGEMENTS

Thank you to those willing to read this book before it went to print. I appreciate your honesty, critiques, and your praise. I know the readers will enjoy this book because of your dedication to this project. Thank you for helping me to end bullying. I appreciate your support. Together, we will make bullying history.

PROLOGUE
Anonymous

I **can't be late.**

If I'm late, they won't let me in. I'll be disqualified. This is the year I win. I can't be disqualified.

I glance in the mirror and adjust my heather gray hood, slide on my black sunglasses, tug on my gloves, and step out of the car. According to my navigation system, this vacant house is my destination, and I have arrived. Eight cars are already here.

The white *FOR SALE* sign in the lawn gives me some comfort that we may be safe here, but this annual meeting is risky. Having all of us in one place tonight could mean revealing our identities to outsiders. Anonymity is our strongest weapon. We can never lose it.

I glance at the cars, trying to match them to possible members in my mind. One license plate reads QT PIE. How can we be a secret organization with our cars on display like this? How can we remain secret if members refuse to be discreet?

My phone says 9:59 p.m. I throw it in the back seat where it slides under my AP Physics book. I have to be inside this house by 10:01 p.m. Forget force, mass, or acceleration. I need to run.

Ten steps. I climb ten more giant steps, sliding into the room as the clock hand clicks into place.

10:01.

A girl locks the door behind me.

An envelope with my pseudonym written on it is on my chair. I am the ninth girl to sit down. I resist the urge to sit at the head of the table, but inside I know this is where I deserve to sit.

One year of effort comes down to this moment. I did my best. Ten people dropped out of school because of me. No one at this table should be able to beat that stat.

Last year, tears fell because of me! Terror reigned because of me! Break ups, friendships lost, hearts broken….all due to me! But will it be enough to be Number One?

We open our envelopes simultaneously. Three years, I have ranked in the top five. This is my senior year. There's no more time to compete. I want to win. I deserve this victory.

I slide the paper out, trying to avoid eye contact with the other members in the room knowing they will attack if they sense fear. Sadly, this envelope contains what I feared:

A Picture.

An envelope with a Picture that does not contain a dime means I have a new target for the school year. It also means someone in this room outranks me. It means I am not Number One. Last year's Number One did not choose me. She had the final say. I should have had enough votes to win if everyone voted based on the evidence.

One at a time, we slide our Pictures toward the center of the table. Strangely, the eighth picture I see looks just like the picture from *my* envelope. Do we have twins in this year's mix?

I look in my envelope once more thinking I might have overlooked my dime. Could Number One have made a mistake and forgotten to put the coin in my envelope?

I hear the sound of a dime hitting the glass table. The dime is reserved for Number One.

Number One rises from her seat and walks toward the head of the table. There are nine heather gray hoods around the table, but only she wears the bedazzled crown.

I watch her toss the dime on the table. When it lands flat on its side we are allowed to speak.

Silence is replaced with the sound of nervous chatter. I watch and listen trying to memorize each voice, height, weight, or any distinguishing feature like a tattoo or a signature scent. Nine heather gray jogging suits. No jewelry. No nail polish. Gray gym shoes. Gray socks.

I believe I may know the identity of everyone in this room, but I'd love to be one hundred percent certain. I have only worked directly with seven of them. Four years of battling with and against them, but I still don't know every member.

"Enough of the whining!" Number One exclaims. "The results are final. This is a new year. This is a new battle. We don't have time to fight one another."

Chastened, the room quiets instantly. Hesitantly, another member points to the two pictures that seem to show the same caramel colored girl with almond eyes and asks, "Are we...changing the rules? I mean, are we putting two girls on the same target? Or are they identical twins?"

Number One adjusts her black sunglasses.

"No," she replies with a fake British accent. "Actually, they are triplets." She pulls out the Picture from her own envelope, showing the group a face with an X drawn across it. It's the same face as the one in my picture, but the triplet in the picture has dimples.

Number One explains that the person who gets both their target and this triplet with the deep dimples to drop out of school will wear the crown. I know that person will be me. I don't care which member will rank last, but I will rank first this year even if it is only for a semester.

CHAPTER 1
Eris
Vita and Varsity

The locker room is silent after the varsity girls whip us for the fifth time since we've been practicing together. The silence allows me to channel my big sister Ebony's zen energy. I decide to give an Ebony-type motivational speech when one of my teammates says she's thinking about quitting and trying out for either dance or cheerleading.

Is she kidding? I've seen my baby sister Emani dance and it ain't easy to do. My teammate can't even make it through practice without her asthma medicine. There is no way she could do dance at C.I.A. Emani says those girls practice longer than we do.

I want to tell her that, but instead I stick to the Ebony-style motivational speech.

"Do you guys think those varsity girls were always that good? They were not. All of them used to be us. The difference is that they have not quit. We have. Some of you quit before we even go on the court. You think you've failed so you fail. Well, I'm no failure. I'm a winner. If you think you can win, shout yes!"

Two of my teammates shout yes. The rest sit silently watching the varsity girls enter the locker room as they sing their usual victory chant. Maybe I should have asked Ebony to write a speech for me because my teammates are more focused on the varsity's chant than they were on my "motivational" speech.

"1-1-2-2-3-3. No one beats varsity. 1-1-2-2-3-3. No one beats varsity. 1-1-2-2-3-3. No one beats varsity."

I hate their chant.

"No one but me," I say under my breath as I slam my gym locker closed.

"You need to turn that me into a WE, freshman," Vita Rowe says as she forms a W with her two hands. I smack her hands before I realize it. What's with these weirdos and the W's?

"I know what a W looks like, Vita."

Vita taunts, "W is for winners like us, freshman. L is for all of you."

I wait for my teammates to say something in our defense, but they just lower their heads like losers. Vita makes an L with her two fingers and walks toward our team's middle back Keyshia. Vita smugly places her L-shaped fingers on Keyshia's forehead.

"Say it, Freshy. Say, 'Today I'm a loser.'"

Keyshia lowers her head. "Today, I'm a loser," she quickly says in a very small voice.

Like lions attacking gazelles, the other varsity girls tease and taunt some of my remaining teammates until Coach comes in to speak to us.

"Coach, isn't hazing against school rules?" I ask and look directly at Vita Rowe, trying to let her know that she doesn't intimidate me. If she ever put her two fingers on me, I'd have two fingers to show her that she wouldn't like very much.

"Absolutely, why?" Coach tenderly, yet forcefully interrogates me like a good detective.

"Ask Vita," I say.

Coach demands that Vita explain herself.

"There's no hazing going on in here, Coach. I think your special freshman recruit is just confused. We were just giving the girls some tips on handling defeat." Vita could teach a class on lying. This girl is gifted.

Vita continues to fib, "I learned how to be humble as a winner from you, Coach. You taught us to keep our heads up in defeat. I was just sharing your wise words with the freshman."

Coach smiles.

Vita is such a good liar that even I am almost convinced as she strokes Coach's ego. Almost.

"You can ask the girls, Coach," Vita brags.

"Is there any hazing, teasing, or taunting going on in here, girls?" Coach asks the Fresh-Soph squad.

"No, Coach." My teammates shout this lie in unison. It is the first time I've heard them speak as a team. I just sit on the bench in disbelief as these traitors look down at the floor.

"With each defeat comes a chance for learning, ladies," Coach says as she squeezes my shoulder like I need a pep talk. She doesn't know it, but I have just learned a very important life lesson. Unfortunately, it was not to be humble.

* * *

In Biology class the next afternoon, my traitor teammate Rochelle pulls me into a corner.

"Eris, I think Vita Rowe is a Dime. You have to be careful what you say to her. She can destroy you."

"A dime? What's that?"

"The Dimes are a group of ten of the most popular and powerful girls at school. No one knows all of the official members, but I do know that they are all upperclassmen, and you don't want to be on their bad list." Rochelle whispers.

"Bad list! Destroy me?" I laugh. "Rochelle. Let me tell you something about me. I survived a school shooting and two school bombings. I lost some of my closest friends to explosions. I'm not afraid of a group of girl bullies."

"Well, you should be," Rochelle says as she puts on her safety goggles.

My biology teacher, Mr. Davies, interrupts our conversation when he asks for everyone to choose his or her lab partner. By the end of the pairings, no one chooses me. I decide to work alone, but I hope that this is just a coincidence, because I do not want to get into any trouble. If these "Dimes" have as much power as Rochelle thinks, trouble may just find me.

*　*　*

I am having a lot of trouble finding my sisters in the lunch room after Biology class. On Freshman Monday, there were only about 175 of us freshmen in lunch C, but today all classes are in here. It is already miserable having the last lunch of the day. Now, I can't find a seat because the sophomores, juniors, and seniors have beaten me to them all.

When they spot me, my sisters call my name and gesture me over to their very crowded table. I have been secretly snacking in class all day, but my stomach growls with unexpected hunger. I hurriedly sit next to them, feeling grateful that my dad made our lunches this morning. In between bites, I tell them about Rochelle's warning to me in science. My sisters laugh at the idea of girls naming themselves after coins.

"Can you even buy anything for a dime nowadays?"

"We should be trying to get coins, not be coins."

"She can stay, but you three have to go," A very tall boy with a full tray says this as he looks down at me and my laughing siblings. Alexis, who is normally in a world of her own, looks up.

"This is a sophomore table." the big guy says as he tries to intimidate me. I stand up. Sometimes I think my strength makes me invincible. This guy is about one hundred pounds heavier than me, but my pride won't let me back down.

As my sisters try to whisper something to me that I cannot hear because of the cafeteria noise, I remind the giant guy that there aren't any assigned seats in the lunch room. Then, I ask him to show me where his name is written on my seat. My Robertson confidence is at an all-time high in this moment.

His sophomore friends urge him to say some more words to me, but are distracted when a petite girl with a sandy-brown complexion squeezes into a seat next to me. She has a brown paper bag covered in grease. Her red checkered flannel shirt does not quite match her gray and brown dress pants or this season of the year, but she doesn't seem to care. As I am taking stock of her and wondering who she is, she does it. She passes gas right here in front of everyone.

"You can have the table, freshman," the sophomore boy exclaims in disgust as he and his crew leave. With a sense of relief, I sit back down, ignoring the pungent odor. I've smelled worse in the girl's locker room, but I am still a bit uncomfortable sitting so close to this strange girl.

"What's your name?" I ask my multicolored, uncultured tablemate.

"Kitten," she replies, and bites into a very greasy hamburger.

Then, she offers me her greasy hand. I offer her a napkin. My sisters act disgusted by the very sight of meat, but I tell Kitten of my fondness for protein. I know my sisters miss my daddy's barbecue, though they won't admit it.

"I'm Eris, by the way. You saved my derriere there. It's been years since I've had to fight a boy."

As she devours her burger, she tells me that she saw me confront Vita Rowe and her bodyguard Shiani Chan at my locker this morning and thinks I could have handled that sophomore boy on my own.

"Thirsty?" I offer her my vitamin drink, though I'm not fond of sharing with folks.

She finishes it in two gulps. My three sisters each introduce themselves in their own way.

"It's a pleasure to meet you," Ebony says with her firmest handshake in her professional motivational-speaker voice. No one would ever know my big sister once was a stutterer.

"Hi, I like your Libra earrings. We have two little brothers with September birthdays," Emani says. Emani can find something good about anyone.

Alexis doesn't speak, but she smiles at Kitten with her eyes, as only Alexis can. We triplets call it the Alexis twinkle. After we stare at Kitten for a while, I look around the lunchroom for Vita Rowe.

There she sits in what seems to be the Senior Section of the cafeteria. Out of thirty lunch tables, the upperclassmen seem to have taken around twenty tables leaving us freshman and sophomores to fight over the few remaining seats available.

As big sis Alexis plays in her food, I secretly wish that I could ask her for advice about this table situation. Normally, she would know what to do. She would have known what to do earlier with that big sophomore boy, too. She would have known what to say earlier to Shiani Chan and Vita Rowe as they double-teamed me at my locker.

I wish I could hear one word from her even if she just screamed at me. I miss that. However, things are no longer normal when it comes to Alexis. My oldest sister is not as brave as she used to be.

I watch Alexis twist and turn her spoon in her yogurt. Then, she gets up and heads toward the security officer who stands at the door. He speaks to her, but she does not utter a word nor make eye contact, so he looks in my direction.

"Should I follow her?" I ask Emani and Ebony.

"We all should," Ebony says as she stuffs chips into her purse. Ebony says the "no food leaving the cafeteria" law is unfair and unrealistic. She plans to change it if she is elected as Chicago International Academy's Student Council treasurer. Emani and I believe Ebony wants to be America's first female President.

I guess Alexis remembers the dean's speech about not having open containers of food in the hallway. We break free from the table of now twenty-five people sitting too close for comfort.

Kitten follows at my heels as I try to keep up with Alexis, who eventually stops in front of the library. When we enter, the librarian asks Alexis for a pass. Alexis reaches in her pocket and gives a pass to the silver-haired librarian. Passless ourselves, we watch Alexis walk into the library toward the tables.

Unable to enter, we all look through the glass. I notice that there are several available tables and chairs.

"Can we eat in here?" we ask in triplicate, expecting a "no" from the librarian. At my old school, there was no eating in the library, but then again, my old school did not have ten custodians like this fortress.

"Yes," she answers, to my surprise, "but you must be very quiet and clean up after yourselves, young ladies. And you still need a pass to enter," The silver-haired librarian points to a sign that plainly states: ALL STUDENTS MUST HAVE A PASS.

Alexis takes out a carton of milk and a honey bun and begins to eat. She takes an eReader out of her purse and positions it on the table. For a mini-moment, I could have sworn she had a smirk on her face. Though my sisters say we should leave, I stare at Alexis for a few more seconds before walking behind my sisters out of the library and into the hall. Emani pulls me away.

"We need to find a nice teacher," Emani says.

"No, we need to find a new teacher," Ebony says.

"Ms. Kelly is new and nice," Kitten says from behind us. I begin to wonder how Kitten got past that security guard. He knows that we're with Alexis, but why did he let Kitten out of that cafeteria cage?

"What does Ms. Kelly teach?" My sister Ebony asks, because she has all advanced-placement classes and does not know any rookie teachers like Ms. Kelly. Ms. Kelly tends to teach students like Emani and me, not those with genius IQ's like Ebony.

"She teaches regular social studies," Emani teases Ebony. They both have what my dad calls our "100-watt grins" on their faces.

"She is also going to be the new faculty sponsor for Student Council," Kitten says to Ebony.

"Well, let's go introduce ourselves to Ms. Kelly," Ebony suggests as we follow Kitten down the hall.

When we meet her, I quickly realize that Ms. Kelly is just as nice as Kitten said she'd be. Even though she's eating lunch, she listens to our pleas. She's also new enough to trust us and give us permanent passes for lunch time to do recycling or research for her, and nice enough to let us out five minutes early from our classes so that we won't lose any of our eating time. Nice and new!

Dad says that Aunty Jay should be my favorite teacher for life because she gave up her job to teach us at home and it wasn't her fault we were homeschooled, but nice Ms. Kelly is my new favorite teacher at C.I.A.

Sorry Dad, Aunty Jay can't get me out of that lunchroom, but Ms. Kelly can.

CHAPTER 2
Ebony
Head or Tail

"**M**s. Kelly, I'm here to get my posters approved for the election," I say as I proudly hold up ten of the thirty posters my sisters and I hand-decorated for my election.

Emani and Eris enter with the remaining posters as Ms. Kelly looks over the first few.

"Sis, some of the glitter came off, but the poster still looks fine. Do you want to keep it?" Eris asks as she holds up a neon-green poster that simply says "Vote for Ebony for Student Council Treasurer."

It's simple, but I nod a yes as my competition rolls in on her wheelchair.

"Charlotte, you're still running?" I ask.

"I may not be able to run, but I can run for Treasurer, Ms. Ebony," Charlotte says with a giggle as she unveils her small poster.

Her poster reads, "A Vote for C.G. is a vote for Victory. Your Money Matters."

I suddenly feel a little more confident in my own victory when I see she only has one itty, bitty poster, no matter how nice the slogan is.

"Only one poster, Charlotte?" I decide to tease her a bit.

I tread carefully, because Charlotte is very quick-witted. She rolls through the halls of C.I.A. like she owns the place and few people dare to comment.

"No, this is a flyer. My crew is putting up fifty of my posters as we speak," Charlotte says as Ms. Kelly stamps "Approved" on her flyer.

Crew? Fifty posters? I look over at my crew of two and begin to get nervous again.

"Charlotte's dad is an owner of Green's Copy Service and School Supply Depot, Ebony. She's going to make 2,000 colored copies of this flyer for free. She has yard signs outside, and she had her posters approved at 6:30 a.m. this morning at zero period like I suggested. Where were you?"

I try to hide my self-doubt as Ms. Kelly says this to me, but suddenly I fear that my homemade posters may not be enough. Where was I at zero period? I don't think I should tell Ms. Kelly that Emani, Ebony, and I were still making these posters. "I'll get the glue and glitter," Eris says when she reads the sad look on my face.

"I'll get the markers and poster board," Emani says.

"I'll try to think of a catchier slogan," I say as I read my own miserable excuse for posters.

Suddenly, "Ebony Robertson for Student Council Treasurer" doesn't seem like enough of a slogan.

"Ebony, how about 'Vote for Ebony Ellen Robertson, Big Money Starts with Small Change'," says Eris's new best friend, Kitten, when she enters Ms. Kelly's class.

"I like it, Kitten, but how did you know my middle name?" I pose this question as I look at Eris.

Eris raises her hand pleading guilty to giving away this confidential information. I toss a marker at Eris's head as Ms. Kelly talks on the phone to the principal.

I'm named after one of my mother's favorite comedians.

I think my parents were hoping I'd be a little less serious. Well, the joke's on them.

* * *

This week, my anonymous school survey seems to be a complete success. I've walked around the school visiting homerooms, telling them my story. Most of them somewhat know about my old school's bombings. I answer their questions and offer a few of my best ideas for making changes at this school. School safety may be my platform. I haven't fully decided.

The students have responded to my one-question survey in large numbers. The only question I asked is this: "If you could change one thing about this school, what would it be?" Replies can be anonymous, and are confidential.

*Long lunch lines—Why do upperclassmen
go first? —Anonymous*

*Theft—They stole my inhaler. I could have died
from an asthma attack. —Anonymous*

*Lies—I have never had plastic surgery—I am
not even done growing yet. Why would I need
liposuction or any kind of work done on my lips,
nose, or assets? No more lies, please. —Anonymous*

*Fees—I had to pay for books that someone
else ruined! —Anonymous.*

*Rumors—They planted roaches in my locker,
and everyone saw them crawl out. I was
humiliated. I may not be live in a mansion, but
we don't have ROACHES! —Anonymous*

*Favoritism—I may not be a millionaire's kid or
have a famous last name, but I deserve the same
education—even from student teachers. —Anonymous*

Teasing—Everyone says I smell bad! —Anonymous

*Confidentiality—They told everyone I had
to cut my hair because I had lice. I'm sure I
didn't tell anyone but the nurse about that!
She should be fired! —Anonymous*

Peer Pressure!!! —Anonymous

*Bullying—Check the internet . . . you're
on there, too. Sorry. —Anonymous*

Gangs . . . oops, I mean the Dimes. —Anonymous

As I look through the rest of the surveys, one name continuously appears: Dimes.

It seems like the students of C.I.A. want to get rid of the Dimes. That seems easy enough, I think to myself as I pull out my laptop.

For no particularly good reason, I wonder what is written about me online, and I search the internet for my name.

LMAO.

Someone is quite creative, but they have too much time on their hands. There are ten pictures of me with different hairstyles on the screen.

It seems somebody at C.I.A. is not too fond of my red hair. A few people have voted on the completely bald picture of me.

They must be joking. Ebony Ellen Robertson will never cut her hair completely off. They'd better get used to seeing red. Red means stop— as in, they had better stop while they are ahead.

* * *

In my head, I practice the speech I am giving today over the intercom. My theme will be "change," because everyone wants to change something about our high school. I get five minutes to tell who I am, what I will do, and how I will do it.

When Ms. Kelly hands me the mic, I try to keep the speech positive and light, so I highlight cafeteria conditions, the need for more extra-curricular activities, and ways to improve school spirit and pride. I forget to say my name, but Ms. Kelly does that after I finish my speech. My Robertson confidence is at a ten on a scale of one to ten when I realize I have just spoken to 2,000 people without stuttering or stumbling over my words.

*

I am very proud of myself until I listen to my opponent, Charlotte Jericho, a.k.a. the Copy Queen.

Charlotte's speech focuses on removing exclusionary organizations from our school, improving equality in all sports, and maintaining a safe school environment. She even says she will turn all of our pennies, nickels, dimes, and quarters into dollars. I am quite impressed with her ideas and try to shake her hand after the speeches are over, but Charlotte does something odd: she won't shake my hand, but congratulates me on my win.

"Win?" I echo. "No one has even voted yet," I reply.

"Oh, but they'll vote for you because you didn't mention the Dimes. I just hope that you aren't afraid to truly bring change," Charlotte says as she rolls away in her decked-out wheelchair.

I can't believe her subtle verbal attack on the Dimes went right over my head. My sisters say I'm the clever one, yet Charlotte found a way to attack the Dimes without being obvious. I have to find a way to do the same.

Today the students will vote. I hope that they will vote for me and not simply against Charlotte, but if the Dimes are in control here, maybe

Charlotte's prediction will come true. Maybe I've already won because they want her to lose.

* * *

Later, as I'm explaining problem number three from last night's trigonometry homework to the class, the principal asks for our attention. The class continues to speak until I yell for silence. Having survived a real school tragedy, I know the importance of listening to an office announcement.

"Attention C.I.A. students, the moment you have all been waiting for has arrived. The results of the election are in…" Ms. Kelly begins, until the principal interrupts her to give a typical mini-speech on the importance of voting and says that we are all winners, blah blah blah…

Ms. Kelly starts again, "For secretary, sophomore Kevin Salley. For treasurer, freshman Ebony Robertson. For vice president, Stephanie Singleton, and for president…Ms. Zyanne Jeffries."

As the other two freshmen in my math class clap for me, I watch Stephan Miles pull out his camera and hand it to his fellow school photographer, Myshell Mangun. Myshell walks over to me and takes my picture and Stephan shakes my hand soon after.

"Well, Red, we all know you're good at math. I just hope you can handle the job," he says through a fake smile. He's usually so nice. I don't know why he's acting this way today. He's the one who encouraged me to run for treasurer and to get involved at C.I.A. Maybe it is because we're in front of all of these juniors and seniors. Sometimes I forget that I'm one of only seven freshmen in my AP classes.

"I'm a Robertson; there isn't a job that I can't handle," I boldly tell him, though inside I am quite afraid of my office's duties. Will there be more speeches? What do the Dimes have in store for me? My mind is racing.

Student council is the brains of the school. It is connected to every club, major event, and student at C.I.A. Yet, I think I can do it if I take it one step at a time. Plus, to be honest, I love money. Student council treasurer is the perfect job for me.

When I leave trig class, I am greeted by my smiling sisters at my locker.

"Madame Treasurer, may I hug you?" Eris brags about my accomplishment as only she can.

"Ebony Ellen Robertson. Today, C.I.A. Tomorrow, CEO." Emani cheers me on as only she can. I decide to ignore the middle name part of her statement.

"Is that what I think it is?" Kitten asks as she points at something on my locker.

We all stop our sister celebration to look at my locker.

A crowd slowly gathers as Kitten points at a Dime taped to my locker. She pulls out a little checkered notebook that matches her flannel shirt and turns to a page with a hand-drawn picture of a dime. Words are scribbled beneath it, but I can't read them from this distance.

"Heads . . . Oh, that's not bad. That means they're watching you. Now, if it were tails, that would mean trouble."

As Kitten says this, I look past her to the crowd that has formed around me. It's like they appeared out of nowhere—sprung up like weeds. Through them, I see another crowd around Charlotte's locker. When I make my way to Charlotte, I see her take a picture of a dime that is taped to her locker: her dime is tails up.

As soon as I reach the circle around her, I am pushed out. By the time I manage to get back to her, Charlotte is sitting in her wheelchair, sobbing and begging for her phone. It's nowhere to be seen. The tails-up dime is gone, too.

CHAPTER 3

Eris
Lockers and Swimming Pools

My big sister Alexis's friend Jeremy walks over to me and puts a dime into my hand. What's with the dimes? First, Ebony has one on her locker. Then, Charlotte has one on her locker. Now, Jeremy has one?

"Where'd you get this dime, Jeremy?" I ask the boy my dad wishes were his son. Though they won't admit to being a couple, Jeremy and Alexis are holding hands in front of me.

"It was taped to Alexis's locker," Jeremy says, as a few of his fellow upperclassmen point toward our direction.

I can't help but notice Jeremy squeeze Alexis's hand a bit tighter and pull her closer to him as the upper-class guys surround us.

"Heads or tails?" I ask.

"Tails, but don't worry. I won't leave her side," Jeremy says as he caresses Alexis's shoulders.

Jeremy is so loud that I don't know if he is speaking to me or the entire crowd. Jeremy is a senior here and one of the most popular girls at C.I.A. is interested in him. Her name is Kylie Calderone, and she is captain of the Stomp team. Emani says Kylie is flawless: smart, gorgeous, and a talented dancer.

I don't know whether to believe Emani, because she's not the best judge of character and she compliments everyone that she meets. For instance, she thought that student council president Zyanne Jeffries was flawless, too. In reality, Zyanne reminds me of sandpaper: she's good at smoothing things out, but her default setting is harsh and hurtful. Like my dad always says, brains and beauty are nothing if you don't have a kind character. I wonder if my sweet sister Emani is wrong about Kylie, too. Do I need to worry about this Kylie crushing on my big sister's friend?

"Jeremy, will you point out Kylie Calderone to me?"

His face can't hide his feelings. His expression turns cold when I mention Kylie's name in front of Alexis, whose usual vague smile has suddenly disappeared. I feel like kicking myself. Will somebody please help me with my big mouth?

"Ebony," Jeremy says tightly, "Why would you want to meet her?"

"I'm curious about Kylie because Emani's trying out for the Stomp team tomorrow, and Kylie is the captain."

"Oh, she is that, but Kylie is also much, much more. Be careful, little sister," Jeremy warns, as he points me toward the south gym.

About one hundred prospective Stomp team members are stretching in the gym. I watch as a brunette bombshell orders the girls to line up by height. She holds a megaphone, but she definitely does not need it. There's a drill-sergeant quality to her speech and movements. Even I am forced to pay attention.

Ten girls step out from the line at the brunette's command, and she whispers something to each one. Emani's reaction to the drill sergeant tells me that she didn't whisper something helpful. I've seen Emani make that sour candy face when her dance instructor, Ms. Jennings, gives her mean-spirited criticism.

On the brunette's cue, the group of ten jumps, kicks, and flips. Then, the brunette shows them a dance combination, which they all repeat.

Still holding Alexis's hand, Jeremy comes up behind me. "So there's Kylie Calderone . . . Are you impressed?"

Kylie begins to stretch, touching her toes flat to the floor, then does splits that prove she possesses amazing flexibility.

"Yes, I'm impressed," I reply, "but she's no Alexis Robertson." Lifting my head, I look into her empty eyes. Alexis' signature twinkle is nowhere to be seen.

"I'm taking Alexis home on my motorcycle, Eris. I'll see you tomorrow."

"Hey, she's precious. Keep her safe, Jeremy!" I say as he opens the glass school door for my big sis. She'll be on the back of a motorcycle. I'll be on the bus. I could just imagine myself on a motorcycle one day, zipping along winding roads as the wind blew through my hair . . . .

My motorcycle mini fantasy gets interrupted by a student barging through the door. It's Stephan Miles. Frantically, I start looking for an alternate exit. Where can I run to? Fire safety codes means that there has to be at least one other exit to this gym, but I don't know where it is. I have a sudden, urgent need to tie my gym shoes. I'm hoping he'll walk by me and not see me.

No luck.

"Hey, newbie. Was that your silent sister leaving with Jeremy Sparks? You must really trust him."

I stand up, square up, and put my hands on my hips. "Actually Stephan, I do trust him. Jeremy is a good guy. He's like my big brother."

I want to tell him that my sister Alexis may be silent, but she's not stupid, but I decide to let him assume what he will about her.

"Good guy or not, Alexis is sexy, and that's hard to resist."

What business is it of his? I stare at him with disgust, then, wordlessly, head to volleyball practice. No surprise, Stephan Miles stays behind to watch the girls practice.

My teammates are already dressed when I enter Olympus. They all look to me for some motivational words, but I don't have any.

"1-1-2-2-3-3. No one beats varsity. 1-1-2-2-3-3. No one beats varsity . . . " The varsity squad chants as they head outside.

I slam my locker twice and sit on the bench in a state of disgust as Kylie Calderone's speech to the one hundred Stomp team hopefuls plays like a movie on repeat in my mind. Kylie was hard on those girls, but she was correct: sometimes things seem complicated, but you can do anything if you take it one move at a time. Getting up, I walk over to Angie and Karen, the only girls on the fresh-soph squad who seem to have a backbone. Though I ask for privacy, our defensive specialist Rochelle refuses to leave the locker room.

"Do you two want to beat varsity as badly as I want to beat them?" The girls look around. Then, they whisper in duplicate:

"Hell yes!"

"Well, if we can get two more people to train a bit more with us, I know I can get us a win." Karen taps her foot on the bench. Angie tugs on her wristbands. Then, they both huddle around me.

"1-2-3-4. They ain't gonna win no more," Karen says in her silly, baby voice.

"1-1-2-2-3-3. We're gonna beat varsity," Angie whispers through a giggle.

I usually reverse the e and the m in the word teamwork to focus on me. My goal has always been to work on me. My strength, my skills, and my mind, but now I'm going to focus on the we. Vita Rowe was right about one thing: It isn't about me, it's about we.

And we need to work on our strength, our skills, and most importantly, our minds. Varsity calls our squad mere mortals and themselves sports goddesses but we soon will see who the true goddesses are soon. I deserve to be here in Olympus. We deserve to win.

After Karen and Angie leave the locker room, Rochelle approaches me.

"You don't fool me, Eris. You may say you want us to win, but you just want to be on varsity. I heard you talking to Coach. If we win, we lose you as a teammate. You're going to join them, but don't worry, your secret is safe with me. I'll even practice with you, because I want to get better, but you can save the "we" speeches. You don't give a damn about us," Rochelle rudely says as she walks away.

Other than me, Rochelle is the only player who seems to try on the court. I have always had the feeling that she did not like me. I sit and think about her words for a minute, because lately, I really haven't thought about what would happen after the win. I just want to win. I have always won. Plus, Rochelle's right. I want to be on varsity. I want to be the best. I want that irritating Stephan Miles and Vita Rowe to know that this newbie is the best athlete to every walk on a court at C.I.A.

I take one last glance at my image in the mirror on my way out of the locker-room and onto the court. For some time I don't even notice Coach standing behind me as I look at my muscular physique and my ridiculously short hair. "I'm expecting you to score," she says in light tones. "You promised me a win!"

With a bright smile, faking confidence I do not feel, I zip up my Illinois jacket and race out the door. I'm thinking that we haven't won yet, but we *will* win very soon.

* * *

Two hours later, after an intense battle with varsity, Coach hands the winning flag to Vita Rowe again. Karen and Angie meet me by the shade tree with their respective best friends, Sylvia and Monica, to discuss our secret mission to defeat varsity.

Sylvia and Monica are both on my team, but they both are not fans of me, especially since I made our teammate Keyshia cry when I called her a weak-willed wimp last week. I apologized, but I don't think they've forgiven me. Rochelle stands behind them. I avoid eye contact with her.

"So what's your plan, Superwoman?" Ms. Malicious Monica says to me.

"Don't call her that, Monica. She apologized for calling us 'mere mortals' weeks ago. Let's start over," the calmer, nicer Sweet Sylvia says to Monica.

"Fine!" Monica agrees to allow the past to remain in the past.

"Fine!" Sylvia repeats.

I explain that we can practice at my house after our school practices and on the weekends, since my father has a workout room and my mother loves making healthy snacks for me and my friends.

"So you're going to put me on a diet and make me go to secret meetings? Now, you're starting to sound like the Stomp squad super soldier Kylie Calderone," Monica half-teases me.

BATTLE OF THE BULLIES Eris

CHAPTER 4

Emani
Stomp Out Payne

"I made the squad!" I scream at my sisters when I receive the call from an emotionless Kylie Calderone.

They ignore my good news and ask me to sit down and watch the news with them.

"Did you hear me? I made the Stomp team. I'm the only freshman on the squad. Is anyone listening?"

At that moment, I see why I am being ignored by my sisters. The face on the screen belongs to Princeton Payne, the man who helped Johnny Turner shoot up and then blow up our former school.

My sister always calls Johnny an evil idiot, but I think Princeton Payne was the mastermind. According to this news report, he's been sentenced to three consecutive life sentences today. He helped to kill almost one hundred people and he will live. I cannot believe it. I listen to her explain how his partner has yet to be caught.

A photo of the accomplice appears on screen: it's Payton Payne, Princeton Payne's sister. I don't really need to see it. I've seen it one hundred times in my mind. How can a woman so pretty on the outside be so evil on the inside? It has been over a year since the evidence against her went missing, then she did too.

According to the police, she may have bought her freedom. The cop who was on duty when the evidence went missing quit his job the day after Payton was released. He was found in Hawaii at a beach house that he allegedly inherited from a relative. The police believe that he was lying, but all of his paperwork appeared to be legitimate.

My sisters and I believe that the evil twins Payton and Princeton played a wicked game of rock, paper, scissors and Princeton had to take the fall for it all. We cannot find any other way to explain Princeton's capture.

Payton Payne is rich, influential and powerful. She does not make a mistake—or at least she hasn't made one yet.

Here she is ruining my moment, just like she and her brother ruined our school.

My big sister Alexis's eyes turn away from the screen when Payton's picture is replaced by pictures of the victims of our school bombings. Though she turns away, I can't take my eyes off of a very handsome picture of Alexis's true love, Zachary Thomas. He was one-of-a-kind. Jeremy is rare, but I know Alexis's heart belonged to Zachary that year. I believe her heart will be Zachary's forever. I think even Jeremy knows that.

"What were you saying, Emani?" Ebony asks, trying to change the subject back to my good news.

"I . . . umm . . . made the Stomp squad!" Suddenly my news doesn't seem as important anymore, as I look at my solemn big sister.

"Wow! Isn't that great, girls? Our sister is a dance star," Eris says, adding that that she's jealous because I beat her to successfully being the only freshman on an all-upperclassmen squad.

I appreciate Eris's praise, but being a dancer on a large squad is not as difficult as making the varsity volleyball team.

"There's no need to be jealous, Eris. I may have been the first, but I can't play volleyball or dribble a ball to save my life," I say.

"Thanks, sis, for trying to make me feel better, but you deserve to be proud. You sweat, you practice hard, and you put on a demanding show. That makes you an athlete, too." Eris says, as Ebony interrupts our mutual praise-fest by telling us about her new friend, Charlotte.

According to Ebony, lately, the formerly-popular Charlotte's been getting the silent treatment from some of her closest friends at school. Ebony says that no one speaks to Charlotte anymore, not even people who worked on her campaign for treasurer, since the "dime" incident. Charlotte believes she's being treated this way because she mentioned the Dimes in her speech to the students over the intercom, but of course she cannot prove it.

"Yesterday, Charlotte was stuck in the elevator for ten minutes before she thought to light a match in order to trigger the fire alarm," Ebony explains as Alexis gets up to leave. We watch Alexis zigzag out of the living room, then Ebony resumes talking.

"Today, Charlotte slid down the hallway and almost through the glass window in the hall because one of the custodians forgot to put up the 'Caution: Slippery Wet Floor' sign out after he mopped the floor and because Charlotte says someone in the crowd gave her wheelchair a slight push," Ebony says.

"Did she see who did it?" Eris asks.

Ebony answers, "No."

Emani jokes, "Well, I didn't see the push, but I saw the slide."

"This is serious, Emani," Eris says. "I think it is the Dimes doing this to her. I think that dime on her locker was a warning, like Kitten said."

"Well," I say, "I think I was attacked by the Dimes, too." But Eris and Ebony ignore me. Instead, they begin discussing who might be members of the Dimes. They think they know the identity of a few of them.

Didn't they hear me? Irritated at being ignored, I try again.

"Listen to me, sisters. It was after swimming class. When I came out of the shower, my clothes were gone from my locker. You guys don't have to take swimming so maybe you don't know, but we are all assigned a second, small locker just for swim clothes on account of them getting wet and all, and mine was empty. No one in the locker room admitted to seeing anything, so I was forced to keep on my swimming suit and walk to my other locker to get my gym uniform."

"You walked in the halls, wet, and in a two-piece swimsuit, and didn't get in trouble?" Ebony asks in disbelief.

"The security guard looked like he was in shock when he saw me, but he didn't say a word, so I got my gym shorts and shirt and put them on. That's when Charlotte rolled by me. I saw a crowd of kids at the end of the hall, but I didn't see a push," I explain.

There are cameras throughout our building at school, but according to Ebony, Charlotte refuses to tell the dean so they can investigate. Charlotte is determined to get her revenge.

I try to explain how I believe that revenge is not the way, but my sisters ignore me again. They both disagree with me.

We all want revenge on Princeton and Payton Payne, but I don't think Charlotte should waste her time on those dime-sized bullies. The Dimes can't really harm her. Can they?

*   *   *

Spirit Week begins next Monday, and the audiovisual team is already setting up cameras around school to get candid images and audio for both the hardcover yearbook and the video yearbook. I offer to help the AV girls set up near my locker when I see them struggling with the camera. I'm sure my height could make their jobs a bit easier.

"Hi, I'm Emani Robertson. This is my first year at C.I.A. I help my sister film her YouTube videos sometimes, and I would love to help with capturing next week on film."

They do not turn around and acknowledge me. Instead, they completely ignore me. I decide to repeat what I just said, only a little bit louder.

"Do you hear something?" The short one says to the slightly taller one.

"Nope!" The taller one says.

Before I can respond, the hallway TVs turn on and I see the two AV girls standing in front of me, except they are onscreen and giving a report on next week's events. Until that moment, I had always thought we had a live TV broadcast.

> "Attention students. Spirit Week begins on Monday. Let's quickly review the week's events. As decided by our lovely student council President, Zyanne Jeffries, Monday will be "Oh –No-You-Didn't-Day," so dress wild and wacky-tacky. Tuesday will be Professional Day, so pull out your Sunday's best or interview clothes. Wednesday will be College Team/Sports Team Day, so represent your future school/university or your favorite team. Thursday will be Twin Day, so dress like someone else. Finally, our favorite day, Friday, will be Class Colors Day. Dare to represent your class or wear your school colors of blue and silver. Freshmen, you're assigned white. Sophomores, you have green. Juniors, we'll see you in red; and Seniors, you'll be in black. This ends our announcements. As always, have a great day! Yours truly, the AV girls."

"Wow, we're good, Ciera." the short one says.

"No, we're great, Darcy," the tall one says.

They aren't wrong. They are good actresses. On screen, they looked nice and friendly. In person, they are not nice or friendly at all. I try to get their attention, but they continue to compliment one another without acknowledging my presence at all.

So I walk away, crashing right into the handsome and helpful Stephan Miles.

He grins. "Congratulations, Curly. I knew you'd make the Stomp squad. You didn't need that extra practice to be perfect."

Out of the corner of my eye, I notice a circle beginning to form around Kitten as Stephan continues to flirt. The crowd is making fun of Kitten's hair, clothes, and eating habits. Kitten does not wash her hair. She does not brush her teeth every day. Kitten's clothes are obviously not clean, stylish, or new. She chews with her mouth open and she isn't afraid to pass gas in front of everyone. She's skinny because she doesn't get food at home. This is because Kitten is homeless.

I figured it out the second week of school when I saw her washing up in the girls' bathroom early one morning. I was at school for zero period to retake a quiz and ran to the bathroom for a quick potty break. Through the crack in my stall's door, I saw Kitten unpacking a little hygiene kit and trying to wash her hair in the bathroom sink. I sat there quietly, not moving or saying a word because I didn't want to embarrass her.

Unfortunately, Mr. Peterson screamed into the bathroom for me to come out and said I had better be in his room in five seconds or I'd be getting another F on my quiz. I exited the bathroom, trying to ignore Kitten brushing her teeth. I hoped Kitten would understand.

She didn't say anything to me in our homeroom that morning after the bathroom incident, but later that day when we were in the library making some copies for Ms. Kelly, she tried to explain her situation to me. I told her it wasn't necessary and that it was her private business, but she kept trying to explain. I listened. Then, I offered to help. She didn't want my help. I had offended her by even asking to help her. Kitten remains a mystery to me.

How did these people find out that Kitten's homeless? How do they know that she basically lives at the fast-food restaurant she works in after school? How do they have pictures of her sleeping with her mom in their car?

"Kitten lives in a car!" someone says again as the circle breaks apart.

When they separate, Kitten is on the floor, crying. There are ten dimes at her feet, one for each insult I heard about her. I hold her as people walk by as if nothing has just happened. Once I have her to her feet, I suggest that she go to the dean, but she refuses saying she won't snitch. **S**ay **N**othing **I**n **T**imes of Trouble 'Cause it Could be **H**azardous to your health. Snitch.

"They know I'm close to figuring out who they all are," Kitten says between sobs. She rubs her tears onto her filthy flannel shirt.

"Who? The Dimes?" I ask.

"Yes, the Dimes. Who else could be this cruel?"

Stephan hands her some tissue. Where did he even come from?

"Who were the people in the inner circle? I couldn't see them. I could only see the outer circle," Stephan says as he examines the few people in the hall with his deep, dark eyes.

Kitten begins to cry again when she says, "It was some of my so-called friends. I didn't see one Dime. The people who did this to me were all people I thought were my friends. I only have a few friends. How could they do that to me?"

Stephan leans on Kitten's locker looking down the empty hall.

"The Dimes can get anyone to do their dirty work. They'll put you in the circle and expose all of your secrets. Rumor is that they give you a choice: either hurt someone else or get hurt yourself. Most people choose to lose a friend instead of exposing their dirty laundry," Stephan says as he gazes around the empty hallway.

"What did you choose?" I ask Stephan. He looks puzzled at my question.

"Choose? What do you mean?" He takes about three steps back from me. He has that surprised look on his face that guys get when they realize that my curly head isn't only for holding a tiara. I'm not stupid. I'm not a genius like Ebony, but I'm not ignorant either.

"You're a junior, Stephan. Kitten couldn't even make it through her sophomore year without an attack so I'm wondering if you have ever been inside or outside of the Dime's circle."

"Neither. I'm not quite an insider or an outsider. I guess they can't find any dirt on me. I don't have any secrets," Stephan says with a smile.

It isn't his usual smile, but he still looks charming. Stephan Miles is adorable.

As he says this, I begin to think of my own secrets. What would the Dimes dig up on me in order to hurt me? What would I do if they made me choose to hurt or to be hurt?

*   *   *

"No pain, no gain!" My dance instructor, Ms. Jennings, says as she stretches my leg out at a 90-degree angle. I want to sit down and get off of my sore tippy toes, but I try not to let it show. I don't want to hear the words *perk up* or *pixie*. Plus, she seems to be enjoying torturing me enough already as she sips on her designer coffee. She enjoys causing me pain now as much as the Paynes enjoyed causing us pain in the past.

"Emani, have you been sticking to our no-meat diet? You do remember that you aren't even supposed to eat fish or chicken. You can have fiber and carbs."

I nod, yes, since I am out of breath; I've been eating like a bird for two weeks now. I hate sunflower seeds and carrot sticks. I need a piece of fried fish in my life right now.

I close my eyes and imagine food dancing on my favorite turquoise blue ballerina plate. The food fairy asks me what I would like to eat when suddenly the dream is interrupted by Ms. Jennings screaming for me to tuck in my derrière.

"I can't tuck it in. It is attached to me. I can eat twigs and berries for a month if you'd like, but this behind is not going to disappear," I say as I gather my bags to leave.

"Quitting? I know you are not quitting when I assured Coach Calderone that you weren't a quitter. I bragged about your talent and work ethic, and look at you, Emani. You are a freshman on a varsity Stomp squad. Are you going to quit because you can't handle the truth? You need to lose some weight, young lady," Coach Jasmine declares.

My bags fall to the floor when I realize that she isn't only telling me that my butt is big, she told me that she used her influence to get that Kylie's *mother*, Coach Calderone, who is also my dance coach at school, to place me on the squad. I almost faint.

"You begged her?"

"No, I didn't beg. I gave you a recommendation. Coach Cassidy Calderone and I are best friends. I'm her daughter's godmother. Do you know Kylie? Her mom and I have been friends since elementary school. I didn't have to *beg* her, Emani. I just had to ask."

I begin to pace across the wooden floor. Then, I walk over to the mirrored wall where I watch myself lengthen my spine and adjust the line of my shoulders and neck. I have been dancing since I was five years old, and not until this moment have I considered quitting. Am I really any good? Did I earn the spot on the squad? Questions cloud my mind. I can't think of anything except questions, questions that I do not have the answers for.

If she finds out I didn't earn my spot, Kylie will destroy me. Every practice, she picks on me about my weight, my kicks, my jumps, and my freshman status. She doesn't like the way I hold my hands, my posture, or my facial expressions. I truly do not need Coach's daughter to come for me on this. I have to find out if she knows that her godmother Jasmine Jennings is the reason I am on the squad.

I decide to approach Stomp squad captain Kylie after our next practice, before she can ambush me.

"Kylie, I have a homecoming routine I'd like to present to the group, if you don't mind," I say as I raise my hand at practice.

Coach Calderone asks me to present my routine while Kylie frowns at me. I explain my entire concept before I begin to dance.

After I finish, Kylie says that the dance is too simple. She does not like my idea of dressing like doctors while we perform. Though I explain to her that there are several medical tools we could use to make beats in our routine, she does not change her mind.

"I don't think we want to wear doctor's outfits or bang stethoscopes together, freshman. The money we raise is going to cancer research, so I think uniforms are very predictable. Everyone will expect us to wear something like that." Kylie says, as the remaining squad members mumble in agreement.

Kylie continues, "We are going to give your sister something unforgettable to post on her little channel."

Coach Calderone addresses the group by saying that she believes my routine is the most creative and complicated piece the squad has done in years. She likes the ideas of the uniforms and wants to meet my mother to discuss using some old medical equipment from her hospital in the freestyle portion of our presentation.

When Coach Calderone finishes giving her opinion she says that the decision is ours, and she puts it up to a vote. Kylie asks our coach (her mother) if she could explain her own idea for the routine to the group. Kylie presents a plan to dress in pink. She calls it a "Pretty in Pink" presentation. We'd wear pink wigs and dress in different shades of pink. We'd use pink canes as props. She does not have a dance prepared, but she tells the Stomp girls that she will think of something that will make my dance look amateurish. The girls seem more excited about Kylie's non-existent dance than the imaginative and innovative (those were Ebony's words when she saw it) one that I had just showed them.

All of the girls vote with Kylie. I'm not surprised.

After Kylie and the girls celebrate, Coach Calderone stands before us with some news of her own. She thanks both Kylie and me for our presentations. Then, she thanks the squad for their vote. Finally, she gives us her reasons for overruling the team's decision. We will wear pink, she says, but we will do my routine. Her reasons were quite similar to the ones I would have said if maybe I were as brave as Ebony or Eris or Alexis. When Coach finishes her final rationale for her decision, we all watch Kylie storm out of the gym.

A few minutes later, I enter the bathroom where Kitten performs her secret morning hygiene ritual. Kylie is standing in front of Kitten's usual sink, staring at herself in the mirror. "Are you okay, Kylie?" I ask hesitantly

There's a long silence. Eventually, Kylie replies, still staring at her own face in the mirror, "I don't know why my mother is so crazy about you, but let me assure you that she is the only one. This is my squad. If you challenge me again, Emani, you won't be wearing a doctor's uniform, you'll be calling one." Kylie says without raising her voice. Then she splashes water in her eyes until tears start rolling down her cheek.

As Kylie studies the effect in the mirror, Coach Calderone requests her presence in the hallway. Without giving me a second look, she leaves, fake tears flowing down her face.

BATTLE OF THE BULLIES   Emani

CHAPTER 5
Ebony
Class Colors

"**S**he cried?" I repeat in astonishment.

"Yes, Alexis cried." Jeremy clarifies.

Jeremy tries to explain to me that he only left Alexis alone for one minute to get popcorn at the movies tonight. He says that when he was coming back to get her, there were a group of girls around her. One of them handed Alexis a folded piece of paper, which he assumed was some sort of movie theatre brochure until Alexis dropped it. When he reached her, he picked it up and he saw that it was her ex-love Zachary Thomas's obituary. Before he could match names with the faces in the crowd, the crowd had vanished. Zachary Thomas's picture had been marked with two X's across his eyes.

Emotionally, Jeremy tells me that Alexis had tears in her eyes as she fell face-first into his arms. She would have hit the floor if he had not been there to catch her.

As Alexis gazes at me with traumatized eyes, Jeremy adds, "I think Kylie Calderone is behind this, Ebony. I can't prove it, but she is so jealous of Alexis. She is so envious of our . . . our friendship. She asked me three times today why I was dressed like Alexis for Twin Day."

"For her sake, I hope you're wrong, Jeremy," I say solemnly, but I half-believe that he's right.

He walks Alexis up to her bedroom.

"I'd like to talk to Alexis alone," he says to me as he escorts her into her room, and quietly but firmly closes the door. I stay in the hall so I can eavesdrop on their conversation.

"Lexi, I know that you do not love me. Your heart still belongs to him, but my heart is yours. I failed you today. I'm sorry. I hope that one day you will forgive me. I came back as quickly as I could. I love you, Alexis Dieona Robertson, and I have loved you since the day I met you."

When I peek into Alexis's bedroom, he is kissing her, but she is looking through him. Her eyes are open, but she does not even try to return his kiss. She doesn't even blink. It is a sad sight so I look away feeling guilty. Poor Jeremy will forever be in the shadow of Zachary Thomas.

A few minutes later, Jeremy finds me sitting in front of the television in the living room. I don't think he knows I was spying on them. "Ummh, Ebony," he says in subdued tones, "I don't think I'll be around for a while. My band has a few gigs booked around town, but I still have to work at my mom's flower shop to make ends meet. I need to start earning some money for prom. College is around the corner, too. You know?"

He doesn't look me in the eye, but I know that he's heartbroken. It's been years, and Alexis is not over Zachary Thomas.

I think this is Jeremy's way of telling me he has decided to quit fighting for her love. He has so many girls after him. His friends are always teasing him about how Alexis treats him. I guess I can't blame him if he's given up on trying to win her heart. It is hard to fight a battle alone.

To lighten the mood, I change the subject. "Hey, Jeremy, is it true that you are producing the music that the Stomp squad will use for the pep rally on Friday?" I ask him this, knowing he will be spending more time with Kylie Calderone.

"Yes! Emani asked me to do it. You should come by the studio to hear it." The thought of Emani's jaw-dropping dance routine makes me smile. I can't wait to get it all on film. I'm proud of my sister for doing this to raise money for such an important cause.

"Are you producing Kylie Calderone's solo performance, too?" I ask as he begins to fidget with his helmet.

"Ummh…yes. I've been working on something with her, too." In my mind I am thinking that she has probably been working on making him her man, but since he seems uncomfortable I do not ask him anything more. Jeremy deserves the best. The best is my sister, Alexis.

"I'm pretty sure she loves the flowers you bring her and the music you play for her," I say when we reach the front door to the house.

"I don't give Kylie flowers or play for her!" Jeremy exclaims.

"I'm talking about my sister, Alexis, not Kylie. Alexis doesn't say anything to you, but she looks forward to spending time with you."

He smiles when I say this. I smile, too.

"The other day Lexi held me so tight when we were on my motorcycle. For a moment, I thought maybe she was enjoying my company, Ebony, but that's the problem. I really don't know if she was holding me or just afraid to fall," Truthfully, I am far from worried about Jeremy being a bad boy. I am more worried about Kylie Calderone being a bad girl. I believe she is a very bad girl.

* * *

Eris, Emani, and I look like angels in our white outfits today. Mom even bought us wings that attach to our shirts. When we get to the bus, we soon realize that we are the only freshman girls in white. There are juniors dressed as red devils. Sophomore dressed like green leprechauns, but no freshmen wearing white. I check my Spirit Week folder to make sure that our class color is white. According to the calendar, today is the day and white is the color.

The AV girls get on the bus after us and stand next to us, taking our pictures with their camera phones. I haven't quite forgiven them for how Emani says they treated her. Eris refuses to remove her feet from the aisle when Darcy purposely steps on her brand-new white gym shoes as they walk by.

After she is safely past my sister's feet, Ciera leans over and whispers that we are so lucky I had the school install the video cameras on the front and rear of the bus. I believe that is her sly way of threatening us, but I try not to react. I can't believe these AV girls are covered in red hearts and holding cupid's wands while spreading so much hatred. It is crazy.

Kitten gets on the bus dressed in a green checkered shirt. On her jeans, she's drawn the words, "Sophomores Rule," in green permanent marker. I sigh because she only has three pair of pants. What is she going to do after Spirit Week? Is she going to wear these pants all year?

We watch her mother drive off, probably toward some bank. Kitten's mom can't get a loan to start her own restaurant, even though she used to have an award-winning one in New Orleans. Kitten sits by us.

*

When Eris almost falls out of the seat we three are all sharing, she decides to take her new gym shoes to the back of the bus before they are ruined by everyone's feet as they walk through the aisle. Behind Eris, Emani walks toward the back of the bus like a supermodel down a runway. There are three empty seats in the back of the bus, but we all know that senior class president Zyanne Jeffries and varsity cheerleaders Natasha Nicholson and LaTosha Rise have not been picked up yet. No one dares to sit in their seats. Not until today. Today, Eris decides to trespass into their territory. I'm the one wearing combat boots, but she is the one who wants to wage war on this yellow bus.

When we reach Zyanne, Natasha, and LaTosha's bus stop, they step up onto the bus dressed in little black dresses that have white lace on them. Natasha and LaTosha are holding their cheerleading uniforms on hangers in plastic dry cleaner's bags.

We watch them walk to the back of the bus. Everyone wants to see what Eris is going to do when they tell her to move. I hope she will be civil, because I do not want to fight today. Eris is the one who takes karate class, not me. She is the one that bullies fear.

I don't want to fight Zyanne Jeffries. It has taken me meeting after meeting to even get Zyanne to acknowledge me as part of the student government.

Zyanne likes to call me A-boney instead of Ebony. She ignores all of my suggestions for school improvements. I finally had to go over her head and present my ideas to Ms. Kelly directly. That is how I got a spring dance approved for underclassmen.

Then, I had to fight for the video cameras on the bus, the site of so many fights instigated by the Dimes. Since no one would tell what they saw to the deans, I suggested the cameras. The deans were happy to help me raise the money for the cameras with my car wash. They made the Saturday detention people wash the cars for me. It was a complete success. The detention boys were okay with me once they saw Emani's dance crew show up to help with the car wash. I don't know if the boys did more watching or more washing, but we made money.

I am still working on another elevator for our handicapped classmates and elderly visitors to the school. Charlotte wants wider doorways and is always in my ear about the one percent of our school population who get ignored because they are obese or handicapped. Charlotte won't let me get a minute's rest. She rolls beside me and doesn't mind stopping in front of me with suggestions for equity at C.I.A. I'm just happy she is speaking to me again.

The day after my cafeteria plan failed, Charlotte was eager to suggest some alternatives. I had asked the homeroom teachers to assign students to certain seats in the lunchroom, since each homeroom has about twenty kids and each table seats about twenty kids.

It sounded like it would work, but it did not. The teachers thought it was too much work to check IDs every day during lunch time to make sure everyone was sitting where they should be. Therefore, they asked kids to sit with their homeroom classmates on the honor system.

Honor? The teachers actually trusted the students to do the right thing. So of course, the fresh-soph students still squeezed themselves onto the back tables or avoided lunch all together for fear of being in a fight, and the upperclassmen continued to sit as comfortably as they had been sitting since their first day of school, which means they sat wherever they wanted to sit.

"Sit down or fight. Make a choice," the young, wild, reckless bus driver says to Zyanne, LaTosha, and NaTasha, who stand in the aisle ordering my sister to move from her seat. How does he focus on driving with music in his ears? Is he supposed to wear those earbuds while driving?

"There's only room for one more and I was here first. So two of you need to grab your brooms and hats and go to the front," Eris says in matter-of-fact tones.

"We're not witches, we're French maids, angel," LaTosha says as she tries to touch Eris's wings.

"Well, you witches could have fooled me, but let me assure you that I am not an angel," Eris replies, but does not move.

A brief stare-down later, NaTasha and LaTosha decide to move two seats up and order some other freshmen to move. The boys move. I don't know what Zyanne says to Eris, but she sits down in the seat next to Eris.

I don't know all of what they say to one another since our reckless driver makes me sit down before I can read any lips (It's a special talent that Eris learned on the court and taught me so that we could frustrate Emani), but when we reach the school, Zyanne suddenly speaks to me. We have had countless meetings, but she has never spoken to me. We have worked hard together for all of C.I.A.'s activities this year, but she has never spoken to me. One word from Eris and suddenly President Zyanne's speaking to me. Wow!

"I'll see you at the pep rally, Ebony," Zyanne says with a wave. She calls me Ebony, instead of her usual A-boney. Wow! What did Eris say to this girl?

Charlotte rolls up behind us as Emani and I wave back to Zyanne. We are both baffled.

"My enemy is your friend?" Charlotte says. She is wearing a neon green wig and green lipstick. Charlotte has tied a scarf with green dollar bills on it to her wheelchair. She has her usual green book bag in her lap.

"Have you seen anyone else in white?" Emani asks.

"About a dozen foolish freshman like yourselves," Charlotte teases.

"You're calling us fools. What's up with that dollar bill across your chest?"

"You know me. I'm about making dollars. I don't care about dimes," Charlotte says.

When she says this, she turns her upper torso, showing us the back of her t-shirt, which has pennies, nickels, quarters, and dimes crossed out on it. We all stare at the ten dimes with the x across them. Then, we look at each other.

"Well, there's going to be dimes on all of our lockers when we go in there aren't there?" Eris says.

"Yup!" Charlotte reports.

"Well, let's go in anyway," I say.

"Let's!" My sisters agree.

Charlotte doesn't say the words, but I think her shirt says enough.

CHAPTER 6
Eris
When the Lights Go Off

When we are dismissed from class, I walk to the gym for the pep rally. I feel at home in the gym. The gym is my happy place. Yolanda Reese approaches me and asks if she can tell me something.

"Eris, the rumor is that anyone wearing white will be sprayed with puffy paint during the rally."

"Thanks Yo-Yo, I owe you one," I say.

"You don't owe me anything, Eris."

Yolanda and I met in Spanish class. She was retaking the class and was the worst speaker in the class. My teacher asked me to tutor her. I invited her to our house to speak Spanish with my family, and she loved it. In about one hour, my sisters and I taught her everything she needed to know to survive Spanish class. We've all taken Spanish since kindergarten and are fluent. Aunty Jay is stubborn, but she was a great Spanish teacher. She truly brought Spanish alive for us.

I used Aunty Jay's teaching techniques to tutor Yo-Yo. After tutoring Yo-Yo for a little while, I noticed that Yolanda tried to pay for everything. No matter where we went after that Spanish tutorial hour, she would try to buy me something. My sisters and I took her to my friend's house party one weekend so she could have an authentic conversation with some friends from our old school who happened to be Latino, and the entire day she offered to pay for our food, our bus fair, and even our outfits for the party we were going to that night. I told her that she had to stop it because it was not necessary, and she started to cry. Yo-Yo is one of those kids at C.I.A. who were selected for admission to the school because of their parents' deep pockets. Kids at school took advantage of her generosity before she met me.

Tutoring Yo-Yo is how I learned that Yolanda was dating student government president Zyanne Jeffries' younger brother, Zechariah. Yo-Yo said when she was with Zechariah and Zyanne's friends, she found herself paying for everything. I was disgusted.

Now, I've seen Zechariah Jeffries, and he is the most popular sophomore at school for many superficial reasons: his pretty face, his big arms, his tattoos, and his earring. So I understood why Yolanda wouldn't want to lose him, but she had to be true to herself. I asked her to stop paying for things. I suggested that she go out to dinner with him, then say that she forgot to bring her purse. That way, she would find out if he really cared about her for the person she was and not for how much money she would spend on him and his crew.

Well. According to Yolanda, Zechariah did notice after about a week that she seemed to always "forget" her purse, so then, on one date, she didn't return, he called her from outside her front door on his cell phone. That's when she told him that she was tired of paying for their dates. I thought that she was quite courageous. Some girls would never risk losing their boyfriend, no matter how badly he was treating them.

Yo-Yo told me that Zechariah rang her bell about twenty times after her confession on the phone until she came back downstairs and that he told her that she wouldn't have to worry about paying anymore. He asked her on another date. She chose the place, and he volunteered to pay.

*

Today, on our first Class Colors Spirit Day in high school, Zechariah Jeffries grabs Yolanda's hand and they walk off into the gymnasium together. After I log them as the cutest couple at school in my mind, I find my sisters and tell them about the puffy paint issue.

We all look down at our brand-new outfits. We are having a triplicate moment, thinking the same thing right now: I don't want to risk ruining this outfit. This outfit is brand new. My shoes have already been abused by these people. This outfit will not be victimized.

Before we enter the gym, I can see Zyanne Jeffries on stage at the microphone. Zechariah's big sister President Zyanne is going to be this year's homecoming rally emcee. Ebony walks toward her, leaving us to find our seats. Emani and I walk toward the bleachers. The next sound I hear is my sister's voice on the mic.

"Freshman, the student council is asking you to sit on the front right. Sophomores, please sit on the back right. Juniors, you need to sit on the front left, and seniors, you need to sit on the back left." Ebony repeats this about ten times until everyone is seated.

Then, I watch her hand the microphone back to Zyanne, who does not look very happy about Ebony taking control of the microphone without permission.

"I can't believe you did that, Sis," I comment when Ebony takes her place beside Emani and me. I can't believe Ebony boldly spoke in front of everyone. She didn't even stutter. She sometimes does that when she gets nervous. It was bold to change the entire gym's seating arrangement. We can usually sit wherever we want for pep assemblies.

"Neither can I, but I thought we'd have a better chance of not getting puffy-painted if we were sitting by our fellow freshmen," Ebony says, as she looks around us at all of the freshmen teachers who are sitting behind us.

I whisper in her ear. "I think what you did was smart, but what I did was smarter. The Dimes can even get freshmen to put paint on us, but I doubt that they can get anyone to do it in front of all of these teachers." I'm the one who lied to the teachers and told them our principal said they should sit on the highest bleachers in the back.

Ebony looks back at all of the teachers sitting behind us, smiling at them. Then, she laughs.

Ebony questions, "Eris, I think you're the smart one. Does that mean I have to be the athletic one?"

"You couldn't be athletic if you tried. You're the most uncoordinated person I know, Ebony, but I love ya," I respond as we share a fist bump.

When the lights go off, the AV girls present their audiovisual footage from the first few weeks of school. I see a few of the pictures that Stephan took of me alongside their clips. I am so happy that he doesn't show the picture of my feet.

The video is like a tribute to the upperclassmen at our school, with a few images of a few of us freshman thrown in just to appear to be fair, but it is still well done. The pictures seem to tell a story of the start of school. The AV girls are very talented. They don't like me or my sisters, but I admire their work.

Everyone cheers when the film ends with the words, "More to Come." The lights come on. The darkness is replaced by our gym's dim, yellow light. The school must really save money on electricity, because this gym is never bright or filled with light.

About ten rows down, I see that the back of Tyra Jacobs's white jacket is covered in spray paint when she stands up to clap for the film. There are about ten other girls standing with the number ten on their backs. When all of the freshman realize what has happened, they begin to boo. All the other sections in the gym cheer.

I look at my sisters, who are already looking at me. Then, I slowly turn in an attempt to look at my own back, even though there are teachers behind me.

"There's nothing there, Eris. I can't believe they would use spray paint. I thought they'd use something that will wash out. Didn't they smell it? Didn't they hear it? Didn't they feel it?" Einstein Ebony asks.

The security guards remove the ten girls and a few of the girls that are sitting around them from the pep rally. A couple of the teachers leave from behind us, probably to go question the girls.

I ask one of the teachers if I can go to the bathroom. She believes I have to go since I am shaking my leg and holding my bladder like I could explode at any moment. With her permission, I force my way down the crowded bleachers filled with either curious, culpable, or confused freshmen.

The teacher who gave me permission to leave watches me from the top of the bleachers until I enter the bathroom, which is under the stage area.

When I get in the bathroom, I peek back out to see if the teacher is still looking. She isn't, so I follow the line of ten girls toward the dean's office.

"What are you doing here, Eris?" Tyra asks. The number ten is black and bigger than it seemed from my seat at the top of the bleachers.

"Isn't there a ten on my back?" I ask Tyra, though I know there isn't.

Tyra frowns at me. "No."

"Oh, well . . . umm, I was just curious. Tyra, didn't you hear it? Didn't you feel it? Didn't you smell it?"

"What? The paint? Yes! But they said if I did this I would be safe all year. So I ignored it and I stood up like they told me to do," Tyra whispers as we walk.

"Who told you to do that?" I ask.

"The girls who were sitting behind me," she explains.

A teacher sees us talking and comes over to search me. The teacher recognizes me from the AV girls' footage of me in our daily broadcasts. She tells me not to say another word to Tyra. Suddenly I think that maybe sneaking into this line was a bad idea. I watch the other line of girls who were sitting around the terrible ten enter the deans' office. They look nervous. I didn't even do anything, but I am nervous, too.

When we reach the deans' office, we are brought to a conference room that all four deans share. They ask us what happened and no one says a word. They search everyone, and no one has anything in their purses or pockets.

"Well, maybe we'll have to conduct a scientific investigation and test your fingertips. Someone here has sprayed spray paint," Dean Norton says, as my science teacher comes in the door. Behind Mr. Davies is the teacher who gave me permission to go to the bathroom. The teacher frowns at me and shakes her head in the disappointed way my dad does when I don't know which tool to get when we are working on one of his classic cars.

Mr. Davies asks, "What are you doing in here, young lady? Do you want to be suspended?"

"Umm . . . ."

The teacher who gave me permission to leave asks, "What's your name?"

"Umm . . . Eris Robertson."

"Well Ms. Umm Eris Robertson, you have a detention with me Monday. You can go," the teacher says to me, as Mr. Davies frowns.

As I turn to leave, I look around at girls who I see in my classes all day long. They all know one another. They are all friends with at least one other person in this room. I can't believe they would do this to one another. Half of them are going to get suspended and the other half have just been humiliated, but the sad part is that the Dimes are probably in the gym enjoying the pep rally. I have to figure out who the Dimes are before they do something to me. I know exactly who to go to for help.

CHAPTER 7

Emani
Costumes and Cases

"Could someone please help me get these boys ready?" I scream as I try to put my twin brothers' superhero Halloween costumes on.

The twin terrors won't be still. They are already so full of Halloween sugar that I don't know why we are taking them to the mall to trick or treat. If mom hadn't given me some shopping money, I would not be anywhere near these little spoiled brats tonight. I always get stuck doing all of the work around this house.

"Should I just do it myself, Emani?" My mother says as she peeks into our room.

Mom looks so beautiful in her Queen of Hearts costume. I can't believe that she made it herself. I'm beginning to regret my decision to wear a store-bought costume this year. Maybe I should have let mom make mine, like my sisters did.

Ebony walks by in her sparkling mermaid suit and lifts her tail when she sees me admiring her costume. The costume hugs her every curve. I am so jealous. I wanted to flaunt my physique tonight, too.

"Can you fix this feather, Emani? I want to look like a 1920's flapper, not a peacock," Eris asks. I can't believe she's wearing fringe, sequins, and a boa. That should have been my costume. I look great in iridescent sequins. One of my dance costumes was covered in sequins.

Suddenly, I am considering giving my share of the shopping money Mom promised to give us for babysitting the twins to my sisters and staying home alone. Dad and Mom will be at their grown-up party and the twins (Tevin and Kevin), Alexis, Ebony, and Eris can go to the mall. I'll just stay here and give candy to the neighborhood kids so they won't toilet paper our house or something. Some houses had eggs thrown last year for leaving an empty bowl out for kids. Why do people do that? Kids don't just take one piece and leave the rest.

"Why are you pouting, baby girl?" Mom asks as I frown at my Greek goddess costume. The picture on the package looked so feminine and flirty, but on me it just looks like a frumpy white and gold sheet.

"Mom, I think I'll just stay in tonight. Halloween is overrated. I'm getting too old to celebrate it," I lie.

"You're never too old to enjoy fun, candy, and the people you love. Hey, won't you go in my room and get my crown?" Mom asks, as my dad kisses her neck.

Wow, they've been together forever and they still act like they have just fallen in love, but do they have to smooch in front of me? Ugh!

I put my brothers on my hips and carry them to Mom's room. They love it when I do that, but they are starting to get too heavy for me to do the double hold.

When I get to mom's room, I almost drop both of the twins because, there on Mom and Dad's bed, is a belly dancer costume in my new favorite color, lilac. I'm still jumping up and down with joy as Mom walks in behind me and asks me, in teasing tones, for her crown. I laugh, because she is wearing it on her head. Mom is the Queen of Hearts and the queen of surprises.

"Is it for me, Mommy? Did you make this costume for me?"

"Of course it is, baby girl. I know you said that you wanted to find your own costume, but I've been making your costumes for fourteen years, so I just had to make you one. Do you like it?"

My dad's mouth is agape. He looks like he'll have a heart attack if I wear this costume.

"No, Mom. I love it!" I say as I kiss my dad's cheek. Mom kisses him too, and he follows her downstairs. I hear him mumbling about our tiny costumes, but she tells him something that quiets him. Mom always knows how to quiet my father.

When they leave, I run upstairs to become a belly dancer.

"It fits like a second skin, Emani," Mermaid Ebony says approvingly. I love it even more thinking of what she would say about this jewel I've placed in my belly button.

"Are you guys ready yet?" 1920's Flapper Eris says, still adjusting the wayward feather on her headband.

Motorcycle Mama Alexis walks in wearing a small, red, faux leather jacket that shows her tiny tummy, and some faux leather pants that show her hourglass shape. Alexis definitely has the best figure out of the four of us. I hope I look like that when I'm her age. One year to go.

Alexis walks over to Eris and readjusts her headband. Then, she pulls two bobby pins from her pocket and secures the headband to Eris's three-minute hair. Eris walks over to the mirror and smiles.

Tevin and Kevin throw Alexis's helmet back and forth to one another until she holds out her hand for it. They instantly give it to her. I can't believe my eyes because I have to beg the twins to get dressed. They run all over the place when I call them to come to me. They make bath time and play time miserable for me, but Alexis doesn't even have to say one word and they obey her. What is wrong with me? Why can't I get any respect?

Our doorbell rings. It's probably my Aunty Jay here to take us to the mall.

I rush downstairs to see her reaction to my costume first. She'll probably faint. When I open the door, it is me who almost faints.

"Hey, Emani. Is Alexis ready?" It is Jeremy Sparks' voice so I know that it is him behind the mask, but I can't stop staring at his mask. He's wearing an evil clown mask. I am deathly afraid of clowns, so I just stand here frozen.

Aunty Jay walks in behind him and asks me if we are ready to go. I still cannot speak or move.

"Jeremy, take off that mask. Are you trying to kill my sister?" Ebony says as she takes off Jeremy's mask before he can do it himself. I hear myself exhale, but I do not speak. I can see that it is him, but for some reason I am still afraid. Clowns are evil. Alexis walks out and he follows her.

"Dad, I thought she was going with us," Eris says as Alexis leaves without a chaperone, as usual. She gets to go on a date with Dad's favorite, Jeremy.

"No, she's going with Jeremy to his family's movie night party. She'll be fine. Your dad knows where she's going," Aunty Jay says as she looks over our costumes.

"Does your dad know what you all are wearing?" Aunty Jay asks.

"He sure does!" I say as I grab my house key and walk out the door with a twin in each arm as a belly dancer.

"Aunty Jay, who are you supposed to be?" Ebony asks, though Aunty Jay isn't wearing a costume. She's dressed in a long-sleeved dress that covers every inch of her flesh, from neck to toe.

"I'm a school teacher," Aunty Jay declares as she rolls her eyes at us. We watch her lock our front door.

Aunty Jay has a very handsome husband, but she doesn't dress to please him. She is always wearing long dresses that I think they wore in the nineteenth century. She used to wear brown, beige, gray, and black all the time, but now everything she owns has flowers, dots, or stripes. I guess I should consider that an improvement, but I do not. I can't believe I'm going to be seen in the mall with her.

My twin tyrant brothers march us around the mall so quickly that it is hard to keep up with them. I don't know where they get their energy. Maybe Mom sneaks sugar in everything they eat.

"Let's stop and get something to eat. I need to sit down," Aunty Jay says after an hour of following behind the twin tyrants.

It's a good thing she doesn't have kids yet because I don't think she could handle any. My sisters and I ask Aunty Jay if we can keep going store to the store with the twins and meet her back in the food court, and she quickly agrees.

Eris, Ebony, and I stop walking when we see a group of boys who appear to be our age walking our way. None of them have costumes on, but I am not surprised. Boys in our neighborhood refuse to dress up for Halloween. They just go around trying to steal everyone else's candy.

I squeeze my ballerina bucket tightly, and my sisters do the same to their candy baskets. The boys call Tevin and Kevin to them and my little friendly baby brothers walk toward them. Mom and Dad have been teaching these knuckleheads not to talk to strangers since they were one-year-olds, but they still walk over to everyone smiling and giving hugs. It is a scary sight to see.

The tallest boy asks my baby brother Tevin for some of his candy, but to my surprise my brother says no. The bald boy then tries to reach in Tevin's basket anyway.

"He said no!" I scream.

"And who are you supposed to be? You look like a genie without a bottle to live in," the bald one says. I can't believe he has the nerve to tease me when he is kneeling there with a shiny, bald head.

"No, *she's* not a genie, but *we* are *his* big sisters, and WE will grant you three wishes. One, we will allow you to remove your hand from his bucket. Two, we will allow you to stand up. And three, we will allow you to walk away without a fight," Eris says as she stands looking down at the boy with the polished head.

"Come on, let's go, guys. I didn't come here for a fight," the cutest one says.

"They're just girls," the tallest one says.

"Exactly! And that's why we aren't going to fight them. Let's go," the cutest one says as he looks directly at Ebony for the second time.

They all follow the cute one when he turns to leave.

"Do you know him, Ebony?" I ask when he looks back at her.

"Yeah, he umm . . . is in the drama club," Ebony says. She met him Thursday at some informational meeting. She's thinking about acting lessons now in order to improve her channel. We tease her a bit more about him when he is out of sight, but she claims that he isn't interested in her. Ebony never thinks any boy is interested in her.

As we tease Ebony, the twins run into a maternity store named Mommy's World. None of us want to even go in the store so we all just beg Tevin and Kevin to come out. They ignore us. We really need Alexis right now.

I don't ever want to see my mother pregnant again, because she doesn't know how to just have one baby, or maybe she just forgot how to have only one after she had Alexis. Besides, I definitely do not want to be seen in a maternity store by any of my friends.

"Hey, ladies," Stephan Miles says as he whips out a camera to take our pictures.

Like usual, he just appears without any footsteps. I don't know if it's a football footwork thing, but one minute he is not there, the next minute he is.

Eris walks over to him and tries to take his camera from him.

"Give it to me, Stephan. Give it to me now!" Eris says as she tries to pry the camera from his huge hands.

He winks at me as she uses all of her strength but does not get any results. I don't think my sister is used to fighting someone stronger than she is. Ebony has tried to explain to her that muscles don't always equal strength.

"Hey . . . I know why you're here, Eris, because I'm here to take pictures of C.I.A. students who weren't cool enough to be invited to Blair's Boo-gy Blast tonight, but why are you here, Red, and Curly?" Stephan says as he pulls his hand and his camera from Eris's grasp.

Eris winces in pain. Then, she tries again to get the camera. Eris is not a quitter. We all know that to be true.

"We're looking for her!" I say when I spot Zachary Thomas's mother at the checkout counter. My baby twin terror brothers are at her feet pulling on her legs.

"Sure you are! Who is she?" Stephan says as if he is doing one of his student spotlight interviews on us for our online school newspaper, *The Pulse*.

We walk up to Dr. Thomas and hug her. Eris and Ebony each grab a twin and put him on their hips. We haven't seen Dr. Thomas in a long while.

"Now, this is a treat, triplets!" She says as she kisses each one of us.

I watch her look around for Alexis. Then, I tell her that Alexis is at home. In my mind, I ask God to forgive me for lying, but there is no way I could tell Zachary Thomas' mother that my sister is on a date with another boy. I know it has been years since her son's death, but . . . I just can't say that to my sister's true love's mom.

The salesperson hands Dr. Thomas a very large bag and I notice that Dr. Thomas has a little belly bump. I don't dare ask her the question, though.

"Are you pregnant?" Eris blurts.

Stephan just shakes his head at Eris's big mouth. Ebony and I shake our heads too. Then, we apologize for our big-mouth sister.

"Yes, but . . . ummh . . . ." She looks at Stephan as if to tell him to disappear, and he must understand because he leaves, but not before taking another picture of all of us.

"Bye, I have a party to get to, ladies."

Eris throws a baby pink noisemaker at him, but unfortunately it does not hit him.

Dr. Thomas does not look very happy about him taking a picture of her without her permission.

"Well, young ladies, ummh . . . my husband does not know about this quite yet. We're sort of separated at the moment. I know you're helping him with the case against *that woman*, so I would appreciate it if you didn't mention this to him."

The twins both reach for her to pick them up. It's been a year since we've seen her, but Dr. Thomas has not changed. She refuses to say the names Payton or Princeton Payne. I try to think of something to say to erase the pain that I see in her eyes.

"Are you hoping for a girl or a boy?" Another pregnant woman in the store says to Dr. Thomas.

Dr. Thomas looks at the five of us.

"I just want a healthy baby," she says as she tries to ease toward the exit of the store without crying.

"Well, you look like you're carrying a girl because you have that glow. You look so beautiful," the pregnant lady says to Dr. Thomas.

Dr. T responds, "I don't feel beautiful. I'm so much bigger than I was with ...my son. I wasn't even showing until my fourth month."

The pregnant woman compliments Dr. T again.

"I hope to see you soon, Dr. Thomas," I say, as we exit Mommy's World.

Dr. Thomas waves goodbye. Tevin and Kevin start to cry for her to pick them up as we leave.

*

Eris seems more quiet than usual as we walk to meet Aunty Jay after our trip to Mommy's World.

"I called Dr. Thomas a few weeks ago," Eris confesses. "She gave me another number to reach Mr. Thomas at. I should have figured it out. Can you believe they are separated?"

"How could you have known? Why did you call Mr. Thomas anyway?" Ebony asks.

"I umm . . . wanted his help with our Dime situation at school. He's caught so many of the people who work for that multiple-murderer Payton Payne this past year that I thought for sure he could help me figure out the identity of a few teenagers," Eris says in the same sad tone as before.

"Well, did you ever talk to him?"

"Yes, he wants us to come by his condo tomorrow, but now I feel so selfish. He's lost his son and his wife and maybe even a relationship with whoever is in Dr. Thomas' tummy. I shouldn't bring him more problems. We shouldn't go. We can find another police officer. Doesn't Dad have a cousin down south on the police force or in the Army or something? Our uncle is in the military. Maybe we should call him?" Eris asks as she watches Ebony and I eat our yummy cinnamon roll, unraveling it section by scrumptious section, bite by delicious bite.

"Eris, we've passed out flyers and answered phone calls for almost all of Mr. Thomas's cases. We're the ones who gave Alexis the courage to point to a picture of Princeton Payne at the trial. Don't you remember? Without her testimony, Mr. Thomas may not have gotten a guilty verdict. I doubt that he'll mind helping us this one time with our situation. Plus, we only see those cousins at family reunions, and I think our uncle is busy with that classified stuff," I say to convince my suddenly depressed sister.

"Are you going with us?" Ebony and I say in duplicate as we hand her our last piece of lip-smacking cinnamon roll.

She takes a small bite and smiles with satisfaction.

"Well, how could I say no to you two?" Eris says.

I ask, "Is that a yes?"

"Yes, sisters. Yes, I am going to Mr. Thomas's house with you. Now let's find Aunty Jay and try to convince her to make over her look and try on some fun costumes. They're all on sale now. Maybe she can wear one home to Uncle Joe?" Eris says.

When I look at her, I am happy because she looks and sounds like herself again. She even wants to find Stephan to tell him how rude she believes he is. Yes, that's my Eris. Handsome as Stephan is, I hope we don't see that boy, for his own protection.

"It's so nice to see you again, Mr. Thomas!" we say in triplicate to Zachary Thomas's father on Saturday.

I am so pleased that my parents allowed us to come work with Mr. Thomas again. He is the best policeman in the city of Chicago. It has been quite some time since they've let us do our mini-detective duties with him. Both Mom and Dad said we needed to take a break and be normal teenagers for a while a few months ago, but now that we're leading pretty normal school lives, they've agreed to let us do whatever it takes to close the case on Payton Payne. We didn't mention that we're opening a case on the Dimes.

"It's Terrence, young ladies. You are like the daughters I never had. You don't have to call me Mr. Thomas," Mr. Thomas says before he invites us into his condo and we sit on the one sofa that is inside. Our parents don't let us call adults by their first names, so we continue to call him Mr. Thomas.

The condo's walls are covered in newspaper clippings, maps, and photos of several schools. I am instantly happy that we decided not to bring Alexis when I see a few pictures of Zachary scattered around the living room.

Mr. Thomas tells us of his own progress with locating Payton Payne. He has captured and convicted several of the people who work for her R.U.N.Pain organization, and he has come close to capturing her several times.

Mr. Thomas has used the R.U.N.Pain members' confessions to build a case against Payton Payne. According to Mr. T none of the members feel that Payton is guilty. They feel that R.U.N.Pain's violent actions are more like community service to highlight the seriousness of bullying. Basically, Payton and her followers are insane in my opinion.

"She is always one step ahead of us, but we will catch her. We have saved several schools from her destruction, but I really can't wait until she is in a cell for life like her brother," Mr. Thomas says while touching a picture of Zachary.

"I was wondering why you were out of town so long," Eris says to him when he puts the picture back on the windowsill.

"Yes, I've been doing lots of TV interviews in order to urge kids not to seek Payton's help when they are being bullied or mistreated. I've given many speeches and appearances at schools to tell our family's story, to tell Zachary's story. The story has been working, but my wife . . . no longer goes with me. It's been too rough on her to tell the story over and over again. I understand why she feels the way she does, but I'm an officer of the law, and I won't stop until justice is served," Mr. Thomas says, though he, too, acts like it's hard to look at Zachary's picture without tears forming. The Thomas's family photo in the dining room is so lovely. They were the perfect family.

Someone wiggles a key in the door until it opens before any tears can form in Mr. Thomas's eyes. In my mind, I am praying it is not another woman. Hopefully, it is Dr. Thomas. Maybe they have made up. Maybe she has come here to confess about being pregnant.

"Hey Uncle Terrence, I didn't know you had help today. I thought it was my weekend to help you out," A very good-looking young man says before introducing himself to us.

His name is Rickey. He says he is Mr. Thomas's favorite nephew. Mr. Thomas says that Rickey is his only nephew who lives in town, so he won the title of favorite nephew by default.

We all laugh.

After we explain to Mr. Thomas some of the things that we have witnessed or heard about at school, he gives us some advice on how to proceed with our "case" against the Dimes. We need to gather evidence and try to get someone to tell the truth about the Dimes. We all look at him in triplicate with the thought that we knew that before we got on the train this morning.

"I'll supply you with anything you need to build a case against these Dime girls, but you must promise me that you will be safe. Let me and the professionals handle this for you," Mr. Thomas says.

Of course we promise to try to be safe, but secretly I know I'll do whatever it takes to protect myself and my sisters, all three of them.

Rickey looks at me as Mr. Thomas's fellow officers and FBI people discuss some "leads" they have on the infamous mastermind behind global school shootings and bombings, Payton Payne. I am really hoping Rickey will try to talk to me first. My sisters and I have a rule: whoever a guy talks to first has the first opportunity to date him. We won't date a guy who has already showed interest in another one of us. We all know that some guys want to date all of us just so they can say they did, but no boy will ever be able to say that he has dated all three of us.

"So you're a dancer?" Rickey asks, while looking at my *Dance like no one's watching* t-shirt.

"Yes. You're in college?" I say, though his college's initials are written across his chest. I hate being tongue-tied, but I don't know what else to talk about. I really hope he's just wearing the college's shirt because he wants to go to college there one day, but since he looks and acts so mature I already know that he's probably in college.

"First year!" he says as I take a few steps away from him.

I knew he wasn't a boy. He's a man, and my daddy would kill him if he showed up at our door trying to date me. Even Alexis's boyfriend Jeremy is just a senior in high school. This man Rickey is in college, and I am just starting my high school journey. He's on a bigger, better journey already. I take another step back and fall on Mr. Thomas's sofa. The cushions sink, as if it has been slept on by someone very often.

"Good for you!" I reply awkwardly. "I hope to go to college one day, too. I want to go to school in New York so I can dance on Broadway and learn while I do it," I say, hoping both or one of my sisters will come over to save me, but they just stand next to Mr. Thomas, pretending to be interested in his latest spy technology gadget.

I know they see me over here sinking.

Help! I try to beg for help with my eyes, but they both just smile at me. They show me no mercy at all. I know Ebony can read my lips saying, "help me," but she is pretending like she can't.

"I graduated early. Have you ever thought about doing that? It's only a few extra classes a year."

When he says this my brain begins to do the math. He's in college, but he's sort of a senior in high school in age. I wonder if Daddy would allow it. Nah! No way! This guy is at least three years older than me. It is not going to happen, but I ask him questions anyway, out of curiosity.

"Do you like cars? Are you any good at sports? Do you play video games or watch historical documentaries?"

"Yes, I have a car. Yes, I like to watch sports, but I don't play. No, I don't really play games or watch the History Channel." He replies with such candor that I think maybe I could at least try to introduce him to my father.

I decide to ask the question that could end this conversation. "How old are you?"

"How old do you think I am?"

I probably have one of those wrinkles in my forehead that I get when I'm a bit frustrated because he chooses to answer my question before I can answer his.

"Sixteen. Do you want to maybe come visit my school? I could give you a personal college tour, Emani."

Though he seems to be asking me on a date, I'm not quite sure. Is he just trying to be nice? When he asks me for my phone number and social media, I begin to think that he is interested in me.

"Sure," Ebony says for me. "She would love to come to your school. Don't they have a great dance program? Here's her number."

"Are you free next Saturday?" he asks, and I am instantly heartbroken.

I don't have dance practice with Ms. Jennings on the weekends anymore, but I have to dance next Saturday at our football game. We're doing Kylie's dance tribute to the '70s. I'm wearing an afro wig that looks like my mother's natural hair and one of the glimmering silver body suits that the queen of designer coffee, Ms. Jennings, donated to our squad. I really don't want to miss the performance, but I don't want to miss my chance at a first date either.

"Of course, she is," Ebony lies. "Can you pick her up at our school?" I excuse myself for a minute and pull Ebony into Mr. Thomas' mini-kitchen.

"Not only do I have to perform at the game on Saturday, Sis, but I have a curfew. How am I going to dance, go to Rickey's college for a tour and a performance, and be back before 10:00 at night?"

"You can leave after the half-time performance," Ebony says, as if she is brilliant or something.

I *could* do that, but dancers are supposed to wait in the stands until the end of the game.

Naturally, Eris walks over, and she and Ebony start discussing my unofficial date with Rickey. "It won't work," I object. "I have to be there the entire time. I'll have to tell him no."

"Ebony got you into the mess," Eris says earnestly "I'm sure she'll get you out. Maybe, she can be you at the end of the game. All you dancers do is shake a little. She can do that," Eris winks.

This makes Ebony squirm uncomfortably. We all know she does not like to dance, mostly because she is horrible at it.

"Would you do that for me? Would you shake a little?" I ask Ebony.

"I'm a redhead, Emani. You're not. Even if I could "shake a little," everyone would know it was me with my hair like this. I'm not dying my hair for one day. Not even for you, sis," Ebony says.

"Emani is wearing a wig that day. Haven't you been listening to her talk about this performance? Do you even listen to our youngest sister?" Eris says as she giggles.

"Why can't you do it, Eris?"

"Muscles, sweety. I've got these muscles. I wish I could," Eris lies.

Her muscles aren't that much bigger than my own. She's just a little bit more chiseled and toned, but in her mind she's a body builder or something.

"Fine," Ebony grumbles. "I'll do it, but you owe me." Then she purposely steps on Eris's newest gym shoes.

CHAPTER 8
Ebony
The Bermuda Triangle

Agreeing to switch places with Ebony today has got to be the stupidest thing that I have ever done. Maybe she'll change her mind and decide not to go out on a date with Mr. Thomas's nephew, Rickey. Then, I can just sit here and collect money from people as they come to watch the football game. It is much easier for me to collect three dollars from people than it is to dance in front of them. What was I thinking when I agreed to this?

"I need you to find someone else to work the gate, Ebony. We have to make an announcement that we are selling that new spirit wear that you designed," Zyanne Jeffries says, with her arms folded tightly across her chest.

I want to tell her that Charlotte actually designed the spirit wear, but I decide against it, since Zyanne and I have been trying to get along since Eris reminded her that she and Zyanne's little brother Zechariah are friends. Thanks to Zechariah, Zyanne is willing to tolerate me, but she hates Charlotte. In fact, Zyanne hates Charlotte about as much as Charlotte hates Zyanne.

I don't know what the problem is between them, but I do know that I hate being in the middle. Charlotte needs to understand that Zyanne is the president and I'm just the treasurer, so I can only do so much at C.I.A., and Zyanne needs to know that I don't let anyone choose my friends for me. Some people feel that their friends' enemies are their enemies too, but I believe my enemies are my enemies and my friends are my friends. It's just that simple.

"Okay, Zyanne. I'll be up there in a minute," I say as I look around for a replacement for me, though I know that all of my volunteers are either at the refreshment stand, in the stands selling blue and silver noisemakers, or on the visitor's side selling bench cushions.

Every school in our conference knows that the visitor side of our field is in need of remodeling. An anonymous former student gave our football program half a million dollars last year to renovate and remodel. but our school has yet to redo the visitor locker rooms, bleachers, or stands. I think we haven't remodeled the visitor's side yet on purpose, and since we're undefeated, I think that it's working. I know I wouldn't want to sit in those cold, uncomfortable stands.

Eris walks over to me with a smile on her face, so I assume she won her volleyball game. I could tell her that I still feel neither her muscles nor her having to play her game today were good enough excuses for her not to have to switch places with Emani for her date, but I choose not to when I see how happy she is with today's victory.

"Another win, Ebony!" Eris says as she does her usual celebration dance.

"Good for you, Sis. Another win is a step closer to your dream of a perfect season," I say, as Zyanne screams at me to come up to the alumni box to do my announcement.

I wish I could stand here and make small talk about how my sister wants to destroy our varsity volleyball team, but since I do not have a replacement to make the student council announcement for me, I give my sister the money box and the little stamp she will need to take my place.

She complains.

"I don't want this, Ebony. I came to see you dance."

I put my finger on my lips to tell Eris to be quiet. She whispers for me to shake what my momma gave me, and I walk off more nervous than I've ever been in my life. I can handle this announcement without stuttering. It's easy to stand behind a glass and tell everyone to support C.I.A, but maybe I won't meet Emani under the stands for our little switch-a-roo. Maybe I'll just refuse to do this switch for Emani. She's my sister. She would forgive me. Right?

When I get to the top of the stands, I step to the microphone for my announcement, but Ms. Kelly stops me before I can speak. Ms. Kelly is one reason I can speak with confidence and without my stutter, but I wish she would stop forcing me to speak in public without warning me.

The Stomp squad is on the field and Ms. Kelly doesn't want to interrupt their performance. As I wait to do my little commercial announcement, I watch my sister dance. She is so precise, so smooth, and such a natural. Dancing is truly her passion. There is really only one thing that she wants more than to become a professional dancer, and that is to find her perfect mate. Boys aren't really a priority right now for Eris and me.

In fact, I'd rather read a good book than talk on the phone to a boy, because at least when you finish the book, you've learned something. The last boy I spoke to on the phone was so boring that I almost fell asleep.

With my promise to help Emani on my mind, I reluctantly hand confused Zyanne the microphone and leave without making the commercial announcement when I see Emani and her dance squad exiting the field.

If Emani only knew the sacrifice I am making for her to go on her first date. Sorry, Ms. Kelly, I can't do the speech thing this time. It is time to switch places. It's time for a switch-a-roo.

"I was so nervous that you wouldn't come, Sis," Emani says, as she takes off her bodysuit, hands it to me, and changes into her date outfit. I do my best to turn myself into her. We are underneath the football stands, but she acts like we are at home in our rooms. What if someone looked under here?

"I said I would. Have I ever lied to you?" I say as I put on the wig she was just wearing for her performance. I like the wig's bangs. Maybe I should wear bangs. I think I'll ask Aunt CC to give me bangs when I go to her beauty shop next week. They won't be like Kylie's wig's feathered bangs or the curly bangs on this afro wig of mine, but I know they will be cute.

"No, but be careful. Don't talk too much. Don't clap, because you do not clap on beat," my sister says as I adjust a sports bra that Eris and I found at the mall yesterday to smash my cleavage. I tell her not to worry, and she winks at me as I adjust the wig again in front of my hand-held mirror. She claims that she isn't worried at all, but I am not as confident.

"Have fun, Emani!" I scream as she runs off. She turns and puts her finger to her lips to tell me to be quiet.

"I will have fun, Emani!" She says as she winks at me again reminding me that I am not Ebony anymore. I am now "Emani."

*

"Emani, where were you? You asked to go to the bathroom, not on vacation." Coach Calderone says to me as she waves me into the stands. I sit next to her and try not to directly look at any of the girls.

"Where's my water, freshman?" Kylie Calderone says to me.

"It's over at the refreshment stand! Won't you bring me one too when you go to get yours?" I say before I realize that the Stomp squad members are all staring at me.

"You want me to get up and go get YOU some water. You must have lost your mind, *freshman*," Kylie retorts. Then she mumbles something else, but her mother has told her to sit down and be quiet, and nobody takes notice of her after that.

The varsity cheerleader captain walks over to Coach Calderone and asks if we can come down on the field with them to hype up the crowd. I look at the scoreboard in disbelief. We're losing? This never happens!

Keeping one eye firmly on that dismal scoreboard, Coach Calderone agrees to send us down on the field. My knees are shaking so badly that I don't know if I can get up. Emani said that I would be in the stands until the end of the game. I don't want to be on the field. I can't dance!

"Are you okay, Emani?" Coach asks.

"I'm just cold," I lie, hoping that maybe I'll just fall on my way down the stands.

Unfortunately, I do not fall. I don't even trip. Slowly, I follow my teammates onto the field, feeling too close to the action for words. I'm not going to move until the band starts playing, and I may not even move then. *I don't know the routine.* As my heart sinks, the band starts to play Ashanti Sullivan's latest hit.

That's Ms. Kelly's cue to announce each of the cheerleaders' names on the upper deck microphone. In response, each Stomp squad member does a signature move as their name is called out. I don't have a dance move. I try to remember something that I've seen Emani do, but my brain is no longer functioning properly. I hope Emani won't be talked about too badly on Monday morning after I embarrass her today with this ridiculous dance I'm about to do.

I watch feathered-wig wearing Kylie Calderone do a back flip, jump up, and land on her feet, only then to do a dance move that seems to shake every one of her body parts. Even my sister Eris claps for her as the crowd roars its approval. And now it's my turn.

"Go Emani, go Emani, go Emani!" the football players cheer.

The crowd joins in. I close my eyes and dance from the inside out. I feel myself drop to my knees, pop up, and shake east to west. Then, I feel myself turn around 180 degrees, shaking every inch of my body. I kick as high as I can and land in a split.

When I open my eyes, the crowd is on their feet. I somehow stand to my feet and place my pom poms back quickly behind my rear. Once I regain my composure, I notice Coach Calderone giving me the thumbs up. The cheerleaders, the rest of the stomp squad, and I turn around to the field to watch the offense get on the field. In my mind, I am taking a bow.

In my mind, I am saying, *you did it, girl,* because I really can't believe that I just danced in front of my classmates and some visitors from another school. Once I start to pay attention to what's happening on the field, I notice the football coach giving a secret signal to the quarterback. After the whistle blows, I see Stephan Miles break through the defense and run into the end zone. Score!

"If we win, you owe me a date!" he shouts in jubilation as he removes his helmet. He thinks he's talking to my sister, not to me.

I suddenly hope that the kicker misses this field goal. As the kicker walks out in into the field, the home crowd falls silent as the visitors stand booing.

George Street positions himself. Makes the kick. We hold our breath . . . the kick is good! It is official. C.I.A wins again! The stands erupt in cheers. We just beat the best school in our conference.

I begin walking to the gate so that I can get off of the field and home before Stephan finds me.

"Umm, freshman. Are you forgetting that we have to go to shake hands with the other cheerleaders and dancers? I hope you didn't forget the cookies, too. Did you?" Kylie says with her hand on her hip, stomping her right foot.

Who does she think she is? I wish I had gotten that bottle of water earlier, because I'd pour it all over her.

I follow the other dance girls around to the visiting side, only to see Eris at the visitors' gate, holding a bag in her hand.

"Missing something umm . . . Emani?" Eris says as she giggles her husky snort. I grab the bag and look in it only to see an assortment of cookies and napkins.

Kylie screams for me to hurry up, and though I want to call Ms. Kylie Calderone a few naughty names, I decide to be quiet.

The Stomp team and I shake hands with the visiting dance and cheer girls and offer them crackers, cookies, juice, and milk. They follow us into the school to share a little snack and congratulate us on our win. The captains ask who choreographed the half-time performance and Kylie proudly brags on her choreography.

"Hey, I have to say that you were awesome in your solo," the visiting cheerleading captain says to me.

"Thank you!" I say, as I bite into a cracker.

"Aren't you on a diet, freshman?" Kylie says as I stare at the cookies.

"I certainly hope not!" A very deep voice says behind me. Even though I hope it isn't Stephan, I prepare myself for it to be him before I turn around.

"Will you let me feed you tonight?" Stephan asks. "I can't think of anyone more worth my time."

Coach Calderone doesn't like girls on the Stomp squad dating football players, but Emani says Coach said it is okay if you are discreet. I watch as Kylie points angrily toward Stephan and me.

When Stephan reaches for my hand, I explain the dating situation to him. I try to emphasize that he needs to be discreet if he is interested in me since he is a football player and I am a dancer. As I say this, he waves to Coach Calderone and Kylie, and then opens his passenger door for me.

"No problem, Emani, I'll drop you off at home!" Stephan yells so loudly that I'm sure everyone within 50 yards heard him.

"You don't know how to be discreet at all do you, boy?" I ask, as I see Eris standing by the home gate, holding my student council treasurer money box and my stamper.

When she sees me in Stephan's car, she drops both the money box and the stamper on the ground. Oblivious to her surprise, Stephan keeps driving with a big smile on his face, totally happy to be with "Emani."

*

First, Stephan takes me to Wild World, a place where a lot of the students at C.I.A hang out and eat Chicago-style hotdogs and deep-dish pizza. My empty stomach is screaming for food, but there are too many classmates here. I ask him to take me some place a bit more discreet.

He drives me to his house. I am very nervous, but I follow him inside. I may not get to eat Wild World's delicious food, but at least no one at school will see us together here. The last time I was at Stephan's McMansion it was filled with folks. The house seems silent this time.

When we enter his colossal kitchen, Ms. Miles asks him if he won the game and he proudly says yes. Mr. Miles walks in behind us and congratulates Stephan on his win. Stephan reintroduces me to his parents and leads me downstairs to his movie room.

"What do you like to watch?" I almost forget that I'm Emani and say biographies, but then I correct myself and say romantic comedies. Emani loves love stories.

I watch Stephan press a few buttons on the remote and then about one hundred titles appear on the large screen. My stomach growls like a lost tiger cub searching for its mother.

"I thought you were going to feed me," I complain, as he explains a little about each film on the menu. Emani would know all of these movies and their plots, but I don't know any of them.

"Believe me, Curly. My mom will be bringing us some food any moment."

As he finishes the last syllable in "moment," Mrs. Miles comes through the door with a plate filled with appetizers. If Emani were here, she wouldn't eat any of this. Cheese sticks, cheese quesadillas, and veggies with ranch dressing? No way; lately, Emani is not the same type of eater as I am.

I devour everything on my plate just in time for Ms. Miles to bring in the main course. Ms. Miles walks in with a salad. Salad?

"I hope you like it. It's my seven-layer salad. Stephan tells me you're a vegetarian." I start to eat the salad, trying to enjoy each bite. It is a delicious salad, but I need something that will replace all of the calories that I danced away.

"Mom, I know you have something else to go with this foliage." Stephan says, as he holds up a piece of romaine lettuce. Mrs. Miles smiles and tells us that she ordered us a fully-loaded vegetarian pizza. I am instantly made happy by her words, but I will be happier in 20 minutes when the pizza gets here.

"So, Emani. Does Eris talk about me often?" Stephan asks as he eats a juicy tomato.

"Not as much as you write about her in the news," I say as I chomp on a cucumber.

"I only write the truth. It's my job to find the story and to tell it," Stephan says, almost choking on his broccoli spears.

"Well, what you wrote about her online last week was completely false," I say, as I remember that my mother told me not to eat and talk at the same time.

"I know she's your sister, but she is also a ball hog. She is all over the court playing everyone's position, and her own. She's the most selfish player I've seen, male or female," he says as he scoots closer to me.

I forget that I am supposed to be my soft-spoken sister and jump into defense mode, "Eris was just offered a spot on the varsity team and she turned it down because she didn't want to abandon her teammates, and since you've been letting her and her teammates practice here at your house for the past few weeks I would think you would know that she is anything but selfish. She's a leader and a teacher. She's as hard on everyone else as she is on herself. She will point out your weaknesses, but she will also praise your strengths. Haven't you seen that in her?"

He puts another tomato in his mouth to avoid answering me, but I do not say another word until he speaks.

"I see that side of her when she practices here, but not at school. At school, she'll do anything to win," Stephan finally says.

"She's an athlete. She wants a perfect season. She's a lot like you," I say and Stephan acts as if he is going to throw up or something.

He acts like being compared to my sister makes him sick to his stomach. We both turn away from one another and look at a black screen. It is going to be a long night. Emani is not going to be happy with this performance. I'll focus on the first half of this show when I give her the details tonight.

"Maybe I should start a movie, Curly."

"Definitely!" I say as I point to the one that at least sounds a little interesting. It is called "A Love of Her Own."

Stephan spends most of his time trying to compliment "Emani" and the other half of his time complimenting me. He admits that he thinks Ebony is a positive, smart individual. He even says that he "likes Ebony's ideas" and that "she" is never afraid to express "her" opinion.

I can't help but smile, until he almost pulls off my wig putting his hand around my shoulders. I use the bad hair day excuse to break away from him. He claims that "Emani" never has a bad hair day, so I thank him for the compliment before I excuse myself to the bathroom to try to readjust the wig. I finally get a chance to take it completely off and let my own hair breathe for a minute once I am in the bathroom.

"The pizza's here!" Stephan says from outside of the bathroom. I flush the toilet though I did not use it, wash my hands, and go directly to my seat. He asks me if I would get him a slice of pizza, and I ignore him, hoping that he will realize that I am not his mother. He gets up and puts a slice on a saucer. I hold my hand out for the slice and he reluctantly hands it to me. I learned that trick from Eris.

"I knew you wouldn't let me mistreat you," Stephan says after eating his first slice in two bites. I listen to him compliment Emani on being beautiful, smart, talented, and soft. He says she reminds him of his mother. I guess that is a compliment.

Ms. Miles comes in with cheesecake and drinks for us. She gives Stephan another piece of pizza and asks him if he needs anything else. She does sort of remind me of how I think Emani would be with her boyfriend: always catering to his every need and desire.

Ms. Miles leaves after removing the dishes we used for the appetizers and the salad.

"So, your mom was a professional athlete?" I ask, though Eris has informed me about every detail of Ms. Miles's life. To Eris, Ms. Miles is a superstar. Eris knows everything about her.

"An Olympian, the best in her sports," Stephan brags.

"What does she do now?" I ask with a great deal of curiosity.

"She's my mom and my dad's wife," Stephan brags again.

Though he doesn't ask, I tell him about my own mother putting herself through nursing and medical school while raising us. I want to tell him that I think you can be both a good mother and a professional, but I don't know if Emani would ever say those words so I decide not to say anything at all.

"How long have your parents been married?" He asks.

"17 years total," I say. He sits up a bit more in the seat.

"Total? Were they divorced?"

"No, separated for a while," I say, as I walk toward the popcorn machine that is in the right corner of Stephan's personal theater.

When I realize that I don't know how to work it, I turn around and stare at him until he gets up to help me. I quickly try to change the subject back to him as the popcorn pops, but as the kernels pop he asks me to be his girlfriend.

BREATHE IN. Breathe out. I listen to the air escape my lungs.

"Let's just take it slow. Stephan, I would like us to be friends first. Plus, we need to be discreet, remember," I say staring at the popcorn maker instead of him.

"Okay, Curly, I'll wait," he says as he fills a bag of popcorn for me.

After adding a bit of butter and salt, I am back on the couch in his arms. I really hope that Emani wants this boy because he surely wants her. When my wig's hair gets in his mouth, he asks me for the third time if I want to take it off, and I tell him again that my hair is a mess underneath. Though he says he doesn't care, I know he would not be pleased if I took off this sandy brown wig and revealed the red mane that is underneath.

I lean my head on his shoulder and he seems to forget what he was talking about.

The movie we watch isn't that bad. It's cutesy and a bit predictable, but I laugh every now and then so I can't really complain.

I watch Stephan look at his watch and then I notice him frown once he realizes that it is time to take me home.

"Curly, will I get to spend some more time with you soon?" He asks as he scoots closer to me.

"Of course," I say as I stand to my feet.

He did compliment the real me earlier without knowing I was in the room, so I think Emani should give him a chance even though Eris believes he is a "spoiled, hormone-filled momma's boy." I believe I quoted her correctly. There seems to be some good qualities about Stephan. Yet a lot of what Eris says is true too.

I follow him up the stairs and out the door only to hear Ms. Miles ask me to come back in and give her a hug. She gives me a hug and a kiss on the forehead like my own mother does before she lets me go.

*

"I knew she would like you," Stephan says as he starts the car we are in.

I don't know if the car is his or his dad's, but I know that my dad would LOVE this car. The car is on, but it doesn't even make a sound. That's the type of engine my daddy loves. Jeremy isn't the only one who listens to my dad. I don't know everything about cars, but I know some things. I know that this is a car some people would dream to have in their collection.

When we get to my house, we sit in the car by the curb until 9:55. Stephan keeps trying to keep me talking, and since he is pretty interesting I listen, but I know I have to be in before 10:00, and not a minute after 10:00.

As we talk, I notice that there is already a strange car in our driveway. I sit up and examine it, trying to remember if I have seen it before. My dad works on a lot of cars, but nope, I don't recognize this one. As I look for what type of car it is, Mr. Thomas's nephew Rickey steps out of the car, walks over to the passenger side, and opens the door for Emani, who happily jumps out.

I try to look away before Stephan notices who I am looking at. He starts to turn his head toward Rickey and Emani, so I kiss him to divert his attention back to me. When I stop kissing him, I see that Emani is still hugging Rickey by the front door. I kiss Stephan again until I see her go inside.

"Wow! I like taking things slowly with you!" Stephan says as he tries to kiss me again.

I push him away when I see Emani walk through our front door.

"Discretion! We need to be discreet," I say as I open my door. When I close the door, I can see that it is 9:59. I run to the door and ring the doorbell as a no-doubt confused Stephan shouts something to me from his car. I don't know what he said, but I do know that he almost hit Rickey's car as he pulled away.

Wow! That was close!

CHAPTER 9

Eris
Tiny Kitten

Wow! I cannot wait to get home and tell Ebony how amazing she was. Of course, I will have to tease Emani a bit, since Ebony's solo dance was as good, if not better, than the one Emani did last week. I count the money that I've collected for student council and neatly put a rubber band around the dollar bills. Ebony has separate containers for the quarters, nickels, and . . . dimes.

"You can give me the money!" Zyanne Jeffries says, holding out her hand to me.

"I am going to give this money to the person who put me in charge of it. My sister Ebony is the treasurer, after all," I say as I tuck the money box under my arm.

Zyanne pulls out a leather envelope filled with money and asks me to put the money into the bag, after reminding me that she is the president of student council.

"Well, I'll need you to sign for it!" I say, though I know I do not have a receipt book or a pen.

"Sign for it? I don't have a pen or paper. This is a football field, not a classroom, freshman," Zyanne says, as if I am a complete idiot or something.

"Well, then I guess I'll have to give it to the person who does!" I say as I walk off.

Some of my teammates huddle around me before I can walk even six steps toward the school.

"So, are you ready to party, Captain Eris?" Angie says. I really like the sound of that.

We walk a few steps before I remember that I need to wait for Ebony. Karen tries to convince me to go to some player's party that I know I wasn't invited to, but since she is so excited about it I do consider going.

"Will varsity Vita Rowe be there?" I ask, as everyone suddenly gets quiet.

I guess that's a yes. Vita hasn't let me forget that we have yet to beat varsity at any of our practices, but I won't let her forget that we haven't lost a game against anyone else yet. The fresh-soph squad and the varsity squad have a little competition going. The first team to lose will have to say Vita Rowe's famous line in front of all of the spectators who come to watch our games. I can't wait to hear Vita and varsity all say, "Today we were LOSERS." It was nice to see Vita have to watch me refuse Coach's offer for me to join varsity, but I want more.

The girls mention that a few athletes who I think may be worthy of a date with me will be at the party, so I agree to ride with them to the party if Ebony can ride with us. Rochelle agrees, but not before pulling me to the side for the same little threat she gave me earlier.

"I think you played great today, and I appreciate all you've done to build the girls' confidence, but I hope that our wins are about US and not about you, Eris. I know you gave up the varsity spot Coach offered you, but was it for something bigger or because you like playing with us?" Rochelle asks.

Before I can answer, the girls pull Rochelle away. As she walks backward away from the field, I think about my decision to stay on the fresh-soph team. She is actually correct. I love playing with the girls now that we actually play like a team, but I love beating Vita Rowe even more. How could I do that if I were on her team? Why did I stay? I don't even know the real answer. Is it for the team or for the chance to beat varsity?

I stand under a ray of light emanating from a street lamp near the football field, wondering if I'm being selfish or not. As I think, I see my selfish sister Ebony sitting in Stephan Miles's car. What is she doing with him? Why didn't she call me? How did she even know I would make it home okay? Since when are they best friends? Who . . . oh, I forgot that Stephan thinks that Ebony is Emani. Now, that is funny. I can't help but laugh since I am so tickled. Ebony isn't being selfish. She is being Emani. Poor girl. I guess I'll party without her tonight.

My teammates ask, "So are you getting in or not, Eris?"

"Oh, I am definitely getting in the car, wait one minute," I say, as I pick up the money hand stamper thingy that I accidentally dropped on the ground.

When I finish, I feel Zyanne Jeffries and Vita Rowe standing over me. As I stand, Zyanne hands me a receipt for the exact amount I told her we made today. I didn't even think she was listening to me earlier when I told her she'd have to sign for the money. I fold the receipt and put it in my pocket, wondering why varsity Vita Rowe won't look at me.

Zyanne takes the money box and the stamper I used to stamp PAID on everyone who entered the game today.

"I guess you're coming to the party!" Volleyball vixen Vita says, though she looks more at the bright light above our heads than at me.

"Yeah, I'll be there."

"Well, I'll see you there, freshman!" Vita says after Zyanne finishes counting the dollar bills. Zyanne puts the bills in her envelope and dumps all of the change on top of the bills. Quarters, nickels, and then the dimes.

I'm not known as the smart one of our clan, but I am sure she was trying to tell me something.

Sylvia honks her horn three times, and I jump into the front seat.

"What was that all about?" Monica says.

Confused, I say, "I don't really know!"

*

Tiny is known for his parties, but this one will probably be described as the party of the year in C.I.A's e-zine because it has music, munchies, and many mini-men. I mean, Tiny's house isn't huge like Stephan's, but every inch of it seems to be filled with bodies, and his father has grilled enough barbecue to feed an army. I find a plate and decide to taste the food that I've read so much about in our school's e-zine and on Stephan's blog. Yes, I admit I do read Stephan Miles's blog.

When I take my first bite, I feel as if someone has bench-pressed me into the air. It's like I'm hovering in beef heaven, a place that my sisters will never see.

I see Kitten walk by, and I instantly come back to earth. I cannot believe my eyes. Ebony and Emani tried to describe how Kitten looked after their little shopping spree last night, but their words just did not paint this picture in my mind.

"I love the new you, Kitten. My sisters did a great job. I'm sorry I couldn't help with your makeover, but you know I had practice," I say as I lick my sauce-filled fingertips.

"It's not the new me, I'm still the same old Kitten," Kitten says though many of the boys are admiring the new and improved Kitten.

After a few of them start barking at her, she pulls me outside in the cold. Tiny's father is turning his last batch of moist, tender chicken and its pleasant aroma still hangs in the air. I take a deep breath to inhale the satisfying scent.

"Eris, I finished it," Kitten says as I watch my breath cloud float toward the sky.

"Good," I say as I start to move to the beat of the music playing in the backyard.

"Do you even know what I am talking about? Eris, girl, stop dancing, you're no Emani," Kitten says as she hands me her little notebook.

I instantly start giggling at her comment, since both Ebony and Emani are Emani right now. Hey, maybe I should go into the party and pretend to be Emani, too. No, my muscles would give me away.

I open the notebook Kitten gives to me to the first page, only to see what looks like algebraic equations on the first few pages. Then, I close it and give it back to Kitten. I'm here to party. I'm not here to do mathematics.

"You're right . . . I'm not Emani, but I'm not Ebony, either, honey. I don't understand that! What type of math is that? Calculus or something?" I say, as I accept a piece of tasty chicken from Mr. Tiny.

Sorry! I don't know Tiny's father's name.

"Eris, it is a code. Each number represents a letter. A plus sign means who they are dating. A minus sign means something negative about them. An asterix means that they are in a position of power at school. A dollar sign means that they have access to money. A pound sign represents their phone number and address. An at symbol represents where they were during fights, circles, and incidents. A greater than or less than sign is what I think their rank is, a colon shows who is connected to who, and a question mark of course means that I don't have that information." Kitten attempts to seem sane as she explains her insane theory.

Perhaps the shopping spree has ruined my simple Kitten. I don't like this new, complex Kitten.

"Of course!" I say, as I try not to show how puzzled I am. Kitten shows me some pictures.

"I was wrong about the Dimes, Eris. A face up dime isn't just that the Dimes are watching you. It is that they are interested in you."

When Tiny steps on the back porch to ask us why we are standing outside in the cold, we decide to go into his hot and hectic house.

"Eris, is your sister here?" Stephan's friend Tyson asks, as he looks over the crowded living room. Why do boys ask that question like I only have one sister?

"Which sister, Tyson?"

He hands me a flyer for the auditions for the spring play to give to Ebony. I fold it into a tiny square and stuff it in my pocket next to that receipt President Zyanne gave to me earlier. Am I like Ebony's messenger girl or something? I follow Kitten to the basement.

Kitten and I both turn around and head back upstairs when we see Tiny's mom on the floor dancing like she's our age. Wow! Ebony isn't the only female who can jump, jump, and shake her rump, I think as I walk backwards up the stairs. Go Mrs. Tiny. Go Mrs. Tiny. I don't know Tiny's mother's name, either.

"Watch where you're going, freshman!" Vita says after I bump into her on my way up the stairs.

I graciously step to the side and let her and her varsity teammates pass. I wish my karate teacher could see me now as I practice humility. He was so wrong about me yesterday. I can be humble.

"Don't forget to give Ebony that receipt," Zyanne says when I get to the top of the stairs.

Zyanne says hello to Kitten, but Kitten does not say one word to her.

"She's not as powerful as she pretends to be," Kitten says as she scribbles something in her little notebook. This time, when we reach the living room, I tell Kitten to follow me. Kitten sneaks up the stairs behind me, and we lock the door to Tiny's room. Tiny has a king-sized bed like we triplets all wish we had. He's huge. His parents seem to understand that about him. Our parents don't think we even need a queen-sized bed.

"Okay, tell me the code again, because I want to figure it out." When I say this, Kitten hands me a page that looks like a list. It still looks like algebra for a moment until Kitten repeats her secret code.

"Go ahead and try it," Kitten dares.

I choose the shortest name to try first. It says "23'8'5'11&'4'9'2'3'." According to my calculations, the name is DRGU&ILDV.

"Do I have to unscramble it or something?" I ask Kitten, and she laughs.

"I'm sorry, I should have said that each number represents a letter in the alphabet if you wrote them how they appear on a keyboard." Someone knocks on the door as Kitten is giggling at me.

We both try to be quiet, hoping they'll go away.

"Open up. You've locked me out of my own room," Tiny says as he wiggles the doorknob.

At first, we scramble for a place to hide. Kitten finally opens the door for him after he screams for us to open it. To my surprise, he smiles when he sees her.

"Oh, Kitten. I mean, Katherine. It's you. I didn't know it was you," Tiny says as he walks into his room and takes off his soiled shirt, quickly exchanging it for another one from his dresser drawer.

Wait, did he just say "Katherine"?

"Timothy, what happened to you?" She asks, as I realize that I didn't know Tiny's name was Timothy nor did I know that my clever, yet confusing, buddy Kitten's name was Katherine.

I wish Kitten and I had some classes together. The teachers probably call her Katherine. Kitten told me her name is Katy.

"It's no big deal. I'm just glad that you finally decided to come to one of my parties. Does that mean you're finally going to give me that dance you promised me?" Kitten gives me a look that seems to ask me if it is okay for her to leave me to dance with Tiny.

I say yes with my eyes.

I didn't even know that she knew Tiny before tonight, but obviously there is a lot I do not know about her.

When they close the door, I open the notepad and try to figure out the shortest name again. I decide that I better make a key somewhere, so I begin searching through Tiny's room for a notebook.

On his desk right next to a spiral notebook is a hat with the word Zippie's stitched into it in green. Kitten works at Zippie's restaurant, too. I wonder if that is where they know each other from, I think as I write down my key from his keyboard then plop down on Tiny's king-sized bed. Wow, I wish I had one of these.

I write my key and set it next to me as I try to decode the name again.

When I finish the first one, I throw the pencil at Tiny's mirror, because according to my deciphering, it says Vita Rowe, captain of the varsity squad. Kitten has marked her as <3, which means that she is the second most powerful dime at C.I.A. I just cannot escape this girl. She seems to use a period to show that someone is a senior and a semicolon to show that they are a junior. I am starting to get this code.

The names are written as:

.<2~11'19'6'12'12'11'&22'11'19'13'3'4'9'25'3

.<3~23'8'5'11&4'9'2'3'

.<4~20'6'11'25'25'3'&17'3'14'14'4'8'3'12'

;<5~22'8'3'4'11&15'9'25'20'11'19'3'20'

;=5~13'11'4'22'6'&3'15'11'25'

.>5-4'3'11'25'11&10'9'2'3'4'12'

;>6-24'4'3'25'13'11&11'15'24'11'6'3'2'11'

.>7-12'16'8'11'25'8&22'16'11'25'

;>8-5'11'5'6'11'25'11'&5'6'12'9'25'

;>9 -2'8'25'5'3'4'&15'9'4'13'9'25'

When I finish deciphering the codes, I discover that this means the Dimes are:

1. *Kylie Calderone, senior, captain of Stomp squad*

2. *Vita Rowe, senior, captain of varsity volleyball squad*

3. *Zyanne Jeffries, senior, president of student council*

4. *Ciera Gonzalez, junior, audio visual, C.I.A. television, C.I.A. e-zine, and yearbook*

5. *Darcy Egan, junior, audio visual, C.I.A. television, C.I.A. e-zine, and yearbook*

6. *Reana Powers, senior, National Honor Society, mathlete, and number one on the top ten list of students*

7. *Brenda Agbayewa, junior, Fashion Forward Designer Models Organization (FFDMO) president*

8. *Shiani Chan, senior cheerleading captain*

9. *Tatyanna Tyson, junior, voice club vice president, drama queen*

10. *Winter Gordon, junior, varsity cheerleading co-captain*

I straighten Tiny's bed, rip the pages I've used to break Kitten's code and a few that are underneath them out of his notebook, and place it where I found it. Then, I turn off his light and head back out to the party.

Since there is no room in my right pocket, I slip Kitten's checkered notepad and my notes into my left pocket. I am so paranoid that something will fall out that I keep my hand in my pocket all the way downstairs.

"Do you want to dance, Eris?" Malcolm McGee says to me.

I instantly look around for Stephan, since the two of them are always together snapping pictures of people who do not want to be photographed. Stephan and Malcolm are both like flies buzzing annoyingly in my ear at school. I-R-R-I-T-A-T-I-N-G!

"Is this dance on or off the record?" I ask Malcolm, who is always misquoting me in the school paper and on his own social media hate page.

He is the king of taking what I say and making me look like the arrogant, self-absorbed athlete I used to be instead of the confident, team-conscious one I have become. Neither he nor Stephan will ever let me forget my first few weeks of school. I call him Mosquito Malcolm because of his personality.

"It's off the record," Mosquito Malcolm says as he holds out the same hand he probably uses to type those mean things he claims I said about my teammates.

I wish I could afford a lawyer to sue him for all the lies he's written in black and white for everyone to read.

"Well, make it quick," I say as I agree to dance with him, since everyone seems to be looking at the two of us.

There is no way I am going to give him another opportunity for a scandalous story headline by saying no. He and Stephan have already made most of the boys at school afraid to approach me for fear that I may crush them or something. It's because of the two of them that boys move out of my way when I walk through the halls. It's because of them that no one dares even ask me for my phone number or my social. I hate Mosquito Malcolm McGee and Sneaky, Self-Absorbed Stephan Miles.

The song ends and I rush toward the front door to get away from Mosquito Malcolm before he finds a way to trick me into saying something stupid into his voice recorder or takes another ridiculously unattractive picture of me to post online.

After I escape through the front door, I wave to Kitten/Katy or Katherine, who is sitting on the front porch talking to Tiny Timothy. She doesn't give me our "ear pull" signal to save her from the conversation, so I smile and continue walking.

Mosquito Malcolm screams my name, but I try to ignore him.

"You dropped this, Eris!" An out of breath Mosquito Malcolm says when he catches up to me.

"Thanks!" I say trying to quickly grab the red, checkered notepad from him before Kitten can see it. How did that fall of my pocket?

Kitten doesn't even notice Malcolm with her notebook because she is too busy soaking in every word that Tiny says to her. I even try an ear pull, but she just smiles at me from across the street. Doesn't she remember that an ear pull means "save me from this conversation right now"? Where are my sisters when I need them? They know the ear pull signal.

Unfortunately, Mosquito Malcolm wants to walk me home. I agree, since I haven't seen my teammates since we pulled up in Tiny's driveway.

I send my teammate Angie a message that says that I am going home and that I had a great time. She sends me a frowny face with the words "Call Me TMRW" after it. I hate to disappoint my teammates, but I can't party with them; this information from Kitten is too important. I must tell my sisters.

A walk that would usually take five minutes seems to take three hours because Mosquito Malcolm doesn't ever stop talking. I don't even think he has taken one breath since we took our first step away from Tiny's house. In our five-minute walk, I learn that he's been everywhere, he's seen everything, and he knows everyone. I don't know why I was ever worried that I would say something wrong. I haven't said a real word in five minutes, just "umm," "hmm," and "uhh huh."

I am so happy to see my house that I could do a back flip right here on the curb. Okay, actually I couldn't. That's Emani's thing, but I would if I could. I could do a closing side kick, but my karate teacher would be upset with me for hurting Malcolm.

When Malcolm and I reach the steps to my home, inside, I am secretly hoping that my father will tell me to come inside, even though it is nowhere near my curfew. Instead, my mother sees us and invites him in to eat dinner with us. Please say no. Please say no. Please say no, Mosquito Malcolm.

"Sure, Ma'am!" Mosquito Malcolm agrees, pretending to be polite.

I think I need to teach my mother the ear pull signal, and soon.

Dinnertime is usually my favorite time of the day, but for some reason, I know it isn't going to be with Motormouth Mosquito Malcolm McGee at my table.

I'd rather have to feed Stephan Miles grapes and fan him after football practice than to eat with Malcolm McGee. I hope my sisters are here already.

CHAPTER 10

Emani
Barefoot Ballerina

I cannot believe that I am going to have my first real date before my sisters have theirs, but since Rickey will be here in a few minutes, I do not have time to celebrate. I take one last look at the football field's scoreboard. I cannot believe we may lose this one. I know that they need me to dance and pump up the crowd, but I have to get to my date. No boy as cute as Rickey should ever have to wait too long.

I rush toward the front of the school building and stand under the flagpole. Rickey pulls up on time, and I smile when he gets out his car and opens the door for me. I take off my hood and fix my hair in Rickey's mirror once I am sure that no one can see me. When Rickey asks me if I'm cold, I giggle a bit, because I am far from cold. Blood is rushing through my every extremity. I am so excited about tonight.

"So where are we going first?" I ask after Rickey turns down his car's radio.

"We're going to park at my job and go to get something to eat before we go to the university," Rickey says as he glances over at me.

"Where do you work?" I ask, trying to ignore my favorite song playing on the radio. I want to ask him to turn it up, but I am trying to be mature.

"I work at The Majestic hotel in Downtown Chicago. It's near the Magnificent Mile," Rickey says with a smile.

Did he just say hotel? I am already sneaking on this date. If my father finds out that I went to a hotel he won't hesitate to shorten my life. He will be ANGRY. And when my Daddy is angry he always says that he brought me into this world, and he'll take me out of it if he has to. Then he looks at me with a frown and says he won't cry when I'm gone because he has two more that look just like me.

"I thought we were going on a tour of your school. I thought you were going to take me out and show me off a bit," I say, though I want to say that I am not going anywhere near a hotel until I'm on my honeymoon.

"Emani, I park cars for The Majestic hotel. I asked my boss if we could park there for free, and she said yes. We're going to go eat some Cajun food at my favorite restaurant, then I'm going to take you to my school for Jazz Poetry Night. There aren't any dance performances tonight, but maybe we can see one on our next date," Rickey says, as he merges in front of a huge truck. His words help me to relax a bit, but I am still nervous about tonight. Wait a minute, did he just say our next date? I think Ebony is right. He does like me.

I talk to him about the Chicago landmarks along the skyline and when he reaches for my hand, I place it in his. My hand seems so small next to his. Usually freshman boys at school are what I like to call "medium rare," because they aren't quite done yet. They are still growing physically, mentally, intellectually, and emotionally. They like to punch you in your arm, pop your bra strap, and tease you about your every flaw. Rickey does not seem to be like them at all.

After we park at The Majestic, we walk hand in hand to Lucille's. According to Rickey, Lucille's is a restaurant that serves New Orleans-style cuisine. It also has live music. I like it already. Live music usually means freedom to dance.

The waitress who takes our order has the same accent that Kitten has. Kitten seems to believe that my sisters and I have Midwestern accents, but she won't admit to having her own Cajun twang. She claims that we say "Shicawgo" instead of "Chicago." We know she says "N'awlins" instead of "New Orleans."

I order my jambalaya "911 hot," even though Rickey warns me that it is really spicy. I think I can handle a little spice in my life right now. Rickey orders some type of Creole chicken, and I begin to wonder what exactly is in jambalaya. I hope it is vegetarian, but I don't think I've ever told him that I do not eat meat anymore.

"Rickey, I don't know if I've told you, but I don't eat anything with a face." He starts laughing and asks the waitress for a vegetarian menu.

The food is deliciously spicy, but our conversation is even juicier. Rickey tells me about how he caught his uncle, Mr. Thomas, and his aunt, Dr. Thomas, kissing in the condo two days ago. Minutes later, they were arguing over Mr. Thomas leaving on another fifty-city tour to talk to schools about trying to prevent acts of school violence. According to Rickey, Mr. Thomas still does not know that his wife is pregnant. I think he must be blinded by love or something, because she had a belly when I saw her on Halloween.

"She's only two months, Emani. You're just used to seeing her with her old abs of steel," Rickey says as he caresses my hand.

A new waitress walks up.

"Hi, Rickey. I see you're here for your weekly pilgrimage to Lucille's. We've missed you," the waitress says as she rubs his shoulders the way my mother rubs my father's after he has a long day at the Auto Shop. This waitress also whispers a little something in Rickey's ear, but he just stares at me without reacting to it. Then, he introduces me to her.

"Umm, Emani. This is Rachel. Rachel, this is Emani." She still does not take her hands off of him to shake my hand so I just place my hands in my lap on the top of my napkin. My hands squeeze the napkin a bit tighter the more she caresses him.

"Oh, is this your little sister or something?" Rachel says as she finally reaches out her hand to me. She sits down at the table when Rickey says that I'm his date.

"Oh, I'm sorry, Emani. You're tall, but you have such a baby face. I thought you were a high schooler," Rachel says.

I fold my arms as Rickey explains more of who I am to her. When he says the word "freshman," I decide to go to the bathroom to avoid further embarrassment. Passing the piano man on my way in, I slide the guy ten dollars and ask him to play something upbeat that I could dance to. He smiles and promises me some music that will get everyone on their feet. I look over at Rickey, only to see Rachel whisper something else into his ear again.

When I'm in the bathroom, I try to call my sisters, but neither of them answers. I send them each a text that says that my date is going well. I know that I'm lying, but I want them to be a little jealous of me for a change.

When I get outside, Rachel has resumed doing her job. From across the room, she throws a fake smile at me as I sit down beside Rickey. The piano player dedicates the next song to me and my date, prompting Rickey to ask me to dance.

On the floor, Rickey shows me that he has a few skills of his own. We dance, spin, slide, and embrace. He smells so fresh. It is like resting my head next to a warm, fresh-out-of-the-dryer blanket when I place my face on his chest. As we rock, I watch the sparks sliding across the logs in the restaurant's fireplace, and I wonder if we are imitating them or if they are mimicking us.

"We had better get going, Emani. We'll be late," Rickey says, though his hands do not move from around my waist as we dance.

I don't want to let go either. This is my first real slow dance. I've danced with boys who were assigned to dance with me before. I have done some sensational stunts with males who could lift and swing me in the air, but I have never danced with someone who I chose or someone who truly wants to be with me.

After Rickey walks me to the table, he pays our bill and leaves a generous tip on the table for our touchy-feely waitress Rachel. He helps me to put my jacket on and we head for the door. I wave at the piano guy as we are leaving, and almost kick my heels with joy when I see Rachel being stopped by one of her customers before she can get to us. Thanks to fellow customers, Rickey doesn't notice that Rachel was headed in our direction, and I definitely do not tell him when he opens the door for me.

We walk past a few beautifully decorated store windows. I love window shopping almost as much as I enjoy real shopping. I admire the displays, the way the mannequins are dressed, and the scenery. It is beautiful. Rickey stops in front of a window and begins pointing at something. When I realize it is a display of my favorite ballerina statuettes, I almost faint.

"I hope to have one of these statues one day," I declare before I begin walking.

"Let's go inside and look at them," Rickey says still standing by the large glass window.

"Nah! There's no use looking at something you can't have," I say as I look at him.

I once thought Rickey was as out of reach for me as those statuettes are now. Rickey asks me about their price and I tell him that he wouldn't believe me if I told him. Craftsmanship and quality really do come with a large price tag. Plus, those statues are collector's items.

"Can I buy you your first statue?" Rickey asks. I look at him puzzled. Isn't he a college student? College students are known for being poor. I couldn't take any of his money. I'm sure his full scholarship can't finance both of our lifestyles.

"I don't mean now, Emani. I mean when I can. When I can afford to buy you one of these, I want to be the person to buy you your first one," I smile at him. He is so . . . unlike any other boy I know.

"So I'm taking you back to my dorm room before we go to the open mic night," Rickey says while trying to button his jacket.

The Chicago wind wrestles with him as he tries to keep his jacket closed. I stop walking and stand in front of him to block the breeze until he is able to button up. Maybe he isn't any different from the boys I know. Did he say his dorm room?

"First a hotel. Now your dorm room. I hope you haven't forgotten that I'm a freshman in high school," I say with a laugh, though I am only half-joking. I don't want to go anywhere near his dorm room. There isn't anything in there that I need to see. I have my own little bed at home.

"Just trust me, Emani. I want to show you something," He says as he leads me back to The Majestic's parking lot.

As I fasten my seat belt, I silently hope that I am safe with Rickey, especially since neither of my parents know where I really am right now. Dad doesn't even know about my date, and mom only knows that I'm on a movie and a meal type of date with Mr. Thomas' nephew.

Mom was impressed by some of the STEM awards I told her he had won in school. She didn't ask how old he was and I didn't tell. She called Dr. Thomas to get some info on Rickey and I guess age didn't come up because she said I could go. I don't know if Dr. Thomas lied about Rickey's age since I'm keeping her little secret from Mr. Thomas or if my mom just didn't ask her usual prepared list of twenty questions simply because it was Zachary Thomas's mother. She and dad have shown us the twenty-question list ever since we were toddlers, and they have threatened to use it ever since we started to be interested in boys. Yes, Mom probably just made an exception. She probably just assumed that any relative of my big sis's first true love Zachary Thomas has to be a gentleman. Well, I hope for my sake, that she is right.

*

Rickey's dorm room looks more like those model apartments my mother took us to when we were looking for a place to live when she and dad were separated. It is like no one lives here because it is just too neat. I am quite surprised, because all of the boys at my house are messy, including my daddy.

Rickey takes my jacket and invites me to take a seat on his futon. The futon is as uncomfortable as I thought it would be, but I adjust a few of his mix-matched pillows and create my own sense of comfort. I look around the room for anything out of place, but I cannot find one item. Rickey stands in front of his closet and asks me if I am ready for his surprise.

Though nervous, I nod yes. He turns the lights off. The room is darker than a starless midnight sky so I grab a pillow from behind me and hold it in my lap. Forgive me, Daddy, for keeping this date a secret from you. Forgive me, Mommy, for not telling you the whole truth. I squeeze the pillow tighter.

I feel him sit beside me.

"Okay, just touch this button here," Rickey says as he guides my hand toward something on his lap. My hand shakes, but I manage to push the button. A circular light moves across his wall, bounces around the room and then seems to float in the air. The larger circle explodes into smaller shapes of light. I watch the vibrant lights ricochet, bend, flex, and dance across the room like fireworks of light. I can't help but to get up and move to their rhythm. Though the lively lights do not make a sound, I can feel the music they make as they travel through the room. They inspire me to sashay across the floor like a barefoot ballerina soaring above a stage and into the sky. The music joins the light and I observe a coupling of rhythm and illumination.

As the last light fades, I find myself hovering in the air. When I land, the multicolored lights have left their impression in me. Though they are gone, replaced with darkness, I somehow feel them in the atmosphere.

Another light returns. This time it is the light from the fluorescent bulbs in Rickey's room. Their beams' brightness in no way compare to the luminosity that I have just witnessed moments ago. I stand leaning on Rickey's closet door trying to catch my breath. The closet opens, and a flood of clothes, books, papers, and assorted items trickle then pour down on me. I instantly start laughing as Rickey rushes to try to clean up his mess.

"I was hoping you wouldn't see this!" Rickey says as he tries to stuff various objects back into a closet that is overflowing and bursting at the seams. I kneel down to help him trying not to giggle aloud.

"That light show was an amazing experience. Did you learn how to do that here?" I ask as I pass him a boot and a dress shoe from this once-concealed mess.

"Yes! You're going to see a bit more of my work on our next date. I have been hired to do a light show for a party on campus," Rickey says as he forces his closet door closed.

"Well, I can't wait to see more, Rickey. It's like you made light and music dance in perfect harmony."

After I speak, some things fall down inside of the closet and I can't keep my giggle inside. Rickey laughs too.

"Emani. At least now you know I don't have any skeletons in my closet." Rickey says as he hands me my jacket and stuffs his last sock into the closet.

"I'll have to take your word on that one." I say as he opens the door for me.

*

Rickey holds my hand as we walk to open mic night and I try to think of a poem that could capture what I've seen and felt tonight. If I were to stand up at the microphone, I would probably say . . .

My first date

When I saw him I had to smile
He was the walking definition of style
Wiser, older, CUTER than most guys
Finally, a boy who looked into my eyes
Wined me and dined me like a fairytale dude
He wasn't selfish, silly, or rude
We talked, we danced
He walked, I pranced
We held hands
We made plans
It was a perfect date
With a perfect mate
From my first disguise
To my first surprise
My first date fulfilled my every wish
And maybe even my first kiss?

Rickey and I did not kiss at open mic night, but he did introduce me as his girlfriend to a few of his college friends. I would have preferred the kiss, but maybe he'll try to kiss me later tonight. All I know is that he had better kiss me soon, because when we get to my house, there will not be any smooching allowed.

He caresses my hand and then kisses my knuckles like I'm the Queen of England or something. I begin to wonder if he will ever put his lips on mine.

When we pull into the driveway, I begin to tap my foot to the beat, mostly out of nervousness, since he wants to say hello to my parents. How do I tell him that speaking to them is not a great idea, because speaking to them would require my parents to see him? And when they see him, they will know he's older. If Dad and Mom find out he's older, our relationship will be over before it begins.

"Rickey, both of my parents work late hours. They come home tired and grumpy. I would prefer if they saw you when they were fresh and in good moods," I lie, trying to convince him to leave before my parents can see him.

"Okay, but you have to let me walk you to your door!" Rickey says as he exits the car and heads over to my side to open the door for me. I hesitate to get out as I realize that the moment I get out of the car this date is truly over and with it, all hopes of getting my first kiss anytime soon.

Rickey helps me out of the car and stops me halfway to the front door for a hug. A hug? Rickey told Rachel we were on a date, but maybe he does see me as more like a little sister than a girlfriend. I mean one minute he's kissing me on my forehead and the next he's telling me how beautiful I am. I don't really know where we stand.

My dad always says the love fire between him and my mom started with a small spark. Maybe there will be glowing embers for Rickey and I in the future.

"So are you going to be able to go to the party with me?" he asks, as he holds me around my midsection again. I nod, yes, though I don't really know if I'll be on punishment or not when my parents find out the truth about Rickey's age, because they somehow always find out the truth.

My mother has eyes in the back of her head, and my father has a unique x-ray vision that not only allows him to see through me, but through any lie that I try to tell him. And when the truth comes out, I don't think I'll be having a second date with Rickey Thomas, whether he is the cousin of the amazing Zachary Thomas or not. No exceptions.

CHAPTER 11
Ebony
Secrets

"**Y**ou're grounded, Ebony. No phone. No social media. No technology. You're grounded because you are late. You know the rules, and there are no exceptions, so save the excuses. Come sit down next to your sister." Dad says when I enter the house from my date with Stephan Miles two minutes after curfew.

I want to argue, but I decide against it when I notice that Emani isn't saying one word. If she can be silent, I know that I can. We both know that the first person who speaks is going to get it worst, so we just sit on the sofa in silence waiting for our punishment.

"What did I do, Daddy? I was on time," Emani whines.

"I would have been on time, too if I wasn't entertaining your date," I say foolishly in front of my father.

"Ebony, you went out on a date with Rickey Thomas? Well, Emani, who was that boy I saw you hugging on our front lawn?" Dad asks us both questions, but neither of us answers.

Emani folds her arms, and I decide to stare at our chocolate-colored carpet.

"You should be asking Ebony who she was kissing in that car outside." Mom says when she enters our living room.

I feel Emani staring at me, but I continue to look at the carpet.

"Kissing? Hugging? Someone had better start talking before I ground you until you're my age." Dad says as Eris walks into the room.

I don't look up at her, but I know her gym shoes anywhere. I don't know how she keeps them so clean. Even her shoe laces are sparkling white. She sits her nosey self down beside us until Dad asks her to leave. Okay, I'm inquisitive, too, but she's worse.

"Oh, Daddy, I was just going to give Ebony this." Eris says as she hands me two folded up pieces of paper.

She doesn't move until Mom asks her if she would like to get punished with the two of us. Then, she decides to abandon us. I watch Eris's sparkling-white gym shoes walk across the chocolate carpet, hoping that Emani will speak first.

"Daddy, we switched places. Ebony pretended to be me, and I pretended to be her until I went on my date." Emani says.

She is smart enough not to tell on Momma. Momma knew about the date, but she told us all that if we ever get caught she would never admit to letting us go on any dates. I guess Mom told Dad some stuff, but I'm not saying a word! I need Mom on my side.

"Switched places? I told you not to do that five years ago. Don't you remember a certain incident at a certain school that got you both suspended? Nothing good ever comes from it. You know I do not like when you all do that, so why did you do it?" Why does my Dad always ask questions that we can't possibly answer?

I stare at the fireplace, counting each tile in my mind. Each Tuscan tile on the left has a twin on the right side of the fireplace. Why couldn't my life be as simple as those tiles? No one would care if I switched one tile for another, but when we try a switch-a-roo everyone gets upset.

"Ebony, who were you on a date with? Who were you kissing?" My mother asks again after I try to ignore her the first time. I feel so guilty, though I wasn't dating Stephan for myself.

"His name is Stephan Miles, Momma." Emani pinches me on my arm when I say this and I try to explain to her that I thought she was interested in him.

All of a sudden my sister isn't interested in Stephan Miles.

Emani says, "Eris doesn't like him. I wouldn't date him. You're the one who told me that I shouldn't try to date him. Now, you've changed your mind. I don't want him. I'm dating Rickey."

My dad reminds her that she isn't dating anyone without his permission.

I want to giggle and scream at the same time. I just wasted hours of my life trying to help my selfish little sister.

"Well, I certainly don't want him, so I'll call and break up with him right now." I say as I pull out my phone from my purse.

Dad instantly takes my phone. Then, he requests Emani's phone, too. He says we won't be using them for a long time.

"This is why I told you two not to switch. This poor Stephan is going to get hurt. No . . . Stephan isn't going to get hurt, because he's going to be your new boyfriend, Ebony. Emani he's going to be your new boyfriend, too. You wanted boyfriends, right? In fact, the two of you are going to date him until you learn that it isn't fair for you to play with people's feelings. That is how my mother taught my twin brother and me. We learned the hard way just like you're going to do." Dad says as he whispers something into Mom's ear.

They both laugh. Neither Emani nor I are laughing.

I always thought that having grandparents and a parent who were twins would help us, but it hasn't helped us one time. My dad's mother, my mom's father, and my father were all naughty, mischievous multiples, but they want us to be perfect triplets.

"Do as I say and not as I did!" Nana always says.

"We expect you to be thrice as nice as we were." Pa-Pa always says.

And Daddy is the worst. He is always telling us cool stories about tricks he played on his teachers, parents, and friends, but he won't even let us switch for one day. How RUDE!

When we are dismissed, I rush to Emani to tell her all about my date with Stephan.

"I can't believe you kissed him." Emani says like she's heartbroken or something. I knew she liked him.

"Emani, I kissed him so he wouldn't see you all hugged up with Rickey. I kissed him for you, not for me." I say, as Eris walks in eating popcorn.

Emani and I look at her in duplicate. We can't believe she's eating after 10:00 p.m. Eris never eats anything after 10:00. It is against her self-imposed dietary restrictions. She offers us some popcorn and begins to tell us about her stressful evening. When she gets to the part where Motormouth Malcolm flirts with her at our dinner table, I cannot help but laugh. Motormouth Mosquito Malcolm winking at my sister? Trying to hug her? Trying to ask her on a date?

Was he the same Motormouth who called her narcissistic, androgynous, and a control freak in our school newspaper? He should've known he didn't stand a chance. Motormouth's chances of dating Eris are almost as slim as Stephan Miles's chances of dating her, and we all know Eris hates Stephan Miles. Sorry, I believe her words were that she strongly dislikes Mr. Stephan Miles.

We watch Eris gulp down an entire grape drink in about seven seconds. Then, we continue our conversation.

"You kissed Stephan Miles? Dis-gust-ing!" Eris says as she pretends to be sick over our trash can.

We all laugh in triplicate.

"Eris, Dad says we have to date him." Eris seems tickled that Emani and I will be dating her enemy. I didn't expect that reaction.

"I just want to be there when he finds out the truth!" Eris claims, but I don't know if I believe her. Eris is a genius at masking her true feelings.

I pull out the folded pieces of paper that Eris gave me earlier from my pocket as I put on my black silky pajamas. They are my favorite: comfortable, cozy, and sexy!

"Drama King Tyson gave you this flyer?" I ask Eris as she slides on her role model Ms. Mary Miles's Rookie #3 WNBA jersey with some pajama pants.

I would tease her that she is wearing Stephan Miles's last name across her back, but I don't think she would laugh at that one.

"Yup!" Eris says as she rubs her chiseled tummy, which is probably in shock from the white cheddar popcorn and grape drink.

As my sisters tuck themselves in, I admire my receipt from today's game's ticket sales and the selling of our new student council spirit wear. We made nearly twice as much money as the last student government did last year at this same time. I bet President Zyanne is tossing and turning in her sleep tonight. I told her that my marketing plan had potential. I can't wait to log in the rest of the receipts, I think as I pull out my receipt book. I am a great treasurer whether Zyanne will admit it or not.

"What are you staring at, Ebony?" Eris says after she asks me to turn off my night light again. I can't seem to make my mouth move.

"What's wrong, Ebony?" Emani asks as she throws her ruffled, lilac pillow at me. I still can't believe my eyes. I blink. I blink again.

Then, I hand the paper to Eris to read it out loud.

"'Meet me in Theatre 3. Row 10 at 10:00 for further instructions.' Was this there the whole time?" Eris says as she stares at the same words I've just read written upside down on my receipt.

"Zyanne gave that to you to give to Ebony? Is it for you or for Ebony?" Emani asks as she re-ties her satin scarf on her head. One of her rollers keeps falling out of the scarf.

"I think she wants you, Ebony. I think Zyanne wants you to be...a Dime," Eris declares in her most quiet voice.

"You think Zyanne Jeffries is a Dime?" I ask though I have suspected her since the first day I met her.

"I know she is. I was going to wait until after church tomorrow to tell you both since you've had a pretty hectic night, but since you asked . . . umm . . . I think I know the identities of all ten Dimes," Eris says.

Emani and I laugh until we notice that Eris isn't laughing with us. We were only separated for a few hours. How did she figure out who the Dimes are? I grab the receipt and look at it again. Theatre three? Maybe, she wants all three of us. Maybe, it's a code or something. I really don't know what Zyanne would want to talk to me about, but if it is to give me an invitation to join the Dimes she is wasting both of our time.

The Dimes represent everything that I dislike: they use power to make things worse instead of better. If I were to become a member, it would only be in order to destroy them from the inside out. When I think of the Dimes, ten words come to mind: obliterate, annihilate, wipe out, demolish, break up, weaken, wreck, and destroy. And those are just the nicest words that I can think of for them.

*   *   *

On Monday morning, I make my way toward the theatre rooms to survey the area, since I promised my sisters I would. I really don't trust Zyanne or the Dimes. Maybe they are trying to set me up.

When I get to Theatre three, there is a class inside doing some sort of silent improvisation. I leave when the acting teacher asks me where I am supposed to be. After my next class, I return to the theatre with the flyer that the drama boy gave to Eris to bring to me. As the theatre teacher explains the plot of the spring dramedy, I look around the room for any potential problems. I don't see any booby traps or any cameras, so I decide to come back at 10:00.

*

"Wow, Ms. Robertson, three times in one day. You must really be interested in performing in this play," Ms. Scott says, as she explains the requirements for trying out for the spring play.

Inside I smile, since I am actually doing a little acting right now. When I reach row ten, there is an envelope on the back of seat ten. It has all three of my initials on it: EER. I discreetly slip the envelope into my purse as Ms. Scott tells me more about the lead role. Though she continues to talk, I continue to walk backwards toward the exit.

"Ms. Scott, I'm more of a behind the scenes type of person. Maybe I could help you with building the sets," I say as she writes my name on her clipboard.

She is looking forward to seeing me tomorrow for tryouts and I just may go out of guilt now that she has written my name down. I am a young woman who keeps my promises.

When I step out into the hallway, I rush toward my next class trying to read the note while I walk. According to this note, Zyanne wants me to meet her in the library during lunch. Why didn't she just write that in the first note? This girl is too complicated.

It is like my entire class knows that I have to meet Zyanne, because they are so rowdy that my teacher keeps us a minute after class. My classmates and I have to listen to a lecture about respect and peacefulness before we are permitted to leave our desks.

When we are dismissed, I quickly make my way to the library and sit at the tenth table from the door. The note does not say where to sit, but the Dimes seem to do everything in tens. After five minutes of watching everyone, I decide to leave. I can't believe I'm missing my one opportunity to eat the only school lunch that is decent for these chicks. I can't believe I let my sisters talk me into doing this.

Before I can reach the double doors, I see Zyanne Jeffries walking into the library with one of the AV girls. They look at me with such disdain that I wonder if it was me that they invited here or not. Maybe the note was for Eris. We do all have the same initials, plus Zyanne did put the receipt into Eris's hands.

"Are you leaving?" Zyanne says while tapping her right hand on her very wide hips.

The less-tall AV girl opens the door for me and asks me the same question while tapping her left hand on her very narrow hips. I turn around and head back to table ten.

Zyanne sits beside me. The tall AV girl sits a video camera down on the table and walks away. My stomach growls.

"So you were going to leave without even giving me ten minutes?" Zyanne asks as she pulls out her lunch from a very large purse. I hope she has some food in there for me. I'm so hungry that I would maybe join the Dimes if she has a nice salad in there for me. She takes a bite out of what smells like a tuna fish sandwich without offering me a crumb.

"Lunch is only 30 minutes. A girl has to eat," I say as I stare at her sandwich wishing I could even have a piece of her wheat bread.

The narrow-hipped AV girl puts a salad on the table in front of me. The other wider AV girl puts a bottled Vitamin water next to it. After the first one adjusts the camera in front of me, they both sit three tables away from Zyanne and me.

"We always take care of our own," Zyanne says as she pulls out a metallic notebook from her big purse.

I guess my sisters were correct. They want me to be one of them.

"So tell me a little about your secret organization," I say as I look into the camera.

Zyanne pretends not to know what I am talking about. In fact, she says that she just brought me here to hear some more of my ideas for improving the school. I instantly laugh since she hasn't been interested in any of my ideas since I joined student government. Usually, when I speak in meetings, she asks everyone in the room if they hear any vexing sound in the room. According to her, I'm always the "exasperating" sound in the room when she's around. She has fought me about my every idea and suggestion since I became treasurer at C.I.A., so I know she's lying.

"Secrets? I'll tell you some secrets, Ebony. There is a girl at this school who goes to talk to a psychologist twice a month because she has nightmares. There is a girl at this school who is supposed to wear glasses, but does not. There is a girl at this school who has severe peanut allergies and has to walk around with an EpiPen on her at all times. Do you know her?" Zyanne asks a question, but I can't believe she knows these things about me.

Zyanne closes her little metallic notebook and tells me that these were only secrets 8, 9, and 10 on her list about me. I am suddenly a bit nervous about meeting her here. Maybe the Dimes did not want to invite me in. Maybe I'm their next victim.

Charlotte told me that the Dimes had "convinced" some girls to cut Diana Eldrige's very long ponytail completely off at Tiny's basement party on Saturday simply because she mentioned their names at lunch last week. Eris told me that one of her technology classmate's car windows were completely broken out because he said the Dimes are immature and infantile and need to grow up. And Emani still believes that the Dimes stole her clothes from her swimming locker. What will they do to me?

I do not respond to Zyanne's question.

"Don't be nervous. We all have secrets. Secrets that are safely hidden. Secrets that only we know about each other. Would you like to know one of my secrets?" Zyanne asks as she leans closer to me.

My stomach growls again since I have barely eaten any of my food. I do not look at her, but my ears are wide open. Then, my mother's words flash in my mind: Always look into your enemy's eyes. This shows them that you are in control, that you aren't scared. I look into Zyanne's eyes trying not to blink. Big sis Alexis, the blinkless champion, would be proud of me right now.

"Not really!" I say as I get up leaving my salad and water behind.

Am I crazy? I need that food. The AV girls stand as I stand. Zyanne quietly asks me to sit down before I can leave. Then, she turns off the camera.

"Look, Ebony. I don't want you, but my sisters do. Because I trust them, I am telling you my secret. Half of us are graduating and we need . . . want you to replace one of us. Do you understand what this could mean for you?"

"What about my sisters?" I say as I glance over at the now-seated AV girls taking very small bites of their lunch with all eyes on me. They look around the room like we are under surveillance.

"There are 5 spots opening up on the Dimes when we graduate. Surely you don't think the Robertson girls will take 3 of them. They want . . . we want YOU. Your sisters will be safe . . . untouched." Zyanne looks at her watch and then tells the AV girls to leave with a flick of her wrist.

When she does this, I begin to think that maybe Eris is correct about Zyanne's rank in the Dimes. Maybe she is #3. She exudes power and influence. I wonder if I am to take her place. What am I thinking? I don't want to be a Dime.

"And what if I want to say no?" I say, as Zyanne slides back in her seat. She hands me a piece of paper that says "No is not an option." I fold it back up and hand it to her as she requests I do.

"Ebony, we will know that you are saying yes if you show up to school tomorrow wearing blue jeans and a fall-colored shirt. If you aren't saying yes I wouldn't come to school tomorrow, if I were you," Zyanne says as she rises, leaving me at the table with barely enough time to eat or drink anything.

As I stuff my face with food, I wave at Stephan Miles as he turns in a book to the library's main desk. *Please don't let him come over here. Please don't let him come over here. Please don't let him come over here.*

"So, Ebony, have you seen Emani?" Stephan asks smiling from ear to ear. I can't believe I kissed this boy.

"Not since this morning, Stephan, but I'll tell her that you're looking for her," I say, after I drink my water in a few gulps.

"Well, when you see her can you give her this for me?" Stephan says as he slides me what feels like a two-page note for Emani. Before I can answer, he leaves to talk to Reana Powers, the smartest student at school. Her picture is first on the wall of top ten students at C.I.A. She is being recruited by every college I hope to go to one day. Hopefully she is tutoring Stephan, because he definitely needs some English skills.

*   *   *

I laugh after every line as I read Stephan's letter to myself. One date, and he is already crazy about me. Which is to say, about Emani. "Watch where you're going, Ebony," Charlotte says when I accidentally bump into her wheelchair in the hall after exiting the library.

Charlotte tries to roll by me without saying anything else, but I stand in front of her. I always know when something is wrong with Charlotte because her face shows her every emotion. She has anger in her cheeks, lips, *and* eyes.

"I saw you having lunch with HER. My worst enemy is now your best friend?" Charlotte says as she rolls over my foot. I use profanity before I can stop myself. Ms. Kelly tells me to watch my language in the halls. I quickly apologize to Ms. Kelly, though I feel Charlotte should be apologizing to me.

"It wasn't what you think!" I protest, as Charlotte rolls away.

Charlotte doesn't even turn around. I wiggle my toes to make sure they aren't broken and then limp after her to try to explain myself. Unfortunately, Charlotte goes into her class before I can catch her. I guess I'll have to talk to her later about Zyanne.

An opportunity to talk to Charlotte later does not come because after my class, I am invited to the principal's office. According to the principal, I have been selected as a student of character for the month of October. As I start to reminisce about all of my hard work last month, I am told that there will be a breakfast held in my honor tomorrow. There were only three people chosen from each grade level, and I was chosen by my teachers. Today is turning out to be a great day for my ego. First, I am chosen by the Dimes. Now, I am chosen by the staff. I wonder what tomorrow will bring.

* * *

When my sister brings me a "fall-colored" sweater to go with my designer jeans, I hold it next to my skin, trying to decide if I will wear it. Orange isn't my color at all. I think about how this sweater clashes with my hair, as Eris and Emani ask me twenty more questions about my meeting with Zyanne yesterday. Eris and Emani both think I should go undercover and destroy the Dimes, but I don't want to have anything to do with them or their diabolical activities.

I take off the sweater and put on my Think! t-shirt. Eris and Emani both clap like I've just given a speech or something.

"I knew you wouldn't do it," Eris says as she hangs the pumpkin-orange sweater back in our closet. She and Emani both put on their Think! t-shirts, too.

"Maybe, you should wear the sweater under the T-shirt," Emani says until Eris pinches her on her arm.

I can tell that Emani is a bit nervous for me. I try to convince her not to worry, but inside I am a bit nervous, too. I know I am doing the right thing, but sometimes the right thing isn't the easy thing to do. The Dimes are said to be responsible for some of the underclassmen getting sick at lunch. If they are willing to poison food to get revenge, what would they do to me?

* * *

By the time I get off of the early bus, my nervousness has tripled. Now I am no longer simply nervous. I am worried, panicky, and extremely anxious as I walk to the principal's office. I sign in at the main desk and sit at the table with Charlotte, who still isn't speaking to me, a junior boy who I do not know, and Reana Powers.

Reana smiles at me and introduces me to Greg Kim. Greg is a junior. He works in the main office with Reana. They are office runners. It is part of their community service for National Honor Society. Reana, Greg, and I talk about what an honor it is to be selected before principal Wells enters the room.

I can't believe I am even sitting this close to principal Wells. She is certainly a heroine of mine. Under her leadership, Chicago International Academy has gained a reputation of being one of the top-tier Illinois schools. We have a 98-percent graduation rate, and a 100-percent college acceptance rate. Unfortunately, I believe that our unexplainable 2% drop-out rate can be directly traced back to the Dimes. Rumor is that if they don't get you to drop out, they find a way to get you kicked out of school.

I shake principal Wells' hand, and Motormouth Mosquito Malcolm McGee takes a picture of us for *The Pulse*. Finally, a Robertson girl will get a good article in our school newspaper. Even Emani has not been covered yet, because Malcolm always writes about Kylie Calderone's dance moves, leadership, and style.

After I leave the breakfast, I walk up a few flights of stairs to go to my locker to get my books for the rest of my morning classes. Charlotte is already at her locker next to mine when I get there. I don't know how she does this, but it must be nice to have your own elevator. Happiness is still not in her eyes, cheeks, or on her lips, but she does finally say hello to me before wheeling herself away. At least Charlotte acknowledged my presence.

I grab my books, close my locker, and walk toward my second class, but before I can get there, someone knocks all of my books out of my hands. She doesn't apologize. She doesn't run. She just stands in front of me as I lean over to pick up my books. The Freshman Dean's words play in my mind: If you fight, you will be suspended.

When I gather all of my books, I walk around the girl and toward my class. This time, someone else knocks my books from my hands. I feel like I've seen her around school, but I don't know her name, either. This time I let the books stay on the floor. Did the Dimes send them? None of the fights we believe were initiated by the Dimes this year have been in the hallway. Usually, the Dimes have people beaten up in the locker rooms or a bathroom where there isn't a camera, but neither of these girls seems to care about the hall's cameras.

A third girl stands on my right side. A fourth girl stands on my left side. Four to one? This is definitely the work of the Dimes. They don't fight fair.

I try to walk forward, but the first girl does not move. I try to walk backward, but the second does not move. In my mind, I hope for a bell to ring. My prayers are soon answered.

The halls are instantly flooded with students, but all I feel are someone's knuckles striking my temple. Instantly, I choose not to listen to the dean's warning playing in my mind. Actually, I believe that I erase the dean's words from my memory all together, because the next thing I know I am whacking, smacking, slapping, and beating anybody who comes within arm's reach. There may be four of them, but I have two fists and two feet. I ain't scared!

It is not until the security guard pulls me off of the fourth one that I realize that Charlotte, Kitten, and my sisters have joined in the fight.

All of us are dragged to the principal's office.

We are separated into two rooms: us in one, them in the other.

"Did you see what they were wearing?" Eris says as she slides her fingers through her three-minute hair. Her hair instantly snaps back into her style. Though I don't have a mirror, I know that mine is all over my red head. Emani tries to fix it for me. As she does this I notice that my shirt is ripped. Thanks to the Dimes, everyone has seen my bra's peace signs.

"Who cares what they were wearing? We are all going to be suspended," Charlotte says as she tries to hide the green book bag she most likely used to fight a few minutes ago. We watch her trying to find a hiding place for her book bag. It makes us all giggle.

"Charlotte, they were all wearing fall colors and jeans. I think they were the Dimes' new recruits," I say as I put Charlotte's green bag on my back. Charlotte looks puzzled for a moment, but a nod confirms her understanding.

I tell her that I'll tell the dean that I used the book bag. Then, I thank her for fighting with me, even though she was mad at me. When she hugs me, I start to cry like a wimp. I just fought four girls, but now I'm in here crying, mainly because my parents are going to kill me when I get suspended. I'm glad to reconnect with my friend. I've missed Charly.

"You guys act like we're going down or something. If those girls are recruits, the Dimes won't let them get in trouble, and if they don't get in trouble, we aren't getting in trouble," Kitten says as she scribbles something into her little checkered notebook.

I wish I had her confidence, but I know that we were fighting directly in front of a working camera. My Robertson confidence is all gone. I hope my sisters have some of their own.

The dean walks in.

"Hello, ladies. You look like you've been in a war. What happened?" The dean says.

Emani, Eris, and I start to say something, but when Kitten shakes her head no, we do not say one word.

"Wow. The ladies next door are as silent as you are, but don't worry, your actions will speak louder than any words you could say. Let's go see you on video." Dean Norton instructs us to leave her office.

We follow her to the room that holds the dime-wannabes and the video footage from the hallway. I worry that we should have confessed. At home, the first to confess gets the lightest consequence. At home, you don't speak first unless you are confessing.

When the security guard comes in empty-handed and whispers something to dean Norton, I feel a bit more relieved. Dean Norton is visibly frustrated and upset, because according to the security guard the video seems to be a little fuzzy.

"No one in the hall saw anything? The camera is hazy? That is okay. I don't need a video or witnesses to know there was a fight here!" Dean Norton shouts.

Her voice shakes a bit as she speaks. She is quite annoyed with all of us.

"Okay, ladies, if there was no fight, there was no fight." When dean Norton speaks these words, my heart muscles finally relax.

Thank goodness.

"But you all are suspended for one day. You four are suspended for walking my halls without valid passes. Ebony, you are suspended for inappropriate dress, Emani and Eris, you are suspended for being nowhere near your next classes, Charlotte you are suspended for misuse of . . . " Before Dean Norton can finish giving out ludicrous and unfair punishments, principal Wells enters with Tyra Jacobs.

Tyra does not look up, but she speaks quite clearly. "I saw the fight." I almost kick the table when she says this. This girl wouldn't even speak up when the Dimes painted a humongous ten on her back at the pep rally, but now she wants to speak up. Now, thanks to her, I'm going to be out for three days instead of one. I could have maybe explained the indecent exposure to my parents, but fighting is never tolerated. Who am I kidding? My dad and mom will kill me for violating dress code, too. While I contemplate my parental punishment, Eris gives Tyra a thumbs up like she's done something good. I just put my head on the round table too overwhelmed to say another word.

Dean Norton smiles.

Tyra looks up and directly at me.

"Ebony was just walking through the hall when Aesha and Marisa book checked her. Grace and Teresa surrounded her, and then Marisa punched her in the face. She had to fight back."

Dean Norton is not satisfied with Tyra's explanation until Tyra tells on my sisters, Kitten, and Charlotte. Dean Norton says that I tried to do the right thing, but she says that my helpers, though they had good intentions, chose to do the wrong thing. She suspends Aisha, Marisa, Grace and Teresa for ten days. She suspends Kitten, Charlotte, and my sister for three days. I am suspended for one day.

We all listen to a lecture on fighting and mob action before we are released by the dean to our lockers, security guards escorting us as we walk down the halls.

"I can't believe dean Norton says she'll call the police next time," Eris says as she gets her jacket from my locker.

"There won't be a next time," Emani says as she puts her jacket on.

Principal Wells walks over to the three of us. Big sis Alexis and her new personal aide walk beside her.

"Ebony Robertson, I want you to know that today's incident will cancel out your student of character award," Principal Wells says before she tells me that I can still win the award later in the year.

When Jeremy hands Alexis's books to me, I suddenly realize that my sister will be here without us tomorrow. I hope the Dimes aren't foolish enough to bother Alexis Dieona Robertson. They may not know her secrets, but I do: you know that saying about being a lover and not a fighter? My sister is a lover and a fighter. She may not talk with her lips, but her fists speak a language of their own.

CHAPTER 12

Eris
The Red Sports Car

Thanksgiving may only be a couple of weeks away, but I already have a few things of my own to be thankful for. First, my mother did not put me on punishment for getting suspended. This is huge because she only thinks we should miss school for the three d's: death, doctor, or disaster. Mom has even let me go to practices with my team at Stephan Miles's house. Thank you, Mom.

Second, my sisters agreed to proceed with my plan to gather information on the Dimes. I am going to concentrate on Ms. Volleyball, Vita Rowe, and Ms. School Spirit, Shiani Chan. Emani is going to focus on the dancing diva, Kylie Calderone, and co-cheerleading chick Winter Gordon. Ebony is going to collect facts on brainiac Reana Powers and actress Winter Gordon. Kitten is going to get data on the AV girls, and Charlotte is going to find some info on Zyanne Jeffries and fashionista Brenda Agbayewa. It is not going to be easy, but with the help of Mr. Thomas's detective spy technology, we believe we will find something to prove that the Dimes are the trouble makers behind all of the negative mess at C.I.A.

And third, Stephan Miles has really been nice to me since he believes that he is "dating" Emani. Not only has he spoiled me with cold water bottles, warm towels, and snacks when I've come to practice with my squad at his house this week, but at school he has waved and spoken to me. More importantly, he hasn't written one cruel word about me in *The Pulse* or online since Saturday. For my sake, I hope Emani and Ebony date him at least for the rest of volleyball season. Thank you, Emani and Ebony.

Ebony says it has been quiet at school since our big brawl.

It hasn't been quiet here, however. The phone has been ringing since Tuesday. Everyone who has called asks only one question: Are we scared?

Scared? Fear has never been an option for me. When I step on the court, I can't be afraid. I could be hit in the head with a ball. I could fall and break something. I have been injured, but I have never been hurt. If I spent any of my minutes worrying about what could happen on the court, I would never enjoy playing. Life is like the volleyball court to me: I may win or lose, but no one will ever be able to say that I did not play my very best.

"Where's Curly?" Stephan says when I ring his doorbell. I try not to smirk, because he usually knows how to read my body language.

Instead, I speak to Mrs. Miles, hoping that Stephan will forget his question. He does. Mrs. Miles flies around the kitchen like she's the sanitary fairy. She cooks, cleans, and converses effortlessly. Since I've been practicing here, I have learned a lot about her, but one thing is apparent: Mrs. Miles takes being a mom very seriously. She always talks more about motherhood than her past awards, medals, or accomplishments.

In fact, every time I try to get athletic advice, she changes the subject. I want to talk about her playing basketball and volleyball around the world, and she wants to speak about her playing basketball and volleyball with Stephan when he was a toddler. I could care less about Stephan Miles or his childhood, but because I love his mother, I listen to her stories.

The doorbell rings, and Stephan seems relieved that he is saved from embarrassing baby Stephan stories by the bell. He races to the door to let my teammates inside. I do not hear the usual sound of five pair of dragging feet. I only hear one pair of feet, and they belong to my sister and not one of my teammates.

"Eris, is Alexis here with you?" An out-of-breath Emani says, while leaning on Mrs. Miles's spotless refrigerator.

"No, isn't she at home?" I say, as I read fear in my sister's eyes. I try to convince her not to fret.

Jeremy always has Alexis home after school on time. He probably took her somewhere to eat, or maybe they are out joy-riding on his motorcycle. I don't think we should be concerned. They don't do that as much as they used to, but maybe they are back to "dating."

I hear Ebony at the door talking to Mr. Miles about Alexis, so I leave the kitchen and head toward her. When I see Ebony's bottom lip trembling as she speaks to Mr. Miles, I begin to get a little nervous, because Ebony is usually solid. When she sits down on the Miles' sofa, I watch her tap her foot thrice before leaning over to attempt to drink the juice Mrs. Miles has brought for her. Her left hand trembles as she drinks.

"Where's Jeremy?" I ask when Emani comes into the room.

Ebony takes a deep breath, but she stutters a bit, "He's out looking for Alexis with m-mom and dad."

"He came by the house and said that he was waiting for Alexis to come outside after school, when Kylie Calderone's pathetic self walks up to him and kisses him on the mouth. Before he could let loose of the lip lock, he says Alexis walked up and saw Kylie kissing him. Then, Alexis ran off." Emani's words stun me. I think of Alexis' delicate condition.

"Why didn't he chase her? Did she get on the bus? Where is Alexis?" I ask three questions before my sisters can even answer the first question, but I am so troubled right now.

I knew those Dimes were going to try to hurt Alexis, but mom insisted on sending her to school without us saying we were suspended, not Alexis. Alexis's aide at school is supposed to make sure that she goes class to class and gets on the bus if Jeremy has to leave school early or something. Jeremy's band rarely has a gig during the week, so it is quite uncommon for him to leave school early, but when he does it is the aide's job to make sure my sister is safe. I can't believe that he did not do his job. I can't believe I was not there to protect her.

The doorbell rings after Mrs. Miles offers us some food. Is she kidding? I can't eat right now no matter how delicious that meatloaf and mashed potatoes smells.

"Did you find her?" Jeremy asks, before he can even get inside the door. I get up and walk over to him to yell at him, until I see pain in his eyes. His big, brown eyes are not as bright as they usually are, though.

"How did she get away from you, Jeremy?" I ask as gently as I can, but I need to know how my sister outran this six-foot, long-legged male.

Jeremy, who is obviously embarrassed, explains how Kylie and her friends surrounded his motorcycle, flirting and complimenting him on his bike and his band's performance last weekend. He says that by the time Alexis showed up, the cycle was powered-up, and the cheerleaders had his and Alexis's helmets, tossing them around to one another.

"I can't believe Kylie kissed me. She's been flirting, but she has never even tried to kiss me."

I look at Jeremy's face as he says this and realize that he truly does not realize how wanted he is at school.

Kylie Calderone is a Dime, so I know she probably did this kissing crap as revenge against us, but I would not be surprised if she really does want Jeremy. Why wouldn't she want him? He sings with a soft, silky, velvety tone that is like no one I've ever heard. He is a gifted saxophonist who plays with instinct and passion. That's what the music critics for our school paper say. And, he is a mastermind at creating beats that I could dribble, dunk, and bounce to. And since he's that suave stud type, he's not my type, but I know he is far from ugly. Of course, Kylie kissed him. She probably had to fight the rest of the Dimes for this kissing duty.

"It's our duty to protect her, Jeremy. Don't beat yourself up about it. You did your best," Ebony says, before I can say the very same thing.

Stephan, who normally is selfish and spoiled, surprisingly volunteers to help us drive around and look for Alexis. Mr. and Mrs. Miles grab their keys, and in a matter of minutes we are on the road.

After a few minutes on the road, my cell phone rings. It is my mommy. Stephan turns down his stereo after I hit him in the back of his big head with a pack of gum. I can't believe this fool is trying to blast this romantic music to impress Emani when my sister is out there lost somewhere. Is he ignorant or just rude?

"When? How did she get there? Yes, we are on our way home, Mommy," I say, as my mom continues to brag on our silent sister Alexis showing some independence by getting home on her own.

If I came in late from school, Mom would kill me, but when Alexis walks in late, Mom is so ecstatic that she made it home without the help of Jeremy or any of us. It isn't fair, but I guess I am happy that Alexis made it home by herself, too.

"Stephan, you can turn around! Alexis is at the house. She got a ride with someone from school." Emani looks back at me from her passenger seat with a frown.

Then, she asks me who Alexis knows with a car. I really have no idea, but I am thankful to whoever it is. After he turns his romantic music back up, Stephan teases me about missing a much-needed practice today, but I ignore him. What happened to him being nice to me? Emani needs to hurry up and kiss this boy or get Ebony to do it again. He is irritating!

By the time we get home, I decide that either Charlotte's or Kitten's mothers must have driven Alexis home, since they are the only people Alexis knows with cars. I call Charlotte to thank her, but she asks me if I have forgotten that she was suspended for three days just like me.

I laugh, since I had forgotten she is stuck at home too, but I am a bit more confused when I get off the phone with Charlotte, now that I realize that Charlotte could not have given Alexis a ride home since she wasn't at school. There is no use trying to ask Alexis who drove her home, so I go to my mom for some clues.

"Of course I remember the car. It was a bright red sports car. She pulled off quickly, but I wrote down the plate number just in case something happened to my baby. Alexis seems fine, though. She's in there watching the news," Mom states while smiling at her eldest child.

I smile since today is the closest I've seen Alexis come to her old self. Therapy, a year of homeschooling from our aunt, serenades from Jeremy or Alexis: I don't know who to give the credit to, but I'm happy to have pre-school shooting Alexis back if only for one day.

I take the paper with the license plate number written on it and head to the house phone in the living room to call Mr. Thomas. We all know that he only answers calls from our phone number, because he was receiving too many crank calls and false tips about murderess Payton Payne on his home line from strange numbers. I'm sort of glad Mom refuses to get rid of this landline phone even though we all have cell phones, because everyone knows our home phone number.

After a little explanation, Mr. Thomas agrees to find out who the license plate number belongs to. I sit on the line waiting while stuffing my face with spaghetti and meatballs. I am very grateful that my mom made both zucchini-noodle vegetarian and meat-filled spaghetti, because I really need this protein right now. I am starving.

Mr. Thomas tells me that he is happy to hear from me and looks forward to seeing me soon. Anticipation builds in my mind as I wait for the identity of the owner of the red car. I quickly promise to come to help him with the case against Payton Payne as soon as possible.

After a little small talk about his progress with his case against mass-murderess Payton Payne, he reads the name of the owner of the red sports car. I almost choke on my meatball. No, I am choking on my meatball.

Ebony comes in and whacks me in my back, freeing my airway. While I try to take small breaths, I watch her pick up the phone and tell Mr. Thomas that we'll have to call him back later.

She looks at me puzzled.

"Did he find Payton Payne?" Ebony whispers as she tries to close our bedroom door.

I finally capture my breath and take a seat on my bed to relax.

"No, but he saved another school from her destruction. He only caught one of her explosive experts. That is not why I was choking."

Before I can answer, Emani walks in with a bowl of veggie spaghetti. I scream at her to close the door behind her. After she slowly closes it, I get up to make sure it is closed all the way and locked.

"Alexis got a ride with Zyanne Jeffries," I whisper, after I peek out the door to make sure my big sister is not around.

"Zyanne Jeffries?" Emani and Ebony say in duplicate.

After a bit of discussion, we decide to try to talk to Alexis to try to get some information from her. We walk to the living room and stand in front of the TV. Alexis does not look away. She stares right through us.

"Alexis, Jeremy did not want to kiss that girl earlier today. He loves you!" Emani says.

Alexis does not react. The little light she had in her eyes lately seems dimmed again.

"I hope you aren't going to let that Kylie girl have your man!" Ebony says.

Again, Alexis does not react. We stare at her for any sign of a response. As usual, she does not blink.

"Umm. Alexis. How did you go from riding with Jeremy to riding with Zyanne Jeffries?" I ask.

Alexis gets up. When she leaves, I see a folded note on her seat. My sisters see it, too. We all stare at the note, but do not dare open it. Alexis doesn't talk, but if I remember correctly, she can beat all three of us in a battle.

When she comes back into the living room, she has a plate of food. She sits next to the note, taking delicate bites out of her meatballs. She does not make eye contact with any of us.

Then, she looks directly at me. For the first time in a long time, she looks at me in my eyes.

I grab the note and open it, read it silently to myself, and then read it aloud to my sisters. I can tell it is a copy and not the original when I open it because the words are almost too light to read like when you make a copy of something written in any color ink other than black.

> Dear Mr. A,
>
> I am so sorry about that kiss the other day. I know that you said that you cannot be with me since I am a student and you are a teacher, but I know we would be great together. You are a brilliant man, and I am a thinker, too. The age thing is not a problem for me. We are only four years apart. Those years won't mean anything in four years when I graduate from college. We'll both be teachers. We'll both be equals. But I can't wait until then. I want to be with you now. Can we please go on a date? Can we try again?
>
> Z.J

"I get that Z.J. is Zyanne Jeffries, but who is Mr. A?" Emani asks, while scratching her curly head.

"I think Mr. A is Mr. Anderson, that new student teacher. The one who is too attractive and too young to be a high school teacher. Alexis has him for chemistry. He and Alexis's new aide went to college together, but how did Alexis get this note?" We all look at Alexis after Ebony explains this to us. Could this note be the reason Zyanne gave our big sis a ride home?

Alexis does not blink. She does not even look at us. I fold the letter and sit it back down next to Alexis.

Ebony says she is going to call Charlotte to tell her that we have a little information on Ms. Zyanne Jeffries's secrets. Wow, it has only been a couple of days and Charlotte's job to get dirt on Zyanne is already half-finished. Thanks to big sis Alexis, Charlotte now has some information on Zyanne, but how am I going to get some dirt on Ms. Vita Rowe?

I look at Alexis, wishing that I could have been there earlier to see her in action. Did she even say a word? How did she get to keep that note? I really wish she had another one from Vita Rowe to a mysterious, mischievous man, but I know that I'm going to have to find my own way to learn Ms. Vita Rowe's secrets.

*

Vita Rowe fake congratulates me after my girls and I win yet another game.

I fake wish her luck on her own game, but inside I am hoping that she finally learns what the word "defeat" means tonight. The girls and I mentally take notes as varsity plays their game trying to locate a weakness. We don't see any weaknesses in their game. Vita and her squad seem to destroy every opponent they encounter. It is like they've won even before they step onto the court. My girls and I need to develop that type of confidence. We need a victory dance of our own. We need a swagger that says we are true champions.

After varsity wins again, Vita and her teammates sit behind us on the bus chanting "We are the Champions." They form W's with their fingers and call each other winners.

As I look around me at my own partners, I see them sinking in their seats or quietly trying to sit still enough to disappear. On the court, we play in the shape of a W, but when we leave the court, we act like losers. My team has had a flawless season. How can they behave like losers?

I decide to chant by myself: "Not one loss, not one defeat, fresh-soph team just can't be beat. Not one loss, not one defeat, fresh-soph team just can't be beat. Not one loss, not one defeat, fresh-soph team just can't be beat."

After three times chanting alone, my squad finally faintly joins in. Angie, Monica, Karen, Sylvia, Rochelle, and even weak-willed, cute Keyshia chant a little louder and with a little more confidence by our third time.

However, when Vita Rowe and her crew stand on this moving bus, stomping noisily, my timid squad sits down.

"Y'all gonna lose! Wanna bet? Fresh-soph team just ain't lost yet," Vita chants.

Vita's girls join in as soon as she finishes the chant. They are so loud and confident that even I decide to sit down, too. For the rest of our ride, I have to listen to Vita's teammates tease us about not winning one game against them. We have a flawless season against everyone else except them. Again, they call us mere mortals and themselves game goddesses.

* * *

"What happened on the bus? Y'all just left me standing there like a fool. Go to the stands," I say as I point to the football stands when my teammates and I are far away from varsity on the field.

The girls begin to whine, knowing that I am going to be very unforgiving as we train tonight after they embarrassed me, their captain, on the bus earlier.

"Come on Eris, it's late. It's dark. The field's lights aren't even all on. Plus, we won our game. Can't we just go home? Our parents are here," the girls say, as I continue to point to the football stands.

"Coach would not approve of this," Monica complains.

The field's night lights turn on as my teammates give me more excuses. Our parents are going to have to wait. These girls owe me ten trips up and down the stands. Maybe next time they'll chant like champs instead of whispering like wimps.

Once we are on the stands, I begin my chant again.

"Not one loss. Not one defeat. Fresh-soph team just can't be beat." This time the girls join in on time.

I do not let them stop climbing the football stands until I hear their faint chants become ferocious chants. Unfortunately, after our tenth trip to the top, I hear Stephan Miles screaming my name above my squad's chants.

I decide to permit the girls to leave when he begs me to come down toward him. The girls happily give him high five's as they leave. I hear some of them whisper "thank you" to Stephan as they pass the two of us.

Stephan's dirty, grimy, stinky self says, "Were you trying to kill them?"

I snatch the water bottle he offers me and head toward the school's entrance without saying one word to him. Vita Rowe and cheerleading captain Shiani Chan start giggling when I trip over my own shoelace trying to out-walk Stephan. Stephan asks me if I'm okay before he lets a chuckle escape from his dry, lip-balmless lips.

"Where are you going? I'm your ride, Eris. Emani says your dad gave me permission to take both of you home," Stephan says as I try to ignore captain Chan and my rival, Rowe.

When I stop moving, I see Vita getting into Shiani's car.

"Don't let them get to you, Eris! They're just jealous," my teammate Angie says.

I frown at her, thinking that there isn't one reason those girls would be jealous of me. Good looks: they've got 'em. Talent: they've got it. I watch Vita's boyfriend kiss her goodbye and wave to Shiani. Like I was saying, I do not think they are jealous of me. I don't have a car or a man, not that I'm ready for either one.

I decline Stephan's offer to drive me home and choose to ride with my teammate Monica instead. Monica's mom agrees to take me home. As we ride along, I stare out the window at the few stars that are sprinkled in the sky. When you live near the city, you love riding along Lake Shore Drive because the night sky is always filled with multi-colored lights. When the dark sky is illuminated, you can really enjoy the skyline. Each building seems to melt into the next one. In Chicago, from our car, I can see each edifice and its shadow. Each shadow is as beautiful as the building it outlines.

In the suburbs, my view is blocked by trees, but I am able to see the steady moon. Its light will never fade.

"Eris, I hope you aren't worried about Vita Rowe and Shiani Chan," Angie says.

I try to focus on the impeccable moon, but Angie won't give me any peace until I answer her.

"Vita and Shiani just seem to be perfect. They are so good at pointing out everyone's flaws," I say, as I look at my muscular arms.

The very same arms that Vita Rowe claims are larger than her boyfriend's arms. I don't know why I listen to her. My sisters tell me I'm not built like a body builder. I'm just toned.

Stephan says I have a brawny body. I haven't looked up the word or consulted Ebony's mental dictionary, but knowing him, it probably means I'm too burly. His mom defended me and told him that I could be the prototype for flawless female physical fitness, but I just asked him why he was looking at my body at all. Shouldn't he be looking at his "girlfriend's" body only? I mean his girlfriends' bodies! Ha ha. I can't wait until Stephan finds out that he is being played.

"Eris, Vita Rowe is dating Shiani's ex-boyfriend, even though they are supposed to be best friends. I don't think they are as picture-perfect as you believe they are," Monica says, as we pull up to my house. I can't believe my marvelous Monica was once malicious Monica to me.

Is Vita a cheater in real life? Is she a player off the court and on the court? My mind spins like Emani in one of her tutus. I suggest that the girls rest tonight, because after I get back from Mr. Thomas' house tomorrow, we are going to practice, practice, practice. This information on Vita is interesting, but it will not help us to beat her on the court. My teammates moan and groan, but I just ignore them. I think only of the end goal. No practice, no progress.

As I walk up our front side walk, Monica's words echo in my head again. Thanks to her, I may have an idea on how to gather some data on Shiani and Vita simultaneously. I just hope that Mr. Thomas can help make my plan a reality.

*

The train ride to Mr. Thomas's condo this morning is quite lonely, since Emani has to cheer at a home football game and Ebony has to collect money. They wouldn't have come anyway, since the fake Emani (Ebony) has a "date" with Stephan, and after a little begging mom is allowing the real Emani to go on another date with Rickey. I guess I only have a date with destiny. Am I destined to be alone?

Mr. Thomas is not alone when I enter his condo. There are officers in uniform, detectives, and volunteers throughout his place. I take a seat on his single sofa and take out the list of items I'll need for my plan.

He reads over the list as he talks to a very distraught parent on the phone. From the bits and piece of his conversation that I can understand, it seems like this parent on the phone believes her daughter may have contacted Payton Payne's company, R.U.N. Pain, Inc., because she is being bullied. The mother gives Mr. Thomas some information, because I see him write something down on his notepad. Another detective talks to the parent when Mr. Thomas gives him the phone. Mr. Thomas walks toward me with my list in his right hand.

"She's calling the new website N.P.N.G., Eris: No Pain. No Gain. This is the seventh name change since . . . the tragedy. We can't keep up with her or her pseudonyms. What am I going to do? I don't have the authority to shut down every website that uses the word pain? Do you know how many medical websites use or mention that word? But anyway, I have a surprise for you," Mr. Thomas says as he grabs me by the hand and takes me toward his tiny bedroom. When he opens the door, I stumble backwards.

"Mr. Turner?" I curiously ask to make sure I am looking at *the* Mr. Turner.

Mr. Turner was the very rich father of Johnny Turner (the boy who brought a gun to our school and hired R.U.N. Pain to bomb my former school). He has helped Mr. Thomas ever since the first bombing, but I have never worked with him personally. Actually, I am a bit nervous to even be in his presence. My life is most likely a painful reminder that his son is no longer alive.

"Hi, Eris. How is your sister?" I nod to indicate she's okay while shaking his hand, knowing exactly which sister he is talking about.

Sometimes people forget that Alexis is not my only sister.

Avoiding eye contact, I take a step back toward the bedroom door.

"Alexis is much better, Mr. Turner. We all are."

Mr. Thomas opens a box and asks me to come look inside, so I reluctantly step toward his unslept-in bed. I can't believe this grown man has a tiny twin bed like me. Does he ever sleep?

"Eris, Mr. Turner bought these for your mission. I told him about your situation and he volunteered to pay for these things for you. We think they could help you to accomplish your goal," Mr. Thomas says, until a former FBI guy requests his presence in the living room. I am not privy to the details of their secret and most likely unauthorized mission.

To avoid an awkward moment with Johnny Turner's dad, I want to follow Mr. Thomas out the room, but I decide to thank Mr. Turner instead for the items.

I feel myself sweating, suddenly. I begin to rock side to side. This is Johnny Turner's dad. This man is innocent. It is his son who was guilty, but I am very uncomfortable in the same room with him. The magazines praise Mr. Turner for his humanitarian efforts. The news reporters treat him like he is Man of the Year, but I only know him as Johnny Turner's father. Johnny Turner changed our whole world. Johnny Turner ruined my big sister's life.

"Eris, this is the latest in spy technology. This is extraordinary equipment. Do you agree?" Mr. Turner's excitement is so contagious that I stop rocking and begin to examine the items in the box a bit more than I did before.

Inside of the box there are two teddy bears, two necklaces, two pair of earrings, two bracelets, and two tiny cameras. As I examine each piece, Mr. Turner explains the technology hidden inside of them. He boasts about the clarity of the sound and picture quality for the hidden cameras inside each item.

Then, he shows me how to use the cameras. He explains how each camera collects data. When Mr. Thomas returns, I finally realize that, thanks to him, I am holding the keys to discovering Shiani and Vita's secrets. Actually, I am potentially holding the keys to discovering all of the Dimes' secrets.

"So, little Ms. Eris, do you still need those other items on the list?" Mr. Thomas asks with a smirk on his face.

I smile, too realizing what an amateur plan I had before. When I say no, Mr. Thomas sits me down to explain how I can view the live video from the hidden cameras we'll give to the Dimes. Mr. Turner and Mr. Thomas have used this same equipment with other kids to collect evidence for schools and school districts now that bullying is a crime. They have designed apps and software together. They are really trying to end bullying forever.

When Mr. Thomas wishes me luck with my case, I finally grasp that I am a sleuth. I am like an honorary police woman or detective diva or something on a mission to battle my own bullies. I don't have a boyfriend or a car, but I have a duty. The Dimes seem to believe that they are perfect tens, but I will find the evidence I need to prove how wicked these terrible tens really are.

CHAPTER 13

Emani
Curfew

Kylie Calderone approaches me in the locker room with a smile that is as phony as our "friendship." Her mother, coach Calderone, is nowhere in sight, so I know Kylie will soon show her true colors. When Coach is around, Kylie is as sweet as banana pudding, but as soon as Coach leaves, Kylie is tormenting me about any flaw she can find.

There is no pleasing Kylie Calderone: either my hair is too curly or my hair is too straight, either my kick was too high or my kick wasn't high enough, either my butt is too big or my tatas are too little. Having her around is like having your own personal critique expert, evaluating and analyzing you, day in and day out. It is like I am a new movie and she's the critic who decides if I'm five stars or not. She walks uncomfortably close to me and gives me two thumbs down on my performance tonight.

I simply smile, knowing that even she can't get me down tonight. I'll be seeing Rickey tomorrow at Mr. Thomas's condo. Then, we are going on another date. I am so excited that I could do a cheer: R-I-C, K-E-Y, Rickey Thomas is my guy. Yeah!

"So how's that sister of yours doing, Emani?" Kylie asks this mostly to rub in the fact that she kissed my sister Alexis's boyfriend Jeremy.

"She's fine. I'll tell her you said hello," I say as I grab my bags.

"Yeah, and I'll tell Jeremy that you said hello when I see him tonight!" Kylie says as she takes out her ribbons and transforms her dance hair into date hair. I know she wants me to ask what she is doing tonight with Jeremy, but I do not. Instead, I slam the door on my way out of the locker room and head directly toward him.

"Hey, sis. Do you need a ride?" Jeremy smiles so innocently that I almost forget what Kylie has just told me. Almost!

"No, but I do need to know where Kylie will see you tonight," I say as my duffel bag's strap falls off of my shoulder.

I am here to protect my best friend and big sister Alexis's honor. Okay, there would probably be a three-way tie for best friend amongst my sisters if I'm being honest.

"Oh, she's going to come to Flava tonight to see us perform. My uncle is going to let me do a few songs at his club. Kylie asked if she could come, and I said yes."

I step closer to him and look into his eyes in order to make sure that I am really talking to Jeremy. Is this the same Jeremy who was kissed by Kylie a couple of weeks ago?

I guess he senses my anger because he begins to explain how Kylie apologized to him and promised never to kiss him again. Jeremy assures me that he is in love with my sister and would never hurt her.

"You do believe in forgiveness, don't you Emani?" Jeremy asks, knowing that I owe him because he convinced my father to forgive me for being all hugged up with Rickey during one of their late-night car chat sessions.

Thanks to Jeremy's talk with dad, I'm no longer on punishment.

"Yes, Jeremy. I believe in forgiveness," I say, though I do not trust Kylie or her apology.

When Kylie walks by the two of us, she has a flirtatious smile instead of the fake one she had for me in the locker room. I want to hit her in the head with my pom poms knowing her ulterior motive, but I can't get suspended again for fighting, so I choose to let her walk away swaying her hips left to right.

When I look up, I catch Jeremy watching her sashay away. Of course, I hit him with my bag. He and Alexis are supposed to be giving one another space, but I know they are still a couple, so he needs to check his eyes and behave like a boyfriend.

"I was not looking at her . . . ." I put my finger on his lips to silence him before he begins to lie to me.

Every boy in this hallway is looking at Kylie Calderone, and he is no exception.

"Jeremy, I need a favor," I say as I reach into my bag looking for the box that Eris gave to me.

Eris has found a way to give both Vita Rowe and Shiani Chan their hidden camera jewelry, but until this moment I did not know how I would get Kylie to accept anything from me without suspecting something. There is no way she would accept a present from me without any questions, but if it came from Jeremy, I bet she would not refuse it. I decide to ask Jeremy to give Kylie the necklace with the secret camera in it and of course he looks at me puzzled.

"You want me to give Kylie Calderone a necklace? You want ME to give Alexis's ENEMY a necklace? Is it going to turn her neck green? Is it stolen? I know you two do not like one another, so what is the story behind the necklace?" Jeremy says, as he admires the precious gems that are in the hidden camera in the necklace I got from Mr. Thomas and Mr. Turner.

I decide to bribe him by telling him that if he does this little favor for me, I will tell Alexis what a wonderful boy he is and how I hope the two of them stay together forever every chance that I get. He seems to be falling for it.

"And what if I don't give this necklace to Kylie?" Jeremy asks as he places the necklace back into the jewelry box.

I begin to pout, because there is no way I am going to say anything bad about Jeremy to Alexis and he knows that. I can't blackmail Jeremy, because I adore him. We all adore him. I reach for the necklace, and he gives the necklace back to me.

"Eris, you know that this time of year is really hard for your sister. I think it was Zachary's birthday sometime this month. Anyway, I've been trying to give her the distance she needs, but maybe if you could convince her to come to my performance tonight, I could give Kylie that necklace," Jeremy says as he holds out his hand for me to return the necklace. I quickly give it back to him.

"Could you sort of pretend that you like her?" I ask, though I know he will probably say no.

"Nope, but I can be nice to her. There is no way anyone at this school is going to be able to tell Alexis that they think I'm into them, and that is exactly what Kylie would do if I pretended to like her for you. I am only into Alexis Dieona Robertson, and I want everyone including Kylie to know that. I'm sorry, but that's the best I can do to help you, sis," Jeremy says as he offers me a ride home on his motorcycle.

I grab my bag and follow him out the door. Maybe the hidden camera necklace will be enough.

*

Mr. Thomas explains how the hidden cameras work to me for the third time before he finally allows Rickey and I to leave for our date. He tells us to be safe one more time before we get to the elevators. Once Rickey and I are in the elevator, I give him the biggest hug I can give. Then, Rickey kisses me on my forehead like I'm a toddler, but I guess a little peck is better than no smooch at all.

"I promised your dad that I would have you back by 10:00 when we spoke on the phone," Rickey says as I look into his warm eyes.

When I'm in his arms I feel so comfortable. I don't let go until the doors open on the ground floor.

He drives us to a building on campus that seems quite familiar to me. It is familiar for a reason. I just saw this building on TV this morning. Some of Chicago's comedy royalty are supposed to be performing here tonight.

"We're going to a comedy show?" I say, before I realize that I've ruined his surprise.

He laughs and tells me that I am way too smart to be dating him. Since I know that Rickey graduated a year early with honors, I decide that he is just trying to flatter me. He is definitely the smartest person in this relationship.

"The show starts at 7 and it should be over at 9. That will give me enough time to get you home and get back in time for the party," Rickey says as he caresses my hand as we stand in line to enter the building.

Party? I want to go to his party. Should I say something, or should I assume that I am not invited?

"So is it your birthday party or something?" I finally say, trying to read his eyes after minutes of driving in silence. His eyes only show affection for me, but I feel a bit betrayed. I think he mentioned a party before, but he hasn't said anything about a party for a while to me.

"No, it's not a party for me. I'm just in charge of the lights. The word is really spreading about my light shows. I've been getting calls to do all types of events. That is how I can afford to take you out, sweetheart." Rickey says as he hands our tickets to the ticket collector.

We have to walk through separate metal detectors before we meet outside the auditorium door. Rickey asks me if I would like to take a picture with him and of course I say yes. Then, we enter the auditorium to find our seats.

We ate at Mr. Thomas's condo, but I wouldn't mind something sweet to eat. I decide to wait to ask as we walk by the sweets. Once we are seated, Rickey reads my mind and offers to go get us some snacks. I simply smile, trying not to let him know just how warmhearted I think he is.

When he returns a while later, he is not alone. That whispering waitress girl Rachelle or Rachel or whatever her name is has her arm around his arm leaving her own date to stand alone holding two red and white boxes of popcorn. She is holding the candy I asked him to purchase for me. She gives the chocolate to me before sitting beside us. I forgot that he told me they went to school together. After our encounter at Lucille's, I was hoping that I would never have to see her again. I guess I'm not very lucky.

"So, Emani, will you be coming to the party tonight?" Rachel asks though I can tell by Rickey's face that he has already told her that I will not be there.

He even elbows her a little when she says this to me. I quickly try to think of something to say. I need something witty or funny or something that says, "Rachel, you don't bother me at all," but nothing comes to mind.

Luckily, my phone vibrates. Unluckily, it is my father. How embarrassing. I get up and walk toward the door, hoping to get some reception and to get out of range from Rachel's listening ears. I am finally able to hear my dad once I am almost outside. He just wants to make sure that I made it safely. "Um, Daddy, I was wondering if I could stay until 11:00, because everyone is getting something to eat afterward," I lie to my father.

There is silence on the phone, but I can hear my mother in the background saying yes. Dad agrees to 11:00, and I suddenly wish that I had asked for midnight.

When I return the show has yet to begin, but Rachel is sitting closer to my date than her own. She is all in his ear like she's his eardrum. Isn't it enough that she has on a shirt that leaves nothing to the imagination?

*

The comedy show is hilarious despite all of the college life jokes that I do not get. I laugh at the jokes anyway, though I don't know much about sororities, fraternities, or keg parties. I do know that Rachel touched Rickey's leg almost every time she laughed, and that was not funny.

"So did you like the show, little lady?" Rachel's date says as we exit the building. He is the exact same height as I am, but he is calling me a little lady. What he should be doing is keeping his eye on his own lady, who can't keep her hands off of my man.

Rickey and Rachel's date go to get the cars for us. I am forced to stand next to her while we wait.

"E-man-i, You're so lucky. Rickey is such a great catch. You met him at the perfect time," Rachel says after stepping closer to me. "I mean it makes perfect sense that he would go and find a little girl after having his heart broken by that woman."

I take a large gulp of air, then find myself asking her what she is talking about. She explains that Rickey's girlfriend of three years broke up with him after he told her that he'd decided to attend a different college than her. "Rickey probably chose you because he can mold you into the type of woman he wants," she says with fake-sweetness "You're adorable."

She manages to say this right as Rickey pulls up. He opens the door for me, and I get in, grateful to escape Rachel and her whispering words.

"So did you enjoy the show?" He asks, with a smile, but I just nod yes trying to fight back my tears that want to slide down my cheeks.

Instinctively, he knows what's wrong. He apologizes for Rachel's behavior and promises me that he had no idea she was going to be at the show. According to him, he's not interested in Rachel. They are "just" friends. He wants me to believe that they are just "friends" when they live on the same dorm floor. He wants me to believe that they are just "friends" when they eat lunch together whenever he works downtown. He wants me to believe that they are just "friends" when I just witnessed her flirting with him all night.

He must truly believe that I am as naïve as Rachel says that I am. My sister Alexis and Zachary Thomas used to claim to be "just friends," too, but we all knew they were in love. "Just friends" usually leads to more. Just wait.

"Did you want me to come with you tonight to the party?" I ask though I am afraid of the answer.

"Of course, I would love for you to come, but I respect your dad's curfew, Emani."

"Well, when I spoke to my father earlier, he said I could stay . . .um . . . later." Rickey tells me that the party does not even start until 10:00 and that it ends at 2:00 in the morning. I try not to seem surprised, but I am in shock. I can't stay that late, but I want to go to this party, especially if SHE will be there.

Rickey picks up his phone to call my dad for a specific time, but I tell him that my dad said 12:00. I can't believe that I am about to go to a college party. I listen to him explain that he will probably be able to get permission to leave a bit early since tonight's light show is mostly on timers.

* * *

For the first hour of the party no one is around but the DJ and the hosts, who are sorority girls. I watch Rickey running around, setting things up. Then, I head over to the DJ to talk about music. I decide to talk to him instead of the sorority girls because they are practicing some secret step routines. I watch them as they practice memorizing each step.

"So you like to dance?" the DJ ask as I stare at the sorority girls. "Are you any good?"

I look over at Rickey, who smiles at me. Then, I say I can show him better than I could tell him. After the song ends, he changes the music for me. The sorority girls continue stepping while I do a few moves. As I do a few more, I notice more and more girls are around me. If there were ten of them, I would get nervous, but these girls are nothing like the Dimes. They just smile and start copying my moves. Before I know it, I am leading thirty girls around the dance floor. It is beyond fun. Some are even tall like me. At my school, my sisters and I sometimes seem to tower above others. Here, there some other long-legged ladies.

The sorority president and I talk after we finish. She would like my help in coordinating a step routine for a dance competition the girls are going to be in. Of course, I say yes.

"I can't leave you alone for a minute without someone falling for you. First the DJ, now the sorority president," Rickey says as he hugs me.

The lights start to flicker. Flickering lights have not been a good sign for me in the past, but tonight, he and I are surrounded by beams of color. My outfit changes color with each flash. I am suddenly wearing pink, green, red, blue, yellow, and every other color in the spectrum.

Rachel walks in as Rickey and I dance under one of the spotlights. When I squeeze him tighter, he turns around to look at who I am looking at. He turns my head toward him and tells me to ignore her, but I can't.

The room begins to fill a bit more. Soon the floor is filled with college kids. They look like more sophisticated versions of the high schoolers at my school. Some are bigger than me. Some are smaller than me. I start to feel like I fit in. That is, until Rachel walks over to interrupt Rickey and me. He seemed so close to kissing me this time.

"Rickey, won't you dance with me? This is my favorite song," Rachel says as she pouts seductively.

Rickey looks at me for an answer, but I just look at the door.

"Maybe, the next one, Rachel," Rickey says as he holds me around my waist.

The sorority president walks up and asks Rickey to follow her for a minute. It is time for the sorority girls to do their official entrance, and they want to make sure the lights are in their sorority colors.

I keep walking toward the exit. Rachel steps in front of me.

"I thought Rickey said you could dance."

Is she serious? Is she challenging me to a dance contest? I am very tempted, but I try to be mature and walk away. There is no reason to battle her.

"Well, if you're scared I understand. I wouldn't want you to hurt yourself."

I spin around until somehow we are back in the center of the room with people all around us. It is a true battle, because she has people cheering on her side, and I have people cheering for me on my side. I decide to pull out some of the moves that my dance instructor showed me, and suddenly the majority of the crowd begins to cheer for me. She tries her best, but I excel at freestyle. I feel the music. I feel the lights. I can't help but move. Rachel keeps up the dance battle until the end of my song, but the crowd and the victory are mine.

I walk up to Rickey with my head held high, but he guides me outside into the hall. He doesn't seem proud.

"What was that all about, Emani?"

"I was just dancing," I say, as people come out to congratulate me and praise me for my moves.

"This Rachel thing isn't about me at all is it? It is about you wanting to beat her."

I follow him down the hall, though I don't know what to say. Maybe I did get caught up in the battle. Maybe I forgot about why I even joined in. I won't be like this with the Dimes. I won't forget that justice isn't supposed to be personal. Otherwise, am I any better than they are? I'm usually the one who is against any sort of revenge. I don't know what just happened to me.

I walk faster trying to catch up with Rickey, but he doesn't slow down.

"We need to get you home!" Rickey finally says once we are almost out of the building, but before we can even walk down the stairs, I see my father entering the building.

Rickey must realize it is my father, too, because he freezes as if my father's mere presence has turned him into stone. When my father reaches the top of the stairs, I stand beside him as he looks at Rickey with fury.

"We were on our way to your house, Sir," Rickey mumbles.

"On your way? It is almost 11:45," my dad says as he grabs my hand.

Dad asks Rickey to give him his phone. Rickey quickly gives the phone to him. Daddy shows Rickey that he has called thirteen times. I knew I felt my phone's vibrations as I danced. I didn't know that it was my father trying to call me.

"Sir, I had my phone on silent because I was at the party. I'm sort of at work," Rickey says to my dad, but does not dare look at him.

"No, you are on a date with my daughter after curfew. I had to call your uncle to find out where you were," Dad shouts, then lowers his voice when he notices that people are watching us.

Rickey looks directly at my father after my dad says this. Then, he looks at me.

"Sir, I was told that I had to have Emani home by 12:00," Rickey protests.

"Who told you that?" Dad asks.

They both look at me instead of one another.

I look at the floral carpet on the floor.

"So, my daughter told you that I said she could stay here until 12:00?"

"Yes, Sir."

"Well, son. I think you should only listen to the words that come out of my mouth in the future because now you will not be seeing my daughter for a long while. And also, keep your phone on vibrate from now on. There could be an emergency." Dad says before telling Rickey to go back to work.

"Sir, will I be able to talk to her on the phone?" Rickey asks.

Dad frowns and says, "The phone she ignored for the last thirty minutes? Let me think about it . . . no!"

Rickey does not argue. He apologizes for the miscommunication. Then, he simply turns to leave. I know that I cannot kiss Rickey, but I wish I could hug him. I know it is a foolish wish.

Instead, I follow my father down the stairs and out the door. He doesn't speak to me until we are in his car.

"I almost killed myself driving here in this car. I have never driven 100 miles per hour in this car and this car can do more than 100 miles. Why did you do this, Emani?"

I don't have the words that I think he wants to hear so I stay silent, hoping that Dad will fill the silence with his voice.

"Speak, Emani Elizabeth Robertson!"

"Dad, there was a girl and she was all over Rickey. I couldn't leave."

After I say this, my dad drives faster. I hold on to my seatbelt after making sure it is buckled tightly. Then, I lock the doors for no apparent reason. Locked doors won't save me when we hit someone.

"Emani, I only have three things to say to you, so you should listen really well. One, I am disappointed that you would lie to me after I trusted you enough to extend your curfew. Two, I am hurt that you're trying to impress a college boy and some girl more than you are trying to impress me. I have news for you: I am the only person you should be worried about. If you're worried about that girl, you're going to drive yourself crazy, because there were a lot of beautiful girls at that party and on that campus. That boy is always going to have girls all over him. You wouldn't want him if he wasn't worth wanting. And, three, I've never told you this, but I think now is the time. Out of all my girls, you have always reminded me most of your mother when she was younger. Tonight, you have shown me that you don't know your worth. You don't know that Rickey is the lucky one. That is how your mom used to be. I bet you Rickey knows he's lucky because I know I'm lucky to have your mother, but it does not mean anything if you do not believe he's lucky. He should be chasing after you instead of the other way around."

My dad speeds down the expressway after he says this to me. He is clearly driving above 100 miles an hour, because I can barely see the cars next to us. They all seem blurry as we speed down the highway. I feel like I'm in a movie that is permanently on fast forward.

"I'm sorry, Daddy!"

Dad slows a bit after I apologize, but he still does not speak to me. I hate for my daddy to be disappointed in me.

Awkward silence . . . a swirling stomach . . . too many tears to count.

"You're forgiven, but you're on punishment until you truly understand what you did wrong. Punishment means no computer chats, no calls, and absolutely no dates with college boys."

I tell him to keep his eyes on the road. I know that he isn't happy with me yet, but I will make it up to him. I won't ever make this mistake again.

*   *   *

The Monday following my disastrous date with Rickey, I make the mistake of arriving at dance practice early. Kylie Calderone practically runs over to me when she sees me stretching.

Kylie sits in front of me, twirling the necklace I asked Jeremy to give her. The necklace that has the hidden camera inside of it. We are not supposed to wear jewelry to dance practice, so I realize that she wants me to say something about it. I do not say one word.

She takes off the necklace and asks me if I know whether or not the stone inside the necklace is her birthstone. She was born in February, so her sign is Aquarius. I say only one word: yes.

Coach Calderone calls us over toward her. When I turn around to see Coach, I see my dance instructor, Ms. Jennings, is sitting beside her. My confidence shrinks a bit, but I still walk with my head held high next to Kylie and the other girls. In my mind, I can hear Ms. Jennings saying *perk up, pixie.*

"Ladies," coach Calderone says, "you will be auditioning for Ms. Jennings upcoming Christmas musical. Ms. Jennings is a prize–winning performer, and several of her famous and influential friends will attend the musical. She will also be presenting scholarships for two of you based on your performances." After listing her one million accomplishments, Ms. Jennings begins to show us her routine. I memorize every step. Then, I mentally rehearse them as I wait to dance.

After she goes through the routine, she lines us up by height. As usual, I am the last person in line. The tinier dancers go first. I watch them as they attempt to do the most complex dance Ms. Jennings has ever taught. I clap when they finish, impressed that no one gave up. Though many of them made mistakes, Ms. Jennings writes very few notes in her notepad after each group. I am in the last group. Kylie is two places to my left. She tells me to break a leg and she means it. When the music begins, I keep my eye on coach Calderone and Ms. Jennings, ignoring Kylie and the rest of my group.

After three minutes, we are finished with the routine. Ms. Jennings writes on her clipboard, but coach Calderone stands up, clapping for our group. She is probably proud of her daughter, but I am surprised that she claps so enthusiastically, because she usually never shows favoritism toward Kylie.

Coach and Ms. Jennings talk over our performances. As they deliberate on who will be in the Christmas performance, the dancers all compliment one another, and I compliment all of them, but no one says anything about my performance. Because I always watch and memorize, the girls think I'm a show off, but I'm not. Dancing is a gift I was born with. I have a photographic memory when it comes to dance. There are entire musicals in my mind.

Coach speaks to the team, "Okay, girls, I sort of tricked you all. Ms. Jennings is going to use all of you for her musical, but the real reason we had you dance is that we were trying to decide who would play the two lead roles: Lady Light and Dame Darkness... Ms. Jennings and I have chosen Kylie and Emani to dance these two leads."

Many of the girls mumble under their breath.

Kylie jumps about six feet off of the ground, but I just smile inside. I am surprised when the Stomp girls come to congratulate me. Ms. Jennings walks over to me with Kylie by her side after the crowd disappears from around me.

"So, Emani, I see you have learned how to perform with confidence. You were great today," Ms. Jennings says as she smiles at me.

"I have a great teacher."

"Thank you!" Coach Calderone and Ms. Jennings reply together, before laughing at themselves.

"So, you two, we've decided to flip a coin on who will play Lady Light and who will play Dame Darkness, because we don't agree on who should dance as whom," Coach Calderone says as she asks us for a coin.

Kylie gives her mother a dime, and calls heads. Coach shows the shiny coin to Ms. Jennings, they flip it, and the two of them announce that Kylie has won the opportunity to choose who she will play.

"I would like to play Lady Light," Kylie says, as she twirls her dime in her hand.

I smile to myself as I think that Ebony won't be the only one who will be acting. If I am playing Dame Darkness, I will definitely be acting. I love light, but I guess I will soon need to find my dark side. I am a good girl, but I'm sure I can become a bad girl for one night. It wouldn't be the first time.

CHAPTER 14
Ebony
Surveillance

The first time Emani, Eris, and I reviewed our hidden video footage, we laughed because the Dimes all have some silly or peculiar habits: Kylie Calderone sings badly with her brush in the mirror, Vita Rowe brushes her eyebrows with a toothbrush, and drama queen Tatyanna Tyson puts on wigs and talks to herself in the mirror with different accents.

We only recently learned this silly secret about Tatyanna when she finally wore her hidden camera necklace home. Before last week, she kept the necklace in its box in her locker, unopened. I'm sure she didn't touch it because the card on it said it was from her favorite actor, Denzel Smith's, fan club.

When I found out that drama boy's sister Tatyanna was a member of the fan club and a follower, I wrote an email thanking her for her support from a fake email address. Then, I sent the official letter and the box with the necklace in it from a fake address to the school. The main office had them delivered to theatre practice where Tatyanna bragged about them to everyone there.

It took everything inside of me not to laugh as she lied about knowing Academy Award-winning actor Denzel Smith personally. Actually, I really feel bad about lying to her, since the letter promises that Denzel Smith will come to our spring musical, but I had to do something to get her to accept the necklace.

Her fraternal twin brother, drama king Tyson, said that Denzel Smith is the only person Tatyanna loves more than herself, so I decided to try it. Luckily, it worked.

Tyson is in the drama club with his sister, but I met him in Spanish class. The teacher had us performing poems in Spanish and acting out skits in front of the class. Tyson thought I had some potential, so he invited me to their first meeting of the year. I never came, but several weeks ago, he gave my sister a flyer inviting me to come to another brief meeting and I was interested in finding out some information on Tatyanna, so I came.

When I got there, I witnessed Tatyanna on stage. Her monologue brought tears to the audience's eyes. She can cry on cue. The monologue was set during the Great Depression, and I thought I was back in the days of the Depression after listening to her. She made me believe that she was a starving, unemployed, mother of four instead of a middle-class junior in high school.

The only person who moved me more on stage was Tyson himself. I was almost inspired to join the cast myself after he performed his original piece, but I decided to stay behind the scenes. I specifically wrote that I was interested in being on the crew on my application, but Tyson somehow found out what I wrote and quickly told me that my being on the crew was unacceptable. The next thing I knew, I was practicing for my audition today.

I am auditioning for the part of Zaria, a young woman who designs and builds armor for soldiers and the Greek god Hephaestus. Tyson wrote the play, but that is all he will tell me about Zaria. He promises that I only have about thirty lines, so I think I can handle the role. I can't believe that I've allowed him to convince me to audition, but I welcome this challenge.

To be honest, I have been inspired by Emani's new confidence. To think, three years ago I couldn't even speak in front of my class without suffering or stuttering— and now if I get this role, I will have the opportunity to perform in front of my entire school and community. Okay, now I'm nervous again. I hope I get this role.

Stephan Miles snatches my script from me as I practice outside of theater three. I watch his nose wrinkle as he tries to figure out what he is reading.

"Red, I thought this was a love note from Tyson to you. Is this what he gave you at lunch?" Stephan says, as he gives the script back to me.

He seems a bit disappointed that it isn't a love letter or secret message. Tyson tells me that Stephan Miles tries to hook him up with girls all the time. I guess Stephan was hoping that I could be a potential mate for Tyson.

I say my lines in my mind, trying to ignore Stephan, as he asks me about Emani's whereabouts. When will I be able to tell Stephan that I am Emani fifty percent of the time? I am the one he kissed. When can my sister and I break up with this boy?

"Red, Tyson told me that you thought he was dating Tatyanna!" Stephan says as he giggles about a mistake I made a few weeks ago.

It really wasn't my fault. While I was at the drama club's meeting watching Tyson perform, I sat next to a girl who willingly gave me all of the gossip on him. She is the one who told me he was dating someone, so when I saw him hugged up with Tatyanna after practice, I assumed she was his girlfriend. I didn't notice that they looked a little bit alike until Tyson told me the next day in the library during lunch time that she was his sister. He almost choked on his French fry when I called Tatyanna his girlfriend. I didn't know they were twins.

All the twins in my family are identical. Tatyanna and Tyson are far from identical: Tatyanna is about five feet, six inches tall, and Tyson is like six feet, five inches tall. Tyson is warm, funny, and full of wisdom, and Tatyanna is none of the above. The only things they seem to have in common is their love for acting and their Nigerian heritage.

"Hey, Ebony. Are you ready to bring my Zaria alive?" Tyson asks, after he gives Stephan a boys-only hug and handshake.

I continue to read the lines in my mind, as Tyson stands over me. I give him the script and say a few of the lines to him. After I finish, I wait for his reaction, but he doesn't smile. In between my student council meetings, I've been working for days on perfecting these lines. He could at least smile at me for trying. I know I am better at counting and collecting money than acting, but I am trying my best.

"You still haven't become Zaria." Tyson says as he reads the male main character's part to me. The character's name is Hephaestus and his wife is Aphrodite, the goddess of love. Hephaestus is abused by his wife. She cheats on him and does not truly love him. She also reminds him of his disability often and criticizes his looks, but yet Hephaestus loves her. He loves her because she is impossible to resist. It is like she has him under a spell.

"Well, maybe I could become Zaria if you could tell me more about her. You have told me Aphrodite's story. You have told me Hephaestus's story, but I don't know Zaria's story. How can I become a girl who I do not know?" I ask.

I want to tell Tyson about my role as my sister Emani this year or my role as Eris five years ago, but I decide against it. Stephan is his friend. He wouldn't understand my dad's weird way of teaching Emani and I a lesson.

Tyson sits beside me and tells me a bit more about my character. When he finishes telling me about her talents and charms, I soon realize that she isn't the minor character he'd promised she'd be. Zaria is the girl that Hephaestus will fall in real love with. She is the girl who will love him for the beauty inside of him.

Tatyanna walks by us with her copy of the script in hand. She is wearing the necklace that I sent to her as her acting hero Denzel Smith. I am instantly more nervous, since I know that my sisters will be able to see me audition for this part soon. Though this theater is closed to the student body, it is not closed to the hidden camera around Tatyanna's neck. When we go to look at the video footage, my sisters will see me. I cannot fail at this. I have to give everything that I have inside of me. I have to become Zaria, or else Emani and Eris are never going to let me forget that I didn't.

Tyson finally gives me the last pages of the script. I've been waiting for them for a week. I quickly look through them, noticing that he has written more lines for me. Since I have memorized the rest of my lines, I think I can handle these. I skim over the stage directions until I read in parenthesis the words "They Kiss."

"You're going to kiss your sister? Isn't she going to play Aphrodite?" Tyson shakes his head at me like he does when I say something naïve or idiotic. I instantly feel guilty for always doing that to my little sis, Emani.

Tyson is one of the few boys who has ever said something that challenged me or made me think, so he is really the only boy to hear me say something naïve or idiotic. He is so special: I can still remember him stopping his friends from taking my little brothers' candy at the mall on Halloween. His friends were rude little thieves trying to steal from babies, but Tyson defended Tevin, Kevin, and us. Tyson is above negativity. He can make any bad situation good. He is also cute and kissable.

"No, Hephaestus does not kiss Aphrodite. Aphrodite has her own suitors and lovers. Hephaestus kisses Zaria." Tyson says as he stands to his feet holding out his hand for me to rise up.

When I look up to him, I find myself looking at his lips. Before this moment, I have enjoyed almost every word that he has said to me. Before this moment, he has used his mouth to teach me acting skills that I never knew I had. I don't want to kiss his mouth, not with my lying lips. I have not told him that I kissed his best friend Stephan or that I am spying on Tatyanna since we suspect that she is a Dime.

I don't want his honest tongue anywhere near my fibbing mouth. How would he feel if he knew what I was up to? Betrayed? His sister? I'm investigating her as a possible Dime. His best friend? I'm pretending to be Emani to date him for Daddy. I think I'm more like Aphrodite than Zaria.

Tyson holds my hand and asks me if I'm nervous. Then, we do the breathing exercises that he has taught me. After he gives me another pep talk, I suggest that he have the characters hug instead of kiss, since Hephaestus is a married man. That is when he tells me that Hephaestus and Aphrodite are no longer married at the end of the play. Hephaestus marries his true love Zaria, and the two of them live happily ever after once Zeus brings her back to life after Aphrodite has her killed by soldiers. Why do writers have to have happy endings? Is life like that? Nope. I don't think I'm going to get my happy ending when the truth comes out.

"So I'm responsible for the breakup of a marriage?" I ask, but Tyson just shakes his head at me probably thinking that I do not understand his fictional romance.

He assures me that he is not going to change the ending of his story, but I want to tell him that it isn't the story's ending that I am nervous about. It is the ending of our newfound friendship that makes me nervous.

CHAPTER 15

Eris
Love Letters and Louisiana

Kitten and I watch nervously as Vita Rowe and Shiani Chan argue for the third time at the water fountain. This time, we hear the name "Dylan," but nothing more once they notice that we both are watching them. "I knew I shouldn't have signed his name." Kitten says, as she takes out a copy of the letter she forged from Dylan Gibson to Shiani and Vita.

It originally was a letter from Stephan Miles to my sister, Emani, but Kitten reworded it a bit and signed Dylan Gibson's name to it. He is an artist, so his signature is on artwork all throughout the school. Kitten sent the same letter to both Vita and Shiani to see if they would tell one another about it. We were hoping they had never seen Dylan's handwriting, since texting is our most popular form of communication.

Well, Vita and Shiani obviously told one another about the letter, since they are arguing over the fact that Dylan is Vita's boyfriend. I think it is odd that they did tell, since they haven't told each other about the gifts we've been sending each one of them from Dylan. I guess Dylan's signature was proof enough to encourage them to confront one another.

We shouldn't have signed his name. Now, they will probably confront him, and he will probably be able to talk his way out of it. Dylan seems so sweet. I hate that he is in the middle, but he was the only connection we could find between Vita and Shiani. He was the only thing we could use to get inside their minds. We needed to turn Vita and Shiani against one another so that we could get some information on whether or not they are part of the Dimes. They both like him, so Kitten and I decided to use that against them, but I think this may backfire on us, and soon.

Kitten and I slowly walk behind Vita and Shiani as they walk into the lunchroom together. I watch as they both sit beside Dylan, both only about a hand-length away from him. Vita kisses Dylan on his left cheek. Shiani puts her hand on his right thigh and he slides her hand away from him slowly. As Vita whispers in his left ear, Shiani puts her hand on his right knee. This time he stands up and walks away. Once he's gone, Shiani and Vita slide together as if he was never there.

I secretly wish that I could see the video on the two of them right now, but I know I will have to wait until this weekend at Mr. Thomas's to see it. I really need to know what they are saying to one another.

*

"So are you still going with me to my grandmother's house?" Kitten asks Emani and me as we wait for Ebony to finish her theater audition with her new special friend Tyson after school.

"Yes, but we can't leave until after Ebony's Thanksgiving celebration." Emani says as she stretches against the brick wall outside of theater three.

Kitten and I watch in amazement as a very flexible Emani slides into a Chinese split. I can feel the pain. She doesn't seem to be in any pain at all. How does she do that? I don't care how warm I get my muscles; they won't ever be warm enough to bend like she does.

"I'll be there. My momma is going to cook for Ebony, remember. I'm so glad that you guys will be able to come with me to N'awlins for Thanksgiving." Kitten says as she eats my last bite of brownie.

Though her mother is an ex-chef and restaurateur, Kitten surely loves to eat all types of my junk food. If it's healthy, she doesn't want it. If it isn't healthy, you had better hide it, or she'll eat every bite.

I am actually a bit shocked that Mom and Dad are allowing us to miss our traditional Thanksgiving and to go with Kitten and her mom for Thanksgiving, but then again, Ebony was so persuasive last week that they could not say no. When Ebony finished her speech to Momma about her wanting to give instead of receiving, to feed people instead of eating, and to serve instead of waiting for someone to serve her, Momma quickly said yes to both the Thanksgiving celebration at C.I.A and our trip to Louisiana with Kitten and her parents. Mom and Dad even volunteered to serve tomorrow at the school's Turkey Day celebration. Ebony is a genius with words. She's a persuasive prodigy. Hey, I like the sound of that. I think I'll call her that to impress her.

Anyway, Stephan Miles walks out of the theater, interrupting my lovely thoughts about my sister. His presence wipes my smile away. I thought that Ebony said this performance was closed to the public. How did he get invited?

"Hey, gorgeous!" Stephan says to Emani after looking around to see if we were alone in the hall.

He always does that look-around thing, I assume to protect his playboy reputation with the jocks. The empty hallway gives him courage to try to kiss "Curly" on the mouth, but she turns away before he can kiss her lips. As he kisses her dimpled cheek, she points to some girl who is about fifty feet away from us on the other side of the school and tells Stephan to be discreet.

I want to laugh, but he looks so heartbroken that I decide to hold it in. Stephan is used to getting whatever he wants. Tyson probably got him in that closed-to-the-public practice.

I giggle when Emani slides out of Stephan's reach. Kitten laughs aloud. She laughs mostly because Stephan uses one of the lines from his letters to Emani. It is a line that we have not only read, but copied twice and given to both Shiani Chan and Vita Rowe when we pretended to be Vita's boyfriend Dylan Gibson. The line is typical Stephan: clichéd and unoriginal.

After ten minutes of watching Stephan unsuccessfully flirt with Emani, Ebony walks out of the theater with a frown. We try to comfort her about her performance.

"I have to kiss him! I have to kiss Tyson!" Ebony, the persuasive prodigy, says before she notices Stephan standing against the brick wall. Stephan smiles and snaps her picture. I punch him in his arm since Ebony does not seem to have the energy. She doesn't even respond to my compliment.

"You are sooo lucky. You're going to kiss Tony Tyson. Wow!" Kitten says as she looks at Ebony as if she's her hero or something.

Ebony doesn't say a word.

When I notice that Stephan is trailing us outside, I get fed up and ask him why he is following us. He points to Emani. My poor sister has to ride with him all the way home on the bus. Why didn't he drive today? Why is he always giving his cousin Kylie his car?

Stephan Miles may be spoiled by his parents, but he also spoils his cousin. I have never seen him tell her no. Actually, I don't think I've ever seen anyone tell Kylie Calderone no. Never. Anyway, I like when he drives or gets a ride to school. It is so much more peaceful on the bus without him here.

"Ebony, I am going to do the best news story on Tyson's play, "Goddess of Love"! I know you have the part in the play. Don't worry!" Stephan says as he gets off of the bus.

We watch him put his fingers to his ears in the shape of a phone in order to ask Emani to call him. Emani slowly agrees to call him. Stephan smiles as the bus pulls away. I frown. Emani does frown, too, once he is out of sight.

"Oh, great, now I have to talk to him over my Thanksgiving break! I already have to see him tomorrow!" Ebony says, as she rolls her script up and hits it against the window. Our wacky speed-racer bus driver asks her not to hit the window again. Ebony apologizes.

Kitten tries to make Ebony feel better by changing the subject to the Thanksgiving Turkey Day celebration, and it works, because as soon as Kitten mentions the celebration, Ebony forgets that she has to pretend to be Emani for Stephan Miles tomorrow and perks up. She is so proud of it.

I decide that now isn't the time to tell my sisters that I do not want to serve people tomorrow for Thanksgiving. I want to be at home sitting with my family around a table with a delicious, buttery turkey that melts in my mouth when I bite into it. Why couldn't the celebration be the day after Thanksgiving? Now, I have to serve on Thanksgiving and travel to Louisiana the day after. When do I get to enjoy my mama's baked macaroni and cheese or my dad's turkey and dressing?

Emani's phone rings. We all look at it, mostly because we haven't heard it ring since she got on punishment for breaking her curfew. Now that she is officially off of punishment, we watch her say "yes," "umhh hmh," and "okay" before hanging up. Then, she laughs.

"What's so funny?" I ask after Emani whispers to Ebony and Kitten and does not answer me.

As usual, Ebony realizes that I'm seriously upset, before my baby sister does.

"Eris, that was Stephan. He just wanted to make sure that you weren't cooking tomorrow. He asked if he should bring something pink to coat his stomach or a brown paper bag to throw up in if you were." Ebony says as she giggles with Kitten and Emani.

I listen to them laugh as we reach our bus stop. Then, I get off of the bus without speaking to any of them. Traitors, they are.

I am definitely going to go to the celebration tomorrow, and I am going to cook something so good that Stephan Miles will fall to his knees and beg me for another bite.

* * *

"This is de-li-cious, Newbie! Did my boo Curly make this?" Stephan asks as he bites into my baked macaroni and cheese at the Thanksgiving celebration. It is the very macaroni and cheese that I made late last night with my momma. I watch him scrape the plate. He doesn't leave one morsel of cheese on the dish.

"Nope!" I say as I tighten my apron.

"Did Red make this?" Stephan asks as he takes another serving from the dish.

I remind him that the food is for the families who have come to the school to eat and not him. The school was opened to feed fifty families, not to feed a rich, greedy, chauvinistic, egotistical jerk such as Stephan Miles. He must read my mind as I think this, because he apologizes for eating another serving.

My mother comes over and asks me to help Alexis bring the senior citizens their plates first. I walk away to do as she says before I can brag to Stephan about my melt-in-your-mouth-mac-and-cheese. Unfortunately, he finds me as I am bringing drinks to the little kids later.

"So it was you who made the baked Mac and cheese?" Stephan asks with a look of surprise on his face.

He acts as if he's discovered a cure for a fatal disease or solved a complex mystery. I do not answer his question. Instead, I go to the dessert table to help Charlotte cut slices of pie and cake.

After Stephan steps to the mic to remind the people at the celebration that the event is anonymous and that picture taking is not allowed, he finds Kitten, Charlotte, and I over at the dessert table discussing what we are going to do in Louisiana.

Stephan asks if he can talk to me privately. I quickly remind him that my name is Eris and not Emani, but since his eyes remain serious, I decide to find out what he wants this time.

"Eris, I am sorry that I misjudged you. My mom can cook a great meal and play a great game. I should have known that you could, too. You two are so much alike that it sickens me sometimes. Anyway, she thinks I owe you an apology. You're my girlfriend's sister and I should be more respectful to you. I'm sorry." Stephan says as he reaches for a piece of chocolate cake.

I watch him eat a piece off of his fork. Then, I see him pick up the rest of it with his hands. He swallows the piece whole. Then, he licks each finger until there is not a crumb of chocolate left. Each moist, spongy piece of chocolate is gone.

Charlotte asks him if he enjoyed it.

He says yes after licking his lips. Then, he compliments her on how yummy it was. She smiles and then tells him that she did not bake the cake.

Kitten laughs when he asks if she made it. According to Kitten, her mother is the cook and she is the sampler. Kitten says she couldn't cook to save her life. That's why she works at a fast food restaurant. We all laugh.

Emani, Alexis, and Ebony walk over to us mid-laugh, sit down behind the dessert table, and grab a piece of chocolate cake. They are delighted to finally have a break from serving the fifty families that fill the cafeteria.

"Eris, you really put your foot into this chocolate cake! It is scrumptious, my sister!" Ebony says.

Stephan walks away. I guess he loses his appetite.

*   *   *

The day after Thanksgiving, I wake up early with the desire to see Mr. Thomas. He was in my nightmare last night, and I really need to see him. All four of us have had nightmares since the school tragedy, but this one seemed so real. I had to tell my daddy.

Luckily, my dad listens to me and agrees to take me to see Mr. Thomas to ease my mind. When we get there, his condo is empty, or at least no one answers the door. I am instantly upset, since I have given up a trip to Louisiana to see him and he is not here. Dad is upset because he almost let me travel on the train here alone and Mr. Thomas is nowhere to be seen.

We leave a note on Mr. Thomas's door and get on the elevator.

As we are exiting the building, I see Dr. Thomas entering. She has a slightly bigger belly, but basically looks the same: beautiful! She is dressed in scrubs, but she somehow looks amazing. She has a glow that seems to emanate from deep within.

My father hugs her. They embrace for a long time. If she were any other woman I would be upset, but since she is Dr. Thomas, she can hug my daddy as long as she likes. I know that Dr. Thomas's hug is innocent. She and Mr. Thomas may have secrets, but their love for one another is no secret.

"Thanks so much for visiting. How did you hear about the accident? You know that he is isn't here? He's still in the hospital." Dr. Thomas says, as I notice that she has Mr. Thomas's weapon "concealed" in her coat pocket.

It isn't visible, but I know the shape of a gun, especially against cotton fabric. I have seen many officers of the law in Mr. Thomas's condo with "concealed" weapons that weren't really that concealed before.

"Terrence is in the hospital?" My dad asks.

"Yes! I thought you knew. He was working late, driving while sleepy. He says a car came out of nowhere, and when he slammed on his brakes, they didn't work as they should. The car made it through the intersection, but it took his brakes a while to kick in. He knocked over a few little trees trying to avoid pedestrians, but the trees helped the car slow down," Dr. Thomas says as we follow her to the elevator.

My dad and I look at each other since Mr. Thomas was in a car accident in my nightmare last night. The only difference is that he did not make it out alive in my dream.

"Does Mr. Thomas believe that Payton Payne had something to do with this?" I ask, but I wish I hadn't when I see Dr. Thomas's face lose all of its color.

I forgot that she does not use that mass murderer Payton's name or like it when other people use it.

"No! Why? Do you think so? My husband thinks it was an accident. I thought he wasn't working on her case anymore." Dr. Thomas says as she pushes the number for Mr. Thomas's floor. Our silence seems to make Dr. Thomas a bit suspicious.

Though we do not speak, my dad and I look at each other again, puzzled, knowing that Mr. Thomas is definitely still working on Payton Payne's case and has vowed not to stop until he puts her in jail for killing his son and all of the other sons and daughters who died in our school bombings.

I watch Dr. Thomas rub her growing middle. She caresses her tummy like one would the head of a newborn. I smile, until I notice the contours of Mr. Thomas's gun in her pocket again.

Dr. Thomas lets me into Mr. Thomas's makeshift office while she looks for clothes for her husband. I hear her ask my dad if he would please not mention her pregnancy to Mr. Thomas. I know my dad is probably wondering, like I'm wondering, how Mr. Thomas could not notice that emerging tummy underneath those scrubs, but I hear him agree not to tell her "secret."

*

As Dad and Dr. Thomas talk, I watch this week's hidden video footage of Shiani Chan and Vita Rowe, but I do not expect to see Zyanne Jeffries. It is Zyanne's face that I see on the screen. The girls appear to be in Zyanne's house, and she is telling them not to let a boy come in between their friendship. She repeats one of their rules: Dimes before Dudes.

Out of her own mouth, Zyanne calls the three of them Dimes. This is evidence. I press "record" to copy the video onto my zip drive. I also send it to my phone as a backup.

Then, I watch Shiani and Vita share information about Dylan Gibson with Zyanne. They tell her about the gifts and letters they have received from him (they are gifts from Kitten and me, but they don't know this.) They tell her intimate information that even I do not want to know. Zyanne does not seem to respond. Her face has a frozen quality as she gets on the phone and tells someone else this information.

Shiani picks up the phone and listens to them. Then, Vita Rowe does the same. Neither Vita nor Shiani seem to like what the voice on the phone tells them, but I hear them agree to do as they are told. They do not discuss specifics about the plan, but I do hear them say that "Dylan Gibson will pay" for trying to play games with them.

I watch all three of them chant "Dimes before Dudes" again. Uh, I knew we shouldn't have involved innocent people, but Kitten felt we had to in order to get the evidence we needed. Now, I regret my decision. Dylan may be in danger.

When the footage starts to wander into purely personal subjects, I press fast forward and stop on the footage from two days ago in the cafeteria, and turn up the volume when Vita begins to speak.

"Dylan, you know that I love you, but I don't mind sharing you with my best friend. Is that okay with you?" Vita whispers in Dylan's ear.

When Dylan gets up to leave, upset, after Vita says this to him, Vita whispers to Shiani that they will have to hurt Dylan where he is most vulnerable, since he is pretending to be so innocent. She says that they will take away something that he loves, since he tried to take away their friendship and made them fight and argue like fools. The two of them agree to make him feel the pain that he has made them feel.

When I hear this, I begin to pace around Mr. Thomas's tiny make-shift office. I try to come up with a plan. Each plan that I create is more miserable than the last one, so I end up throwing one balled up piece of paper after another into the wastebasket.

I have to save Dylan Gibson from any pain, but how will I do that? I need Mr. Thomas, but he is in a hospital room dealing with his own problems. I need my sisters and they are on their way to Louisiana. The Big Easy. I guess I'll have to figure this one out on my own.

CHAPTER 16
Emani
Road Trip

I hate leaving Eris alone, but there is no way I am going to miss a road trip with Kitten's family. I don't know why Eris wants to go to see Mr. Thomas, but I want to see New Orleans. Some of the best musicians, art, and food come from the Big Easy, and I don't want to miss this chance to see Louisiana with my own eyes. I've read about it. I've visited it through the Internet, but this will be my first time experiencing it for myself.

I suspect Eris wants to see the secret videos for this week, but I can see them later. I am tired of the Dimes monopolizing my time and my energy. I need a break. I've given too much of my time to the cruel people in this world. I want to enjoy some normal, nice people for a while. I want to laugh and to smile.

Kitten's father is the funniest man I've ever met, so I know he will make this 14-hour trip a fun experience. Kitten says he used to have his own business, but I think he should have been a comedian. Whenever he drives us somewhere, he makes my cheeks hurt from laughing so much. I have never seen a frown on Kitten's father's face. Now that his finances are doing a bit better and they have been promised a place at a shelter after break, Kitten's dad has been smiling and joking more than ever.

Kitten's mom has packed lots of Thanksgiving leftovers from the celebration for us, but I also see a few containers with some new snacks in them. I am excited that she has made some treats for us, because Kitten's mom is a superb cook. I can't even cook on a stove, but Kitten's mom finds a way to feed us without one. Kitten says her mom volunteers around the city and suburbs cooking delicious meals for the homeless. Kitten says no one at the shelter realizes that her mom is homeless, too.

As we exit our home state of Illinois, I open one of my lengthy letters from Rickey to read. He always sends me three letters at a time, so I am saving the other two for later. I only have a couple of weeks left before I can see him again, so his letters help me to feel close to him, though we are so far away from one another. I prefer these letters to any brief text message he could ever send to me.

"Is that letter from Stephan or Rickey?" Ebony teases, though she knows it is from Rickey.

Rickey's letters aren't drowned in cologne like Stephan's. Rickey's letters aren't two-page tributes to my body parts or my beauty.

"Emani doesn't smile like that when she reads Stephan's letters or messages. That's definitely a letter from that college boy." Kitten says. Kitten's father looks back at me in the backseat and teases me about Rickey.

I giggle until I realize that if Kitten's dad is looking at me, he isn't looking at the road. I suddenly have a flashback of my dad doing 100 miles an hour jumping lane to lane after I broke curfew.

Last night, we served food at Ebony's Thanksgiving celebration, and now I am finally able to sit down. Finally, I am off of my sore feet. My hips have healed, but my toes are tired.

Kitten's dad pulls into a gas station and Ebony and Kitten jump out to go shopping for souvenirs like we're in Louisiana. We still have an hour to go, but they are filled with energy. I decide to stay in the car with Kitten's mom. She is more quiet than usual, so I try to get her to talk since everyone is gone.

"Mrs. Johns, Kitten says you haven't been back to Louisiana since that big hurricane hit a couple of years ago. Are you excited to be going home after so long?" She stares out the window before finally turning around toward me.

"Emani, I told you that you could call me Kyla or Aunty Kyla. Mrs. Johns is my mother-in-law—and honey, I am nothing like her," she says before she turns back around and stares out the window. I love Mrs. Johns' accent when she talks. I feel like I'm at Rickey's Cajun restaurant, Lucille's, talking to the owner all over again.

Kitten told Eris and me all about her grandmother, and from what Eris has told us, I would say that Mrs. Johns is a lot like her mother-in-law. They both love Kitten. They both love to cook. They both spoil Kitten's dad.

Kitten's dad has us singing silly songs as soon as the wheels hit the road again. We all sing in different voices. All of us sing except for Mrs. Johns——I mean, Aunty Kyla—who sits silently, looking out of the window for the rest of our drive. She only opens her mouth to ask us if we're hungry. Of course, I say yes. Lately, I have been more and more sleepy and hungry.

After we cross into Louisiana, Uncle Ken announces that we are only minutes from his mother's house. His smile widens. Aunty Kyla does not have a smile.

*

Kitten is our tour guide as we travel along the road. She points out every building, store, and street that she feels we should know. She has a story for each building, storefront, and road. Kitten knows Louisiana like I know Chicago. If I closed my eyes, I could draw a picture of downtown Chicago. Each landmark, each building, and each magnificent mile is forever etched in my mind.

My eyes widen when we pull into a massive house with a wraparound porch. It isn't as large as Stephan's, but it has much more personality. The house seems to have its own story. It looks like someone has pulled it out of a historical magazine. The house has seen through its windows. It has heard through its doors. To me, it wants to speak, but cannot. It wants to tell me how it has survived.

I follow Kitten, Ebony, Uncle Ken, and Aunty Kyla toward a slender, warm, amber woman with dark brown hair. Her skin is silky smooth, her smile is warm, and her eyes are focused on Kitten.

"Katherine, come give yo' Gram a big ole kiss," she says. Grandmother? This woman cannot be Kitten's grandmother. She doesn't look like she could have a child the size of Uncle Ken. She looks so young. New Orleans's fresh air must be good for you. I watch Kitten hug her. Then, I watch Uncle Ken do the same. She invites us into her historic house.

I soon learn that Kitten's Gram lives in this huge house alone. She gives us our choice of which room we would like to stay in for the weekend. Ebony and I smile, because each bedroom has its own queen-sized bed. Finally, I get to be a queen in a queen-sized bed, instead of a triplet in a twin-sized bed.

After we choose our rooms, Kitten's grandmother surprises us with a room filled with movies, snacks, spa supplies, and dress up costumes.

She gives us each a laptop or tablet so that we can get the music we like and tells us to her call her if we need anything. When I look around the room, I think to myself that I will not need to call her any time soon.

Ebony, Kitten, and I dress up in these huge dresses from Kitten's Gram's closet that are mostly tulle and satin. As I look in the mirror, I think of my Aunty Jay. She would love these dresses because they do not show any skin, but she'd hate the way the dress accentuates your cleavage.

Ebony finds some Louisianan music to play. The rhythm makes me stand to my feet, prance around the room, and finally jump almost out of my dress. Ebony and Kitten jump on the bed, and I join them when they begin to have a pillow fight.

Our pedicures, facials, and manicures are interrupted later by a delicious aroma that lingers in the air. It tickles my taste buds so much that I find myself by the door, sniffing outside.

Kitten says the smell is probably her grandmother's gumbo and her cobb salad. She reports that the dishes have seafood in them, but I still want some. If I weren't allergic, I would try it. That smell is difficult to resist.

Before we get to the kitchen, we can hear Aunty Kyla and Mrs. Johns arguing. We stop on the stairs, but our curiosity causes us to continue to listen to them.

"Why won't you let my son accept the money from me? I am just trying to help you," Kitten's grandmother asks.

"We don't need your money or your help. I am taking care of my husband and my daughter, Mrs. Johns."

Kitten's dad comes through the front door, interrupting our eavesdropping and Kitten's mother and grandmother's argument.

"So who is going to help me finish putting up the Christmas decorations?" Uncle Ken asks.

"These girls don't want to work, son. They want to shop," Grandma Johns says, as she gives us all a fistful of money. I assume she is giving us some of the money we just heard her offer to her daughter-in-law.

Kitten waits for her mom's permission to accept the money, and when Aunty Kyla says we can go shopping, we all follow Kitten out the door.

* * *

"I have to buy something for Tiny for Christmas," Kitten says when her grandmother's driver drops us at the mall. Ebony and I tease Kitten about her crush on Tiny (Timothy Armstrong). She does her shy smile then changes the subject to the Dimes.

Ebony has yet to find a way to give Zyanne her hidden camera necklace, so we try to come up with a plan to give her one. Without more information on Zyanne than her fling with the student teacher, we won't ever be able to get rid of the Dimes. The problem is that Zyanne does not wear jewelry.

The three of us go to the jewelry department and buy ourselves some charm bracelets. Then, we go to Kitten's favorite boutique to buy matching outfits. Kitten insists on buying an outfit and a bracelet for Eris, so we all split the bill for Eris's items. She is absent, but she is with us always.

When I check my phone, Eris has not left me a message. It is not like her to let a day pass without speaking to me, but maybe she is mad at me. I should have stayed with her. Alexis is there, but she won't be any company because she won't say one word for the entire Thanksgiving break.

I feel guilty joking, traveling, playing, dancing, singing, snacking, and enjoying myself without all of my sisters.

Ebony's phone rings, and I instinctively know that it is Eris when Ebony steps away from me to talk. Ebony speaks very low and constantly looks back at me.

"What did Eris say? I ask of Ebony when she hangs up her phone. She looks like she does not want to tell me.

"Eris has a plan that could affect Vita Rowe, Shiani Chan, and the AV girls, but she is a little nervous that you won't want to do it because if we fail, we could all be suspended and on punishment for a long time," Ebony says as she looks for agreement from Kitten and me.

I put my hand in my pocket, touching my three little hand-written letters from Rickey. I don't know if I can handle not seeing him for even more time, but I do not want to fail my sisters, either. Should I risk it?

"I'll help with the plan," Kitten says, as she tries on sunglasses like its summertime.

She looks like a celebrity trying to hide tired eyes from the paparazzi. I remind her that she is supposed to be looking for a present for her boyfriend, Tiny.

Kitten and Ebony look at me like they are waiting for my answer about the plan. I begin to look around in the glass case that holds the jewelry instead of responding. They follow closely behind me.

When I see a watch that Rickey owns in the glass jewelry counter, memories of him flash across my mind: our conversations, our walks, our hugs. Yet, my mind also flashes back to a moment when I said I would do whatever it takes for my sisters.

I once said I would do whatever it takes for justice, and I meant what I said. I meant it then, and I mean it now.

"Tell me the plan, Ebony. Tell me every detail," I say as I spray on some French perfume.

CHAPTER 17
Ebony
Gram's

Yesterday, Kitten, Emani, and I bought some delicious fragrances from the mall, but none of them smell as good as what's cooking in the kitchen today.

I try to straighten my bed before I head downstairs. Usually I'm a bit messy at home, but since this is someone else's house, I am on my best behavior.

I run down the steps, almost crashing into Kitten and Emani, who are frozen at the bottom of the staircase.

They seem to be listening to Kitten's grandmother and mother arguing in the kitchen again. I sit beside them on the steps and try to use my eyes more than my mouth to ask for an update. Kitten does not whisper.

"Well, my mom said that she has been trying hard to get a loan to open up a restaurant in the Chicago suburbs, but she can't seem to get one. And my grandmother says she doesn't have to get a loan, because she'll give her the money, but Mom won't accept it. Now, they're talking about how Mom lost her restaurant to the flood. They are talking about Hurricane Katy, so we are staying out here. I don't want to remember that hurricane. Why did they name something so horrible after me?" Kitten says, as she walks toward her grandmother's beautifully decorated living room, which Gram calls her sitting room.

Emani and I follow, though I would prefer to go to the kitchen and eat some of that delicious breakfast.

Mr. Johns walks in with his usually gigantic grin. His smiling is contagious. I smile too, as I watch him untangling some more Christmas lights and singing.

Last night when we came back from the mall, he made us all smile when we pulled up to this house and saw him almost fall off the roof outside hanging Kitten's grandmother's lights. When we got out of the car, he asked Kitten to hit a switch. The house lit up like a Christmas tree, literally.

Kitten had never mentioned that her dad decorated houses for all seasons of the year. His former business did holiday decorating for television shows, the news, and several celebrities' homes. We have always decorated our own home for the holidays, but Mr. Johns used to make a living doing it for others. Last night's decorations proved that he is very good at what he does. He even coordinated the beat of the Christmas music he used with the movement of the angels in the yard. I have never seen anything so beautiful.

Emani said the Christmas lights reminded her of her boyfriend Rickey's light shows, but I doubt Rickey's light shows could be as beautiful as Mr. Johns's light and sound show. I wish he'd decorate our house. My parents work so much and it gets so cold that we have very few decorations outside. The inside of our house is decked out, though. We even have our own mini-Christmas trees in our rooms.

"Hey, Mr. Johns, if my dad hasn't already done his miserable attempt at decorating the outside of our house, would you be willing to do our decorations? How much do you charge?" I ask as Grandma Johns exits the kitchen.

Grandma Johns assures me that I couldn't afford to pay Mr. Johns what he is worth, but I ask him the question again anyway.

"Ebony, I'd decorate your house for free," Mr. Johns says still smiling at me. My own dimples deepen as I grin.

"Son, how are you going to support your family if you do work for free?" Grandma Johns says, as she offers us some freshly squeezed orange juice.

It is a bit too bitter for me, but I drink it all since no one will let me go in the kitchen to eat.

Mr. Johns stands next to his wife and tells us that he has news for all of us. We all look at him. I secretly hope his news is that we need to all eat before we die of hunger, but it is not. My stomach growls from all of the junk food I ate last night.

Last night, we spent most of the night exploring Kitten's gram's house and her family's photos. Kitten gave us a history lesson we won't soon forget. I wonder what our classmates would say if they knew about Kitten's pedigree. This house alone is probably worth more than a few of Kitten's critics' fortunes. I am surprised that she just doesn't tell them at school that her family is Rich, with a capital "R."

"I have been hired by most of my old neighbors to decorate their homes," Mr. Johns proudly announces.

I admire Mr. Johns's desire to work when he really doesn't have to work at all. I love raising money for others, but I love making my own money, too.

Mr. Johns's wife drops his hand and reminds him that they do not have any of the tools he typically needs to do his work. She also reminds him that we are leaving today.

Before he can respond, Grandma Johns offers to buy the tools he needs for him and to allow him to stay at her house for a while in order to finish his new jobs for her neighbors.

We all look at Kitten's mom for a response, but she just goes into the kitchen without saying a word to Grandma Johns or Kitten's dad. I gladly follow her and begin making my plate. Solving problems is usually my area of expertise, and I'd love to help them, but I can't think until I eat.

It is a very silent breakfast.

"Well, you finally separated us, Mama Johns. Neither a hurricane nor homelessness has separated us, but one visit with you and my husband wants to leave me and my daughter," Kitten's mother says, as she gets up and begins cleaning our unfinished plates.

I hold on to my plate tightly, so she moves on to Emani's. Emani manages to get a biscuit from the plate before Kitten's mom takes the plate away. Kitten grabs a sausage and sips some juice before her mom takes her dishes away.

I stuff my mouth with food and swallow my juice in two gulps when I see her coming toward me to take my plate away again. After she takes the plate from me, I head upstairs to pack up my things, since she commands me to do so.

Kitten and Emani come into my temporary room to complain about us leaving early. I tell them that I really wish I could pack up this room and take it to Chicago with me, and that I am a little disappointed that Mr. Johns was unable to give us his official tour of New Orleans. I'm sure it would have been fun, but I guess I'll never know.

"I don't want to leave, Ebony," Kitten pouts as she watches me pack up my things.

Emani repeats Kitten's words in her sweetest voice as she complains about not having any souvenirs to bring to Rickey, who she says loves Louisiana's cuisine and culture.

"Why are you both looking at me? I don't want to leave either, but Mrs. Johns has her mind made up, and I don't think anyone can change it," I say as I stuff my dirty clothes into my black luggage.

Emani frowns at me when I do not fold them, so I try to fold a t-shirt. Then, I give up when I realize my folded-up t-shirt looks just like a crumpled piece of paper.

"My mom really likes you, Ebony. She would listen to you. You convinced her to cook for fifty families for Thanksgiving. I know you could convince her to stay until tonight," Kitten says with a sweet smile.

Kitten's slanted gray eyes convince me to listen, but I do not give in. I continue to stuff my toiletries into my luggage until she tells me I'm like her little sister, the little sister she wishes she had, but never had. She hugs me tightly, then looks up at me with her catlike eyes. When she lets go, I walk out the door and down the steps to try to talk to Mrs. Johns. I don't know what I'll say, but I'll try to speak to her from my heart.

Mrs. Johns listens as I tell her how Kitten probably feels when her family argues in front of her. She pays close attention when I tell her how hurt I was when my parents argued in front of me. I told her how my parents were separated and how I felt miserable being in the middle.

"I don't want to be separated from Ken. I love him, but he loves his mother more," Mrs. Johns says as she dries the semi-dirty dishes.

"I do not love my mother more, Kyla. I love her one way and I love you another. You're my wife, and she's my mother. That's why I need to work, so I can make both of you proud. I believe you are going to get your restaurant, but until then, I need to make some money. I need to be a man. If I stay here I can reconnect with some of my old clients. Once I'm established, I can come back to Chicago to be with you and Kitten. Maybe I can get some big contracts or referrals," Mr. Johns says when he walks into the kitchen in the middle of our discussion.

"Kitten and I can help you to get some clients in our neighborhood so that when you return, you'll have more jobs. We'll walk door to door, Mr. Johns. Most people hate organizing and hanging Christmas lights. I know that I do. There have to be other people out there like me. I know that we can get you some customers," I say, though I haven't okayed the plan with Kitten.

Mr. and Mrs. Johns smile at me as I speak. Their smiles disappear when Kitten's gram comes into the kitchen. She gives Kitten's mother a business card and explains that it has the number to her banker on it. Kitten's grandmother insists that Mrs. Johns call the banker on Monday to get a business loan.

Gram Johns declares, "I don't know how I became the enemy, Kyla, but I only want to help my children. I have always considered you to be my daughter. I know that you want to be independent, but you need to learn how to use the resources you have. I don't want my son here with me. I have my own life now that my husband is in Heaven. You are welcome to visit, but I'm not trying to keep anyone here against their will. I am trying to invest in both of you so that my grandchild won't be living in a car anymore."

When Kitten's gram says this, we all stare at her, since she isn't supposed to know that Kitten and her parents were living out of a car. Kitten's mom lowers her head in shame. Kitten's dad sits down and puts his head in his hands, ashamed, too. I try not to look in Kitten's grandmother's direction.

Kitten walks in, smiling, until her grandmother reveals that Kitten is the one who told her that their family lived in a car the last time she called. Kitten's gram also explains how she sent Kitten four train tickets to New Orleans. Kitten had told us a while back that the train tickets were for my sisters, me, and her to travel from Chicago to Memphis to Mississippi to Louisiana, but her grandmother says that the train tickets were for Kitten, her parents and a friend of her choice to take a scenic road trip to New Orleans.

Kitten looks at her father and mother, and then she leans against the refrigerator, staring at her own bare feet. I suddenly realize who probably financed Kitten's mini-makeover. I had assumed Kitten had used her paychecks for a makeover, but now I realize it was her Gram's money. I also realize that Kitten is in BIG TROUBLE.

No one is speaking to anyone.

"Look, I know you won't let me buy you a house, but I am so sad that neither one of you have come to me for help. Am I the enemy? Is my money evil?" Grandma Johns asks, before she starts to cry. "Your father and I worked hard so that the next generation would not have to work as hard. Why won't you let me help you?"

This is really not the vacation I thought it would be. What happened to the laughs? Why all the tears? New Orleans looks so cool in Eris's favorite vampire movies.

I ask, "Excuse me for interrupting, but does everyone here love one another?" They slowly look at each other and say yes.

Emani walks in with her lilac luggage, frowning and pouting since we won't get to see New Orleans and she didn't get to shop for herself or Rickey.

"Well, I think you all are wasting time arguing over nothing. Grandma Johns wants to buy you a house and help you start a business. Why not take the money? You're still going to have to pay the bills and keep your customers happy. Just because she pays for the restaurant doesn't mean she made it a success. Your hard work makes it a success. You all win if you work together. That's what my mom says. The way I see it, Kitten will have a house, Mr. Johns will have his business and a place to keep his tools, and Mrs. Johns will have her restaurant. And Grandma Johns, you will have the opportunity to help your family, which is all you seem to want to do. How does that sound to everyone? Plus, I'm hungry and we should just sit down, pray, and eat some real food." They do not speak, so I continue to munch on my apple. I can tell that everyone wants to say something, but they do not speak.

Emani interrupts the silence when she suggests that they hug and they embrace.

I wish I could do this at school. I wish I could stand in front of the school and ask the Dimes to stop torturing people and ask the tortured to forgive the Dimes. I wish I could get everyone at school to hug and make up, but at school there is no love. In this kitchen, there is love, and when there is a bit of love, there is always hope for change.

Mr. Johns tells us to change into our new matching outfits and to get ready for a tour of the Big Easy after he kisses all of his ladies: his mom, his wife, and his daughter. I tell him that I will join him right after I eat. He laughs and watches me make another big plate of Gram and Aunty Kyla's delicious breakfast cuisine.

*

My phone rings, and I answer it quickly when I see it is my personal acting coach and friend, Tyson's phone number.

"Hello, Ebony Robertson. This is Tony Tyson calling to congratulate you. You will be playing the part of Zaria in my drama entitled, "The Goddess of Love." Do you accept this role?" Tyson speaks in a strange voice that is so serious that I momentarily forget it is him.

I scream, "Yes! Yes, I accept the role!"

My sister and Kitten tease me when I whisper that it is Tony on the phone, so I walk to another room. Tyson tells me about a few people he had to call to inform that they did not get a role in the play. I am sad for them, but I must admit I am very happy for me.

"So our first practice is Monday, but I want you to come over my house today so we can go through our lines, Ebony," Tyson says in his deep voice.

I kick the sofa in the sitting room, as I tell him that I am in New Orleans and won't be able to come to his house to practice. Inside, I know that my father probably wouldn't let me go to Tyson's house anyway, but being in New Orleans is a less embarrassing excuse so I decide to use it.

Tyson sounds disappointed, too, but he tells me he is looking forward to practice on Monday. I wish I could say the same, but I am suddenly nervous again about having to kiss him for the first time in front of a room filled with people. I hope we don't have to practice that part of the play.

I ask him about the rest of the cast. The cast list is just as I knew it would be: the star of the show will be his sister Tatyanna. Her costar will be Tyson. And a few upperclassmen that were at the auditions will be in supporting roles. The behind-the-scenes crew is mostly made up of freshman and sophomores, but there is also a sophomore playing Athena, the Goddess of War.

As Tyson talks to me about the play he wrote and will star in, I imagine myself on the stage in front of my friends and family. In my vision, my family members are giving me a standing ovation after my fantastic performance. I take a bow and receive flowers, and when the curtain closes, they beg for an encore. In my vision, Tony comes back on the stage with me and tries to kiss me, but before he can put his lips on mine, a stage light falls on top of me, crushing me.

* * *

"Are you okay, sis?" Emani asks as we walk down Bourbon Street behind Mr. Johns a bit later, but I am still imagining myself on stage, smashed by a stage light.

"I'm okay, Emani. I just have a wild imagination," I say as I snap out of the daze I have been in for an hour.

I don't know why I keep imagining myself being injured, because I really don't have to worry. Sometimes my nightmares come true. Sometimes they do not. Besides, the Dimes are cruel, but they aren't that cruel. Right?

CHAPTER 18

Eris
It All Started at the Lunch Table

I sit down on the right side of Vita and Shiani's boy-toy, Dylan Gibson after I enter the lunchroom Monday. Even he is surprised when I do, since I am the only freshman at his table. The entire table stares at me as I talk to him. Dylan tries to help me out by telling everyone how I am sitting there because I know his girlfriend, but the people at the table continue to eavesdrop on our conversation and give me foul glances.

"Are you lost, freshman?" Vita asks as she sits beside Dylan. Shiani sits beside me and asks me the same question.

"No, I was just getting to know your boyfriend so he would know the freshman girl who will beat you at varsity volleyball," I say to Vita, who quickly rolls her eyes at me.

If body language were a weapon, I would say that her eyes could pierce my heart.

Vita makes some unfunny remark about my hair that I ignore, and Shiani teases me about my man muscles. I continue my conversation with Vita's very sweet boyfriend, Dylan Gibson. He tells me about a piece of art that he will be unveiling this weekend at the opening of the alumni building. I listen to him, but I do not take my eyes off of Vita.

Shiani Chan compliments Dylan's artistic abilities before she asks me why I'm not hiding in the library with my sisters and the rest of the scared freshmen. She calls my sisters copies, then she and Vita laugh simultaneously. They have airy, breathy laughs. They are the kind of fake laughs you do to impress boys. Real laughs aren't that pretty. Real laughs start in the belly and end in the mouth. Their laughs were all in the throat. Vita and Shiani's laughs were as phony as their "love" for Dylan.

When Dylan Gibson tells someone at the table that he has been working on his sculpture since this summer, I realize how much it probably means to him. When he says he may use a picture of the sculpture in his portfolio for college, I begin to believe the sculpture is probably what Vita and Shiani will try to destroy to get revenge on Dylan. I could be wrong, but I doubt it. Ebony is the smartest one, but I am usually the first to solve a mystery or a puzzle. I can fix my dad's rubix cube in thirty-three seconds.

I get up after Tatyanna Tyson sits at the table, but not before I see a fellow freshman bring Tatyanna a lunch tray filled with food and quickly leave. I do not see Tatyanna give the freshman any money, so I assume he bought the lunch for her, and since he left so quickly, I assume he did not volunteer to or want to buy it for her. I have heard about the Dimes forcing people to feed a few chosen upperclassmen, but I did not know they made people pay to feed them, too. I don't mind feeding the needy, but not the greedy. Tatyanna is definitely not needy.

As I am leaving the table, the freshman is bringing Tatyanna something to drink. I look back and watch, hoping he will pour the liquid on her head, but he does not. He doesn't even look her in her eyes. The Dimes seem to control boys and girls at this school. They have too much power.

I walk over to the security guard to ask for permission to leave, and he allows me to go. I can't wait to tell my "copies" what I just witnessed. I also tell my "copies" my plan.

* * *

All week, Emani tries to convince me not to go through with my plan to divide Vita, Shiani, and the AV girls. One day, Emani is confident that we will succeed. The next day, she is afraid that we will fail.

On Friday night, I begin to feel a bit of nervousness about my plan, too, as Kitten, Emani and I hide in the bushes outside of the alumni building with our video cameras.

Emani sends me a text that says, "Where R they?"

I reply "IDK," because I really don't know. I was sure that Vita and Shiani would try to destroy Dylan's masterpiece before the unveiling tomorrow, but it is pitch black outside, and they have yet to arrive. Maybe Kitten is right. Maybe we should leave before we miss our curfews.

As I rise, I see three figures slowly approaching the statue. They are dressed in dark clothes, but when I switch my camera to night vision, you can clearly see that it is Shiani Chan, Vita Rowe, and, to my surprise, varsity cheerleading co-captain Winter Gordon.

I ignore Emani's next text message, but I'm sure she is saying "OMG." I hate to be her echo, but oh my God! What is Winter doing here? We both thought Kitten was wrong about innocent-looking Winter Gordon being a Dime.

I continue to videotape, trying not to shake my hands, but it is difficult not to react as the girls spray paint Dylan's meticulously detailed sculpture. In fact, I almost drop the camera when I see pretty, petite, Winter Gordon take out a blow torch and begin slicing pieces of the sculpture off.

The air is silent and still, so I am able to hear Emani drop her camera, but the Dimes do not seem to hear her, so I continue filming. It is 9:35, according to the time on my camera screen, but the Dimes don't seem to be in a hurry. They slowly spray paint and slice as if the school's cameras are of no concern to them.

I scan the area with my camera and land on a security vehicle entering our school's parking lot. When I turn the camera back toward the sculpture, the Dime girls are running away. The security vehicle slowly drives into the parking lot and pauses in front of the alumni building. Kitten screams, 'Great plan, Eris" from her side of the bushes. I cannot believe we are going to get caught here while the guilty girls get away.

Kitten is right. We do look guilty. Uh oh. We can't get caught. I decide we should run. I quickly change my mind when the security vehicle's bright light floods the grass and bounces off of the weeping willow trees.

I hug the cold earth closely, trying not to be seen, as I silently hope that Kitten and Emani are doing the same.

The security vehicle shines his bright light around the alumni building again then stops for a moment near the main entrance. He sheds light on everything except Dylan's statue or Emani, Kitten, and me.

When he leaves, I do not move from the dirt. I wait about five minutes before I run toward the gate. Kitten and Emani quickly join me there. We all frantically look around for Ebony and Jeremy, who are supposed to meet us here.

"We aren't going to make it, Eris. I'm going to be on punishment again. We'll never make it home by 10:00. Rickey and Rachel will be dating by the time I see him again," Emani says, as she shakes the school's gate in frustration.

I try to calm her, but she is too frantic to control.

Kitten taps Emani on her shoulder, smiles, and points toward the street, where I see Jeremy's dark car parked with its lights off. We swiftly run toward our getaway car. Emani even outruns me.

"Did you get them on video?" Ebony asks in front of Jeremy.

I do not answer because he is not supposed to know anything about our plan. Ebony was supposed to just trick him into coming to pick us up without giving him any information. I just stare at her until she tells me that she had to tell Jeremy our plan to get him to leave the studio and to come here to get us.

"Yes, we all have video," I say, as Jeremy starts driving full speed down the street.

I am able to buckle my seatbelt at the end of the block when Jeremy finally stops at a stop sign. Thank God for that little red octagon.

"Jeremy, I know what your motorcycle can do, but can your car make it to our house in ten minutes?" Emani asks frantically.

"Emani, your dad built my engine. This car can definitely get you home in ten minutes," Jeremy says as he races through a yellow light.

At 9:59, Jeremy slides into our driveway. Emani and Ebony beat me to the door, but we all make it in by 10:00. My dad laughs when he sees us piled up on top of one another by the front door. As he teases us, Alexis helps us to get back on our feet. She looks out the window, watching Jeremy pull away in his car. She doesn't blink.

"We did it!" Emani says, as we watch Kitten get into her mother's car across the sheet.

"We're only half way there, Sis. The hard work begins tomorrow," I say, as I clean the grime out of my favorite blue jeans.

* * *

Thanks to Kitten's security guard friend, we easily sneak into the AV room the next day. Charlotte is already there when we enter.

"Where's the evidence?" Charlotte asks without looking at us. I give her our footage. She looks up at me and smiles at the videos.

"You know me, Charlotte. You're holding my plan A, plan B, and plan C," I say, as I look out the door to make sure the AV girls are not around.

They aren't supposed to be here until Monday, but Kitten's security guard buddy says they sometimes come in to pre-record their show early.

Ebony walks in and heads directly toward me.

"It's time to go, girls. The police are outside by the alumni building. Poor Dylan looked heartbroken when he arrived. Vita and Shiani are both out there pretending to comfort him. It was nauseating watching them and not being able to say anything," Ebony says, as she looks over Charlotte's shoulder at our videos.

"Don't worry about Dylan. I'll take care of him. He has been a true friend to me," Charlotte says, as she tells us to leave her while she works.

I offer to stay and protect her, but Charlotte insists that she doesn't need any protection, so we leave.

* * *

On Monday morning, my sisters and I meet at my locker after homeroom. We eagerly stare at the TV screen that hangs above my locker. Always punctual, the posing perky AV girls appear on the screen.

Our own news producer Charlotte wheels herself next to me and looks up at the screen, smiling ear to ear. I want to ask the cunning Charlotte how the newscast went this morning, but I decide to watch it for myself. I know that she told Ebony the AV girls almost caught her editing the videos in the AV room Saturday, but she was able to talk her way out of it. Charlotte is amazing.

As usual, everyone in the hall stops to watch the school's favorite news reporters, the AV girls, give us our weekly report. After they welcome us back from a hectic weekend, they report on sports, the cast of the upcoming spring play, and the success of student council's Thanksgiving food drive and celebration.

It is a positive report, until pictures of homeless students eating with their families flash across the screen. When this happens, my sisters and I demand an explanation from Charlotte. The celebration was supposed to be anonymous. Ebony promised the students and their families that everyone's identity would be kept confidential. The only people who were supposed to know the identities of the homeless families were people who were there at The Thanksgiving celebration.

Charlotte tells us that there were not any pictures from the celebration with the copy of the positive story the AV girls submitted to her this weekend. She said there were only pictures and video for the sports highlights section of the broadcast.

As Charlotte speaks, a picture of Kitten stuffing her face sits on the screen. Across the hall from my locker, Zyanne Jeffries smiles and waves at us, as the AV Girls report on the "needy" students at C.I.A. who attended the celebration. We listen to them say specific names and show pictures and video. I almost lose my balance when I see my family and a few of my new friends. I guess Charlotte wasn't the only one editing the video this weekend. These AV girls are ruthless. How could they embarrass so many people who can't help being in need of help?

When the AV girls move to the next story about the vandalism to Dylan Gibson's statue, Zyanne stops smiling. A look of surprise, and then anger, is on her face. When the video of Shiani, Vita, and Winter plays on the TV, Zyanne accidentally drops her metallic notebook on the floor.

It looks like the very notebook Ebony believes contains the information we need on the Dimes. We watch her scramble to call someone on her phone, and I am tempted to grab her notebook, but I resist.

The majority of the people in the hall are silent when they see Vita, Winter, and Shiani's faces on the screen spray painting and slicing, but we do hear a few giggles and whispers.

"Laugh now, but you'll cry later," Zyanne screams threats as she talks to someone on the phone.

We watch the AV girls run over to Zyanne, most likely trying to explain their broadcast.

"You should have seen their faces as they read the teleprompters this morning, girls. Darcy even asked our faculty advisor and producer, Ms. Smith, if she had to read the story. It was amazing," Charlotte says, as she looks through her book bag for a flyer that she says we must see.

"Where are Vita, Winter, and Shiani now?" Ebony asks, as she stares at me, staring at Zyanne's notebook on the hallway floor.

It has been kicked a little closer to us somehow.

"They're in the office!" Kitten says as she approaches us, visibly upset.

All four of us try to apologize to Kitten for her picture showing up in the broadcast, but she remains upset. She screams at Ebony for promising to keep the celebration anonymous and confidential. Then, she accuses all of us of trying to make her look like a fool in front of the entire C.I.A. student body.

Zyanne and the AV Girls, Darcy and Ciera, stop arguing and begin to look our way as Kitten screams at all of us.

Kitten finally stops screaming and leaves when her security guard pal tells her to hush herself and get to class.

"Do we proceed with our plan?" Emani asks once Kitten is gone. After we discuss the Kitten situation a bit more, we decide that she will probably just need some time to heal. We were all on the video. We are sure she will understand that it was not us that did this to her or the other families. In time, she will realize it was the Dimes, once she has time to think.

Once Charlotte realizes Kitten is not in the mood to listen to anyone, Charlotte tells us that she's going to comfort poor, innocent Dylan Gibson some more. Then she gives us all flyers for Fashion Forward Designer Models Organization (FFDMO) and encourages us to come to their meeting this Thursday after school. Modeling? Me? I don't know what Charlotte's plan is, but if it is based on any of us modeling, it is bound to fail. Our mom tried to get us into movies and commercials as toddlers. We were not hired.

"I guess that is a yes!" Ebony says, as she reads over the FFDMO flyer.

Stephan Miles tells us that we are going to be tardy for class when he walks by us. Then, he walks over to talk to Zyanne. We all go in different directions toward our classes, but not before I quickly bend over and pick up Zyanne's metallic notebook and slide it in between my books, since she is distracted by Stephan Miles's spell, which seems to work on everyone except me.

When I finally get to class, I am instantly sent to the dean's office. My teacher does not explain why I have to go, but she does look solemn when she gives me my pass. I am already shaking from trying to get Zyanne's notebook without being seen. Now I am shaking because I have to face Dean Norton again. She once warned me never to return to her office again.

When I get to the dean's office, I nervously sit and wait. Instead of the dean's face, I see Vita, Winter, and Shiani's sad faces as they exit their own dean's offices.

National Honor Society president Reana Powers walks into the office and sits beside me. I hold my books tighter, trying to conceal Zyanne's notebook, just in case Reana is a Dime. Unlike Kitten, we do not believe Reana is capable of being a Dime, but we were wrong about Winter, so . . . Kitten may be right. Reana was voted as a "student of character" by students and staff, but Kitten hasn't been wrong yet.

"Why are you here, Ebony?" Reana asks with genuine concern in her voice.

I relax a bit. Then, I laugh, since no one usually mistakes me for Ebony. Most people know that Ebony is the redheaded triplet and I'm the bald-headed triplet with three-minute hair. Now I'm sure that Reana isn't a Dime. She would definitely know who I am.

I smile at Reana and tell her who I am.

"Reana, I'm actually Eris. Ebony has the red hair. Emani has the curly hair. I'm the one with this um . . . short hair."

Reana smiles and compliments me on my hair.

As I finish my explanation, Dean Norton walks in and gives Reana Powers a few passes to deliver to some other freshmen students. When I hear the names of the students, I get nervous, because they are all troublemakers. Maybe I am in trouble, but what did I do? Reana is an office runner, which means she gets paid and gets out of class. Unfortunately, the job is only open to the smartest kids in schools, which is not me.

Dean Norton invites me into her office. When she closes her door behind me, I begin to wonder if I should have come with a lawyer, not that my mom and dad could afford one after paying this ridiculous school tuition times three. I personally think we should all have full scholarships, but C.I.A. doesn't believe in those, no matter who you are or will be in the future.

It would be nice if they extended scholarships to some of the homeless students in the community. There were quite a few kids my age at our Thanksgiving Celebration that probably have great potential. I bet they wouldn't be here waiting in the dean's office to be punished like me.

"Ms. Robertson, I was hoping that I would not see you so soon, but here you are again in my office. Do you know why you are here this time?"

I try to count the stars on the flag behind her instead of answering her question but lose count after 33. That is when I look down on her desk and see my ID still on the lanyard. I haven't seen it since last Tuesday or Wednesday.

Dean Norton watches as I reach for my ID and place it around my neck.

"I think I lost it the day before break," I say limply as I wipe dirt off of the plastic case.

"You think?" She shakes her head. "Well, your ID was found next to Dylan Gibson's vandalized artwork. Do you have any idea why it would be there?" Dean Norton looks across her desk and into my eyes.

I try to channel Alexis. I try not to blink and I don't dare look away from her.

"No."

Sighing, Dean Norton gets up and takes a quick peek out her door. She seems to be looking at Winter, Shiani, and Vita. After a minute or so of staring at them, she closes her door and stares at me.

"Do you know those girls outside?"

"Everyone knows who they are. They are three of the most popular girls at school."

"Are they your friends?"

"No."

Dean Norton believes that the girls outside did not work alone. She feels there was someone who came up with the plan. I want to tell her that I agree, but I decide to listen instead.

She tells me that she has decided that Vita, Winter, and Shiani will be on a beautification committee instead of being expelled from school, since they are first time offenders and Dylan Gibson's parent won't press charges against them. Then, she warns that whoever actually planned the destruction of Dylan's sculpture will be found and expelled from school.

Judging by the way she looks at me, she believes I am the brains behind the destruction. I wish I could tell her that I am not the smart one.

Reana Powers walks in to tell Dean Norton that Shiani, Vita, and Winter's parents are here. Dean Norton dismisses me. I am so nervous as I leave that I trip and drop my books and Zyanne's metallic notebook. I quickly pick them up. Luckily, no one is paying me any attention.

*

At lunch time, everyone in the school discovers what the "beautification committee" is, because Vita, Winter, and Shiani walk into the cafeteria wearing custodian uniforms. They follow the custodians around like they are their shadows, cleaning up and picking up our trash. It is odd to see pretty, petite, Winter changing garbage bags with her long fingernails.

Emani, Ebony, Alexis, and I leave the cafeteria after we see an upperclassman throw his cookie wrapper on the floor and order the girls to pick it up. He says that the girls missed a spot, and many of the people in the cafeteria laugh as Vita, Winter, and Shiani wipe off the rude boy's table and pick up his trash. I can only imagine what the Dimes will do to him later.

Tyra Jacobs's real phone number was posted on the internet only moments after she made her confession to the dean about our fight with the Dime recruits. She has been harassed since then every day. I believe she told Ebony it said "for a good time call Tyra" next to her phone number. Ebony says Tyra has tried to change her number but they always seem to discover it.

No one is safe from the Dimes, so I really feel sorry for this rude boy. He must have no idea what he may be in store for in the future. The Dimes may seem to be weak right now, since Winter, Vita, and Shiani have to clean up people's messes, but the remaining seven Dimes still have followers. They still have power.

If the powerful Dean Norton had more evidence, I would have been on the beautification committee, too. I am so grateful for that video.

We triplets follow Alexis to the library after Kitten's security guard buddy permits us to leave the cafeteria.

When we enter, I am surprised to see Stephan sitting with the AV girls, until I notice his cousin Kylie sitting with them, too.

He walks over and sits beside Emani when he notices us.

"So, Eris, I guess you're on your way to varsity now that Vita is suspended for the rest of the season," Stephan says, as he takes his voice recorder out of his pocket and points it at me.

Someone needs to show this boy how to do voice memos on a cell phone. I mean, welcome to the twenty-first century. When I do not respond, he snaps a picture of me with his paparazzi camera. I am temporarily blinded by its flash. Cell phones take pictures, too. Can someone please teach Stephan Miles a few tech tricks?

"No comment!" I yell, as I get up to leave.

The librarian asks me to be quiet.

I don't want to be quiet. I want to scream. I want to walk back into Dean Norton's office and tell her everything I know about the Dimes. The only problem is I don't know enough and she still seems to suspect me.

When I get to the end of the hall, I go into the bathroom and close the stall door behind me. This is probably the safest area in the school. There is no camera for the AV girls to control. I slowly open Zyanne's notebook, hoping to read something that will help my sisters and I to get rid of them.

*

The first ten pages of the notebook are blank, but on the eleventh page I see words and symbols. The notebook is written in code. I instantly think about Kitten's code. I really need her help, but I don't think that now is the time to ask. Kitten's complex mind could probably break this complicated code, but after being embarrassed in Charlotte's and the AV girls' television broadcast, will she? And if Kitten won't help me break this code, can I do it?

CHAPTER 19

Emani
The Notebook

Thanks to Charlotte's parents' business, Eris and I were able to make copies of Zyanne's notebook last week and put it back where Eris found it before Zyanne could miss it, but we haven't been able to break the code because Kitten won't even speak to us. Kitten was supposed to go around with Ebony finding clients for her dad's holiday decorating service, but she never showed up. Eris and I helped Ebony to convince our neighbors and some local businesses to sign up for the service ourselves, but Kitten didn't even say thank you when we gave her the list of clients to give to her dad.

We've tried everything possible. I thought maybe the code was the alphabet backwards, but it isn't. Eris thought that maybe the code was based on a keyboard like Kitten's, but it wasn't. And Ebony is trying to use a phone to figure it out. Nothing has worked.

We have been able to break apart the AV girls and Vita, Winter, and Shiani, however. They argue whenever they cross paths in the hallway and according to the hidden video we saw last weekend when we went to visit a very healthy Mr. Thomas, they truly have not forgiven one another.

Though they are all still unofficially Dimes, Zyanne is always trying to keep the peace between them in the hidden camera video footage, but it doesn't seem to be working. The AV girls are on one side, and Vita, Winter, and Shiani are allies on another side.

Rickey was not at Mr. Thomas's condo this weekend, but he is supposed to come out to see me around Christmas break. I am counting the days until then, especially since my dad is going to finally let Ebony and I break up with Stephan. Thank goodness.

Stephan is a nice guy, but he is just not the right guy for me. Actually, he is not the right guy for either of us. Ebony has her Tyson. I have my Rickey.

I am supposed to go out with Stephan tonight, but I am not looking forward to it. I wanted to go to a movie so that we wouldn't have to interact too much, but he wants to take me to a Chicago Bears game. I really wish I could switch places with Eris, but even if I could, she would not trade places with me, even for her favorite football team. She does not like anything about Stephan Miles.

*

"You cannot wear those to a game, Emani," Eris says as she frowns at my outfit. She is pointing to a new pair of heels I am wearing with my favorite blue jeans.

Ebony walks in to see what we are talking about.

Ebony asks, "Emani, do you want to catch frostbite? Do you want to lose those little twinkle toes of yours? How are you going to dance with no feet or toes?"

As my sisters tease me about my runway wobble walk, I hear my mother screaming that Stephan is here to pick me up. Though I beg Ebony to take my place, she just stubbornly sits on her bed next to Eris, looking through copies of Zyanne's notebook. We still haven't broken that code.

*   *   *

Stephan Miles compliments me for the tenth time when we find our seats in the stadium. I thank him for bringing me a seat warmer. Then, I try to pretend to be interested in the game. I know the game of football. I've been on the sidelines since sixth grade. Of course, I know the game, but I pretend not to so that we don't have to discuss any delicate topics. "So Er-Emani, are you cold? Do you need a kiss to warm you up?" Stephan says as he holds my auburn gloved hand in his hand.

"Oh, I'm always warm. I have a warm heart," I say as I smile at him, hoping he will not ask me for any more kisses. I ignore the fact that he just almost called me by my sister's name. The two of them have definitely been spending too much time together lately.

"Well, my heart is beating so fast, just sitting here next to you." I look at Stephan's mother and father sitting in front of us when he says this, because I cannot believe he is flirting with me with his parents in such close proximity.

If he spoke like that in front of my dad, he would be thrown on the field or through the goal posts.

I decide to talk to his parents instead of to him. Mr. and Mrs. Miles tell us about how they met at a Chicago Bears game. Stephan smiles as his dad says how the cold Chicago air can bring two complete strangers together.

As I look at Mr. Miles in his business suit at a Bears game and Mrs. Miles in her jogging suit, I realize how different they are. When they hold hands, I realize how in love they are with one another, despite their differences. It is inspiring. Mrs. Miles is five years younger than Stephan's dad, but it doesn't seem to make a difference.

Maybe when I'm older, the age difference between Rickey and me won't matter either, but now it seems like we are from different worlds. He speaks of the future in his letters. He is always dreaming. He is always planning for tomorrow, but I am just trying to make it through today. I am just trying to take it one day at a time.

"Do you want to get married one day?" Stephan asks.

"Yeah, in like ten or fifteen years," I say as I sip a little hot chocolate, hoping for any excuse not to continue our conversation.

"Will you work?" Stephan interviews me like I am applying for the job of being his wife.

"Of course I'll work, but to be honest, dancing isn't work to me, Stephan. It is like breathing. I can't live without doing it."

Since he doesn't respond, I talk to him about my upcoming part in the Christmas musical. I tell him how wonderful it is going to be, and before I realize what I'm saying I am inviting him to come and see me perform. I guess I want to prove to him that dancing on a stage is as challenging as what he does on the football field.

"Oh, I can't come, Curly. My family always goes on vacation at Christmas time. I won't even be in the country."

I smile inside, but try to keep a straight face in front of him. That is the best thing Stephan has said all night.

*   *   *

"So you went on another date with my cousin?" Kylie says as we warm up with the Stomp squad in front of Ms. Jennings and Coach Calderone. It has only been one day since my date with Stephan, but I guess he shared the details with his curious cousin.

I sit on the polished gymnasium floor and stretch, trying to ignore Kylie.

Kylie's hidden video footage so far shows her constantly flirting with my sister's boyfriend, Jeremy, at his friend's studio. She goes to his group's events. She compliments him and tries to seduce him every chance she gets. It makes my stomach turn when we watch her on video trying to tempt Jeremy to betray Alexis. Luckily, Jeremy has yet to fall for her charms.

"I went to a football game with Stephan. I wouldn't call it a date. Stephan and I are just friends," I say as I do a backbend.

"Well, Jeremy and I went on a date, too. He and I are becoming great friends," Kylie says before she does a forward flip.

I want to tell her that I know she is lying, but I can't because I would probably have to reveal a certain hidden video camera. If she went on a date with Jeremy, it must have been on a day that she wasn't wearing the necklace. I know Jeremy, and I doubt he is dating Ms. Kylie behind my sister's back. Kylie is irresistible to most boys, but Jeremy Sparks is not like most boys, plus he is one-hundred percent devoted to Alexis.

Coach Calderone asks Kylie and me to do our first dance from the musical. I wipe my nice smile off of my face and prepare to be naughty. It is time for me to dance as Dame Darkness.

* * *

There are ten days left until Christmas break. Charlotte says that last year around this time, the Dimes increased their wicked activity, but we have yet to see any evil actions. In fact, according to our videos, half of the Dimes haven't been communicating with one another much at all.

Ebony is forcing me to help her with student secret Santa today whether the Dimes are supposed to attack or not. We are in the lunchroom signing people up who want to participate in the gift giving. So far, several people have signed up, but not the ten people we are hoping will sign up. We are expecting more upperclassmen participation, especially Zyanne, Reana, Tatyanna, and Brenda, because Ebony has requested the support of all C.I.A. organizations and clubs for this fundraiser. The clubs are supposed to have their members buy a ten-dollar gift for a fellow student. Ebony and I are here to sign up students so they can pull a name from our jolly jar. The jolly jar holds all the names of the students who have signed up for the secret Santa program.

We are hoping that the rest of the Dimes sign up so that we can send them some special gifts, gifts that have a certain secret camera inside.

Reana Powers walks up to the table with a ten-dollar bill in her hand.

"Oh, I just want to donate to the charity," Reana says with a smile.

Ebony hands her a thank-you card that reads: "Giving is the true gift of life," and Reana wishes us luck with the fundraiser. I don't understand how Kitten could dislike Reana. Kitten is suspicious of everyone. Reana is a good person.

Zyanne and Brenda walk up together. As student council president, Zyanne signs herself up, and FFDMO president Brenda tells me she is so sorry that I won't be modeling in the Valentine's fashion show. She informs me that my designs were accepted by the executive board of FFDMO. Then, she congratulates Ebony on being chosen to model my designs. We both ask her if Eris will be in the show. In so many words, she tells us that Eris does not have "the look" they are going for this year. Brenda is judge and jury when it comes to fashion crimes at our school. She isn't just the fashion police. She gives out life sentences for those who fail at fashion in her blog.

When Brenda says this about our identical triplet sister, we both look at Brenda from head to toe. Brenda Agbayewa wears a Mohawk hairstyle. She is around six feet tall in her heels and is extremely thin. She always wears shimmer and shine make up and about four layers of multicolored clothes. She has a runway walk, even when she is just walking down the school's hallway. Anyway, Brenda is not afraid to show off. However, she is completely wrong when it comes to Eris Robertson. Eris is beautiful. We all have "the look." We all look good.

Zyanne asks Ebony about the money we have made so far from the secret Santa sign-up special, but even she is speechless when the beautification committee of Vita, Winter, and Shiani stroll into the lunchroom behind the head custodian.

When Zyanne opens her notebook and writes something inside, Ebony's dimpled cheeks seem even deeper than when she normally smiles. I smile back, knowing that though we do not know what she is writing, we soon will know everything, thanks to hidden video cameras.

When Zyanne and Brenda leave the lunchroom, a food fight breaks out. I see the same rude boy who has been teasing the beautification committee get a cookie wrapper shoved in his mouth after being punched in the mouth by a fellow upperclassman.

It is then that Ebony and I gather the signup sheets and jolly jar. We ask Kitten's security guard buddy for permission to leave. He won't let us leave. I guess there's a first time for everything. Without Kitten on our side anymore, we don't have our same privileges. We can't escape this horrid, loud lunchroom without her security guard's permission. No Kitten. No exit.

Right outside the cafeteria door, we see Kitten walk by us and look into the lunchroom. We wave to her, but she does not wave back to us.

Instead, she walks over to Brenda Agbayewa and Zyanne Jeffries. Then, the three of them walk away together.

*

"There is no way Kitten would join them!" Charlotte says after school when we tell her that Kitten was spotted with Brenda and Zyanne.

"I agree. Kitten is like our sister!" Eris says as she twirls her volleyball around her arms and shoulders.

We all walk toward the gym to watch Eris's semi-final game, or whatever it is called. All I know is that she and her squad are undefeated and her championship game is right before Christmas break.

"Besides, if Kitten wanted to join the Dimes, she would have done it last year when they wanted her," Charlotte says as we enter the gym.

Ebony grabs Charlotte's wheelchair and wheels her right back out of the gym. Eris ignores her teammates as they call her to come warm up for the game and joins us outside the gym to hear some gossip from Charlotte.

I ignore Kylie as she tells me I need to be in Stomp practice. Is Kylie crazy? I wouldn't miss this game for anything. Eris always comes to everything I dance in. I may not know a lot about volleyball, but I know how to cheer for my sister. I'm going to have to miss today's dance practice. I'll let Lady Light have the spotlight this one time.

*

We finally get Charlotte into a quiet corner in the hall. Ebony looks around for a camera, but there isn't one.

"I'm sorry. I thought Kitten told you that she and I were both invited to a secret Dime meeting last spring. I didn't go, because I did not trust them, but Kitten was new to C.I.A. and didn't know any better, so she did. She had just transferred in and they wanted her. She thought it was like a secret sorority or something. She now thinks she was invited because the Dimes knew how much money her grandmother is worth, but then she thought they liked her personality. Anyway, Kitten says she showed up after school to an empty classroom with a note on the desk that said for her to turn off the lights and blindfold herself. I would have never done it, but she says that she did. The next thing she knew there were ten voices asking her questions. I guess they didn't like her answers, because that was the last meeting she received an invitation to go to, but she was the lucky one. The Dimes didn't like my disregard for their invitation. I can't prove anything, but I find it quite a coincidence that I was hit by a car less than a week later."

I am speechless when Charlotte matter-of-factly says this to us. My sisters are speechless, too. We all look at Charlotte's wheelchair and then into her eyes again. If what she says is true, the Dimes aren't just bullies, they are criminals. My parents say that bullies once stole lunch money or called people vicious names, but destroying people online and crippling them in real life is going too far. The Dimes must be stopped.

"I still don't think she'd join them. Kitten is a decent human being. The Dimes are little wicked women," Eris says, as she holds her volleyball on her head. We follow her back toward the gym after she tells us that we can't stop playing the game against the Dimes until we have a victory. As I look at Eris, I realize that I love my sister's style. She isn't a diva or a supermodel, but she is a winner because she never quits.

CHAPTER 20
Ebony
Let the Battles Begin

"I quit, Tyson," I whisper when our director tells me I am not giving one-hundred percent to my character, Zaria. Is she kidding? I showed up today after someone tried to hurt me yesterday. If that's not giving one-hundred percent, I don't know what is.

Ms. Scott insists that the stage light falling down right where I was supposed to be standing was an accident, but I know better. Tatyanna's face was filled with terror when Ms. Scott told her to stand on my mark and show me how I should deliver my lines. She even jumped out of the way before the light fell halfway down from the ceiling. I know that the Dimes wanted that light to fall on me. I was just lucky enough not to be hit by it.

"You can't quit, you are my inspiration for this play!" Tyson says when he whispers back into my ear.

I suddenly feel a little more able to say my lines for the tenth time after he whispers into my ear.

Tatyanna limps into practice on crutches. She announces to everyone that she has ill-defined fractures in her foot from when she fell off of the stage. Everyone rushes over to her to offer her sympathy. Everyone except for me. Even I can't act that well. I do not like or trust Tyson's sister Tatyanna Tyson —not at all.

In fact, I don't walk over until I notice that the person carrying Tatyanna's books has the teddy bear I left by her locker this morning. I guess Ms. Tatyanna believed what I wrote in the letter. I guess she believes that someone wanted to make her feel better by buying her that little teddy bear. I try not to look at it, but I am very pleased that it is so adorable. That adorable teddy bear's secret camera may be the key to finding the information we need to destroy the dangerous Dimes.

They have made the last week of school miserable.

Eris, Emani and I even made a rhyme about them. We call it the Terrible Ten.

On the tenth day before break, the Dimes gave to us
a food fight in the lunch room.

On the ninth day before break, the Dimes gave to us
an explosion in the lab that went "boom."

On the eighth day before break, the Dimes gave to us
a sophomore beat down at the bus stop.

On the seventh day before break, the Dimes gave to us
a locker search and visit from the drug cops.

On the sixth day before break, the Dimes gave to us
posted pictures on the net of kissing couples
doing secret naughty things.

On the fifth day before break, the Dimes gave to us
five freshmen suspended for fighting
though the Dimes were instigating.

On the fourth day before break, the Dimes gave to us
a fire in the girls' locker room.

On the third day before break, the Dimes gave to me,
a spotlight that fell from the sky and went bang.

We know that the Dimes have more surprises planned, but Emani, Eris, and I came to school anyway. Mostly because my mother would not allow us to stay home unless someone was dying, there was a natural disaster, or we had contacted a deadly disease. We are at school because Mom believes in perfect attendance, but also because Eris's championship game is tonight. CIA's policy is that if you don't attend school for at least half of the school day, you cannot participate in after school activities.

Aunty Jay felt the same way when we were homeschooled.

Anyway, I walk to my locker after play practice to get the rest of my books, only to see that someone has turned my lock around backwards. In fact, someone has turned around ten of the locks around my locker backward. I instinctively step back from the locker. I walk past one security guard and head toward Kitten's friend the security guard to tell him about my lock and my locker. Despite the fact that he hasn't been doing any of us any favors lately, he does call the dean.

Ten minutes later, when Dean Norton arrives, she has on gloves. I watch her cut the lock off. Then I take a step back as she begins to fidget with the locker to open it. When it doesn't open on her first try, I take three more steps back, remembering how that idiot blew up our school using empty lockers last year.

She opens it, and a white powder shoots out after a popping sound is heard. I think it is a balloon, but Dean Norton calls it an explosion. She frowns at me when she turns around covered in talcum powder.

"So you are claiming that you found your locker this way?" Dean Norton asks. I believe she thinks that I planned this little explosion because of my distance from the locker.

"Yes, this is how I found the locker. Maybe you should check the video," I say.

"I already did. The only person who came to your locker was you. I couldn't see the face, but I did see your red hair, your green sweater, and your blue jeans." I don't even know what to say as she leads me to her office by my shirt collar.

The AV girls couldn't have done anything to the video. They weren't even here today. I sit in the dean's office trying to figure out just how miserable my Christmas is going to be when my mother gets another call from Dean Norton about this powder incident.

Tyson walks into the office and says that he has been looking for me. He is ready to go with me to Eris's game.

I tell him about what happened and suggest that he leave the office without me because I'll probably be here for a while getting punished.

After listening to me, he walks into Dean Norton's office without her permission. I am shocked, but I just stay in my chair and wait for him to be kicked out.

Dean Norton calls me into the office after a few minutes.

"So, Ms. Ebony, your friend here tells me that you have been practicing for a play without a break today. He also tells me that you were wearing a costume. I am told that your clothes could have been grabbed by anyone on the crew. Is this true?" The dean asks for clarification.

I look at Tyson and wish that I could go back to a little earlier when I couldn't stop giggling long enough to kiss him on stage. I bet you I could kiss him now for saving my derrière.

"Yes, Dean Norton. I guess I have a few enemies," I say, hoping Dean Norton remembers a certain fight I had at the start of school.

"Oh, you certainly do, and I am going to find out their identities. I don't know what to say about you Robertson girls," Dean Norton says as she releases me.

When I get into the hallway, Tyson shakes his head at me.

Then, he tells me that his sister told him that he should check on me. He starts a long story, but I kiss him before he can finish, until Stephan Miles walks up to us and interrupts our moment.

"Red, I wish you would get your sister to give me a little lip love," Stephan says as Tyson hugs me. I feel a bit awkward in between the two of them, especially since I have now kissed both of them. Until this year, I would have never thought I'd be the girl in between two friends, but here I am fake-dating Stephan and wanting to date Tyson.

"You want lip love from Eris?" Tyson teases Stephan, though he knows Stephan does not want Eris in any way.

"Yuck! Man, don't make me lose my lunch right here in the hallway. I would never put my lips on that . . ." Stephan sees my evil glare and decides to stop speaking meanly about my sister.

Tyson and I walk down the hall toward the game. When we get there, we watch my sister and her teammates destroy Princeton high school. The Princeton fans go from chanting "PHS is the best" at the start of the game to complete silence by the end, due to my sister and her winning squad.

At the end of the game, Eris shakes hands before being presented with her MVP trophy. I watch Stephan go up to her to interview her and take her picture. To think that last week she was being accused of taking performance-enhancing drugs by some of the varsity girls and this week she is a champion. I don't know who spiked her water bottle, but I know that whoever they are, they have to be very upset right now. Their plan to destroy my sister has failed. Scouts were back watching her play the day after her second test came back negative. I can't even believe the school even thought she'd cheat. Eris would never use steroids or any drugs. Eris Robertson would never cheat to win.

"Congratulations, Sis," I say as I hug her.

Eris looks over at my cute mentor and friend Tyson in the bleachers and says congratulations to me. I guess she saw him kiss me on my cheek mid-game. Eris notices everything.

I take a few steps back when a few fans surround her. When I hear her use the words "team effort" to our school press and her loyal fans, I realize just how much my sister has matured. Eris was proud once to be the "me in team" and "I in win" type of girl. Now, I can see she values her teammates and teamwork.

She is a valuable member of our triplet team, too. I don't know what

I'd do without my sister. I don't know what I would do without any of my sisters.

Though Eris is a champion and I am an actress, Emani is the happiest of us all. Today, she is officially off of all forms of punishment. I am too, but unlike her, I do not have a date tonight. I don't know how she convinced Mom and Dad to allow her to have college-boy Rickey over to our house, but he is coming for dinner.

Today is our last day of school before the New Year. When we return from inter break, it will be a new year; a new start. I am beginning to get a little excited, as well.

"Don't you two have to break up with Stephan today? Can I watch?" Eris says as she teases Emani and me. Emani frowns. I mope. Eris continues to grin from ear to ear.

"Let's just wait until he comes back from his vacation!" Emani suggests.

I quickly agree. Eris's smirk disappears, then she asks why we are waiting. We ignore her cruel intentions toward Stephan Miles.

As we are walking down the hall toward our homerooms, I accidentally bump into Kitten when she steps out of Ms. Kelly's room unexpectedly.

"Sorry!" I say.

"Yeah, you are sorry. You are a sorry excuse for a friend," Kitten barks at me before she walks over to Zyanne, Brenda, and Tatyanna.

After I watch Zyanne walk, Brenda strut, and Tatyanna limp away on her crutches, I notice that Kitten's checkered notebook has fallen by my feet. I pick it up and begin to walk toward her to give it to her, but then I see my name written in Kitten's code on the first page. Underneath my name it says in code "Alphabet times ten."

My brain begins to calculate and unravel. I think Kitten's code is trying to tell me that the key to Zyanne's notebook is to multiply the number of the letter by ten. So since A is the first letter of the alphabet, it would be ten. B would be twenty. C would be thirty, and so on.

But how does Kitten know I have the notebook? Oh no, I think the Dimes must know. The Dimes must know that we have copies of their notebook. Kitten wouldn't have risked giving me the key to the code in front of them unless it was very vital. They know, but they just don't know that their newest recruit Kitten is still on our side.

*

"Ebony, I need to see you in here," Ms. Kelly says as she closes her door behind me.

I can tell by Ms. Kelly's face that she is very serious.

Ms. Kelly begins: "Ebony, I wanted to talk to you before I spoke to the principal. We are missing some funds from our account. Now, I know I made my deposits, but our statement says there have been some withdrawals. Neither you nor Zyanne are supposed to be able to make any withdrawals from our account without my signature. I spoke to her earlier and she says you have been making some large purchases lately. Is this true?"

I am not a thief, but I do not answer until after Ms. Kelly says she is going to check my locker. I know that there is probably something in there that makes me look guilty. The Dimes can get into any locker in this school. They've proven that time and time again. The Dimes didn't just let Kitten in. I bet she had to give them something on me. She is the only person other than my sisters who has my locker combination. I don't know how to get out of this one. I would bet money that there is something inside my locker that will get me kicked out of school. The Dimes would do anything to get rid of me.

"Ms. Kelly, have you ever seen me do anything without first getting permission from you? I don't even sign my own pass to class when you are in a hurry. I just wait for you to sign it. Why would I forge your signature to steal?"

Ms. Kelly tells me to expect a pass to Principal Wells' office after she tells me how disappointed she is in me. I don't dare argue with her because I have no proof of my innocence, but like Eris says, I may not have it yet, but I will have it soon.

*

"They made you resign," Emani says at lunch time as we sit in the library.

"Yes, Charlotte is going to be the treasurer. The principal says she will conduct an investigation, since I refused to confess. Right now it is my word against Zyanne's, since she has access to the same funds as I do. I had to lie about those things they found in my locker, the things the Dimes planted in my locker to entrap me. I told them they were Christmas gifts for the charity. I told them they were gifts we were able to buy because of the secret Santa sign-up special."

Eris kicks the bookshelf, rattling the books.

"The Dimes are ruthless!" Eris says as she picks up a book on World War II.

We all look at one another when she shows it to us.

"This is war!" we say in triplicate.

CHAPTER 21

Eris
Keyshia and Kisses

"**O**n the second day before Christmas break, the Dimes gave to us some powder in the dean's face. On the last day before Christmas break, the Dimes gave to us another Treasurer to take Ebony's place," Emani sings as we try to make our sister feel better, but we know that Ebony is in big trouble. Her flawless record is slowly being destroyed. Her character is being assassinated. Both of these things mean a lot to Ebony. I have to find a way to protect her. That's my job. I am the protector.

My teammates approach me. Vita Rowe and the rest of varsity walk behind them.

"Eris, I missed your little game the other day. I was busy cleaning toilets and washing windows, but you already know, that don't you," Varsity Vita says.

I look down at the floor at my teammate Keyshia's new pink and purple shoes that I designed for her. I admire her glittery laces until I hear Keyshia tell Vita she should leave before someone gets hurt. Then, I look up at Keyshia with pride. To think, I once thought she was a weak-willed wimp. To think, I once made Keyshia cry. I'm so proud of her for speaking up for herself. I'm so proud of her for speaking up for me.

I am very glad that Keyshia and I have become friends. I owe her and Stephan for telling Coach that the water in my water bottle did not look normal after my first drug test came back positive for performance-enhancing drugs. If Keyshia had not said something, I would be a disqualified athlete instead of a champ. I would never have been allowed to take that second drug test to prove my innocence. Vita tried to threaten Keyshia and to turn her against me, but Keyshia spoke up for me to Coach.

Coach never told me who accused me of taking drugs in the first place, but I did notice that she has benched half of varsity throughout their playoffs. Yet despite all of the drama, varsity still managed to win their final game.

Vita approaches me, saying, "I am not afraid of you. I don't have anything to lose. I came here to challenge you to a real battle. Varsity will play against your little squad. The winner will be the true champion. Are you afraid to defend your title of MVP? Most Vain Pipsqueak."

"You just tell me when and where!" I say as my squad stands beside me. I am most proud that Rochelle stands beside me, too. She convinced Keyshia to stand up for me and now she stands with me against Varsity Vita.

"We will battle you at Stephan Miles's house right after school," Vita says as she walks away. Our varsity team marches behind her.

"Eris, we don't have anything to prove to them. We are winners. We are state champions. You led us to victory. Let's just start our vacation," Rochelle says.

I look at Rochelle and remember what she told me after we won what was supposed to be our final game together: We are a team and we win because we play as a team.

"1-1, 2-2, 3-3, who is going to play with me?" I ask as I look at them. All of my teammates raise their hands instantly. That's my girls!

*

Stephan greets me with a half-smile, half-frown at the door when I come to his house after school. He hands me a bottled water and tells me that it isn't poisoned. I laugh.

As I get up to play, he pulls me back down next to him. I'm not too fond of him touching me, but I quickly get over it, knowing it won't ever happen again.

"Good luck, Eris. I hope you win," Stephan says almost silently.

"Not yet, but soon, Stephan. Not yet, but soon," I say as I head toward my hero, Mary Miles's court. Mrs. Miles sits in the stands next to her husband as an unofficial referee.

When I walk on the court, I see that Vita has invited a few people from school to fill Stephan's benches. Emani's enemy number one, Kylie Calderone, walks in with Ebony's enemy number one, Zyanne Jeffries. I wish my sisters were here, but I told them to go enjoy their first day off of full punishment. I don't think Ebony will be able to enjoy it, since she's probably being placed on partial punishment as I warm up here, but I am sure Emani is getting dressed for her date and special college-aged visitor.

*

Varsity wins the coin toss. We can't seem to score for most of the game. When I realize that my squad is beginning to let varsity get inside of their heads, I call a time out.

"You made me your captain because you knew I could help you to win. I don't think I've ever told you that I only accepted because I knew you could win. You all have talent. Don't let them take that away from you. The battle is in the mind. Say it with me, 'my mind is mine. My mind is mine.'"

The girls repeat my words.

"Unbeat-able, invinc-ible, un-de, feat-ed," we cheer for ourselves, since we do not have any student fans here to cheer for us. Mr. Miles cheers.

Varsity does their usual cruel chants as we take our places on the court.

My squad plays better than we've played all season once the whistle blows. We match them point for point for a while, until we begin to outscore them. Once the scoreboard shows a tie, the crowd starts to boo. We play harder and ignore them.

Mrs. Miles steps in to watch us again. She gives me the thumbs up when I am up to score the winning point. I look around at all of Mrs. Miles's jerseys on the walls and momentarily imagine that the jerseys are mine now. I am the champion. The ball is in my hands and so is the game. I watch as the numbers get smaller on the clock. Then, I hit the ball. Vita spikes it toward Keyshia. Keyshia spikes it. Vita dives for it, but misses. We win.

"1-1-2-2-3-3, we just beat varsity!" My team chants, until they see me signaling for them to stop. Once the squad is silent, I walk over to Vita to shake her hand, but she refuses. She also refuses to say that today she is a loser, but I do not need her to say it, because I know I am a winner. Today, all of my teammates are winners. The rest of varsity forms a line and we all shake one another's hands.

Stephan offers to drive me home after his mom gives me a few pointers and tells me how proud she is of me, and I try to say no, but he won't allow me to walk alone so I reluctantly accept.

"Do you think Emani will like this?" He asks as he hands me a jewelry box. When I open it, I see a charm bracelet inside with little dancing ballerinas on it. There is also a shimmering, platinum "E" on the bracelet.

"Emani will love it Stephan, but I think you should maybe give it to her after winter break."

I say hoping he'll just drop me off and drive away. What if Emani's real boyfriend is at our house already? I don't like Stephan, but I'd hate to see him get hurt when Emani does not accept this charm bracelet. The bracelet is nice. I imagine it with a basketball or volleyball charm on it. Then, I repeat my suggestion to Stephan to postpone the gift exchanging as he drives toward my house.

Stephan ignores my advice. Then, he compliments me on the way I played today. Stephan Miles says several kind words to me, but I do not know how to respond, so I just sit in the passenger seat, quietly looking out of the window at the snow-covered scenery. I've already thanked him for speaking up to Coach about that water bottle, but I don't want him to get used to me being too nice to him. I know I will have to be nice to him since his mother has offered to play with me and mentor me after school, but we don't have to be best friends.

After a while, we pull into my driveway. It doesn't take long for me to notice that Emani is hugged up with Rickey Thomas against Rickey's car. It takes Stephan a bit longer, but once he does notice their body language, Stephan honks his horn until Emani and Rickey separate.

Stephan jumps out of the car before it is fully in park. I quickly push the gear into park all the way and turn off the engine with his key as he runs toward them. Then, I sit and watch the show.

What I see is Stephan showing his shimmering gift to Emani. Then, I see Emani saying something to him. Ebony walks outside. She tries to quickly walk back in the house before she is seen, but Emani calls her over to receive Stephan's wrath, too.

Rickey listens to the three-way conversation between Emani, Ebony, and Stephan for a while. Then, he goes inside our house. I watch Stephan as he turns left to right, screaming at my sisters, who are on either side of him. When he begins kicking snow, I get out of the car.

"Newbie, did you know about this too? Were you all in on this?" Stephan says as I shake my head yes, and then no.

I try to explain my sisters' side of the story to Stephan, but he won't listen. He tells Emani to go to Rickey, since he thinks she wants to be with him. Stephan tells Ebony that she should tell his buddy Tyson what she has been up to for the past few weeks because he won't lie for her if Tyson asks him any questions. Then, he tells her she owes his friend an apology since she's been lying to him. Both Emani and Ebony walk away after unsuccessfully trying to apologize to Stephan.

Seeing him alone in the cold isn't as amusing as I thought it would be, so I offer to give him a hug.

He hugs me, too.

"Eris, I , , ," He seems to be struggling with getting his words out, but before I can ask him what he wants to say, he kisses me on my mouth. HE kisses me on my mouth? Then, he jumps in his car and rides away.

What just happened to me?

Maybe Stephan wants to be the first guy to say he's kissed all three of us, but whatever his intentions were, I feel a weird feeling right now. The kiss was unexpected, but it wasn't awful.

*

"Get in here now!" Ebony says with authority when she sees me standing in the cold.

I guess she saw the kiss. I run up the stairs still a bit in shock from my peck with Stephan.

When I get inside, I am shocked to see Alexis's boyfriend Jeremy there, but of course I hug him when I see him. My pseudo-brother Jeremy hasn't come for dinner too much lately, but he has an open invitation from my parents, so I shouldn't be too shocked he's at our home.

"She spoke to him, Eris!" Jeremy says as he scratches his head.

I look to Ebony for clarification. Maybe it is the weird Stephan kiss that has me confused, but I don't know what Jeremy is talking about.

"Alexis spoke to Rickey Thomas, Eris!" Ebony says, as she whispers that Alexis also hugged Rickey.

Alexis hugged Emani's boyfriend Rickey Thomas? Okay, this goes on record as the strangest day of my life so far. Jeremy is dating Alexis. Rickey is dating Emani. But, Alexis is hugging Rickey and speaking to him when she hasn't even spoken to us since the tragedy. We are her sisters. This is crazy.

Emani walks into the living room and plops down on the sofa. She has tears in her eyes.

Considering who I just hugged and kissed, I decide there must be an explanation. I don't understand why everyone is so sad. Alexis finally said something. We should be celebrating.

"What did she say, Jeremy?" Jeremy doesn't look at me or answer me.

Neither Ebony nor Emani say anything either.

"Ummh Eris, Alexis called me Zachary," Rickey says, before he asks Emani to come speak to him privately.

Emani doesn't move from the couch.

My parents walk in, each holding one of Alexis's hands. Alexis stares at Rickey Thomas as if he is her lost love Zachary Thomas. The love she lost in our school shooting and bombing last year. I begin to see the problem. This is the first time she has seen Rickey since Zachary's funeral. In fact, I don't remember her ever saying she met Rickey at the funeral. This may have been her first time ever seeing Rickey Thomas.

Wow! I never really noticed, but Rickey does look a lot like the late Zachary Thomas. They could not have been identical twins, but they could have been brothers or maybe fraternal twins. You can certainly see they are kin. I could see how Alexis could mistake Rickey for Zachary.

"If Emani hadn't walked in the workout room, she would have kissed him," Jeremy says as he twirls his keys in a circle.

I can tell that he is upset. He always twirls his keys like that when he is upset. I remember him twirling his keys the day Kylie Calderone kissed him and Alexis witnessed it. The difference, of course, is Jeremy did not want to kiss Kylie Calderone. Alexis was in love with Zachary Thomas. I'm sure if he were still alive, she would be with him and not our pseudo-brother Jeremy.

My father tries to assure Jeremy that Alexis is just a bit confused, but Jeremy does not seem to be convinced.

"Mr. Robertson, I have been here for her. I have loved her with everything I am. I have stood by her side and she hasn't even tried to hug or kiss me. She sees this guy one time and she speaks, hugs, and tries to kiss him. I think she has made her choice. She'd rather have a fake Zachary Thomas than the real me," Jeremy says as he gets up to leave. He slams our front door as he leaves, but my dad doesn't say a word about it.

Now I know Jeremy is Dad's favorite, because Dad would have killed me if I slammed the door like that.

Alexis's eyes remain on Rickey. Emani's eyes are on Alexis. Rickey's eyes are on Emani.

Rickey asks Emani to talk to him privately again, but she ignores him. He gets up and walks to the kitchen.

Ebony's phone rings, and I hear her trying to explain herself to Tony Tyson. The conversation is only about one second long, because He hangs up on her before she can explain anything about her fake relationship with Stephan.

To make matters worse, my dad asks for her phone, reminding her about his conversation with a certain principal earlier today about a powder bomb in her locker. Did he say bomb? That word is outlawed in this house.

Ebony pouts when Dad takes the phone, so he explains that he believes her side of the story, but that he is punishing her because he knows she isn't telling him the whole story. As always, my Dad is correct.

I know that I can convince Jeremy that Alexis loves him, and I know that I can help Emani and Rickey, but I do not know if my Dad can handle the whole truth. If we told him the whole story, he would transfer us out of C.I.A. Dad believes we have dealt with enough drama for three lifetimes. He wouldn't let us solve this Dime issue if he knew the truth.

I walk away from the drama and up the stairs to get our copy of Zyanne's notebook. I know Ebony has said that we three need to decode this together, but since my sisters are all a little busy right now, I think I can figure this out.

I can't believe Stephan Miles kissed me on my mouth.

After a few minutes of decoding, I deciphered Kitten's code. I am quite confident that I can do the same for the Dimes code.

CHAPTER 22

Emani
Should Sisters Share?

E ris broke the Dimes' code yesterday, but she doesn't want to give Zyanne's notebook to Dean Norton until we make sure that everything in the notebook is genuine. Ebony seems to believe that some of the members listed couldn't possibly be Dimes because they are some of the sweetest, kindest people at C.I.A. She and Eris are way too naive: they don't think good girls do bad things.

I have tried to tell them that there is a thin line between nice and naughty. For example, the character that Kylie Calderone is playing in Ms. Jennings's Christmas musical tomorrow is nice until she loses her brother. When her brother dies, she becomes very naughty and almost evil. In fact, once Lady Light loses Lord Dawn, she begins to go insane, punishing all in her kingdom. Lady Light's misery makes her want to make everyone else miserable, so she forbids dancing and singing and promises death to any who disobeys. My character, Dame Darkness, is a victim of Lady Light's punishment.

Like Lady Light, I think that the goody-goodies in Zyanne's notebook may have a dark side, too. I know I do. When I dance as Dame Darkness, I instinctively become her, because there is a bit of her inside of me. All of the disdain I have for Kylie comes out as I move. All of the pain I have from being an outcast on my squad comes out as I dance. The pain caused by Princeton Payne, Payton Payne, and Johnny Turner flees from me as I dance.

Dame Darkness has to save the very people who exiled her from their kingdom for her ability to fly. I can relate to her. I have a special talent that makes people jealous of me, too. Then, I have to smile and dance with those very jealous people. Sometimes, I have to trust them to catch me or allow them to toss me into the air. I have to join their team knowing that they envy me. And, tomorrow, I have to dance on a stage with the most evil of all my enemies: Kylie Calderone, also known as Lady Light.

Kylie's cousin Stephan says he hates my face. When I go to the mirror, I am disgusted by my pimple-filled face, too. Of all the days to get pimples, I get one today. Mom says it is because I haven't been eating right since the Rickey and Alexis thing, but I don't believe her. I think I'm just cursed. My sisters have perfect skin. I get pimples. My sisters can eat whatever they want, but if I eat an ounce of junk food it lands on my behind.

Alexis walks in the room and sits beside me on my bed. To think, I was once her favorite sister, and now she wants my boyfriend. Well, my ex-boyfriend. Rickey hasn't answered my calls or letters since I asked him to pretend to be Zachary Thomas for my sister's sake. My parents were willing to try anything that may help Alexis since Rickey was able to get her to speak. Though the light in Alexis's eyes has returned, Rickey didn't think it was a good idea to pretend to be someone who is gone to Heaven. He thinks it will hurt her more when she realizes the truth, but he has agreed to help now. I think his aunt Dr. Thomas convinced him that Zachary would have wanted Rickey to do anything it took to help Alexis to recover from his death, because Rickey showed up yesterday more willing to talk with her than ever before.

So now instead of reading letters from Rickey that say "can't w8 2 c u, 2 b with u, 2 hold u, 2 hear your voice," I have had to overhear him reading Zachary's poetry to my sister for the last two days. I have had to watch him read letters to Alexis that Zachary wrote but never sent to her when he first fell in love with her. It has been a very difficult thing to see. It has been an even more difficult thing to hear the person you care for tell someone else that they love them. I hate to be selfish, but I wish those words would leave his mouth and land on my eardrum.

I wish those brilliant poems and flattering letters were for me, but when Alexis smiled yesterday when she finished talking to him, I was grateful to Rickey for saying each word. Whatever it takes to make her happy again is worth it. Whatever it takes. She is my sister. She is my very best friend in this whole world.

Alexis holds my hand tightly, and I look at her beautiful pimple-free face. I would trade my pimple face for hers or Ebony's deep dimples any day. She looks at me in my eyes, and I try not to cry. Yet, the tears fall without my permission.

"Zachary loved me!" Alexis says as she turns and looks into my eyes for the first time in a long time.

"Loves!" I say, still in shock that she just said three words. I love my sister's voice.

"Loved!" Alexis says as she lets go of my hand. I watch her walk toward the door, but I cannot move my legs to follow her. Did she just say loved?

Rickey stands in Alexis's doorway zipping his coat. I read his college's initials on the right side of the coat.

When I finish reading, my legs decide to listen to my brain. I stand up and walk toward him. "Rickey, did you get my letters?"

"Yes." It could be my imagination, but he seems to notice the pounds I've gained since I've been doing a lot of late-night munching since we broke up. I don't know why my appetite has increased so much lately.

I watch him look over every inch of me without even a slight smile, but I know he has to like what he is seeing, because he can't look away.

"My calls?"

"Yes," he says as he puts on his hat.

I want to ask why he didn't respond to me, but I already know the answer to my question. He speaks again, but I take a step back into my room when he finishes talking. According to Rickey, my mother has asked him to take me to Ms. Jennings's house for our cast sleep over tonight. Rickey is going to take me to Ms. Jennings's house on his way to Mr. Thomas's house. I quickly grab my purse as Rickey gathers my luggage.

"I thought you were only leaving for one night!" My dad says as he peeks into my room, most likely to see why Rickey is in my bedroom. I laugh as Dad acts as if my luggage weighs as much as I do.

"A girl is always prepared for what if" I say as I look at Rickey.

"I wish girls would stop worrying about what if and take it one day at a time," Rickey says as he heads toward the stairs.

My dad agrees with Rickey before I can respond to what he says. Once we are at the door, Dad offers Rickey some gas money, but of course Rickey doesn't take it. I warned Rickey a long time ago about Dad's gas money test: my dad says if he can't pay for gas, you shouldn't be driving with his @$$. I know it's vulgar, but Dad will always be Dad.

My mom winks at me when Rickey opens the door for me. Then, she kisses me goodbye like I'm leaving for two weeks.

The car ride is very uneventful for about five minutes until Rickey turns down the radio and says, "Are you ready to talk?"

I look at him with a look that I hope says "I've been ready to talk to you for a long time."

Rickey explains, "Emani, my last girlfriend and I broke up because she gave me an ultimatum: either I go to her college or we couldn't be together. I was hurt, but I let her go so I could follow my dreams at my own college. Now, you've hurt me."

I turn the radio back up before he can say the words. I haven't even had enough time to officially be his girlfriend and now it's over. No love? No kiss? No boyfriend? Pimples? An extra five pounds? I lay my head back on the seat's headrest and look out the window, ignoring his attempts to speak to me. I can't handle any more bad news.

Besides, I have to sleep with the enemy tonight at Ms. Jennings's house, so I better rest now. There is no way I can close my eyes and sleep around Kylie Calderone. If I did, I may wake up with a knife in my back. I think about Kylie the back-stabber as I close my eyes in Rickey's car.

When I open my eyes, I am shocked to see Ms. Jennings's home is in the heart of the city. I was expecting lakefront views, balconies, or at least security, but I don't see any of the above.

When Rickey unlocks the door, I look back and ask if he is sure this is the address of my snooty, snobbish dance instructor. Rickey glances at the address he has entered into his phone. Then, he assures me that I am at the right place, so I hesitantly unlock my door.

When I grab the door's handle to leave, he locks the doors again before I can exit.

"So this is it?" Rickey says, as if he is surprised.

"It is what it is, Rickey. Am I supposed to beg you to be with me? Am I supposed to apologize for asking you to do what I thought was best for my sister? Alexis needs you to be Zachary, so I need you to be Zachary, too. Thank you for what you are doing for her, but those are the only words I can say to you," I say as I unlock and open my own door.

"What about what I want to say to you?" He asks, as I reach into the back seat to get too much luggage.

"Tell it to Rachel!" I say before I can take it back.

"Rachel?" He asks as he gets out of the car.

Then, he shakes his head at me like I'm a child or childish. I know it was immature to mention his "friend's" name, but I'm hurt. Without looking at me, Rickey places my luggage by the door and rings Ms. Jennings's bell, though I tell him I can do it myself.

I quickly introduce myself to the dancer who answers the door before Rickey can start a conversation with me. She introduces me to about seven other girls who come to the door. I watch them look at Rickey with more than interest, so I introduce him as my "friend" to let them know that he is no longer taken. Then, I enter Ms. Jennings's place as the girls swarm around Rickey like bees to his honey-colored self. It stings, but I guess this is goodbye.

The inside of Ms. Jennings's house is even more unlike what I expected. In a word, it is comfortable. I was expecting showroom furniture that I wouldn't be able to touch or relax on, not comfy couches. I was expecting plaques, trophies, medals, and certificates, but all I see are pictures of dancers who look a lot like me and those eight girls outside. Ms. Jennings's has sculptures and paintings of dancers and none of herself. Each corner of her living room tells a story. I see a folk dance story, a hip hop story, a ballerina's story, and a tango story. How can the queen of designer coffee Ms. Jennings have such a warm home and be such a cold, cruel, criticizing, chick?

"You made it, Pixie!" Ms. Jennings says as she enters from her kitchen with Kylie and Coach Calderone behind her.

Coach speaks to me before Kylie says one word. In fact, Coach has to ask Kylie to say that one word to me. I quickly repeat, "Hi" back to her. It is going to be a long night.

I watch Kylie walk over to the door after complaining that the girls are letting cold air into the house. She smiles when she sees Rickey outside. She makes some comment about Rickey's coat, since it has his college's name on it. Then, she tries to make me jealous by saying Rickey's smile could melt the snow outside.

Is she kidding? He's hot, but he's not that hot. It is about zero degrees outside. This is Chicago, the city of wind. Kylie is so full of hot air.

"But . . . you don't have to worry about those girls do you? It's your sister who is your competition, huh, Emani?" Kylie says, as she and I watch Rickey walk to his car.

When he waves to me, I close the curtains. Kylie takes this as an opportunity to share how well she and Jeremy are doing, now that Alexis is interested in Rickey. I believe she and Jeremy are talking too much, since she knows all of my business, but I doubt she and Jeremy are doing as well as she pretends they are.

I want to plop her onto Ms. Jennings's comfy couch, but I decide to be mature and congratulate her on getting my sister's sloppy seconds. Okay, maybe that wasn't mature, but she deserved it.

"I'd rather be second than to not place at all," Kylie lies; we both know Kylie Calderone never wants to be in second place.

Her mom asks her to stop bickering with me, and I laugh when Kylie whines that Coach Calderone is taking my side. It doesn't help when Coach Calderone tries to change the subject to dance and says that I remind her of herself when she was a teenage dancer. Kylie almost faints when her mother tells the girls what a quick learner I am.

"Thanks, Coach. You are a great teacher," I say without sticking my tongue out at Kylie.

Coach gives me a quick squeeze and smiles.

"She's a great mother, too," Kylie says. On cue, Coach Calderone begins her pep talk to all of us by saying that we are all like her daughters. I think we all hear Kylie mumble "like" under her breath, but Coach continues her motivational message.

When Coach finishes, Ms. Jennings thanks us for giving up our Christmas morning to practice and our Christmas Eve to bond.

As Ms. Jennings talks of what her mentoring program and giving back to her neighborhood means to her, I stare at Kylie. Usually I can't read lips, but I am sure Kylie mouths "I HATE YOU" to me.

I continue to look at her as she throws mental darts at my eyes, my heart, my legs, and everything else. I know that the bull's eye she wants to hit is my mind. Kylie Calderone wants to know what it takes to break me. She wants me to cry, crumble, or collapse, but she doesn't know my strength as a Robertson. I may bend, but I won't break. I may fumble, but I won't stop running the race until I win it. I learned that from my sisters and my parents.

I promised my dad that I would dance tomorrow as if he was the only person in the room. He advised me to focus on him, because I am most comfortable when I dance in front of my daddy. Tomorrow, no matter how many people arrive at Ms. Jennings's musical, no matter how many friendly, famous faces are in the crowd, no matter how well Kylie does, I am going to do my very best. Like Dame Darkness, I am going to fly.

*

I don't quite fly to the bathroom that night at Ms. Jennings's, but I do dash to the restroom when I feel cramps on the right side of my abdomen. My stomach hurts. This pain is beyond an ache. I feel wounded.

Hor-ri-ble! Help!

I just got my period for the first time in my life! I just got my period and my mommy and my sisters are not here to help me.

Kylie stands outside the door asking me if I am okay, probably because either her mother Coach Calderone or her mother's best friend Ms. Jennings has commanded her to check on me. I lie and tell her that I am okay.

Why today? Why do I have to menstruate the night before the biggest day of my life? Is this my fault? Did I dance too hard when we had the dance contest earlier? Did I eat too much? Why can't I be in the family room enjoying my facial, manicure, and pedicure like everyone else?

"Emani, can we come in to help you?" Ms. Jennings and Coach Calderone say. I am instantly mortified. They are the last two people I need right now. I need my mother. I want to be at home opening my Christmas gifts. This isn't a gift. It is a curse. Why couldn't I become a woman in a couple of days?

The door opens. My head lowers in shame. My mother packed me an emergency period kit at the beginning of the school year, but it is at school in my locker. What am I going to do?

I watch Ms. Jennings take a few items from one of her drawers before I realize what they are. She hands the items to me without any emotion on her face.

"This is all you'll need for now. If you need anything else let me know, but you will dance tomorrow, Pixie," When she leaves, I look at the tampon and cry. My mom told me everything. She even gave me a demonstration using a water bottle, but I need her.

Coach Calderone gives me a pep talk before she exits the restroom. She does a good job, but she isn't my mommy. I don't think her talk will be enough. I need my momma.

I am in the bathroom for about an hour, but I figure it out. When I exit, the girls cheer like I've danced a perfect salsa or something.

Ms. Jennings pulls me to the side.

"Pixie, you think I am hard on you, but I see the fire inside of you and I won't let it die. I am always hard on the student who has the most potential, because the road ahead for you will be very hard. Keep your head up and perk up, Pixie," Ms. Jennings says as she hugs me.

When she leaves, I smile. When Kylie walks up to me, the smile leaves.

"You steal my praise. You steal my attention. Now, you steal one of the few mother-daughter moments I have had with my mom. Tomorrow, you will not steal my scholarship, Emani. Tomorrow, you will be second, and I will be first," Kylie whispers.

Then, she hugs me when Coach walks toward us. I swear Kylie has two personalities. Both are evil. She may be playing Lady Light, but she is filled with darkness. She is nothing like Coach.

"Are you ready?" Coach asks, as I warm up my muscles for our performance.

When I peek out into the audience, I see only my father in the front row. I know that there are many other people there, but his smile is all I need to become Dame Darkness.

The lights flicker when the narrator sets the scene with his first three words: "a sinister shadow." I step onto the stage to prevail both as Dame Darkness and Emani Robertson.

The lights are so bright on stage, but the audience is completely dark except for the flashes from their cameras. I cannot blame them for taking pictures of us in these costumes. We look so artistic because each costume is handmade with such attention to detail.

At the end of the performance, I am attached to a cable that allows me to fly through the air. As I fly through the air, the performers sing and dance through the aisles and onto the stage. Kylie and I embrace on stage as sisters. Then, the curtains close and we quickly break away from one another.

After the rest of the cast takes their bows, Kylie prances on stage to accept many flowers and a great deal of applause. When I join her, we both receive a standing ovation. My dad walks up to the stage to give me a dozen yellow roses. When I lean down to kiss him, I finally make eye contact with the entire audience. I blow kisses toward Ebony, Eris, Aunty Jay, Uncle Joe, Alexis, my mommy, and Rickey. Rickey? I didn't think he would come, but there he sits next to the rest of our very large family.

"You were FABULOUS!" Eris compliments as I hand her one of my pieces of luggage.

"Yes, you were awesome, but what did that have to do with Christmas?" The always-inquisitive Ebony says as she grabs a suitcase.

"It was about love conquering all. It was about unconditional love. Isn't that what Christmas is about?" My mother says, as she watches me looking around for Rickey.

I try not to react when she says that Rickey had to leave.

Coach Calderone approaches us to congratulate me on my performance, but I am not really listening to her when I see Ms. Jennings walking toward me with award-winning actor, artist, entrepreneur, model, and mogul Denzel Smith on her arm. Ebony and Eris introduce themselves to him, since I cannot seem to speak. My mother even admits that she is a fan of his movies. Oooh, I can't wait to tell my daddy.

"Emani, this is Denzel. He is one of our largest patrons. He is the person who will be financing your education. I just wanted you to meet the man who will be paying for your scholarship," Ms. Jennings says as she grabs my hand and puts it into the iconic Denzel Smith's hand. I can feel him shaking my hand even though the rest of my body is numb. Why won't my mouth move? Did she say scholarship? Did I win?

"Jasmine told me that you were a very special young lady. That's how she got me here on Christmas, but she didn't tell me that you were phenomenal. My wife and my daughters thought you were spectacular. Would you sign this for them?" Mr. Denzel William Smith says as he hands me the playbill from the musical.

Ebony takes my hand and helps me to sign my own autograph. Then, she steps on my tender toes until I muster up the courage to speak to him. I have never been this close to a true celebrity. Ms. Jennings believes she is a celebrity, but the entire globe knows Denzel Smith.

"I would be honored to sign anything for your family, Mr. Smith. Could I meet them?" I ask finally getting control of my tongue.

Ms. Jennings races away to get Mr. Smith's family, but while she is gone, Ebony takes the opportunity to ask for a favor of her own. Mr. Denzel Smith agrees to allow her to record him saying hello to his number one fan, Tatyanna Tyson. Ebony even gets him to thank Drama Queen Tatyanna Tyson for being his greatest fan. I don't know what Ebony will do with the video, but I know she has a plan. Her eyes always gleam when she has a plan being born in that brain of hers.

Kylie Calderone and her father arrive just when Ms. Jennings arrives with Denzel Smith's family. When she refuses to make eye contact with me, I realize that she must know that I received a full scholarship. Kylie isn't too happy when the girls ask for my autograph either. The look on her face as I sign my name is the greatest gift I could have received for Christmas. Some things are more valuable than money.

*

Dad offers me some money to buy a dress for Dr. Thomas's New Year's Eve party in order to change the subject at the dinner table. When my mother continues to talk about how he has four young women in the house, he reaches in his wallet and gives us each a credit card. Mom smiles when he gives her his entire wallet and goes to sit in front of the television, leaving his dinner on the table. As we are leaving, she gives him a kiss and his plate again. Dad smiles.

Aunty Jay and Mom went shopping for dresses yesterday, and Mom says Aunty Jay chose something a bit more revealing than usual to wear to Dr. Thomas's New Year's ball. We are all shocked to hear that our prudish aunt and former homeschool teacher is going to show some skin tomorrow night at the party. I don't think I have ever seen Aunty Jay's arms, and I've been on a few vacations with her and Uncle Joe. I can't wait to see my aunt in something that fits her body, because even though she tries to hide it in crazy coveralls and patterns, I suspect that she has a nice bod. My mother has had five children, and she still has a nice bod so I know my youngest, childless aunt possibly has one underneath all of that material she wears.

"Emani, that dress is hugging you a bit tightly. You may have to go up a size," Mom says, as she gives me the thumbs-up on a very short halter dress I have chosen to wear to Dr. Thomas's 'Shades of Blue'-themed party. Eris is the only one of us who is not wearing a dress. She has chosen a blue pantsuit instead. I don't know if Ebony's business suit jacket and miniskirt count as a dress or not, but I like it.

Tomorrow night is going to be quite exciting. New Year's Eve in Chicago is second only to New Year's Eve in New York. Fireworks, food, and fun in the Windy City is something everyone should experience.

Eris and I were supposed to ride with Aunty Jay and Uncle Joe, but they are running late, so we squeeze into Dad's newest experiment. He calls it his Magic Machine, but my sisters and I call it his Magic Mess. The car doesn't run on gasoline and it's not powered by the sun, but dad won't tell us what it is powered by. We just know that he and his engineers made it too small for a family of seven. It is also a bit slow.

Dr. Thomas's party is at the Majestic, which makes me nervous, since Rickey will be there parking cars if we ever make it there before midnight in this small, slow contraption of Dad's. Anyway, if Rickey isn't working on one of the busiest nights of the year, he will probably be at his aunt's party. Either way he will be there.

I wish Kitten was coming, too. Her dad was hired to decorate the party for Dr. Thomas, but when we asked if she'd be there, she claimed she and her mother had plans. Plans on New Year's Eve? Kitten's family is never separated on holidays. They are like us, always together. I miss Kitten. Our secret mission against the Dimes has caused us to sacrifice our time together.

When we get to the Majestic, Rickey is in the parking garage, as I suspected he would be. I want to open my coat and show him this jaw-dropping cobalt blue dress I'm wearing, but the temperature outside is saying if you show any skin, I'll freeze you. I don't need frostbite. I need every toe to dance.

Rickey gets a hug from everyone in my family, except for my dad and me, after he parks Dad's slow, small Magic Machine. Dad shakes his hand. I try to shake his hand, but Rickey hugs me without my permission.

"Emani, I invited Rachel to my aunt's party because she didn't have any plans for tonight. I told her I was working until midnight. Could you keep her company until then?" I look at him to make sure he isn't joking, but he seems serious.

He wants me to babysit the woman who wants to be his girlfriend. Rickey may be older than I am, but he is clueless when it comes to females. Well, I guess he did take care of my sister Alexis for me. Maybe he isn't clueless. I should do this for him. I owe him.

"Sure, Rickey. Will your ex-girlfriend be here, too?" I ask half-joking, but half-serious.

"Actually, she is already here. How'd you know?" Rickey says without a giggle or a smirk or any clue that he may be joking. I do not ask for an explanation. I simply follow my family into the warmth of the Majestic hotel. Clueless!

We are all surprised to see Aunty Jay and Uncle Joe are already here, but surprised or not, we all walk quickly to see what our aunt is wearing under that long, faux fur coat.

Before Uncle Joe can remove the panther-colored coat, Aunty Jay runs into the girl's bathroom. My mom runs behind her. I run in behind them though mom asks my sisters and me to stay outside.

"I can't do it, sis. I love the dress, but I'm not ready to do this tonight. I'm going to go home. Joe and I can toast at home. We can pop our own balloons. We can watch the countdown on television. We can even dance there. I'll do this next year!" Aunty Jay says as she looks into the mirror.

I am even more eager to see the dress when she says this, but my mom asks me to get out of the bathroom. When she gives me the evil eye, I decide that I had better leave right now.

My sisters have gone into the party when I step outside, but I overhear my uncle and my father talking about Aunty Jay.

"I don't know why she is so worried about the scars. They're almost gone. I think she's beautiful, but it is so hard to get her to see it sometimes," Uncle Joe says until he sees me behind him.

Dad gives me a strange look. "What did you hear, young lady?"

I know not to say anything, because Dad can always tell when I'm lying. I decide to tell the truth. Uncle Joe walks away when Dad asks him to leave.

"Emani, Aunty Jay doesn't really want you to know. She made us promise that a long time ago, but since you are so nosey, I guess you should know the whole story." I decide to ignore the nosey comment, since I am inquisitive, not nosey, and listen to my father. His other daughters are the nosey ones. We walk and talk.

"Emani, you were only four years old. Aunty Jay was babysitting for your mother and me while we worked. She didn't teach in the summer so you all spent a lot of time with her in the summers. She babysat you a lot. Do you remember her babysitting you?"

"I think so, but I'm not sure, Dad."

"Well, anyway, one day you were dancing around in the kitchen when she was trying to cook you guys a special snack. You know our family rule is that you have to be as tall as the stove to be in the kitchen. Well, Aunty Jay made up that rule. She told you to leave, but you kept twirling around. You danced closer and closer to her until you danced into the stove. The pan was about to fall on you and Aunty Jay got burned trying to shield you from the hot grease inside the pan. She was burned badly, but thanks to her you don't even have one scar," Dad says with pride in his sister-in-love, as he calls Aunty Jay.

There is nowhere to sit in the hall, so I just lean against a mirror that is on the wall to keep my balance. As Dad tries to explain that the incident was an accident, I turn to look in the mirror. I've been complaining about my pimples when my aunt has never once complained about . . . anything. I am Emani. I am the triplet with the curls, the dancer, the so-called cutest one. Without Aunty Jay, I would have been . . .

Dad hugs me and says, "Emani, look at me. This wasn't your fault. You were just a baby. Aunty Jay doesn't blame you and neither do I. You cannot tell her that you know. You're a young lady now, so I know you can handle this. She can never know that you know. Do you understand?"

"Yes," I say as Aunty Jay and Uncle Joe walk up to us to tell us that they will be leaving the New Year's Eve party early.

"Happy New Year, niece," Aunty Jay says as she hugs me tightly.

I hug her tighter than I ever have in my life. Then, I kiss her on her cheek.

"Happy New Year, Aunty. I hate that you are leaving. I was so hoping to get one dance with you."

"You were?" Aunty Jay says as she tries to hold her coat closed. A bit of a blue beaded dress can be seen when she moves her hand to touch mine.

"Wow! Can I see that dress?"

Aunty Jay looks around, then offers to give me a peek at the dress.

When she opens it. I am genuinely impressed. Aunty Jay's figure is fantastic. She has curves where I only wish I had curves.

"You really like it?" She says as she rubs her shapely hips.

"I love it, Aunty!"

"Me too," my sisters say when they come out of the ballroom and compliment Aunty Jay as only they can. By the time Ebony and Eris are finished, Aunty Jay is smiling ear to ear.

"So what about that dance, Aunty Jay?" I ask, as Uncle Joe offers to take her coat so she can dance. She hesitates before she answers.

"You won't be embarrassed to dance with an old lady on the floor, will you?" Aunty Jay says as she removes her coat.

I watch as my triplet sisters' eyes get a bit larger when Aunty Jay's coat is completely off. They both look away when they see her remaining burn scars.

"I would never be embarrassed to be with my favorite aunt," I say, as I grab her hand and walk her toward the ballroom.

As we walk, I listen to my sisters compliment Aunty Jay some more on the back of her royal blue dress. They are telling the truth: her dress is wonderful from all angles.

After my dance with my aunt, I realize that she is not the person I thought she was. I thought she was strict because she didn't want us to have fun. I thought she was always concealed because she had forgotten what it is like to be young. All of these years, I believed my aunt was the lucky one to have such a handsome husband who was a first-class fellow.

But, after one dance with my aunt, I realize that her true self has been camouflaged. She is strict because she's learned that breaking the rules has consequences. She's concealed because she knows how cruel onlookers can be, but inside, she is a true hero, because true heroes never have to brag or show off. True heroes know who they are inside, even when we (as Eris would say) mere mortals do not. Uncle Joe is the lucky one.

"Can I dance with my wife?" Uncle Joe says as he twirls her around. I step away, watching the two of them as they spin and step and spin and step.

"Beautiful, isn't it?" A sistah's silky-smooth voice says behind me.

"Yes, true love is beautiful," I say as I turn around to see the face I have been hoping not to see tonight.

It is the same face I've seen on the internet a dozen times. It is the face of the daughter of the owner of this hotel. It is the face of my ex-boyfriend's Rickey's ex-girlfriend McKayla Hayden. The woman who made him choose between her and his dreams.

Before I can respond to McKayla's introduction of herself, Rickey's "friend" Rachel walks up to us. Where are my sisters? I am outnumbered here. I pull on my ear, hoping someone will come to my rescue, but no luck. No one comes.

"Wow, you two even have the same taste in colors," Rachel says when she sees that McKayla and I are both wearing the same shade of cobalt blue. Rachel re-introduces McKayla to me.

I suddenly wish I had chosen baby blue like Eris.

I quickly try to change the subject to the weather, entertainment, and decorations for the evening, until Rachel informs me that she has saved a place for my sisters and me at her table. She invites McKayla to join us. McKayla, foolishly unaware of Rachel's true motives, accepts Rachel's invitation.

As the two of them talk about Rickey, I look around the room, hoping that someone will ask me to dance soon. No luck.

Rachel repeatedly interviews McKayla about her many years as Rickey's girlfriend, and though she looks uncomfortable, McKayla answers Rachel's many questions.

My sisters finally find me. When they try to sit at Rachel's table, I give them the evil eye until Ebony suggests that we should go to get drinks. I quickly stand up, until McKayla informs me that she can have a waiter bring refreshments to our table instead. Oh GREAT!

The superstitious say that the way you spend your New Year's Eve and Day are the way your year will be all year. Well, the night is not at all what I thought it would be, until Rickey walks in. In the distance, I watch him walk up to his aunt and kiss her. As he stands at Dr. Thomas's table, I admire his ebony tuxedo, blue tie, and blue vest. I mean, he was handsome to me earlier in his leather jacket and cold-weather wear, but this is more of what I imagined him wearing last night in my dream.

I glance at the dance floor, imagining the two of us strutting our stuff. Then, I remember that he won't be dancing with me. I'm just like McKayla Hayden: I'm Rickey's ex-girlfriend now.

I head to the dance floor to dance alone. My sisters follow me onto the floor.

"That McKayla is hard to hate, huh, Emani?" Eris asks, as she almost falls in her brand-new silver high-heels.

Ebony and I try to hold in our laughs, but a few giggles escape our mouths. It serves her right to get teased after all the teasing she did to me after my miserable runway walk for FFDMO's model tryouts.

"Do you get the feeling that McKayla thinks Rickey and I are still together?" I ask Ebony.

"Yup!"

As Ebony answers, McKayla walks onto the floor to dance with us. The four of us have a lot of fun for a couple of songs.

"I really like you, Emani. I was soooo glad that Rickey didn't choose Rachel, but if I can't have him I'm happy that you do. You're a cool chick," McKayla says as she points to the boy that she thinks is my boyfriend.

I thank her for telling her dad to let Rickey off a bit earlier so that he can enjoy the New Year's countdown, and I accept her advice to go spend some time with him when she gives it.

I walk 33 steps until I get to Dr. Thomas's table. She stands up to hug me, exposing her bulging belly. When she pulls me to the side, I am told that she has not told Mr. Thomas about the pregnancy or the baby who will be born sooner than later. Her tummy is quite round in this form-fitting dress she's wearing. Isn't she afraid that he might find out from one of their many friends at this party?

"I think your secret's out, Dr. Thomas."

"No, I think the people in this room will keep my secret, just like they kept Terrence's secret about working on Payton Payne's case. People know how to mind their own business. You and your parents kept my husband's secret, didn't you?" Dr. T asks a question and my guilty eyes tell on me before I can explain myself.

"I'm sorry!"

"That's okay. Tonight is a celebration. Terrence and I have never spent a New Years apart in twenty years, but tonight he is probably somewhere in front of a computer, looking for that lunatic lady who ruined our lives, instead of spending his evening with the woman he promised to love for life. He's probably looking for clues on the whereabouts of the woman who tried to kill him instead of being with the woman who loves him. Did you know he knew that it was her people who tampered with his brakes? He knew she was behind that explosion in his building last week? Well, if he wants to let her kill our marriage like she killed our . . . anyway, Emani, as I was saying, I don't think anyone will tell Terrence anything, because everyone knows that our marriage cannot take any more friction. Terrence is not ready to be a father or a husband. He's too busy for us." When Dr. Thomas's eyes begin to fill with tears while rubbing her belly, I hug her.

Her hormones are probably out of her control. I feel awkward, but I can only imagine how she must be feeling. I feel guilty. My hormones have been weird lately, too.

Rickey hugs her when she and I finish our embrace, and by the time he finishes talking to her, she is smiling again. I guess he may know a little bit about females after all. I take back my earlier clueless comment.

"You look beautiful in blue, Emani," Rickey says when his aunt walks away. I do not speak.

"I didn't know if you would dance with me while Alexis was here, but I'm glad you came over," Rickey says as he holds out his hand to me.

I take his hand, but I do not head to the dance floor. I walk him toward the exit, though he reminds me that the countdown will be starting soon.

"Why haven't you told them about us, Rickey?"

"Who?"

"Rachel and McKayla."

"They do know about us, but to be honest, what happens between us is not their business. It's OUR business," Rickey says as he tries to spin me toward the dance floor.

"Well, why don't they know about OUR break up?" I ask.

He drops my hand like it is a hot skillet. "Our WHAT?" Rickey asks as he steps toward the door, adjusting his tie.

"Last week. Our break up. Don't you remember breaking up with me?" I ask, as I follow him out into the hall where there is less noise, since he claims he couldn't hear me well.

"You thought I broke up with you last week? Is that why you haven't called me since? You thought I broke up with you and you were perfectly okay with that. Huh?" I take a moment to try to understand his questions, but I am confused by his reaction to the words "break up."

He acts like this is news to him. Isn't he the one who said he was breaking up with me because I broke his heart?

I say yes when he asks me to answer his questions.

"Wow, Emani. Now I am convinced that you don't want me. First, you practically give me to your sister. Then, when I think I believe that you were just being a good sister to Alexis, you prove that you really don't want me. After all, you have proven that you could care less if I am your boyfriend or not. What I don't understand is why you care if I'm with McKayla or Rachel. You don't want me!" Rickey says as he glances at the very same mirror I looked in earlier.

Before I can respond, my sisters interrupt us. We listen to them tell us that the balloons will be falling after the countdown in three minutes.

McKayla and Rachel both ask Rickey and I to come back to the dance floor. Rachel grabs Rickey's hand and McKayla looks at me like I should stop Rachel or something. When I do nothing, McKayla takes Rickey's hand and places it in mine. Then, she pulls Rachel to the floor against her will.

Rickey and I stand in the center of the floor, hand-in-hand, when the DJ turns off the music. I smile at him when the lights start to flicker, knowing that he most likely had something to do with our mini light show. Flickering lights normally make me nervous, but not now. I continue to smile, ignoring a flashback to a tragic school year long ago. He doesn't smile back at me, however.

Ten . . . nine . . . eight . . . seven . . . six . . . five . . . four . . . three . . . two . . . one . . . I stand in the middle of the floor with him, as every other couple in the room share their first kiss for the New Year. I don't think we will ever have a first kiss.

When the music comes back on, husbands dance with wives, sisters dance with brothers, mothers dance with sons, daddies dance with daughters, and my ex-boyfriend dances with . . . his other ex-girlfriend. I dance with a complete stranger. Happy New Year to me.

CHAPTER 23
Ebony
Hood Robin

I wish a new year meant a good start, but I am very afraid of what this new year will bring for me. I couldn't really tell what Mr. Thomas's mood was on the phone, but I hope he has good news to share with me. Mom is going with me this time, since she is very nervous about me going to a place that had an explosive device in it less than two weeks ago. Plus, Mr. Thomas told Mom that he has been receiving threats on his life for continuing his investigation on Payton Payne. I admire his honesty, courage and strength, but his timing is not very good. Mom has already become a protective lioness since my school wants to punish me for something I did not do. Now, thanks to Mr. Thomas, she is worried about my safety, too.

When we get to the condominium, we are searched by armed policemen and then quickly directed to an unfamiliar area. I am surprised at first when we reach a condo that is not the one Mr. Thomas has lived in since the beginning of last year, until I realize that Mr. Thomas has probably moved on purpose.

I then realize that Payton Payne's crew bombed the wrong area of the condominium a couple of weeks ago because that is where they probably thought Mr. Thomas lived. I bet she and her crew were quite confused and surprised to discover that Mr. Thomas had already moved to a different location, a location that was only a few floors away.

Now, what I am confused about is the fact that the old Payton Payne, who blew up my school, would have blown up the entire building and not just one area. I wonder why she only planted the explosive device near Mr. Thomas's condo, but who am I to try to think like a criminal mastermind. She is an insane woman. I am a logical girl.

"Hey, beautiful ladies! As you can see, I am on my way out of town, but not before giving you something that will put a permanent smile on your faces," Mr. Thomas says this as he smiles, holding a large brown envelope. I smile instantly, but I am a bit distracted by all of the things I see packed up in boxes in his condo. He says he is going out of town, but his condo seems to say that he isn't planning on coming back here anytime soon.

I reach for the envelope, but he directs me to the flat screen TV that we always watch video footage from the Dimes' secret cameras on, before handing the envelope to me.

Mr. Thomas explains, "Don't open it quite yet. Let me show you what caused me to do a little investigating of my own."

Mr. Thomas presses a button, and I see Kitten in what I have come to know is the bedroom of Brenda Agbayewa. On the video, Brenda and Kitten do a little bit of small talk. Then, I hear Brenda tell Kitten not to worry about how some of the other girls (the Dimes, I believe) are treating her. She says it is all part of her initiation. Then, Brenda walks Kitten through her massive walk-in closet, showing her enough clothes for three lifetimes. Most of the clothes still have tags on them.

"How is this going to help me?" I ask, but my mom asks me to hush. Mom is all about listening more than you talk. I'm working on that.

I watch as Kitten describes a secret meeting she's had with the Dimes. Then, I realize that Kitten must be on our side. She knows she's on camera and she is giving us a lot of information about what they said, when they met, where they were, and why they met, but for some reason she does not mention who was there.

Maybe I already know who was there. Kitten always says that it isn't always important what people say, but what they don't say that is most important. Maybe she isn't saying their names because I already know their names. Maybe!

Mr. Thomas tells me to listen very carefully to what Brenda says next, so I lean closer to the TV like a toddler trying to watch cartoons on Saturday morning.

After Brenda says only three sentences, Mr. Thomas cuts off the television. Now, usually I am pretty smart, but I did not hear Brenda say anything about me. Brenda called Zyanne "Robin Hood." Brenda said that she loves designer labels and can't resist anything with a designer's name or logo on it, but now she doesn't have to worry about things like that.

Then, she tells Kitten not to worry about Zyanne, because Zyanne will have her back in the end, no matter how rough she seems now. Where in those words was the key to get me out of trouble before Monday morning when I have to sit in front of Ms. Kelly and Principal Wells and explain where the school's money has gone? I don't know Principal Wells very well, but I do believe she isn't going to care about Kitten's issues with Zyanne or Brenda's desire for designer labels.

"Did you hear her?" Mr. Thomas says as he unplugs the TV and asks one of his police pals to pack it away for him. I believe he is packing that TV away prematurely. I need to see the video again.

"I was listening, Mr. Thomas, but I did not hear anything," I say as my mom says the same thing with a frown and her hands folded across her chest. Mr. Thomas does not know it, but that usually means Mom feels like she has just wasted a few precious moments of her life listening to nonsense. She folded her arms just like that as Emani and I tried to explain our way out of dating Stephan. She folded her arms just like that when I tried to talk her out of coming with me today.

"Well, my little sleuth. I'm sure you noticed that Kitten called Zyanne "Robin Hood," which makes me believe that the Dimes have secret names for one another, but it also tells me that Zyanne must be like Robin Hood. What did Robin Hood do?" Mr. Thomas asks.

"Steal from the rich to give to the poor," My mom says with a grin before I can. Mom acts like she's going to get a million dollars or something for answering first. I smile, but I still don't get it, especially since Brenda Agbayewa is far from poor.

"Exactly! Ding! Ding! Ding! You get to open up your envelope," Mr. Thomas says as he rolls his luggage toward the door. Why are adults so odd? Actually, Mr. Thomas's son Zachary was goofy at times, too. Maybe it is a Thomas trait to be silly.

I open the envelope with my mom looking over my shoulder. After only about a minute of reading, I decide to sit down on one of Mr. Thomas's many boxes. Hey, where is his little comfy couch? Why are there so many boxes?

"Zyanne has a record for theft?" Mom asks, as she leans on the very bare living room wall.

"Not officially. She was a juvenile when that stuff happened, but yeah, I found this documentation. Her parents were probably just trying to teach her a lesson for that first one, but the other one seems a bit more serious. Ms. Zyanne Jeffries not only stole from her parents and the banks they both work at, but also her parents' friends and the banks that they work at too. Her parents may have gotten these records to disappear with their money, power, and influence, but I got my hands on them, and you can make them reappear on Monday," Mr. Thomas says as he glances around his condo, seeming to soak in every inch of it, most likely for the last time.

Mom goes over to the door to hug him before she walks into the hall. We both thank him from the bottom of our hearts.

Mr. Thomas said he would help me to get out of trouble. He promised my mother everything would be okay. I really think this information is going to help the school to discover who the real thief is at C.I.A. She's not just a poor teenage girl with a crush on her student teacher. Zyanne Jeffries has stolen more than once. I plan to expose her for who she really is to the principal and the dean.

When I hug Mr. Thomas, I whisper to him to go see his wife ASAP. When he asks why, I simply say, "Trust me." My relationship with Tyson was ruined by secrets. I don't want Dr. and Mr. Thomas's relationship to end because of secrets. I know I promised to keep both of their secrets, but oh well, I think they both will forgive me.

*

"So tell me something, Ms. Ebony Robertson. Did you see anything else on that video that you could say was interesting? Do you have any theories?" Mr. Thomas's FBI pal says, as Mr. Thomas turns off the light and locks his door.

I smile, trying to think of anything else I can remember. The Dimes do not wear jewelry to their meetings. They dress in the same grey outfit. They are not permitted to bring cell phones or anything other than themselves. Only nine of them meet at one time. So where is the tenth Dime? Who is the tenth Dime? Do I already know? Maybe there never were ten of them. Maybe it was to fool everyone. Is Kitten the tenth Dime?

"I have a Dime theory. That Brenda girl said that she loves designer labels, but that thanks to Zyanne, she doesn't have her "bad habit" anymore. I bet she was a thief, too. She probably does it for the thrill, because she probably doesn't wear any of those clothes to school. Does she?" My mom says, interrupting my thoughts about the identity of the tenth Dime with her theory. Mom is really handling our secret mission well.

"No, Brenda wears her own wardrobe creations to school, so you just may be right, Mom. Brenda probably steals for the thrill," I say, as my mom smirks.

"Mommy is always right, baby. Mommy is always right!" I laugh, because to be honest, I would never tell her to her face, but so far in my life my mom has always been right.

The threat of expulsion or suspension caused me to confess to my parents, but I'm glad I did. We haven't told them the whole truth. They don't know how much we've helped Mr. Thomas, but now they know we have a few dime-sized problems to solve at our school.

When we walk into the school early Monday morning, Reana Powers is right there to greet me. Her eyes look a bit weak, and she has the sniffles, but she manages to smile when she sees me. I feel sorry for poor Reana, but colds and the flu come with living in Illinois. All of the teen helpers in the office are coughing and sneezing.

"Good morning, Ebony. Good morning, Mr. and Mrs. Robertson. The principal will see you soon," Reana says as she sneezes. My mom offers her a cough drop, but she says she is allergic to them.

"You seem sick. Why are you at school?" My medical-minded mom says. Mom has very high standards for missing school, but she does not like when people send their sick kids to school.

"I never miss school. I have had perfect attendance since elementary school. Plus, I wouldn't have missed school today for the world. Principal Wells found out she will be promoted to superintendent of schools over break, and many of the principals from surrounding schools will be here to celebrate with her. One of the principals was the principal of my elementary school. I'm sure she'd want to see how I've turned out," Reana says as she walks us into the principal's conference room.

Though I am prepared to face Zyanne with my evidence, I am nervous. My dad holds my hand as Ms. Kelly walks in and sits across from us. Zyanne and her parents enter a few minutes later. We all sit in silence until Principal Wells enters the room with a voice recorder that I have only seen in interrogation rooms on crime TV.

Ms. Kelly gives her statement first. Then, Principal Wells asks Zyanne and me some basic questions, but I stutter as I answer them. I am instantly embarrassed when Zyanne smirks and giggles. When Principal Wells asks Zyanne why she laughed, Zyanne claims she was just clearing her throat.

My mom and dad ask Principal Wells for a brief break to talk to me, but she declines. Mom and Dad squeeze my hands under the table, and I feel a sense of strength, just knowing that they are both by my side. I silently remind myself that though I had a stuttering problem, I have given many speeches this year. I can do this interview.

"My daughter should not even be here. Zyanne is innocent. This young lady was found with evidence against her in her locker. She had the opportunity to steal the money and we believe she has the motive to do it, since she is the one with the financial need," Zyanne's mother, Ms. Jeffries, says.

My mom and dad do not let go of my hands, but I do look at both of them to see if that statement hurt them at all. Did she just call us poor? My mother is a doctor. My father is a mechanic. Our family does not come from old money, but we have a little new money.

I wait for my parents to say something, but they do not. They just look in Principal Wells's direction as she begins asking Zyanne Jeffries some questions. Zyanne is a practiced liar, so I am not surprised that she answers each question perfectly, without any slips of the tongue. She is so poised that even I am convinced of my guilt.

Dean Norton walks in holding the file that Mr. Thomas gave to us yesterday evening. My mom took the file to Dean Norton's house last night in preparation for this meeting. Dean Norton said that she had to handle some "administrative details" before presenting the file to Principal Wells.

Mom trusted her with the file mostly because my mom made a copy of the contents of the file at Charlotte's mother's copy service and school supply depot last night, too. Charlotte's mom is a notary. Mom always has a plan B. I know she has that copied file in her purse. She's the type of mom that has everything in her purse, just in case.

I watch Dean Norton hand the file to Principal Wells. Then, I watch her give Principal Wells another letter that appears to be on school letterhead. Principal Wells reads the letter for a few minutes. Then, she says she will need to take a break. The Jeffries family does not want to take a break, so Principal Wells pushes the record button on the crime TV voice recorder again as she begins to speak.

"It has come to my attention that Zyanne Jeffries, though a stellar student and leader at C.I.A., has a history of taking things without permission." Mr. Jeffries sits up in his chair and asks for his lawyer to be permitted to come into the room, when Principal Wells begins to list some facts from Zyanne's file. Dean Norton smiles, gets up and ask the Jennings' lawyer to enter. She asks the school's attorney to enter also. Mr. Jeffries continues to sit on the edge of his chair.

Principal Wells states some very serious facts about Zyanne, which neither Zyanne nor her parents deny after Principal Wells holds up the brown folder with the FBI seal on it. Principal Wells says she cannot give away the identity of the person who gave the school Zyanne's file, though the Jeffries ask for the person's identity. My dad adjusts the blue color on his work shirt as Principal Wells mentions a few more white-collar crimes from Zyanne's past, after denying her parents' requests for a break to talk with their lawyer privately.

Soon after Principal Wells shares the highlights from Zyanne's file with us, Zyanne hesitantly confesses to her past crimes and the current one. Once she admits guilt, the Jeffries' lawyer quickly asks Principal Wells not to expel her. The Jeffries offer to pay the school back all of the money Zyanne "borrowed," but Dean Norton informs them that the school board president has told her she wants Zyanne to be expelled. Principal Wells slides the letter she was given earlier from Dean Norton to Mrs. Jeffries, who reads it rather quickly. Then, she hands it to her husband, covering her face with her manicured hands.

"My daughter is supposed to graduate with honors in five months. She made a mistake that is correctable. She has made a few poor choices in life, but it will be quite embarrassing for both the school and us to have the news headlines read that your prestigious C.I.A.'s student council president was expelled for improper removal of school funds. You should really think about what you are doing! We could use all of our resources to fight this!" Mr. Jeffries says as he hits the wooden oval table.

Principal Wells asks me to close the door when it opens slightly. Then, she turns off the crime TV-style recorder. The Jeffries' lawyer objects, but Principal Wells doesn't seem to care.

"Mr. Jeffries, when your daughter stole money from you, you probably told her she was naughty and not to do it again. When she stole from your friends and their banks, you probably told her she was really naughty, paid her debts and told her not to do it again. Now, she is stealing from you, your friends, banks, and schools. I am not her parent, but she should be punished, because she will do it again. If she weren't a minor, she would be in jail for forgery, theft, and a long list of crimes, so I would suggest you use your resources toward helping her instead of fighting us. The headlines could read, "Student Council President Expelled," but if I know you, you'll be long gone before that headline appears in the news. You'll take those resources you're threatening to use on us and move your daughter to another school to be their problem, but wherever you go her record will go, too. I promise you that! You squashed her juvenile record, but you cannot squash her school records. I'm sure you'll buy her way into a prestigious college, but it will have to be without my recommendation and in spite of her record. And since I am a teacher first and a principal second, I am going to help you to teach her a lesson. Let me also share some words of wisdom with you, since parents should be their kids' first teachers. Remember, you will not be able to buy her way out of federal jail!"

Principal Wells pushes the crime TV-style voice recorder's record button again. My parents and I listen as Dean Norton and Principal Wells apologize for false charges being brought against me. I smile brightly when they say I am reinstated as treasurer of student council. I smile brighter when Dean Norton tells the Jeffries that she will be paying special attention to me and that I will be under special surveillance for my protection. Dean Norton says she will not be afraid to personally press charges if anything peculiar like exploding lockers or falling lights happens at this school, even if Zyanne Jeffries is no longer a C.I.A. student.

Zyanne just looks out the window. She does not smirk. She does not smile. She does not giggle. She is speechless. She's correct. I may be a stutterer, but she is ex-exp-expelled!

When I exit the office with my parents, I smile a 100-watt smile. My dimples probably look like miniature caves in my cheeks. My parents hug me. Mom then walks over toward the school nurse and poor sick Reana to offer some of her home remedies for colds. Reana's ruby-red nose reminds me of a certain popular Christmas reindeer, and her eyes do too.

* * *

I stand eye-to-eye with Tyson at play practice after school. He cries to me, only because he is in character. He is crying because I am Zaria and he is Hephaestus and because the scene requires him to shed tears, not because I am Ebony who broke his heart by kissing and dating his very best friend Stephan.

When the scene ends, we go our separate ways.

"You lost the best thing you had going for you," Tatyanna says, as I prepare for my next scene. Shouldn't she be on stage being a very mean Aphrodite instead of backstage being a very mean Tatyanna?

I grab a fake blow torch and read my lines aloud, as Tatyanna stares at me.

"Tatyanna, what do you want me to say? I know I lost the best thing I had. I made a mistake, and he doesn't believe in forgiveness. He's the one who said I was a better actress than he thought I was. That really hurt," I admit.

"Did it hurt as much as you hurt him?" Tatyanna asks.

I do not answer, but I think I probably hurt Tyson a little more than he hurt me with the actress comment, because I know I was never acting when I was with him. I was acting with Stephan. I guess Tyson deserves to be a tad upset with me. Okay, he deserves to be extremely upset with me.

"No . . . I think I hurt him more," I say as I watch him on stage.

He is a brilliant thespian. Even with all those other people on the stage, you know that he is the star. He is a three-dimensional object in a two-dimensional world.

"I hear your father is a mechanic. My brother is artsy, but he loves racing. It is the only sport he is into. I believe people should write their own stories, but this one time I'll make an exception and help you with this scene in your life. You can thank me later. Ask him on a date now," Tatyanna says as she walks onto stage like the goddess she believes she is.

I thought that sending her that recording of Denzel Smith would help to gain her trust, but I could have never expected to gain her loyalty.

I watch the twin Tysons on stage. They both are truly gifted, but I can't help but wonder why Tatyanna would really help me. The Dimes believe in Dimes before Dudes. Does it count if the dude is your brother?

*

I ask Tony, "Ummh, Tyson. Are you speaking to me yet?"

"No!"

"You just did!" He does not laugh. I just stand there as he takes off his shirt and puts on part of his armor.

"Well, Tyson. Ummh. My dad has built quite a few cars. He even knows a few racecar drivers. I was wondering if maybe you would like to come over this weekend to . . . "

He interrupts me with a very quick "No" again.

Tatyanna mouths to me to try again, and though I read her lips, I don't have the courage to try again. I think I used all of my courage this morning, trying to prove my innocence and Zyanne's guilt.

"Is this another lie to get my attention?" Tyson says, as I try to look in his eyes instead of at his brawny chest. I didn't know he had real muscles. I thought it was the armor. Stephan is the athlete. Tyson is an entertainer who is always covered up. He's a cool dresser with a unique style, but I didn't know he had a few muscles of his own.

"I'm not lying. You can ask anyone," I say, though no one is around us to ask.

I step closer to him and look deeper into his tender eyes.

He holds my hands and asks, "Well, if you can promise me that you do not have any more secrets and that you will not lie to me again, I will be at your house on Saturday. If you can't make me that promise, let's just keep it professional. You are Zaria and I am Hephaestus. So who are we? Tyson and Ebony or Zaria and Hephaestus?"

I break our eye contact to look for Tatyanna, but she has disappeared.

To be honest, she is the only thing standing between us being together. I believe she is a Dime. I would be lying to him if I said I had no secrets, because I am secretly investigating her, and if Tatyanna is a Dime, I will not hesitate to expose her and her evil deeds.

"I guess for now we are Zaria and Hephaestus only," I say as Tatyanna approaches us.

I don't think Tyson was expecting that answer, because his face seems to lose all of its coffee-with-cream color. His face is nowhere near the color of his chest. He walks away without saying another word to me.

"I hope that you aren't doing this because of me," Tatyanna whispers as she puts on more make up.

I don't even know what to say to her. Does she know that I know?

CHAPTER 24

Eris
What Not to Wear

I know I should be happy to have my first verbal offer for an unofficial athletic full-ride scholarship, especially since I was in jeopardy of losing it. I'm only a freshman. I thought it would be junior year before I would hear those words.

I should be even happier to have achieved victory over varsity, but now I have to begin again with basketball season. It will be basically the same girls with a few new faces sprinkled here and there, but with every new team there is that honeymoon period when you are trying to figure out what each other needs to succeed. I hope I can work the same miracle with these girls as I did with my volleyball squad.

"Hey, Stephan!" I wave at him, but he does not even say a word to me. I didn't know how he would respond to me after our kiss, but he has been acting quite weird.

He kissed me. I didn't kiss him first. If he didn't want to kiss me, why did he?

After being ignored by Stephan for my entire practice, I walk into my basketball coach's office after he requests that I see him in private. I am a bit nervous, because I have never had a male coach before. I have never been on a varsity basketball team before either, but I guess this is what I have always wanted. It is too late to be afraid now. Who am I kidding? I am petrified.

"We have high hopes for this season because of you, Ms. Robertson."

I smile when he says this. "I am going to do my very best, Coach!" I say with a grin.

The Coach says, "I also have a few concerns given a certain episode you were accused of having with steroids. Now, Coach Keyes has assured me that you were innocent, but I need to hear from you that you have not used, are not using, and will never use performance-enhancing drugs of any sort as an athlete at C.I.A."

I look at the dull gray carpet of Coach Reed's floor, mostly because I am humiliated. Do I look like a body builder? I have never done drugs of any kind. Why do people think I have? I eat well. I exercise. I sleep. I drink water. I practice. These are not secrets. These things are what all good athletes do. Why can't they just believe that I am a first-class athlete instead of a cheater?

"I promise Coach. I am not a fraud. I am the real deal. I will make you proud." He puts his hand out for me to shake, and I shake it.

As he walks me out, he tells me not to fear the cameras, the scouts, the crowds, or the pressure associated with C.I.A. varsity basketball. I look up at him with my most confident expression. After all, I am a Robertson.

*

"Are you nervous?" Keyshia asks.

"Are you scared?" Rochelle asks.

I look at both of them before I prepare to confront him.

"Yup!"

I knock on Stephan's door. My hero Mary Miles answers with a genuine look of happiness to see me.

"Are you all here to see Stephan?" Mrs. Miles asks.

Keyshia and Rochelle start to step backwards. Then, my sneaky teammates tell Mrs. Miles that I am the only one here to see him before they run, jump in Monica's car, and ride away, abandoning me to confront Stephan alone.

"He's not here, Eris, but I have wanted to talk to you." Why didn't Mrs. Miles tell me Stephan wasn't at home before my ride rode away?

Now, I will have to walk home. Plus, Stephan's car is in the driveway. Where is he at? Maybe he's with Kylie. No, the two of them would be in his car. Kylie is always in Stephan's car.

I follow my hero onto her court and watch her remove a basketball from her secret slot. Stephan showed the secret slot to me when he gave me my first tour of this place. He also told me how important the ball is to her. It is the ball she won her last championship with. She signs it and hands it to me.

"I can't accept this, Mrs. Miles. I'm not worthy yet," I say as I look around at all of her medals, trophies, and framed jerseys. She is a true legend.

"I'm not giving you this ball for the reason you think that I am. I want you to ask my son why I am giving you this ball," she says as she stands up and tosses me another ball for us to practice with today.

"I would ask him if he were talking to me, but he isn't talking to me much these days. Are WE going to play?" I ask, as she stands, looking quite confused.

I throw the ball to her and we begin to play.

Two hours later, I take my last shot and break our tie. I pinch myself just to make sure I didn't dream the whole thing. The stinging sensation I feel reminds me that my victory was real. I really beat Mary Miles at her house. I'm dancing inside.

"So, where's your victory dance?" Mrs. Miles asks, as I try to remain calm.

I stand facing her and ask her for permission to celebrate. When she grants me permission, I take her championship ball and place it in her face.

"I beat you in your house, with your ball, on your court . . . oh I mean my court. I rule this court. Go me. Go me. Go me." As I dance, Mrs. Miles laughs a real belly laugh that reminds me of Emani's laugh.

Emani's laugh always starts in her tummy and land on her tongue. It also ends with a snort. Emani is such a pretty girl that no one ever expects that obnoxious laugh to come out of her mouth. It is hilarious!

"So Eris, will you ask him about the ball when the two of you are talking again?" Mrs. Miles asks while looking me directly in my eyes.

"I promise, M&M," I say.

She laughs again. For some reason I believe no one has called the woman who had the sweetest snap of the wrist in basketball M&M for a long time. Maybe MOM, but not M&M.

Though Mrs. Miles and I had a great conversation and b-ball challenge, Stephan and I haven't spoken in weeks. He has, however, spoken to Emani and Ebony. He goes out of his way to speak to them. My sisters are even back to being friendly with him, but he has avoided me, for some reason unknown to me. I'm the one who didn't pretend to like or date him, but I am the one he is choosing to ignore. I don't understand boys.

I am focusing on my games, though. It was fun irritating him and I miss it, but I am not one to worry about some boy. Maybe in time he'll spontaneously mature and face me like a man.

*

I hand my love questionnaire to the owner of the Soulm8tes agency instead of Brenda Agbayewa because to be honest I don't trust her. Brenda is most likely a Dime. Ebony believes she's a shop-lifting, designer bag-stealing Dime who plotted against her with Zyanne Jeffries, but I only care that she is a Dime, and therefore my enemy.

Soulm8tes claims that they can find your perfect match out of the 2000 students who are on our campus if your potential mate completes a questionnaire, so I'm trying it. I can't let the Dimes cost me a chance at a love life. I don't understand boys, but I do like them. I've seen some great love stories begin with an app or an online date. I've seen some horrible horror stories of loves that have gone wrong, too, begin the same way. This Soulm8tes questionnaire won't cost me a dime, though. It's free.

*

Over the last few weeks, the remaining Dimes have been in attack mode. I know they wish they could hurt Ebony, but since they can't, they've focused on Eris, Emani, Charlotte, and the rest of the innocent C.I.A. student body.

There have been too many fights to count. In fact, one was the very next day after our Martin Luther King, Jr. Day Peace Celebration. There has been vandalism to the school and students cars: Charlotte's house and her brand-new self-driving car was toilet papered and covered in graffiti. Charlotte is just happy it wasn't destroyed, given its price tag; not that my dad wouldn't fix it for her for a reasonable price.

Anyway, there have been very cruel false things posted on the Internet about Emani's promiscuity (my sister hasn't even had her first kiss yet) and my alleged bisexuality.

Stephan drops his love questionnaire into the box behind mine. He doesn't speak to me, but he speaks to everyone at the table including Brenda, Ebony, the new student council president, Cari Sinclair (number two on C.I.A.'s list of top ten students) who took Robin Hood Zyanne's place, and Mrs. Wright, the owner of Soulm8tes.

"Hello, Stephan. My name is Eris." I put my hand out for him to shake. He doesn't shake it.

"Oh, so you can kiss me, but you can't shake my hand."

The entire table stares at him, and then at both of us, when he escorts me away by pulling me into the hallway. Why does this boy think he can touch me? I have been taking Tae Kwon Do since I was seven years old. I will body slam this boy.

Once we are a bit farther away from onlookers, Stephan decides to scream at me. Has he forgotten who I am? Is he letting a little peck make him forget that I will dropkick him to his knees in three seconds flat and not even help him to stand back up?

He foolishly puts his five fingers across my lips. "Watch your mouth, Eris!"

"I only said the truth, and get your sweaty, probably unwashed hand off of my mouth, Stephan Miles!" He decides to remove his hand.

I watch him look up and down the hall as if he is expecting a visitor before I decide to speak.

"Stephan, the kiss meant nothing to me. Let's just pretend it didn't happen and go back to being frenemies. I miss the cold water bottles you bring me and I know you miss everything about me. I mean you wouldn't even have a column in the newspaper, a fan following, or a blog if it weren't for me. Get out your camera, your notepad, and your voice recorder. Don't you have a job to do? I'll give you an exclusive. You don't even have to thank me." I laugh because I'm joking about most of what I say, but he doesn't even move one muscle, especially not any facial muscles.

Stephan knows I'm not as arrogant as I was seven months ago, so why is he taking me so seriously? I was simply teasing him. It is what we do. I mock him. He makes fun of me. I guess that ridiculous lip lock has ruined everything between us.

Stephan walks away, after telling me not to talk to him again. I hope he doesn't think that he is hurting me. Not talking to him is quite fine with me.

*

None of my sisters have dates to the Valentine's party that will take place after the fashion show, so I don't feel too out of place when we pull up to C.I.A. solo tonight. I'm not in the fashion show, but I will be in the audience, cheering my sisters on. Emani will be beside me, since she's a designer and not a model. I don't understand Brenda's thinking with that one, but I don't really know fashion. I think members of FFDMO fell in love with Ebony's red hair and gave her Emani's spot. But Emani says that in the fashion industry it isn't about just being pretty, you have to be unique. I think the fact that there are three of us should disqualify all three of us from ever being supermodels, then. The Dimes have people calling us copies, but we all know we are quite different from one another.

*

My sis Alexis sits down right next to Emani, who is sitting right next to me. Alexis should be three rows in front of me with her boyfriend Jeremy. Instead, Jeremy is three rows ahead of us, sitting next to Kylie Calderone. I don't understand their seat separation, but if Alexis would give me five minutes with Kylie, I bet I could convince Kylie to switch seats with my eldest sibling.

I pull out our family video camera when the lights dim and prepare to watch the show. The zoom and night vision on this thing is amazing, thanks to my ingenious dad. Though it is dark, I feel someone sit next to me. I try to focus on the stage, since my sister is walking the catwalk, but when the person drops something on my lap, I almost drop the camera.

Once Ebony is off of the stage, I turn the camera off, only to see an empty chair next to me. I ask Alexis if she saw anyone sit down next to me, but of course she just looks at me as if I am speaking a foreign language (other than Spanish, since she speaks that one). Emani didn't see anything but her fashions on the runway.

I resume my filming when the next scene is introduced by future felon or fashion icon Brenda Agbayewa herself. Brenda commentates for each scene with enthusiasm and personality. Everyone in the audience seems to respond to both her voice and the inimitable way that she speaks about clothes.

If it were me up there on stage, I would say Ebony is wearing a yellow dress, but Brenda describes it as a golden gown. She talks about Ebony's sparkling ruby hair accentuating the bright glow of the sunlit outfit she is donning, and I almost walk out of the show. Does she really have to decorate every word she uses to describe a yellow dress? She really is a pompous princess. I suddenly think of her walk-in closet, filled with items she has never warn and price tags I could never understand.

When the lights come on, I can finally read what is on my lap. Alexis seems to be reading it, too. She looks at me when we both finish reading at the same time. We may not be triplets, but our sister senses are in sync.

The note says, "Do not let Ebony walk on the stage for the finale." For a brief moment, I sit in my chair, trying to figure out who could have given me this note, but I quickly rise when I realize I really do not know. The person had on a hood. The physique looked female. Ebony says that Kitten mentioned the Dimes wearing hoods on Brenda Agbayewa's hidden video footage, but why would a Dime help me or Ebony?

I try to get backstage to talk to Ebony, but Brenda blocks my entrance, first blaming it on the camera in my hand.

"We are about to do the second half of the show, Eris. I'm pretty sure you aren't on the list," Brenda says, though she doesn't even look at the list. She knows she didn't put me in the show. I look at her and come to a decision. She's taller, but I'm stronger. The next thing I know, she is on the floor and I am headed backstage to talk to my sister. I still have my camera in my hand.

Backstage, all I can see is chaos. I step over tossed high-heels and piles of worn wardrobe before I finally get in speaking distance to my sister.

"You pushed me!" Brenda says from behind me before I can speak to Ebony.

I turn around to apologize to Brenda, only to see Ms. Kelly and Dean Norton's frowning faces. I quickly apologize for my "accidental" push, but Dean Norton says she saw me shove Brenda to the floor. Dean Norton is never around when the Dimes' puppets are insulting people in huddles of humiliation. She is never around when underclassmen are intimidated in the cafeteria or if any non-Dime is being harassed, but she is always there to see the Robertson girls make mistakes. It is so frustrating!

As Dean Norton asks me to report back to my seat, I am a bit relieved to get a warning, since I was expecting a Saturday detention. She asks Ebony if she is okay, and as Ebony speaks to her, I quickly mouth to Ebony not to get back on the stage. Ebony seems to have read my lips, but I guess I won't really know until I'm back in my seat.

As I approach my seat, I realize Emani has also left to try to get backstage to Ebony. I notice Emani has been caught by Dean Norton when I see her standing beside the dean with her classic, "why can't I get what I want" pouty face.

Alexis does not look at me when I return. She is focused on Jeremy and Kylie again. Then, she focuses on the extended stage the FFDMO crew has added for the conclusion of the show. I glance at my watch, hoping that maybe the time allotted for tonight's festivities has somehow run out. Maybe the first half of the show was too long and the second half will be canceled.

No luck. Brenda Agbayewa is back on the microphone. No one would even know she had been pushed down in her six-inch high heels moments before. I look away from her supermodel self. When I see Ebony step back on stage, I begin to perspire. I don't even sweat this much on the court. Why am I sweating now?

Alexis gets up and begins to walk toward the stage. She really has improved since her sessions with Rickey, but the emotion I see in her eyes right now seems to be a mix between fear and panic. I follow her, though there are many people screaming vulgar words at us when we block their view of the stage.

Surprisingly, Ebony's walk goes flawlessly. There was no need to worry. There was no need for concern. I take a few steps to the side of the stage when Stephan Miles demands that I move. I try to ignore the fact that he calls me a male, but he will pay for that remark later.

When I look back on stage, I am shocked to see Ebony on the microphone and the rest of the models on the floor. Where is Brenda? For every scene she has given us a story for each outfit and a description of each piece in her and Emani's collection. Where is she now? I listen to Ebony do an average job of commentating and try to ignore the disrespectful and offensive males behind me who are acting like they have never seen girls in swimwear.

When the swim collection turns into an evening-wear collection, my mouth widens in awe of Brenda's gorgeous gowns. I know she is allegedly a thief who is addicted to labels, but she truly is a rare talent. This girl's creations make me wish I was going to prom this year. I would wear that metallic one in a microsecond, even though it reminds me of one thousand shiny dimes.

The crowd's reaction is genuine wonderment. All I hear are vowel sounds like "ah," "ooh," and "oh."

Brenda walks out in a flesh-colored beaded gown that makes her look both radiant and nude. The boys seem to be paying full attention as she walks almost to the end of the runway, then stops before she gets to the side that Alexis and I are standing near. Our entire section seems to be leaning forward to get a closer look at her gown, but she avoids our side as if she fears being ambushed by the mostly male crowd.

Principal Wells walks out on stage when the boys behind us start to act like hormone-filled hooligans. Before the principal can get to our side to most likely lecture us, Brenda steps in front of her. I don't know what she says to her, but Principal Wells only stops momentarily. She races toward us with her finger already in the air.

Dean Norton follows behind her with the microphone as Brenda slowly tries to exit the stage.

I do see the red light, but it is too late. The stage that the dean and principal stand on crumbles before my eyes like sand in an hour glass. Alexis and I only have time to save ourselves from the crash.

Though Dean Norton is in the rubble, she somehow manages to hold on to the microphone, because I hear her send the security guards to the exits and tell the custodians to turn on all of the lights.

My mind instinctively races back to my old school after the first explosive went off. I have that same feeling of vulnerability as I did that infamous and tragic day. I don't know what the future holds. Should I pray or cry?

I would love to tell you that I say a quick prayer, but I do the other thing, the thing I normally never do. What is worse, though, is that I do it in front of Stephan Miles and several other C.I.A. boys who hate me because of Stephan Miles.

Motormouth Malcolm McGee gives me a tissue, but I try to wipe away my trickling tears with my hand first. I decide to use the tissue when I continue to feel moisture on my cheeks. I hate crying! Crying is for private, not for public.

"Are you okay?" Mosquito Malcolm asks, as a security guard screams that he found something that looks suspicious in the balcony area.

When he says detonator, I almost sit down in Stephan's lap. Luckily, Stephan moves before I can take a seat. The crowd erupts with nervous noise. Another security guard tries to tell the crowd everything is alright, but no one is listening.

Once Principal Wells limps her way out of the remains of the extended stage, she quiets everyone down, cancels our Soulm8tes-sponsored dance and sends everyone home.

I am happy to be alive, but many of the students complain about not getting their results from the love questionnaires back as they were promised. Are they serious? What is more important, love or life?

I watch them line up for their results as I quickly try to exit after we are released by the real police. That was not an accident. Someone sabotaged that stage. I only care about that other four-letter word that begins with an l and ends with an e, life.

Ebony, Emani, Alexis, and I hug each other tightly outside when we find one another, especially when we realize we are the first four people in the parking lot. When I see Ebony, she isn't even completely dressed, but she is not in the building, either. We have certainly learned from our last tragedy. We always know multiple ways to exit a school.

Jeremy walks over to Alexis and hugs her, as Kylie pretends not to be watching them from across the street. When he kisses Alexis, I want to scream at Alexis to do something. This boy loves her. Doesn't she care?

We watch Jeremy remove a stray curl that has fallen into Alexis's eye, and we hug him once he finishes hugging her again.

"That was scary!" Jeremy says.

"No, this is scary!" Charlotte says as she brings us all our computerized love questionnaire results.

I guess the little mini-explosion has caused forgiveness to spread at C.I.A. I think, as I see Charlotte smile at us and finally speak to me.

We all look at our results in triplicate since Charlotte has already opened them for us. Only she would take the time to gather love data before exiting the ramp for safety. She was amazing in the fashion show, too. I have to remember to compliment her once I stop shaking.

We exchange Soulm8tes lists to see what is so scary about the results.

Charlotte is right, as usual. There are only ten names on each love list because the computer only gives you your top ten matches in the entire school. And, according to Soulm8tes, Ebony's tenth match is the same as Emani's seventh match, which is the same as my first match. I frown when our so-called match walks over to us, mostly because I am disgusted. I can't bear the thought of Stephan Miles being my most eligible Valentine. I guess there's always next year for love to find me. I clean my off my new gym shoes, admiring the fact that they really do glow in the dark.

"Are you okay, Curly?...Red?...Sexy Lexi?" Stephan says to my sisters.

I watch him apologize to Jeremy about calling Alexis sexy, and I am repulsed when the two of them share a man hug like they're best friends or something. Stephan leans over to hug Charlotte, but she sits her green bag on her lap to block him. I love Charlotte. That slippery snake Stephan kisses her on the cheek, though. I detest him again.

Tyson walks over to tell Stephan something and we watch them chuckle before they share the fact that the back of Brenda's beautifully-beaded dress tore as she was exiting the stage. I hadn't even noticed that because I was so focused on Principal Wells and Dean Norton. Obviously, I missed Brenda's semi-striptease show, but of course, Stephan did not miss it at all. He and Tyson give us all of Brenda's undergarment details.

"You did a great job, Ebony!" Tyson says as he leaves with Stephan.

We all are in shock because Drama King Tyson hasn't been speaking to Ebony at all since the switch-a-roo truth came out.

Ebony's dimples deepen when she smiles, but she does not respond to Tyson. She watches the two boys in her love triangle walk away. Ebony's love triangle seems more like a love square or a love pentagon to me.

I compliment my friend Charlotte on her catwalk slide.

"I guess that little shake shook some sense into some peoples' heads," Charlotte says, as I look at Stephan Miles walking away with Tyson. Stephan Miles is such a stubborn, immature knucklehead. Yeah, some people.

*   *   *

A week later I watch Mr. Knucklehead Miles walk into the gym with his teammates to practice on the boys' basketball team's side of the court. I continue to shoot baskets until I hear his irritating voice behind me. Though I did miss his voice a tiny bit.

"So, how was your Valentine's Day?" Knucklehead Stephan asks as he hands me a cold water bottle.

I consider not accepting it, until my mouth reminds me of my thirst.

"It was great. I spent it with my sisters. We had a girl's night with our mother at the mall. Then we went indoor rock climbing. Mom says you can't let fear paralyze you or stop you from enjoying your life," I say, though I don't owe him any explanations of my whereabouts or activities.

I begin to dribble again and move about the court after I take a few more sips.

"Won't you come and sit on the bench with me, since you've been sitting here a lot lately?" Stephan teases.

He is telling the truth. I have been on the bench lately because my game has been off since the stage explosion incident. I usually have a sweet snap in my wrist like Stephan's mom, but lately I've been shooting air balls. Coach says I need to relax and unwind a bit. Coach Reed even suggested I get a deep tissue massage, so I did on Valentine's Day, but I still feel tense. I'm not afraid. I'm just a bit anxious.

As Stephan continues to tease me, Tyson walks into the stadium and tells Stephan that Tatyanna is being accused of tampering with the stage at the fashion show.

When Tyson actually notices me sitting here, he says a quick hi. Most likely because he is back in like with my sister Ebony. Ebony likes him, too. I'm hoping one of the guys from my Soulm8tes list will admit he likes me soon so I can keep my mind off of explosions and basketball. I don't have to fall in love. I don't mind falling in like.

Stephan claims he'll talk to me later, but I don't have faith in anything he says. I ignore him. I dribble. I shoot. Air ball. Ugh! I only smile because the ball almost hits Stephan in the head.

*

"You want a ride, Newbie?" Stephan asks as I walk toward the parking lot later with my teammates.

"I've got one, thanks, Knucklehead," I say as I try to talk to my gifted teammates.

I need as many tips as they can give me to get my game back sweet. Stephan continues to ask me the same question, despite my attempts to ignore him. Can't he see I'm trying to get some advice from my upperclass playmates? I don't want to speak to or ride with his no-class self.

My teammates and I watch Stephan park his car and exit the car to walk beside us.

"Eris, Could you help me with my jumpshot?" Stephan asks.

My teammates laugh since all I shot was airballs today.

Stephan teases, "How do you keep the ball in the air without hitting the basket?"

I smile.

"It's in the wrist, Stephan. It takes skill."

He offers me his hand. "Can you show me?"

"Stephan, I'm sure my teammates need me. Right ladies?"

They all murmur some form of no.

I grab his wrist. "Ok, Stephan. What's in it for me?"

He picks me up off the ground and begins to carry me toward the car, my teammates just wave goodbye to me and let him take me. What kind of a team am I on? Don't they care about me? I'm the youngin' on the team. It is their job to protect me. I watch them pretend to shoot jumpshots as we drive away. That's foul.

"I need to talk to you, Eris!" Stephan says as I try to exit the car. The sound of my real name coming from his mouth makes me close the door to the car. This must be serious.

"I'm going to be leaving C.I.A. I'm transferring to another school down south where my uncle lives!" Stephan does not seem happy about the information he is giving me, and I can understand why he'd be unhappy to leave C.I.A. since he has scouts coming to see him here next month—or at least that is what his new best friend Emani tells me.

"Why should I care?" I ask, as he drives me in the wrong direction.

Is he abducting me or something? We live south, not north! I ask him where he is taking me, but he doesn't respond.

"Eris, you may read some things about me after I'm gone, and I want you to know the truth. I don't really care what anybody else thinks of me, but I want you to know it all from me." Suddenly, I begin to focus my eyes on the road.

It is cold outside, but I feel warmer.

"Okay, I'm listening, Stephan."

The frosty breeze gets too strong to hear Stephan's words, so though I love fresh air, I let the window up so that he won't have to compete with Mother Nature.

As he drives, he tells me about a time when he used pain killers too much. He admits to once being addicted to them. He also tells me that he used drugs to bulk up his first year at school. I listen to him tell me some of his deepest secrets. Yet, all I am thinking is why is he telling me this stuff. He hates me.

"So why are you telling me this, Stephan?" He points out some Chicago landmarks before speaking again about his past mistakes.

Then, he tells me something I could have never prepared myself to hear. Stephan Miles works for the Dimes.

"I didn't want to work for them, Eris, but thanks to Kylie, they know all of my secrets. They know stuff that could ruin me. I'll never go to the NBA or the NFL if they decided to talk about mistakes I've made." I look at him, mostly because I am speechless, and looking is all I can do.

"Secrets? What did they make you do? Have you done illegal stuff?" I ask, until he takes his eyes off the road and looks at me.

"Kylie knew how I felt about you since the moment I saw you, but she had no problem making me get information on all three of you. They weren't worried about Emani, but they fear you and Ebony, so it was my job to get close to her in order to get close to you two. Kylie forbade me from showing any interest in you, since she knew you were all that I wanted. She threatened to tell all she knew about me and my momma. Nobody knows that Mary M&M Miles dated her college coach back in the day. They could claim favoritism. They could tarnish her records, her legacy."

I ask Stephan to pull over at the first parking garage he sees so we can walk and talk, but he refuses, saying he's said too much and he doesn't even know if we're being followed. Followed? I ain't scared of the Dimes.

Stephan pulls over into a garage after looking behind his car several times. I thought I was the anxious one, but he seems paranoid right now. We walk and talk.

"Besides Kylie, who do you work for?"

"I've never seen anyone, but Zyanne, Vita, and Kylie. I know there is one person higher, but I don't know who they are!" Stephan says as he tries to put his jacket around my arms.

After he sees the look on my face, he decides to wear his own jacket.

When we arrive at Navy Pier, we sit in silence for a couple of minutes. I am able to mentally outline each boat docked here, small or tall. Lake Michigan is a tub and each of these boats are rubber duckies floating on waves. Instead of a lullaby, the seagulls provide a stimulating soundtrack.

"Stephan, I have a solution to your problem!"

"But, I just told you, Eris . . . You have a solution already?"

"Do you want to hear it or what, Stephan?" When he frowns at me I decide to speak a bit softer to him.

"Let me hear it, Eris . . . it couldn't hurt."

I try to explain to Stephan that he doesn't have to quit. Sometimes the best defense is a great offense. If his enemies already know his weaknesses and are planning on using them against him, maybe he should beat them to it.

"You want me to put my drug use in the news. Are you serious? I think you still hate me. I have hundreds of scholarship offers that will instantly dissolve if they even suspected I used anything illegal," Stephan says as he stands near the edge of the pier.

"Stephan, you and Malcolm have written some great fiction about me. Here is your chance to write something real about how you overcame your problems and became the all-star athlete you are now. If you really are a journalist, prove it. Write and inspire some people to make better choices. Nobody expects you to be perfect, except for you."

He stares into the air like Alexis does when we come here to admire the skyline. I watch him closely as he tries to unravel the puzzle he is now in. He turns away from the lake and toward me.

"Um . . . Eris I did more than give the Dimes information on you. I am the one who spiked your water bottles with anabolic steroids." He steps back as if I am going to hit him after saying this to me.

Since he is out of reach, I consider running toward him and pushing him into the lake. He could have ruined my liver, my kidneys, my reputation, and my future. Tainted cold water bottles from Stephan Miles would have been my downfall. I am furious until I look at him.

When he lowers his head, I hold his hand. Silence.

"So what is the story behind your mom giving me her championship ball?"

He smiles a sly smile, still looking down at the concrete beneath our feet.

"Mom said she would only give it to a person she felt was meant to be my mate, and she would only give it to her if she felt I was ready to be a good mate, too."

"So what you're saying is I should probably give her ball back, Stephan. I'm only a freshman in high school." I could also say that potential mates should not poison their potential partners in life, but I choose not to dampen the mood.

"When my dad met my mother, she was in junior high. They didn't get married until much later in life. It's just a ball, not an engagement ring, Eris. There's no pressure."

He stands behind me and begins rubbing my shoulders. The nerve-racking, nail-biting, anxious feelings I've been experiencing for the past week seem to fade away when he touches me. I don't know if he absorbs all of my tension and anxiety, but I don't feel it any more.

I know how I could or should feel about him, but all I feel is like a winner. The Dimes tried to use everything they could to make me lose, but I still won. Even Mary Miles believes that I am a winner. I hope Stephan knows that I still feel like he is a winner, too. More importantly, I hope that he doesn't run away from a battle. I hope he chooses to play to win.

CHAPTER 25

Emani
The Ex of Your Ex

"You lose again, Eris!" I say as I beat her in yet another board game. We've played every game we have for amusement on our family night shelves, and I haven't lost yet. Eris bet me her allowance two games ago, so now she owes me her future fortune. Now, she wants to be my partner instead.

Maybe I'll take those new shoes she received from Stephan Miles that she can't stop smiling at. I wonder if Malcolm saw those shoes Stephan special ordered for Eris. Malcolm used to have a crush on my sister, too. Stephan convinced him not to pursue Eris, and look at who is buying her shoes now. Malcolm is probably kicking himself somewhere.

Well, the shoes have been working, because Eris has been winning on the court, but at home, I've been the champion. I'm the game night family champion of the week. I even beat Alexis on her favorite video game.

I think it is my trips to Rickey's school that have given me my confidence. I went to his school during our winter break and a bit since then, but he and I haven't really been talking on the phone since the new year began, because he has been working so much and for personal reasons. He sends me an occasionally friendly message, but I haven't received any thought-provoking hand-written love notes. Though I haven't seen him, he has continued to help with Alexis's recovery so I can't complain.

Besides, I didn't go back to the school for him. I went to choreograph a step show routine for the lovely ladies of Alpha Delta Sigma sorority at his university. The president of the sorority contacted me and my dad took me down there to help with their routine. When dad couldn't take me, Jeremy drove me there. It took quite a few weeks, but I coached the sorority girls to their first step show victory in years.

Believe me, it was a challenge, because I am a natural dancer, but not a natural coach or choreographer. I had the ideas in my mind, but I had to find a variety of ways to get them to make my vision a reality. It was fun showing them how to remember the routine.

It was even more fun seeing them perform my steps and stomps for a very picky crowd. I need to thank Ms. Jennings and Coach Calderone for teaching me how to teach others. I was hard on the Alpha Delta Sigma's, but when we were finished, their dance routine was amazing.

Despite the unforgiving crowd, the sorority girls were flawless in their performance, and I have it all recorded on video: every step, every hand gesture, and every twist and turn.

*

My sister hands me the phone, most likely to distract me so Eris can win, but I can beat this girl with two hands tied behind my back and my eyes closed. She just isn't any competition for me tonight. I have my Robertson confidence turned all the way up to high.

"Hello," I say as I deal the cards to my opponent, who has now become my partner.

I recognize the voice on the phone instantly. I drop the phone to the floor. Eris smiles at her hand puts a card on the table. Ebony and Alexis stare at one another across the table. Then, Alexis puts down the same suit of card. It is the king of hearts, which lets me know that I am probably going to lose this hand, since I have a hand full of baby hearts.

"McKayla, how are you? I'm sorry that I missed your call on V-day, I was with my mom and my sisters. We are actually playing games right now." I say, trying to get off of the phone before I hear the word I know she will be saying soon.

"Why is Rickey dating Rachel? I spoke to him on Valentine's Day and he says that he was on his way to dinner with her. What happened to you two?" Rickey's ex-love McKayla asks.

Eris forgets that she is my partner and slams a spade down on my queen of diamonds. I just shake my head at her need to win everything. Then, I remind her we are now on the same team. She makes fun of my laugh as I lay on the sofa, trying to speak to Rickey's true love.

"I was just the rebound girl, McKayla. He still wants you. Rachel tried to tell me that, but I wouldn't listen. I think he sees me as a little sister and not his girlfriend. I can tell you still have feelings for him. Don't let me get in the way! I really want to be with him, but not if he really wants to be with you!" I look at the baby hearts in my hand, trying to figure out a strategy on what card to play.

Eris screams for me to come back to the card table to play, but I do not move from my soft spot on the sofa. I love the feel of suede against my skin. It really beats dad's cold leather sofa on his "man" side of the rec room.

"Emani, do you remember my dance with Rickey on New Year's?" When McKayla asks this question, I remove my mouth from the phone and silently scream before I speak to her again. Of course I remember her dancing with my boyfriend, leaving me alone on New Year's Eve.

"Yes!"

"On the floor, I knew he was looking at you, so I asked him why he wouldn't just go over to you and dance. Do you want to know what he told me?" McKayla inquires.

I really hate when people ask questions that have only one obvious answer, but I do respond yes.

"He told me that he thought he wouldn't find anyone that could ever take my place until he found you." I can hear a smile in her voice, but I am not smiling.

I don't want to take anyone's place. I'm not auditioning to be someone's back-up dancer to fill in when they can't dance. I want to be the starlet. I want to be the prized performer.

"Oh, great! McKayla, I guess I should run up to his school and beg him to take me back now," I say as Eris pleads at my feet for me to come and play with her. I know she won't quit until she wins at least one game tonight, so I get up.

"No, but you should go back before Rachel steals him completely. She is willing to do anything to keep his interest. She doesn't have his heart or his mind, so believe me she'll try to go for his body." McKayla says.

"What do you want from him, McKayla?" I ask as my sister tries to pull me back to the card table.

I guess I am walking too slowly. Eris is too strong to fight, so I decide to sit back down and play with her. I may just let her win so she won't put any bruises on my body. I threaten to step on Eris's new shoes. She leaves me alone for a minute.

"I don't want anything from him but friendship. Our love was puppy love. It wasn't real. I've moved on and so has he. I like being your friend and his." McKayla speaks with such candor that I believe her instantly.

"Well, you are going to be very disappointed, because I am not going to chase after him. A wise person once said that I am worth too much to chase a boy, and I believe him. If Rickey wants me, he'll come to me, and if he doesn't, we weren't meant to be." I say before I hang up with McKayla to finish my card game with my competitive sister.

I am really not surprised that Eris and Stephan Miles have become such a good couple. They both are aggressive spirits forever in search of their next conquest.

I pick up my hand filled with hearts. I wish I had some different cards. Eris is going to kill me if Emani and Alexis beat us.

My phone vibrates and I look down to see words I haven't seen in what feels like an eternity: "Can't w8 2 C u, 2 B with U, 2 hear ur voice, Call me please!!! Your friend, Rickey."

Before I can dial the numbers, my dad walks in to tell us some news about Jeremy. We see him smiling so we know it is good news, but knowing my father, it could be anything. He and Jeremy could have finally finished that race car that is just sitting in the garage, or he and Jeremy could have negotiated Jeremy a million-dollar music recording contract, since dad claims he is Jeremy's agent. Who knows with the two of them.

"Okay, girls. Jeremy just told me that some singer named Ashanti Sullivan is going to use one of his beats on her new album. He's upstairs playing it for your mother. That Stephan boy is up there too, Eris," Dad says in his completely clueless way.

Doesn't he know that Ashanti Sullivan is the best singer in the world? Doesn't he know that I wake up to and go to bed to her music every day? Doesn't my dad know how cool this is?

*

I watch Dad smile at and hug Jeremy upstairs, and I realize that my dad could not care less about Jeremy's deal with Ashanti Sullivan. Dad is proud of Jeremy for following his dream and succeeding at something he loves. Dad feels like Jeremy is his son, and he looks at Jeremy as only a proud papa can.

I'm not even a bit jealous of Jeremy, because I am following my dream, too.

Alexis does not come upstairs with us. Jeremy definitely notices that she does not, but his mother and my mother take his mind off of Alexis by teasing him about the first time he played his saxophone. Jeremy's mom says Jeremy played all day and night until his lips bled and he sounded like a duckling when he finally spoke.

I walk downstairs to try to convince Alexis to come upstairs to see her man and to congratulate him or something, but she is downstairs playing with my phone.

"You can't hide from fate, big sis!" I say to Alexis, as she smiles.

She knows Jeremy is meant to be with her. Mom says the key is to find a guy who loves you more than you love him. If that is true, Alexis and Jeremy will be married for a lifetime one day.

Alexis hands the phone to me when I ask her what she is doing with it or to it. The phone is already ringing when she gives it to me, so I put it up to my ear. Who has my sister called?

I watch her walk upstairs, still smiling, after I hear his voice.

"Ummh yeah . . . hello, Rickey!"

"YOU called. I didn't know if you would call. Do you have time to talk? Can I come to your house to talk to you?" Rickey asks.

I lay on mom's soft suede sofa and ask him to talk to me over the phone.

"What was that? Who was that in the background?" I ask as I sit up on the sofa.

When he says Rachel's name, I stand up and walk over to dad's cold couch.

"Nah! You should stay where you are. We have company tonight. Jeremy is here and I don't think he would want to see you. I don't think I want to see you either," I hear him say my name as I hang up the phone, but I do not dare call him back.

I just stare at my phone hoping it will ring. Why is love such a game?

Unfortunately, he does not call me back either. Was I immature? Did I overreact? I don't think so. I think I was right. It's late. Why is Rachel with him this late at night? Where are they?

*

It has been a week and Rickey still hasn't called. I have almost called him a few times, but I resisted the urge to do so. I put my phone in my duffel bag and slip off my sweatpants so that I can dance. Last night, I went to Ms. Jennings's studio just to dance away some of my anger. How could he call me and be with her? At any rate, I have a job to do. It is my job to inspire C.I.A. students and staff to dance.

The C.I.A. boys' basketball team will win tonight. We never lose. C.I.A. dominates in every sport: football, volleyball, basketball, tennis, and everything else played with a ball, net, team, squad, or partner. Yet Princeton's players are giving us a true challenge tonight. Usually, they play hard, but tonight you would think they were getting paid to play, or at least paid to destroy Stephan's dreams of ever playing college ball.

I hope Stephan can pull out a win from his bag of tricks. He better show those scouts some of those gifts he claimed he had in his news article three weeks ago. We all read his article, titled "The Magnificent and Marred Miles," but now he needs to show his critics why he is worthy of a second chance.

Stephan Miles wrote his own tell-all article on himself. The subtitle was "There are no shortcuts." He said something about life being a mile race and athletes needing to run every lap. He claimed he was a gifted athlete who tried enhancing his gifts without good-old fashioned hard work. He brilliantly told his story to all of C.I.A. and whoever else reads our online paper, but that story will mean nothing if he doesn't win this game.

If Stephan loses tonight, the news reporters will probably say he should have used less marijuana to increase his appetite and popped fewer potent pills. If Stephan wins, they will probably praise him for turning his life around. It is just the way things go.

I hope all those private practice games he's been having lately with Eris at his house are going to pay off for him tonight. His fans and critics are wondering what will be his outcome. Will it be success or failure? I am rooting for him. Stephan needs to win. He forgave me. I forgive him.

The dance we do pumps up the crowd, but I can only hope it is enough energy in this auditorium to inspire a victory. The crowd chants Stephan's name when he steps back onto the court. His mom and dad hold hands in the crowd. When Stephan begins to dribble, Mrs. Miles stands up to cheer him on. She pulls Stephan's dad to his feet. Though Mr. Miles has always been reserved when I've I met him, I can't help but laugh when I see him start to scream at the refs when they call a foul on Stephan again. I have never seen Mr. Miles raise his voice or show such emotion.

I don't know all the rules of basketball, but I do know that Stephan is in foul trouble. I've been on the sidelines enough to know most of the rules. I can also see the clock. Time is running out. C.I.A. is three points down, and Stephan Miles, our number one scorer, is in foul trouble. Our coach sends him back on the floor after taking a quick final time out.

I finally find my sister Eris on her feet in her new favorite gym shoes amongst many lively fans and skeptics in the stands. She told Alexis, Ebony, and I that she wasn't going to come to the game tonight, but we all knew better. She may not love Stephan yet, but we all know she is quite fond of him, whether she admits it or not.

Stephan takes what I think will be the last shot of the game. There are only seconds left. The majority of the crowd joins Eris by standing to their feet once the ball releases his grasp. I watch it spin through the air. It hits the rim and bounces high into the air. Stephan turns to look at Eris and shrugs his shoulders. When I look away from the two of them and at the ball, I see it fall in through the hoop. The game is tied. He fans himself like he is on fire and the crowd goes crazy.

I didn't ever realize there could be a tie. I guess that was a three-point shot.

When the game begins again, Stephan is on the bench. Eris sits pouting in the stands. Oooh, I can't wait to tease her about that. Mr. and Mrs. Miles still hold hands. It is not until the very end of the overtime that Coach puts Stephan on the floor. No points have been scored, so it really is only a need for one point, but even I know that you get two points per basket in basketball, unless it is a foul shot.

The player who has been attacking Stephan all night comes at Stephan just like I saw Eris do a few nights before on Stephan's home court. When Eris did this, she stopped right in front of Stephan, causing him to get some type of a foul, so I know this guy is trying to do the same thing to him. Stephan seems to hear my thoughts, because he anticipates the guy's moves and spins around him, jumps and dunks the ball.

C.I.A. wins. Eris gets another kiss before I can even get one kiss from anyone. When will I ever get my first kiss?

*

Coach Calderone and Kylie Calderone walk over to Stephan, and I watch Kylie hug him, though I know she is probably feeling miserable right now.

According to Eris, Stephan has already told his mommy about Kylie bribing and pressuring him, and Mary Miles has already told her sister Cassidy how Kylie has been blackmailing her son. Kylie may not be in trouble at C.I.A. yet, but she sure is in trouble at home with her family.

Coach Calderone marches behind Kylie like a drill sergeant training a new recruit. I wish I could say I feel sorry for Kylie Calderone, but I do not. Family is all you have in this world. How could she hurt her flesh and blood? I hurt Stephan, too, but he has forgiven me. Maybe, he will forgive her, too.

CHAPTER 26
Ebony
Backstage Beware

Forgive me. Forgive me. Forgive me.

Dr. Thomas repeats her question, "Did you tell my husband to come and see me, Ebony?"

Dr. Thomas asks this question as she rubs her humongous belly.

"I may have mentioned that a few months ago," I confess.

I take a few steps back, just in case she can still swing her arms. Though I doubt she can, as I look at her booming belly.

"Ebony, I'm not going to hit you, silly child. I came here to help you, since you helped Terrence and me to get back together; to fall back in love with one another. It is because of you that he did not give up until he saw me. I mean, the man stalked me at work, home, and play until he found me. He knows that all of the weight I've gained is because of our baby now, and he has promised to give up searching for that lunatic lady who killed our only son."

When Dr. Thomas hugs me, she says Zachary's name. Though it is faint and almost inaudible, it is the first time I've heard her say his name since the "incident." I squeeze her a bit, but not too much, since she is probably carrying someone extraordinary in her womb. Someone extraordinary like Zachary Thomas once was. He was a gift to all of us.

"So what is with the presents? Aren't we supposed to bring you gifts? You're the one having a baby," I say when I see four shopping bags in Dr. Thomas's hands.

"You can bring gifts to my baby shower next month. These are for you girls. They come with a bit of an explanation, though."

I scream to my sisters to come down stairs after I peek into my own shopping bag. Dr. Thomas somehow knows my favorite color, or did my hair give it away? Alexis, Emani, and Eris come down the stairs. Eris is eating, as usual, but she does put her fork down long enough to hug Dr. Thomas.

I watch Dr. Thomas caress Alexis's face for a minute before the two of them embrace. Dr. Thomas has an obvious favorite out of the four of us, but who can blame her. Zachary Thomas loved Alexis, and he probably would want his mother to love her, too.

"Well, Terrence told me about your money investigation," Dr. Thomas says when my mother walks in with grocery bags.

We know she is talking about the Dimes, but I guess she doesn't know that my mother already knows about the Dime investigation. Mr. Thomas has told her details about both of his investigations, and even a few that he didn't tell me. For example, Mr. Thomas told my mother about his plan to fake his death to fool Payton Payne way before it happened. We only found out about it because of Mom. Mom knows everything.

"I already know about it, Doc so keep talking, but put some groceries away while you talk. You haven't had that baby yet. This might help you to encourage labor," Mom says as she hands Dr. Thomas the milk.

She quickly snatches it back when Dr. Thomas says she is only seven months pregnant. We all stare at her huge midsection and call her a liar. That is not a seventh-month belly.

Tevin and Kevin come in and grab each one of Dr. Thomas's legs. They want her to pick them up, but of course she cannot. She does stoop down to their levels long enough to kiss each one of my little twin brothers. I am shocked when they do not wipe her kisses off. They always wipe off my kisses. Little brats!

"I'm having twins, but I don't know their gender. Anyway, like I was saying . . . ." Before she can finish, we are all holding or touching her belly.

Mom says any woman having multiples should be prepared to become public property. Alexis even puts her ear to Dr. T.'s belly. Wow! I hope that if I ever have children in the far far far far future, I will only have one baby at a time.

Though we are in awe, Dr. T. explains how she asked a very famous friend of hers who is a very prestigious designer to exclusively design the purses that she has brought here for us today. She tells us that once she saw the purses, she just had to buy us outfits to go with them, since she knows our birthdays are this week.

Dr. T says that Detective Thomas had a very complicated plan for catching Brenda Agbayewa shoplifting. She says he gave out Brenda's picture to every posh place he could find in New York, Paris, and California, since we told him that Brenda, her sisters, and their mother only shop at the most expensive and exclusive boutiques in the world.

But when Brenda did come in to shop at one of them last week, a salesperson followed her so closely that it infuriated Brenda enough not to even attempt to shoplift. So Dr. T. came up with the plan to tempt Brenda with these chic, one-of-a kind bags. Dr. T. says her designer friend only made seven of them. She only makes seven of everything; that is why her fashion line is called Seven.

"I think it is a great plan, Dr. T, but Brenda is a professional thief, and we can't rely on our school cameras to catch her. She'll have all four of our bags home before we even know they are gone," Eris says as she begins to chomp on a salad covered with poultry.

That poor bird didn't know it would have to die just to end up in Eris's belly with a million other pounds of protein. Eris is such a carnivore.

"See, that is why I asked my friend to build in a GPS sensor." We all explain what a GPS sensor is to Emani when she acts like she doesn't know anything about global positioning. I don't believe her ignorance about GPS. Emani is probably tracking Rickey and Rachel as we speak. My sister is so good at playing dumb.

"So if, no, when she steals the purses, we will know where they are?" Emani says, as we all congratulate her on solving such a complex riddle.

I swear that girl can pretend to be dim-witted better than any damsel in distress in any fairytale ever written. Emani reminds me of one of my favorite fictional characters, because like Lilly Laramie, Emani is quite clever, but she knows how and when to hide it. Nevertheless, I know she has a reason for acting dim, and I ain't falling for it.

"Hey, I think Emani should be the person to lure Brenda first." When I say this, Emani starts to frown.

I knew it. She wants to keep the purse. Her fake ditsiness is all about the purse. She was going to play the "poor Emani" role so Eris or I would have to be the bait. Wow! What won't this girl do for a designer purse?

I can't believe she had the nerve to talk about Kylie selling out her cousin Stephan to the Dimes. Emani and Alexis have fashion designer's names all over their walls. They would do almost anything for fashion. I want to travel to see the world and do community service. They want to travel to be front row at fashion week. However, unlike Brenda, Emani and Alexis would never steal.

"Eris should do it! I like my lilac purse. What if Brenda does make it home before we catch her in the act? Then I'll never see this beautiful handbag ever again. Seven is my favorite number."

Yes, I know I am supposed to be the actress, but Emani should be on that stage Friday night instead of me. She would probably get a standing ovation in Tyson's play. Emani could probably out-act Tatyanna Tyson.

Once Emani realizes she is being ignored, she stops whining, allowing Mom, Dr. T., my sisters, and I to discuss the plan a bit more. I am quite glad to have these wise women on my side instead of against me. The Dimes are in for a battle that they won't even see coming.

"Have the Dimes cooled down a bit? My husband says he hasn't spoken to you much lately. He sent some equipment here, too, for you guys, since he is no longer investigating that lunatic lady. It's in my Jaguar." Dr. T. smiles at Alexis as she mentions her new Jaguar, because she knows it is Alexis's dream to drive a Jaguar the moment she gets her license.

Mom and Dad don't believe in us getting expensive cars for our first cars, even though Daddy could easily make it happen. Mom and Dad say that their first cars were old clunkers and ours will be, too. It is sooo depressing.

Dr. T throws her keys to the Jaguar to Alexis. Emani and Eris decide to follow Alexis out to the car to get the equipment. I bet you they wouldn't volunteer to help get the equipment if Dr. T. rode in a clunker.

"The Dimes have not cooled down at all, Dr. T. We believe that they poisoned Eris's boyfriend's dogs and tried to burn his house down last week, but we have no proof that it was them. Everything always looks like an accident. Stephan's dog is okay, but the house has fire damage. We also suspect that it was them that turned our school's Olympic-sized swimming pool's water red and wrote that threatening note against us. They didn't mention our names, but they said someone was going to end up in the E.R. We are three of only a couple of handfuls of girls in the school with the initials E.R. I'm the only one with the initials and the red hair." I walk to the door to open it for my scrawny sister.

Emani punches me in the arm almost as hard as Eris would when I call her scrawny.

Mom holds up a few of her special ingredients for our birthday cupcakes as I hold my sore arm and give Emani my evilest glare. Though I am in pain, I am also so excited. Tomorrow we will wear our new outfits with our new purses. Purses created without animal cruelty. For once we will not have a debate about what to wear.

Tomorrow we will wear our birthday crowns, or at least I hope Eris will wear her crown. Tomorrow we will share our birthday cupcakes with our true friends at C.I.A. The Dimes won't even get to smell them, let alone taste them. No sweets for those rotten Dimes.

"Happy birthday, Ebony," my once-Drama King Tyson says as he hands me a little red teddy bear.

We haven't been speaking to one another as much, but ever since the stage fell down at the show I modeled in, he has been just a bit nicer to me. His sister almost got in trouble for causing the collapse, but of course what little evidence Dean Norton and Principal Wells thought they had miraculously disappeared. Tatyanna is free and clear from any charges.

Even the student teacher, Mr. A., who first said he believed he saw Tatyanna Tyson on the balcony later changed his story, too. I guess maybe he and Zyanne had more than a crush going on, because she is long gone and Dr. A. still is afraid to speak up. Anyway, Tatyanna will be acting on Friday right beside me, though she is most likely the stage smasher.

"Don't eat that!" Tatyanna says as she smashes my deliciously-homemade cupcake.

I unhappily watch the cupcake hit the floor. Then, I grab another one and eat it in two bites before she can smash it. What is wrong with this girl? She stares at me as if she expects something to happen to me. I know she isn't concerned about my calorie intake so what is with the smashing?

"I thought . . .You're okay?" Tatyanna says, as she scratches at her flawless face.

Maybe I should get her autograph now, because with her ability to switch personalities, I know she is going to be a movie star one day. Well, if she isn't in jail or something.

I eat another bite of the pizza my mom had delivered to the school for us. Everyone in the lunchroom seemed to want a slice as we walked to our table. It is nice to be envied for one day out of the school year.

I feel lightheaded even before I finish the bite. I grab my throat because I feel like I can't breathe.

BLACKOUT

> *Tyson kisses me so softly. He says I love you, Ebony.*
> *I know my sister is evil and you are going to put*
> *her in jail for hurting people if she is the head of*
> *the Dimes, but I still love you. Be my girlfriend.*
> *Be my love. He kisses me again and again.*

"Are you awake, Ebony? Wake up, Ebony Robertson!"

Was that the sound of our school nurse? Did I pass out? When I wake up in the ambulance I realize that I did in fact pass out.

"It was your allergies, Ebony. Thank God for your EpiPen. Your sister saved your life," Nurse Sue says.

Please don't let it be Emani. Eris and Alexis would not ever even mention saving my life, but Emani Robertson will never ever let me forget it.

"I'm so glad you're okay. I love you, big sis," Emani says at the hospital, after putting her purse on the table next to my bed. She hands me the red teddy bear Tyson gave me before I lost consciousness. I kiss the teddy bear and name him Tyson.

"You are so strong, Sis. Mom says the last time you had a reaction to peanuts and you almost died, but look at you; you're fine," Eris tells me Tyson caught me before my face hit the lunchroom floor.

Alexis squeezes my hand.

"Tatyanna knew. She did this to me," I say, but my sisters tell me that Tatyanna confessed to them that it was Kylie and Dime Number One who planned this one. They claim that Tatyanna cried when she confessed, but I personally know that Tatyanna Tyson can cry on cue. I still think she cannot be trusted.

"Maybe she is the Number One Dime and she is trying to gain our trust. I don't believe her," I say this to my sisters, but they don't seem to believe me.

"She tried to save your life!" Emani says, as she slides a curl from her teary eyes.

"No, one of you saved my life. Who was it?" I ask, wondering who is the one who stuck me in my thigh with that EpiPen needle and saved my life. They all just stare at me without saying a word.

"We got Brenda, Ebony!" Emani says to break the tension in the room. For a moment, I can't even remember who Brenda is, but when I glance at Emani's Seven purse, I quickly remember.

"You left your dying sister to go and try to catch a Dime. Wow!" I say, as I watch the nurse fill my cup with water.

I ain't drinking that. I don't trust anything unless I know who or where it came from. Alexis must know what I'm thinking, because she gets the nurse's attention and points to her bottled water. The nurse frowns, but agrees to go and get me one. Where is my momma?

Mom walks in with Dad beside her.

"Okay, baby. Your dad and I let you guys handle the Dime thing because you said you wanted to do it. You also said that they were just bullies. Bullies don't try to kill people. Bullies harass. Bullies fight. Bullies hurt people's feelings. Murderous maniacs try to kill people. Your dad and I want to end this thing with the Dime gang. We are going to go to Principal Wells and Dean Norton. Then, we are going to go to the police." Mom strokes my hand so softly that I do not even try to debate with her.

Maybe she is right. We are just teenagers. Maybe we need help.

"I'll help you!" Tatyanna Tyson says as she walks in with Tyson and his luscious lips. I look over at my birthday present, my little, red Tyson teddy bear. There are many words to describe Tyson: tempting, tall, talented, and too good to be true. But there is only one word to describe his sister Tatyanna: terrible.

Tatyanna starts with the tears right away this time, but I am not impressed. I'm not impressed until she says she is willing to give us everything that she knows on the Dimes if we can promise to protect Tyson.

Mom and Dad try to convince Tatyanna to go to the principal and the dean, until Tatyanna says she does not know who the head of the Dimes is. Tatyanna tries to stress the importance of not going to the authorities until the true identity of the top Dime is found, but I do not know if my parents are willing to listen.

"Your daughters have scared the Dimes. We were once impenetrable, inseparable, but now we are divided. We've turned on each other. Our meetings are not the same. Our meetings are non-existent. We rarely have our mandatory five people in attendance. No one trusts anyone, and everyone is scared of what the other may do to her. I don't know what they'll do to me, but I am willing to help you guys. Now is the time to find the head of the snake and cut it off. Believe me, if you just chop off a few pieces, the Number One Dime will just regroup and transform into a new, more deadly creature." Tatyanna says, as Tyson rubs her shoulders.

"What is your secret?" I ask, just to test if Tatyanna is truly willing to let us inside her world, or if she is just sharing another well-rehearsed monologue.

I am shocked when Tyson begins to speak for her.

"My parents were killed when we were very little. We were bounced around among relatives until we finally landed with our paternal grandmother. Grandma hadn't really planned on raising tween twins, but she tried her best. She wasn't fun, but she was functional. What she wouldn't do or couldn't do with us, we did with each other. We learned to entertain each other. I guess that's why we can act. We've been acting for a long time."

Tatyanna smiles a bit when he says this. She looks at him with love. She looks at him the way I look at my sisters and sometimes my little twin brothers. The Robertsons are a clan that will never be divided. I guess the Tysons are the same.

"Well, Tatyanna got it in her mind to try to end some of our pain one day, and I agreed to it. However, instead of ending up in heaven with our parents, we ended up in the hospital. Then they tried to put Tatyanna in a mental institution. She began cutting herself in places people could not see, at first. Then she quickly advanced to cutting her arms and legs, before ultimately trying to take her life twice with no success. That is when my maternal grandmother stepped in. We've been living with her ever since then. Tatyana's records are supposed to be protected, but I believe whoever heads the Dimes has access to school and medical records. I think Dime Number One knows all," Tyson says, as Tatyanna lowers her head.

I didn't expect her to share such an intimate secret. Maybe she can be trusted. Maybe.

"Ebony, Eris, Emani, Alexis . . . I have been ordered to hurt you many times, but I haven't. I did do the stage thing, but it was for fear of my own and my brother's lives. I tried to warn you about the stage and the food. Life is important to me now, and I did not want to die. I know that I'd die if they ever hurt Tyson. I also know that our, rather, The Dimes' leader has something you want, and I am prepared to get it for you, if you can promise that you will get her," Tatyana says as she rises to leave.

She says we need time to think about her offer.

"By the way, girls, the purse thing was brilliant!" Tyson says as he leaves.

I wish my dream earlier was real. I wish Tyson would walk back in here and kiss my forehead, my nose, my cheeks, my lips . . . .

Tyson walks back in before he can kiss my hand. "Ummh, sir. Do you think I could come over when Ebony is well to see your car collection? I'm a big Votti fan, and I hear you know him. You worked on his car?" Tyson says to my dad.

"Yeah, Votti owes all of his NASCAR victories to me. What good is a dynamite driver without an excellent engine? He drives and I give him something worth driving," Dad says as he walks Tyson out of the room.

I can hear them talking as they leave.

I blow a kiss at them both, though they are gone.

"Girl, you are so crazy! Dad is gonna steal that boy and you ain't never getting a kiss!" Eris says, as she calls to check on Stephan on her phone.

I almost gag when they start to do that kissy-face stuff on the phone. I can't believe she is putting her lips on that bacteria-packed, germ-filled phone. Yuck!

"Don't be jealous, Ebony. You'll get to kiss Tyson on Friday!" Emani says as she holds my hand.

Mom looks at me and smiles, but she doesn't smile too big. Her smile says "you can kiss him in the play, but not in any other way."

"Mom, did you see Tyson shake his head when you said you know Tatyanna will be safe? That means he doesn't believe you. Can we really guarantee she'll be safe?" My mother gets on the phone to make some calls without answering me.

Tatyanna convinced Mom not to go to the Principal or the Dean yet, but Tatyanna did not convince Mom not to do all in her power to protect us.

* * *

I look around the sterile hospital room at my sisters. The room looks plain, but we look great! It's our birthday. We can't let the Dimes ruin our day. Despite their best efforts, I am still alive. I think we should play charades or Pictionary or something. I feel good enough to draw some pictures or do a little impromptu acting.

"Hey, where is my purse?" I say once I realize that I am the only one missing my new prized possession.

"Your purse? Umm . . .well during the commotion, Brenda stole it, and now principal Wells has it for evidence," Emani says as she grabs her luxurious lilac purse before I can reach it.

"Well, then I'll just take yours!" I say as I try to take Emani's, but I quickly realize I am still a bit weak from everything I went through.

She holds her designer bag tighter than I've ever seen her hug Rickey.

Mom stops talking to whomever she is talking to and tells us to stop fighting.

"Ebony, your sister saved your life. Don't steal her purse!" Mom says before she begins to speak on the phone again.

When mom says this, Emani speedily says that it's no big deal, but I know that it is. She saved my life. My little sister saved my life.

*

The doctor said that I was healthy enough to perform in the spring play, but I still feel a bit ill. I feel ill until Tyson walks over to me and holds my arms. I love when he gives me his big pep talks. Suddenly, I believe I'm an Academy Award-winning actress instead of a girl who just learned how to memorize lines a few months ago. I feel like a powerful speaker instead of a poor former stutterer. I will do this because I can do this!

"You can do this, Ebony. Break a leg!" Tyson says, as the narrator finishes his monologue that opens the play.

Everything is in fast forward until we get to the scene where we kiss. K-I-S-S. Ms. Scott told us to kiss and stop and kiss and stop and kiss and stop when she trained us, so that the audience could get the full effect, but Tyson decides to give me one lengthy lip-lock instead. I like to improvise. Improvising is good! We kiss just long enough for me to take in the moment before we separate.

"Your death scene was perfect!" Tyson says before exiting to perform in the final scene. In this scene, he is supposed to beg the king of the gods to bring me back to life. Once his wish is granted, I become his mortal wife. Aphrodite, who is his immortal wife, is forced never to bother the two of us again as long as I live.

After the play ends in happily-ever-after style, the actors, the crew, and Ms. Scott take our bows on stage. We receive a standing ovation, but Tyson receives another one when Ms. Scott tells the crowd that Tyson actually wrote the play with his sister.

When Tatyanna comes out on stage, the crowd rises to their feet to celebrate her again. She receives flowers from a few more of the boys in the audience, but I'm sure the flowers that mean the most are from her role model, Denzel Smith, who has been sitting in the front row for the entire second half after sneaking in through C.I.A.'s side door.

Emani asked her coach to try to get Denzel Smith to come to the play months ago when Emani first started mentoring a group of Coach Jennings young, budding dancers. We were planning on using Denzel Smith to trick Tatyanna, but now that he is here on good terms, I am glad it is for a good reason. She really does respect him as an actor and a family man. I bet she will just faint when she finds out he is coming back stage to see her later.

*

Tatyanna faints on stage. It is not the fake faint Ms. Scott taught us actors when we first began practicing for "Goddess of Love." Ms. Scott's fake faint requires you learning to use your body to cushion your fall. Tatyanna's faint is real. I watch her fall to the floor with only her wig to cushion her head as it hits the floor.

My mother's medical muscles flex and she is on the stage before Tyson and I can even get to Tatyanna. Mom says she believes Tatyanna was stung by a bee and bit by a spider. I watch her pull out the bee's stinger. Then, I watch her puts something near Tatyana's nose that wakes her up. Mom searches Tatyana's costume for a spider. As she does this, I turn to look for Dimes in the crowd. When I do turn around, I see a silent audience turn into a frantic one.

"There are spiders everywhere!" Tyson says though it is quite obvious once the stage and theatre lights are on.

Mom grabs Tatyanna and heads toward backstage. I follow her toward the exit when Tyson says he has to go back and get his grandmother. There are elderly people and babies here at the performance. The Dimes have too much money and not enough respect for other human beings. I know it was them. C.I.A. may not be able to pass a white-glove test for cleanliness seven days a week, but this didn't happen because of cleanliness. These spiders are here to cause harm.

Back at the hospital, I sit next to Tyson, who is holding his grandmother's hand. I try to comfort him, but he seems so stressed that I do not know what to say.

"Will you hold my hand, Ebony?" Tyson says, and of course I hold it. I listen to him tell me of his sister's last life-threatening reaction to bee stings. I share a few stories of the Robertsons' bouts with allergies, until Dr. Mom comes out.

Tyson stands up.

"Oh, you can sit down, sweetie. She'll be fine. The bee sting was bad, but it was that bite that I was worried about. Have you ever seen what a brown recluse spider does to human flesh? She's going to be fine. It is a good thing my friend found that spider. It is always best to bring in the tiny culprit," Mom says, as she rubs her hand across Tyson's head.

Mom's friend, who is also a detective and friend of Mr. Thomas, gives us an update on the school. He even makes us laugh when he tells us that he and his undercover buddies have dealt with a lot of complicated criminal circumstances, but nothing like a spider attack. Though we laugh, I know that my enemy is serious about harming us, and I am glad that there weren't any more serious casualties.

*

"How are you doing, Spiderwoman?" I tease Tatyanna when I enter her room the following morning. She points to her neck and asks me how bad it is, but it is covered, and I can't see anything.

"Tyson went on the internet and found a lot of horrible pictures of spider bite victims, so I am afraid," Tatyanna says, as I shake my head at Tyson.

What kind of a comforter is he? You don't scare people in the hospital. I tell Tatyanna that I bet she would have been able to even perform in the play tonight if they hadn't cancelled our performance.

Tyson must begin to feel guilty about scaring his sister, because he suddenly declares his devotion for his sister and promises not to leave her side until she is released from the hospital. Tatyanna instantly forgives him.

"Hey, I wanted to give this to you after our performance tonight so you would be able to concentrate on the play, but since it is canceled, I know you will want to see it now," Tatyanna points to a box that is sitting in the corner.

It has my favorite color ribbon on it.

I suddenly feel guilty that Tatyanna did not get a chance to see our secret gift to her, Denzel Smith.

Tyson urges me to open the box, since he doesn't know what it is either. When I open it, there is a red folder inside. The name on it almost takes my breath away. The folder says Ms. Payton Payne. Tyson's face seems puzzled as he looks over my shoulder at the contents of the folder.

"I have seen everything in this folder before, Tatyanna. Where did this come from?" I ask.

Tatyanna sits up in her hospital bed with a very angry look on her face.

"You've seen everything! Do you know what I had to go through this week in order to steal that folder, copy it, and put the original one back?" Tatyanna says before plunging backward into her pillow.

Tyson rushes over to his twin sister to massage her forehead.

I look over the contents of the folder again hoping that there is something I have not seen in what looks like the same information that was in Mr. Thomas's enormous, stolen Payton Payne file. Why would the Dimes care about Payton Payne?

After a slower, closer look, I notice a couple pages from an old newspaper. The yellowish newspaper is folded so that page 3 is showing, so I read the third page for clues. At the bottom right side of the page I see a story on a boy named Philip Payne found beaten to death near a park in my old neighborhood. The paper seems to suggest that the boy could have been a member of a gang. I read on to page seven, where the story is continued. There is no mention of Payton's name, but the last name of the boy is enough for me to investigate.

I close the paper and walk over to Tatyana's bed to tell her what I found interesting in the folder. She smiles when she sees that her hard work was not in vain. There is one thing in that folder that we need to know ASAP: who is Philip Payne?

Tatyanna thanks me for Denzel Smith being in the audience. I am pleased that she did see him before she fainted.

"I can ask my friend Reana if she can get any information about Philip Payne. Her family owns an international chain of funeral homes. They have one in that area. Maybe they handled the funeral," Tatyanna says.

I show Tatyanna the date on the newspaper so that she knows that it was ten years ago.

"Wait, are you talking about Reana Powers?" I ask as, Tyson and Tatyanna look at me like there is only one Reana at C.I.A.

I could tell them that there are three Reana's at C.I.A., but why argue. I know better than to try to come between relatives, especially multiples.

"Yeah, Re-Re is my best friend. Her picture is on the wall across from the main office where she works. I know you know her. Everyone knows Reana. She is the face of C.I.A.," Tatyanna says.

At first, I consider not mentioning that we suspect Reana, but I can't risk Tatyanna telling her best friend any information, so I tell her that Reana is on our top-ten list of suspected Dimes.

Tatyanna laughs despite her pain. She touches the area where she was bitten. It's amazing how something so small could do so much damage.

"Reana is the sweetest, kindest, most honest person I know. She would never hurt anyone. I couldn't even tell her I was a Dime because I know she would be against it. She hates the Dimes! Haven't you read her brave quotes against violence and bullying in *The Pulse*? She was even attacked by the Dimes her first year of school. They vandalized her parents' business and spread untrue rumors about her and her family. Plus, she would never hurt me or Tyson. She has a crush on him. Don't worry—Tyson is all yours, Ebony."

Tatyana's speech sounds good, but I have learned to protect myself.

"Let's not tell anyone! Maybe Reana isn't the queen of the Dimes, but maybe she is friends with her. Until we know who the queen is, can we agree to keep outsiders out?" I ask Tatyanna, as she folds her arms and rolls her eyes, refusing to believe anything negative about her best friend.

Tyson reminds her that my sisters and my plans have been working so far, and she reluctantly agrees with him. We will not share any information with anyone, best friends included.

"I won't say a word to Re-Re, but we need a plan soon, Ebony. I got the folder, but our anonymous leader somehow always knows, sees, and hears all. I don't know what she'll do if . . . when she finds out."

CHAPTER 27

Eris
Dime in Training

"How did you find me?" Kylie Calderone asks me, as I walk up to her at her grandmother's house.

My sisters said that I should not physically punch her, so I decide to do it mentally. When I finish telling her what a miserable person I think she is for hurting Stephan and Tatyanna Tyson, she starts to cry. If she really knew me, she would know that tears do not work on me. I hate tears!

"I'm here to offer you one chance to redeem yourself, Kylie. I offer you this chance only because you are my boyfriend's flesh and blood."

Kylie shares her goal of wanting to be the Number One Dime with me. She tries to help me to understand why she wanted the crown, but I can't understand her willingness to sacrifice everything just to rank first amongst evil human beings. The Number One Dime gave her an envelope, but she chose to do the crimes.

"What do you want me to do, Eris?"

She seems so weak right now. She seems nothing like the drill sergeant who once gave my sister pure hell. It saddens me to see her hiding from the Dimes. She hasn't even come to school for a week now. It is a shame. She has been discarded by them and she was willing to sell her soul for them. Kylie Calderone can't offer the Dimes anything now. She's already given them everything.

"Whatever it takes. Will you do that, Kylie?" I ask, as I smile at an Easter picture of Kylie and Stephan as toddlers on their grandmother's mantel.

*

Later, handsome yet impatient Stephan interrogates me when I enter his new bedroom in his parents' makeshift mansion—the other one is getting repaired for fire damage. "What did she say?"

I open the door a little wider so that he can see that Kylie is with me. She runs over to him to apologize. I watch them embrace.

Once the love fest is over, I tell Kylie and Stephan the first part of our plan. Ebony and I decided that, since we do not know who to trust, we can only let people know parts of the plan. Kylie has to prove that she can convince the rogue Dimes to help us before we can even begin to trust her. If she can get the Dimes to follow her, we may be able to tell her how we plan to take down both mass murderer Payton Payne and the nameless Number One Dime. However, we have to strike now, while the Dimes are weak, separate, and full of fear. We will use their own methods against them in order to destroy them.

* * *

"I found the cemetery!" Charlotte says when she meets me at Zippie's.

I'm listening to her, but I am also watching for Kitten to enter. According to my research, she is supposed to work here at the restaurant tonight. Tiny is supposed to be working here, too.

Charlotte whispers how she found the location of Payton Payne's son Phillip's tombstone to me as I watch Kitten's boyfriend Tiny (Timothy to Kitten only) take Alexis's order.

Alexis walks away from the counter with her burger, fries, and shake. I don't know how Alexis communicates with people without words. It still amazes me. People somehow know what she wants without her having to say a word. I need that gift.

"Eris, how sure are you that Payton will visit her son's tombstone?" Charlotte says after telling me that she has stopped smoking cigarettes, thanks to her boyfriend Dylan's help. Vita Rowe and Shiani Chan's ex is now my friend's boyfriend. Wow.

Charlotte confided in me a long time ago that she had started secretly smoking after her accident. My sisters and I were all curious about why she had those matches to start that fire in our school's east elevator, but I was the only one who didn't mind asking her.

She was very honest about using cigarettes to cope with possibly having to be in a wheelchair for the rest of her life. I was equally honest about my disdain for cigarettes. I told Charlotte that if her dad could invent a way for her to be able to drive, she could learn how to overcome her addiction to nicotine. The impossible is always possible.

Stephan and the best artist at C.I.A., Dylan, sit down next to us in our usual booth. Stephan tries to convince Dylan to draw him on the cover of some sport magazine that Stephan wants to own one day. The self-centered dreams of some boys make me laugh.

I listen to Dylan brag on the painting of his beautiful Charlotte in her wheelchair that he feels earned him a full scholarship to college, but when Kitten walks through the doors, I instantly get up. I don't even know what else Dylan or Stephan said after Kitten walked into Zippie's.

Charlotte stops me and hands me the ten-dollar bill that I am supposed to give to Kitten. It has a secret message to her on it. We tried to keep it simple, but I know Kitten knows her own code by heart, so she will know what it says right away. I know I wrote the message correctly. I triple checked it.

"Did Kitten give you the ear pull signal?" Charlotte says in front of Dylan. I just shake my head no, though I am not pleased that Charlotte is talking about our plan in front of outsiders.

Dylan is a good guy, but he has also been both Vita Rowe's and Shiani Chan's boyfriend before, too. In my mind that means the odds are two to one that he is against us. Once a Dime lover, always a Dime lover. Charlotte likes him, however so he will be a part of our plan. I prefer a simple plan with fewer people, but Charlotte's mind works best in complexity.

"Charlotte has been doing so well. Did she tell you guys she stood up on her own?" Dylan says, before Charlotte interrupts him.

Even I know that Charlotte never wants to talk about her progress in therapy. Her parents have taken her to every specialist in the world to help her to recover, but she doesn't want to get her hopes up too high. I know she is happy about her improvements, because Charlotte's face can't ever hide her happiness. When she is happy, her eyes sparkle, her lips widen, and her cheeks become the size of golf balls. If Dylan is part of the reason for her happiness, I guess I can give him a chance. People do change. Kylie has. Tatyanna has. Well, at least I believe they have changed.

After watching the two of them flirt a bit more, I ask Charlotte to come with me to the restroom so that I can ask her how much Dylan really knows.

"He knows everything that I know. He is the one who helped me to find out the information about Payton Payne's son's tombstone," Charlotte says.

I trust Charlotte, so I have to believe she isn't blinded by Dylan's professed love. I know how blinding love can be. We don't know if the Number One Dime is male or female. Could Dylan be working for the Dimes like Stephan was?

"Do you think Kitten will agree to meet Payton Payne with you?" I ask Charlotte, since she has known Kitten longer, but I do believe in Kitten.

I believe that she is on our side. She may be a Dime in training, but she is our friend to the end.

Later, Charlotte and I wait in Tiny's (Timothy's) living room for Kitten to arrive. When I look out the window, I see Vita Rowe drop Kitten off in front of Tiny's house. My heart does a triple beat. Maybe it was a bad idea to meet here.

"Why are you here?" Kitten says as she frowns at Tiny (Timothy).

After he admits to allowing us to secretly meet her here, he hugs her and looks into her gray eyes, complimenting her as only he can. She seems to forget that Charlotte and I are even in the room.

"Ummh, Kitten, we only have a week, so let's get on with the plan," Charlotte says after Tiny leaves the room.

"Who said I would help you?" Kitten says as she walks so close to me that I can taste her mint green breath.

"Are you trying to get hurt? They see all! You don't think you're being followed. I cannot be seen with you. I am too close to finding out who Number One is," Kitten says.

"I thought you already knew! Plus, this isn't about the Dimes. Didn't you read the code? We need you to help us take down Payton Payne so we can use her to get to your Number One Dime."

"Are you sure you aren't just using the Number One Dime thing as an excuse to get to your true enemy?" Kitten asks.

"Are you sure you aren't consumed with revenge for them deciding not to keep you the first time they offered you a spot on the Dimes?" I rudely ask Kitten, since she sort of hit me below the belt by bringing up Payton Payne.

Kitten kicks Tiny's mother's sofa just when his mom is coming into the living room to bring us some lemonade. I start to laugh nervously, but Kitten quickly tells Tiny's mother that she thought she saw a spider on the sofa. Tiny's mother starts to look for the invisible spider.

When Kitten mentions the spiders, I am sick in my stomach again. Did Kitten help them plan to take Tatyanna down? Is she still our same sweet Kitten, or is she the Dimes' new favorite pet until she runs out of her nine lives?

"Like I said Kitten, we need you. You have certain gifts. Are you willing?" I ask, as Tiny's mother goes into the kitchen to look for some bug spray.

I watch Kitten claim that she killed the spider with her shoe when Tiny's mother returns.

Tiny's mother smiles at her and goes back into the kitchen to finish cooking.

After three minutes of silence watching Kitten look through her notebook, Kitten says yes to helping us, but she says we have to do things her way. There can be no hidden video. There can be no secret cameras.

I watch Charlotte apologize again for Kitten's family's faces being shown on our TV as needy families, and I watch Kitten tell Charlotte that she knows it was not her fault for the tenth time. I am so proud of the both of them. Friends before Pretends. Finally, we have our Charlotte and our Kitten back.

"We can do it your way!" I say to my friend Kitten.

"So when do we do this?" Kitten asks.

"Not yet, but soon!" I say.

*

I hit another ball into the corner pocket of our pool table, though Stephan tries to distract me. I will win this game. I hate the fact that he beats me sometimes. I'm supposed to be the winner in the relationship. Stephan steps from behind my elevated derrière when my father comes down stairs. I bend over more to get the perfect angle. Then, I sink another pool ball into the side pocket of the pool table.

"So Stephan Miles, you've dated all three of my daughters. Which one is your favorite?" Dad says, before Mom hits him on his arm with her magazine.

I miss the next ball completely. Stephan doesn't answer right away, so I hit him with the pool stick. Then, he decides to say I am his favorite.

"My brother and I both dated my wife before she chose to marry me," Dad confesses to Stephan.

Stephan laughs, but my mother does not.

"Wow! Really?"

Mom says that my dad and his brother tricked her with a switch-a-roo. Then, she says she thinks she married the wrong one.

This time, my dad rolls up his magazine and hits Mom on her arm. When they start to smooch, Stephan and I both look away simultaneously. Disgusting!

When we turn around, they are still making out. Ugh!

My little brothers come downstairs and turn right back around when they, too, see our parents kissing.

I wouldn't mind trading places with my sisters right now. I'd do a switch-a-roo so I wouldn't have to witness all of these parental pecks. Ugh!

"No, I guess I married the right one!" Mom says as she invites Dad to sit beside her on her soft sofa. Dad sits on the cold leather one and invites her to come and sit with him.

Stephan and I head upstairs before we find out who won that battle.

"I love your parents!" Stephan says as he tries to eat some of my chips.

"I love yours, too, but I don't like to share. I don't like to share anything. What's mine is mine. Remember that when you go to the NBA or NFL, or wherever you end up." Stephan laughs, though I am completely serious.

He removes his hand from my bag of chips.

My sisters come downstairs to tell me that Charlotte is on her way in. I try not to act surprised, but I was so nervous that maybe she would not make it out alive. I hoped that Payton Payne would believe Charlotte and Kitten's stories of being bullied, since they are both true, but I didn't know if she would really be there to visit her son's grave. I guess Kylie was telling the truth. Payton Payne does visit her son's grave once every year.

Kylie says she believes she can convince the AV girls, Ciera and Darcy, to help us with our plan, since they are no longer loyal to the Dimes. And I believe Tatyanna will help as much as she possibly can to bring down Payton Payne so that Payton will bring down the Number One Dime.

I just hope that Payton Payne does not find out about my connection to Kitten and Charlotte. My last name is Robertson, and unfortunately, Payton Payne probably remembers that last name. It has only been a couple of years since the Paynes destroyed a certain Robertson's will to live and ability to speak.

Alexis sits beside me with a notepad, and I try to explain to her that none of us can be directly involved in the plan. She does not blink, but I know that she is upset with me. I was never Alexis's favorite, but I know for sure that I am not her favorite today when I ask her to leave the kitchen.

Alexis looks around the kitchen at all of the people who will play a part in our plan before she walks out. I hope she knows that I am trying to protect all of us.

*

"You should have seen Kitten, Eris. She didn't even sweat. She was fearless. Payton had bodyguards everywhere. I'm sure she had some snipers that we couldn't even see, but Kitten spoke to her as if it was just the three of us at the cemetery," Charlotte says as she passes me a piece of paper with what I believe is some sort of a riddle on it.

Before I read it, I stare proudly at my two brave girlfriends. I don't know what I would do if I were that close to Payton Payne. They were both so fearless.

"What is this supposed to be?" I ask as I hand it to Ebony. Charlotte smirks as Ebony tries to figure it out, too. The paper travels around the room and back into my hands.

"Do you guys give up?" Charlotte says, with too much enthusiasm.

Didn't she just meet one of the evilest people in the world? Why is she so happy?

"It's a riddle. Kitten says she believes it is the time and day we are supposed to meet with Payton Payne again. Kitten already convinced Payton to meet us in a public place. It was so cool. Kitten suggested three places and she told me that she made sure the last place was the one she wanted. But she seemed the least excited about it. Payton agreed to have a sit-down meeting with the information on the Dimes at Kitten's mom's new restaurant, Kyla's Kitchen, just as Kitten hoped she would," Charlotte says. I stare down at her in her wheelchair, wondering why she is so joyous. This could be a deadly, dangerous meeting. Payton Payne is pure evil.

I look at the paper and figure out that the time is 3 p.m. I also figure out that the day is this Sunday.

"Payton Payne believes she will know the identity of the Number One Dime and all of the other Dimes in one week?" I ask, as Charlotte shakes her head yes, still smiling from ear to ear.

Payton Payne is rich, cruel, and more arrogant than I ever thought she was if she believes she can solve a mystery that has taken us almost an entire school year in one week.

"How much did she request for payment?" Ebony asks.

"That was the best part. I mean. Kitten almost had her in tears telling our story and all of the devilish deeds of the Dimes. Payton feels like she is a savior or something for the bullied. Kitten kept complimenting her work. You would have thought Payton was a hero. Kitten was so witty, the way she convinced her to meet at the restaurant, but when she started explaining how her family used to be homeless and my family may be rich, but a lot of my money goes to my rehabilitation, Payton decided that she could wave her R.U.N.PAIN organization's normal fee. Kitten even admitted how rich her grandmother is, but Payton had already made up her mind. It was priceless!" Charlotte says as she grabs my chips and begins to eat my last precious few.

Those crumbs are always the tastiest ones. Why don't people respect the fact that I do not like to share? I stare into my now-empty bag of chips.

"You can't hide anything from Payton Payne. Kitten was smart not to do so. Let's just hope Payton won't discover that we all know one another. We have to plan everything today, since we will not be able to communicate all week," I say as I look out the front and side windows of our house.

I wonder if Charlotte was followed. Hopefully this is a sacred day for Payton Payne. Hopefully she is mourning the loss of her son and not researching who Kitten and Charlotte are. But, if I know Payton Payne, she is doing her homework, so we'd better do ours.

"I wasn't followed, Eris. I've been watching my back for a long time. I know that I was not followed," Charlotte says as she opens her green book bag and begins to share both her and Kitten's ideas with us.

After Charlotte gives her ideas, I try to share a few of my own, but Emani and Ebony open and close their hands like an alligator's mouth to tell me that I talk too much, so I stop.

We'll stick with Kitten's plan. If she really is the closest person to the Number One Dime now that Zyanne Jeffries is gone, I guess she knows what she is doing, or at least I hope for all of our sakes that Katherine Kitten Johns knows what she is doing. I know that Payton Payne knows exactly what she's doing. She's been causing pain for a long, long time. It's what she does best.

CHAPTER 28

Emani
The Perfect Plan

"What are you doing, Alexis?" I say when I go upstairs to check on my big sister.

When I see the twins' old baby monitor is in her hand, I realize that she has probably been listening in to our entire conversation downstairs.

She does not even try to hide the baby monitor from me.

"So you know the plan, Alexis?" I ask, as she looks directly into my eyes.

"Do you think it is a good one? Tap your foot or something if you think it is a good plan." When I look at her feet she does not tap. I don't worry, because that doesn't really mean anything. Alexis only moves, gestures, or responds when she wants to. I may be her favorite little sister, but I am not surprised that Alexis won't even move for me.

I sit next to her and put the shimmering lip gloss that I just bought for her on her lips. I've been trying to convince her to go to go with me to see Jeremy's live recording with Ashanti Sullivan Sunday at his studio, but she has refused. I know Sunday is now going to be a very busy day, but I really feel she should be there with him while we try to get some evidence against Payton Payne and Dime number one. I don't want to miss seeing him or Ashanti Sullivan, but his recording is at noon. Eris says we all have to be in our positions by 1:00. I wonder if I can do both. What if Sunday is my last day on this earth? Shouldn't I spend it fulfilling one of my dreams? I love Ashanti Sullivan. I'd love to be one of her dancers one day. Plus, I love my sister and want her to be with Jeremy.

I get up to leave when I hear Ebony screaming for me to come downstairs. When I get to the door, I feel a pillow hit me in the back of my head. When I look at my obviously guilty sister, she taps her foot on the ground. The plan is Alexis-approved.

I knew I was her favorite.

Drama King Tyson and Stephan stop me at the top of the stairs before I can go down. I threaten to kick both of them, but they do not move. Tyson asks me to put on a blindfold. Is he kidding? I try to walk down the stairs, or at least through the two of them. When Stephan realizes it will be a rough fall down the staircase, he says that I have a visitor downstairs who wants me to wear the blindfold. I instinctively look down the empty staircase, but I do not see anyone. If it is who I hope it is, I think I should put on the blindfold.

"The blindfold looks good on you, Curly, but now WE can push YOU down the stairs," Stephan's voice says. He and Tyson tease and taunt me about that switch-a-roo swap with Ebony as they guide me down the stairs, step by step. They remind me that they never did get their revenge. I am now a bit more nervous, as I allow them to blindly lead me down our staircase. A dancer cannot fall. They wouldn't push me, would they?

"I don't believe in revenge, guys. You should forgive me," I say.

"We do forgive you!" They both say together.

"Do you forgive me?" I know it is Rickey's voice, but I can't find the courage to remove the blindfold.

"Do you forgive me?" I answer his question with a question.

"I drove here again with Rachel to apologize, even though the last time I came here with her, you wouldn't even let me come in!" Rickey says.

I remove the blindfold so that I can tell him how I feel about him bringing my enemy to my home, and I see him in my living room, holding a little statuette of a bronzed ballerina from Telia's collection. It is the very same statuette he promised to buy for me on our first date. That little ballerina from the window is now in my home in his hands.

*

Rachel holds another statuette, as does each of my sisters. When eavesdropping-Alexis comes downstairs, she has one in her hand.

"When did you do this? How did you do this? How did you pay for this?" I say.

"Well, I know I couldn't just buy one for you from the collection. You Robertson girls are all about multiples. I missed Valentine's Day and your birthday, so I'm trying to catch up. Plus, I got another good job. I want to take you there tonight," Rickey says as he reaches for me.

I hug him as tight as I can because I really do not want to be without him again. I watch my sisters make the little statuettes dance and twirl in the air like me. The little brown ballerinas are so lovely.

"Emani, I'm sorry that I tried to take advantage of your separation and your relationship troubles, but once Rickey told me how he felt about you, I did stop," Rachel says as she tries to hand me the last statuette in the Telia Royalty collection.

I do not let go of Rickey. Rachel places the statuette on our living room table. Everyone else does the same with theirs. I cannot believe I have more Telia statuettes than Coach Jennings. She is going to flip when she finds out.

I smile at Rachel, shake her hand, and look up at Rickey and ask him where exactly we are going tonight.

"We're going to see my light show at the Circus!" Rickey says.

Ebony and Eris let go of Tyson and Stephan's hands long enough to come over to me and whisper for me not to ruin Rickey's surprise. I can't believe I never told him that I am afraid of clowns. I am really afraid of clowns. I can't even convince my legs to walk, until Rickey leads me toward the door.

Alexis walks in front of us with Rachel and Rachel's real boyfriend that I met at the comedy show. Mom and Dad wave goodbye to us once we are in our cars.

"Are you ready to go, sweetheart?" Rickey asks such a simple question, but I don't really have an answer.

He kisses me on my forehead and my cheek.

Hmmh. Maybe he'll kiss me for the first time tonight. Maybe I can think about the kiss or those beautiful statuettes and not those evil, scary, multicolored clowns.

* * *

"Mom, Rickey's light show was amazing! Rickey really got us some great tickets, so we were right in front. I even enjoyed the cyclists and the contortionists, but those clowns still scare me. What are they hiding under that make up? Why do they paint fake smiles on their faces? What is with those baggy, raggedy clothes?" I give my mom a quick update on my date with Rickey and a few more details on the traveling circus he has a contract with now.

She tells me how sweet she thought it was for him to ask her and Dad's permission to begin dating me again. She thinks he is a keeper. I know that he is definitely a keeper, but the clowns must go.

"Only a fool would give Rickey up!" I say, as my mother and my sisters frown at me.

"So you're a fool?" Ebony says until I give her an evil glare and a pinch to remind her that I saved her life.

"What I meant to say is only a fool would give Rickey up again. I'll never give up on him again," I say, as the Robertson females share a laugh at my expense.

Ha! Ha! Ha! I laugh, too.

*

"How expensive is Prom?" I ask when I overhear Eris and Ebony talking about junior-senior prom with our parents.

I know for sure that Eris would prefer to wear any one of Brenda's gowns as featured in the fashion show, but I hope that Ebony will wear one of my designs. They've been treating me like an outsider, since I am the only Robertson female who will not be attending the prom this year. I'm not dating a junior or a senior. I'm dating a college student.

"Too expensive! No, too expensive times three," Dad says as he tries to exit the kitchen.

"You wouldn't say that if Alexis was going with Jeremy! Don't you like Tyson and Stephan? Is Jeremy your favorite?" Eris asks.

Dad runs his fingers through Eris's three-minute hair to try to mess it up and tells her that she'll never know. Her hair falls right back in place like always.

"We don't have a favorite. Stephan, Tyson, Rickey, Jeremy: we dislike them all equally!" Mom says as she exits the kitchen after Dad.

I know my parents are joking. They like our boyfriends. Well, at least I know they like mine.

*

The remaining Dimes do not know of our plans this weekend, but they seem to be getting as much bullying as possible done this week. Brenda, Vita, and Shiani are an inseparable trio at school. Whereas Kitten and Winter seem to be the dynamic duo. Little Winter Gordon always seemed so out-of-place with them to me anyway, but Kylie says that Winter really is a fire starter, a true pyromaniac.

The fire alarm rings.

We hear principal Wells over the intercom saying that this is not a drill.

"Most of the Dimes are graduating in two weeks. Why would they set the auditorium on fire?" Ebony asks once we are outside with the rest of C.I.A.'s student body. Maybe the fire and police department will solve this case for us, I think, as I exit the building and line up with my classmates outside in the rain.

"I think these flames were probably just a test of Winter's loyalty. Kylie says the nameless Dime number one has asked everyone to prove their loyalty lately," Eris says, as we watch a few fights break out on the school lawn.

It is chaotic, but we four stand on the lawn back to back. Alexis looks north. Eris looks south. Ebony looks east. I look west. If a fist flies this way, we will react. I don't believe in revenge, but I do believe in reaction.

*

Later, our recruited former Dimes (Kylie, Tatyanna, Ciera, and Darcy) wait for our reactions after they remind us of some of the crazy stuff we did this year. Well, mostly they talk of the crazy stuff they did or tried to do to us. They tell us how they were told to strike back and how they feel they never did even the score. I listen while trying to learn from the former AV girls, Drama Queen, and Lady Light.

"Emani, I can't believe you put that video on the web. It was hilarious. Emani sucks . . . lemons, lollipops, and her thumb. The pictures were so funny. We've brought people to tears just by writing what we wrote about you, but you made it into a joke. Your response got more comments than our original video," Ciera says as she admires our hidden cameras.

She has some state-of-the-art equipment of her own, but she and Darcy are fascinated with ours. I guess the audio-visual girls may learn something from us after all.

"You will plant these at the restaurant for us before you set up at the pet store down the street?" Ebony asks as, the AV girls say yes for the tenth time.

"Don't worry, we will take care of all video. We'll have Payton Payne from every angle. You'll see her every flaw, if she has any," Darcy says.

"Payton looks flawless on the outside, but inside she is rotten to her very core!" I say as, Tyson practices his lines.

He is our backup just in case we cannot get sound. It will be his job to let Kitten and Charlotte know whether they need to speak up, since he will be acting as their waiter. We may need him to wear one of those wires we found amongst Mr. Thomas's equipment. Ciera and Darcy are still trying to make sure they can figure out how the hidden wire works.

"You do remember that I saved you from getting into trouble for that powder explosion, Ebony!" Tatyanna says as she smiles at Ebony.

Ebony thanks her.

"Yeah, but Tatyanna, or should I say TNT, is the one who planted the powder," Kylie says as she gives Eris and me our ear pieces.

Rickey and I will be in the kitchen. Eris will be across the street at Charlotte's supply service with Stephan. We believe Payton will not allow us to keep the files on the Number One Dime, so we have a plan to copy them. Stephan is the fastest runner, so it will be his job to bring the files to Eris to copy.

"Who stole my clothes from my swimming locker?" I ask. They all look at me as if I should know the answer to that one.

"Brenda?" Their silence tells me that I am correct.

We discuss and review the plan again just in case, but we are all more than ready for tomorrow. By tomorrow, the runaway Dimes will know who is the true leader and we will finally get Payton Payne to confess.

"I don't want you to do it!" Rickey says, when I tell him all the details of our plan on the phone.

I quickly remind him how he promised he would be there with me tomorrow. Then, I listen to him whine about my safety and the plan being too risky. He threatens to call the police and tell my parents. Is he serious?

"No risk, no reward, Rickey. What if you hadn't taken a risk? We wouldn't be together right now. Trust me. It will work out. Payton Payne will give us the evidence on Dime Number One and we will get Payton to admit to her crimes, too."

Though I tell Rickey this with confidence, I am more nervous when I hang up with him. I once said I'd take whatever risks I had to take, but tomorrow I'll . . . we'll be risking our lives.

After church Sunday morning, we typically go to have our traditional breakfast as a family. It is probably more like brunch, but Dad likes omelets, so we go no matter what time it is when our pastor finally stops preaching.

Today, Pastor was not long-winded, so we are out at 11:00. We sit down to eat at 11:11. I know the times, because Alexis points to my watch to show me.

As I eat, I begin to worry about what is going to transpire at Kyla's Kitchen later on today. I'm glad I do not have to look my enemy in her eyes, but I hope that when I do finally see Payton Payne, it is because she is being punished for wrecking so many people's lives.

I look at my sister Alexis and think of how beautiful she is, how talented a singer she once was, how great a person she could have been had Payton not completely ruined her will to dream, speak, and live. Alexis is recovering, but she is someone new because of Payton Payne. Alexis is not the person she was two years ago.

Alexis points at my watch for the third time.

Dad starts to tell us how proud he is of our courage, strength and honesty, and as I look around the table, I read guilt in all of our eyes. I'm surprised that our parents can't see it.

Dad congratulates Ebony on actually getting her student of character award this time, and I almost tell him everything we have planned today.

Alexis stomps my foot under the table.

She gestures like she is playing an instrument when I look at her. I smile. She stomps my foot again. This time, she takes her fork and begins to pretend to sing. I smile and tell the table about the first song Alexis sang to me.

Alexis stands up and puts her napkin on the table. She waves goodbye to us. I feel so dumb when I finally figure out that she wants to go see Jeremy's performance. I tell my parents I'm going to walk Alexis down the street to Jeremy's studio. Dad says how frustrated he is that he has to miss the session, but he has to drop off a car he's been working on to a friend before we drive all the way to Aunty Jay's new house tonight for her special announcement to the family.

When I give him the signal, Rickey reluctantly offers to drive my sisters and I to Aunty Jay's so that my parents can spend more time with their friends before we get together as a family. Dad quickly agrees, before Mom can say that she wants us to ride as a family.

Alexis, who is too eager for words, points at my watch yet again.

"Why didn't you just say something?" I say when Alexis and I get outside.

She stares at me. I laugh, but she does not. She kicks at me, but I move before she can bruise my body.

Alexis is walking so fast that I have to do a bit of a jog just to keep pace with her.

"Do you know what you're going to say to Jeremy?"

She stops walking when I say this. Uh oh. Maybe I should not have said that to her. She turns around and starts walking back toward Priscilla's Pancake and Waffle House. I run in front of her and turn her around in the direction of Jeremy's studio.

"Your presence will be enough, Alexis. He just wants you. Kylie told me that she tried and failed to get his attention. Many girls have tried and failed to get Jeremy's heart. I don't know if Ashanti Sullivan is trying, but according to every gossip magazine I've read about her, she is only three years older than he is. She is allegedly single. Do you really want to let her have him?" I ask this, hoping my sister will be motivated to make a move.

Alexis stops walking. I watch her twist the necklace Jeremy bought her for their anniversary around her index finger. When she points to my watch, I tell her that we need to get to the studio before his session with Ashanti begins in ten minutes.

We run.

*

I scream in my loudest voice, "We ARE on the list. This is his girlfriend. They know us here. We've been coming here to this studio for at least a year. Just go ask Jeremy. Tell him that Alexis and Emani Robertson are here to see him."

I can't believe this security guard suddenly has amnesia when we've been coming here before this place even had one celebrity guest performer. Ashanti Sullivan is here one day and now he suddenly wants to do his job. I've never spoken to this particular security guard, but I've seen him in the studio many times, pretending to guard people.

Ashanti Sullivan's manager comes out to tell us that the session is only open to people on the list. He hands us an autographed picture of her in an attempt to pacify us. Mom says neither Alexis nor I ever sucked on pacifiers or binkies or whatever they're called. I guess we aren't easily satisfied or pacified.

Alexis grabs my hand, pulling me away from the entrance. When she pulls me to the back parking lot, I smile, thinking we will just sneak in a secret back door or something, but I do not see a door of any kind back here.

I do see Alexis getting on Jeremy's motorcycle. When she starts it up, I decide to get on the back. I love my sister, but boy, am I nervous. It has been a while since we have had one of Dad's illegal driving lessons.

Alexis revs up the engine and heads past the line of folks standing outside and straight for the front door. The security guard with the poor memory tries to block the door, but when he sees that she is not slowing down, he opens the door.

Once we are inside, I jump off the bike and run behind Alexis toward studio B, after picking up the keys she drops on the red-carpeted floor. We may need these later.

When Alexis opens door B, Ashanti Sullivan is inside, but Jeremy is not. I run to Ms. Sullivan for the chance to take a picture with her, forgetting for a moment my purpose for coming to the studio. Alexis reluctantly snaps the picture with my phone.

Jeremy walks in with the rest of his band.

When Alexis walks closer to him, he begins to twirl his own keys. Alexis twirls her set of his keys. The two of them do not say one word to each other. I am actually the only one talking. I'm talking to Ms. Ashanti. She is so cool!

"Why are you here, Alexis? Did you and Rickey break up?" Jeremy says as he steps over toward the microphones.

"Umm, Rickey is all mine! Watch your mouth, brother. Alexis came here for you!" I say, before I compliment Ashanti on her outfit and her flawless makeup.

I love her lashes and whatever shade of blush she is wearing. Her brows are perfectly arched. Her edges should be on the cover of a hair magazine. She says she buys her own clothes and does her own make up. Maybe I could be a stylist to the stars or her backup dancer.

Trying to make up with Jeremy, Alexis opens her arms for him to hug her, but he just slips his guitar strap over his head and walks away.

"I don't want to be third choice, Alexis. If Zachary were here, you'd choose him. If Rickey were here, you'd choose him. You don't love me. I'm the only one who uses those words, remember. I think you should leave," Jeremy says as he shows his drummer how he wants him to play.

The forgetful security guard comes in after knocking on door B three times. He doesn't forget to tell Jeremy about our motorcycle incident in the lobby, however.

"Alexis is number one on the list. Why didn't you just let her in?" Jeremy asks the pretend security guard.

It is a great question. I can't wait to hear the answer.

"Ummh, it just says 'Lexi' on the guest list," the not-too-bright security guard says.

"That's my name. Alexis Dieona Robertson, also known as Lexi to the . . . man I . . . ." Alexis says. Alexis speaks!

"Love . . . She wants to say the man she loves. Give her a break, Jeremy. She hasn't spoken this much in two years," I say, even as I notice Ashanti Sullivan has a huge diamond ring on her finger.

I know Jeremy did not buy that ring. He may have a recording contract now, but he hasn't got that kind of five-carat flawless diamond money yet. Maybe she really is still engaged to Stephan's hero, Roderick Isley, of the Chicago Polar Bears. Gossip columns can be wrong sometimes.

"Is that what you want to say, Lexi? Do you want to say, 'I am the man you love'?" Jeremy asks.

She asks him for one of the microphones in the room. I sit down next to Ashanti Sullivan and prepare to hear a voice I haven't heard since I was a middle schooler.

My sister sings,

> "Those three words are so hard to say
> When the last time I said them my love went away
> But you're my future, not only my past
> That love, it ended; our love will last
> You're more than my love; you're my friend
> You've stood by me through thick and thin
> You've been my voice, the wind beneath my wings
> You know my heart and you're the reason it sings
> So today I sing those three words
> The three words from me you've never heard
> You I love, you love I
> I love you and you know why
> Because you're my future, my present, and my past
> Because you may not be my first love, but you'll be my last
> You're more than my love, you're my best friend
> You've stood beside me again and again
> You've been my voice, the wind beneath my wings
> You know my soul and you're the reason why it sings
> My soul sings I love you
> My hearts sings I love you
> Jeremy, I love you
> You love me and I love you, too
> I love you
> I love you
> I love you."

The band, Ashanti, and I clap and cry, but Jeremy is still standing where he was standing. You can hear the people who came to listen to the recording session outside cheering, too. I hope they know that was not Ashanti Sullivan singing. That angelic voice was the voice of my big sister, Alexis Dieona Robertson. Ashanti hugs my sister and tells her the song was touching.

"Can I hug you?" Jeremy asks before he squeezes my sister.

Alexis kisses him.

When I look away from their long overdue lip-lock, I look down at my watch and realize I need to get going. I am tempted to just leave Alexis here, but I still fear my sister, so I ask her if she wants to go with me. My other sisters should have found a way to separate themselves from our parents by now.

"No, I think Jeremy needs me here! I know you are going to do just fine." Alexis says as she hugs him again, and hugs me, too.

After seeing Jeremy and Alexis together, I can't wait to see Rickey again. A week ago I was getting a great hug like that one. I couldn't hug him at church or at breakfast, but I will hug him when I get a chance tonight at Aunty Jay's house. If I get a chance.

*

"Are you trying to sabotage our plan? I told you she didn't want us to try to get revenge, Eris." I remind my sister.

Eris responds, "It isn't revenge, Emani."

"We are just trying to make sure Payton Payne never does what she did to us to anyone else," Ebony says, after I exit the studio.

My staying here with Alexis has only made us a little bit late. We'll make it there on time.

"Was that Alexis singing? They wouldn't let us in," Eris asks, as the security guard with memory loss looks strangely at the three of us.

"Are you . . . ?"

"Yes, we are triplets" I say, before he asks the obvious question.

"Triplets? Oh, that's nice, but are you on the list?" the security guard with amnesia says, as we three get into Rickey's car.

Rickey kisses me on my cheek and tells Ebony to stop giving me a hard time for being a bit tardy. Ha! Take that sister!

Rickey parks three blocks away from Kitten's mother's restaurant, Kyla's Kitchen, and we all walk our separate ways after saying our newest sister slogan: "No male, no female, no money, not even death. Inseparable even after we take our last breath!"

*

"I can't breathe, Rickey. All I smell is seafood!" I say, as Rickey and I hide in the walk-in refrigerator section of Kitten's mom's kitchen.

"Just don't touch anything," Rickey says, now that I've confessed my allergies to him.

I feel my hand and throat beginning to itch as soon as he says these words to me. We have to get back in that cabinet Kitten's mom cleared out for us. She thinks we're doing an exclusive investigation on her chef's sanitary habits, so she was happy to help us, but I may have to blow our cover story if I can't stop itching.

"Oops!" I say as I accidentally touch a few of the jumbo shrimp that were in the bowl I just saved from hitting the floor.

"Emani, we still have a half hour to wait here before Payne even arrives. You cannot get us caught. When that last chef goes to the front, we have to make a run for it," Rickey says as he peeks outside the freezer.

He turns around and tells me to run, but not before looking at me with sheer horror. I run behind him, though he keeps looking back at me.

"What's wrong, Rickey?" I ask.

He hands me a mirror and I see that my eyes and lips have tripled in size. I have to listen to him lecture me about how I need to take allergy medicine before I think I will encounter seafood in the future, but I do listen, since he is going to risk being seen to try to get some medicine for me now from Kitten's mom.

"Are you sure she has some medicine?" Rickey asks, though I have told him that Kitten and I share the same allergy.

I know her mom has something to help me. I've always felt bad for Kitten, because so much of her family's cuisine contains seafood. It's no wonder she eats everything else she can.

When Rickey leaves, I listen for any type of noise, but I do not hear one word. I hope there is silence in my ear because Payton Payne has not arrived and not because our sound system is not working. I will personally kill the AV girls, Ciera and Darcy, if our audio is not working. If they have betrayed us, they will pay for their decisions. They pledged their loyalty to our cause. They claimed they wanted to be better people. For our sake, I hope they have truly become our allies.

Ten minutes later Rickey returns with some medicine. He reaches in his pocket and asks me if he can take my picture, but I do not allow him to document my hideous self. I can't even look at him right now. He isn't even supposed to have a phone, anyway.

"I'm sorry, Emani. I'm just teasing you. I don't really have my phone. You have nothing to fear. You're beautiful to me," Rickey says as he touches my super-sized smackers.

I should bite him with these large lips.

"Kiss me, Emani!" When he says this I lean toward him and plant my great big mouth on his.

We kiss until I finally hear Charlotte's voice clearly in my earpiece. The audio is working clearly. The AV Girls are on our side.

BATTLE OF THE BULLIES Emani

CHAPTER 29
Ebony
Bodyguards and Bathrooms

"I can't hear a thing. We need to get closer to the restaurant," I tell Tatyanna, as she tries to park in the tiniest parking space I've ever seen.

We are in her grandmother's minivan, so I am surprised that she can fit into the space. I wonder how we will get out. How are we going to be the getaway car if we can't get away? I hate parking in Chicago. We should have taken one of my daddy's compact cars, but he guards them like a pit bull guards his master.

Tatyanna prepares her props for when it is time for her to distract Payton Payne's bodyguards. Drama Queen Tatyanna is prepared to fake a seizure in Kitten's mother's restaurant while Charlotte is in the bathroom with the file. Then, Stephan can get the file of proof on the number one Dime from Charlotte through the bathroom window and then take it over to Eris to be copied.

Stephan should be on his way over to bathroom side of the building in exactly ten minutes. I hope Charlotte can convince Payton Payne to permit her to take the file with her to the restroom to look it over. This would have been easier if P.P. permitted us to have our phones.

CHAPTER 30

Eris
Copies and the Original

I'm bored. P.P. hasn't said anything to Charlotte and Kitten that we don't already know. Plus, why do I get stuck doing Charlotte's job? Who wants to make posters and yard signs in the middle of a mission? Not me.

Stephan hasn't stopped teasing me since we got here. Charlotte's mom is nice, but she really is making us work, because she doesn't know what we are up to at all. Charlotte promised that we would have a light, no-pressure day at this location because it is Sunday, but I guess everybody decided to wait to the last minute to make their copies for their Monday morning meetings, because I've made too many copies so far. Stephan and I have been copying since the moment we arrived.

"I'm leaving, Eris. Do you want to kiss me, just in case I do not come back?" Stephan says, as I throw some of Charlotte's mother's precious resumé paper at him.

"Just go get that file!" I say as I listen to Payton Payne softly tell Kitten about Dimes ten through two in my earpiece. We already know their order. Kylie gave us their true order and their nicknames when she was trying to prove her loyalty. Then, she helped us to recruit those runaway Dimes that we could reach. That's how we got the AV girls on our side. P.P. is wasting our time. She confirms what we already know.

10. Tatyanna Tyson-TNT...Recruited

9. Winter Gordon-Blaze

8. Shiani Chan-Bruiser

7. Brenda Agbayewa-Bandit

6. Ciera Gonzalez-Eyes…Recruited

5. Darcy Egan-Ears…Recruited

4. Vita Rowe-Psycho

3. Kylie Calderone-Fox…Recruited

2. Zyanne Jeffries-Robin Hood…Replaced by Kitten

We already know how they were recruited and what secrets Dime Number One used to blackmail each of them, too.

Wow! Now we did not know that Aesha King, Marisa Chu, Grace Vinson, and Teresa Peterson are still being trained to be future Dimes. I guess Dime Number One is still a bit desperate. I guess she believes she can replace runaways Kylie, Darcy, Ciera, and Tatyanna with them, or is it that she has four senior spots to fill once Vita, Shiani, Kylie, and she graduate?

Whatever Dime Number One's thinking is, I know that she has to be desperate, because those four girls may be willing, but they couldn't even beat Ebony in a knuckle contest. They wouldn't stand a chance against all four of us. In fact, if my memory is still accurate, I believe we have already beaten them literally in a fist fight. Dime Number One should give up on any hopes of her legacy lasting passed graduation.

CHAPTER 31
Emani
Reality TV

I repeat my words to my guy, "She hasn't said one word about the number one Dime, Rickey."

"My uncle says all we need is for her to admit to any act of violence," Rickey says as he kisses my neck.

His lips feel so nice against my now itch-free skin.

"Your uncle! You told Mr. Thomas about our plan, even after I asked you not to? He is retired from the case. Isn't he?" I ask as I push him away.

I hear Charlotte's voice again, so I believe phase one of our plan was a success. Charlotte is still breathing, so she must have given Payton Payne the file back after Stephan secretly copied it for us.

"Emani, I care about you. I couldn't just let you risk your safety like this. I wasn't going to tell him, but when Uncle Terrence called me this morning to tell me my aunt had gone into premature labor, I took it as a sign to tell him," Rickey says as he rubs my hand.

I let him kiss my hand, but I am very upset with Rickey Thomas.

"Mr. Thomas is not coming, is he? If Payton Payne senses any professionals are even in the near vicinity, she could suddenly become mute or violent, and we would never know who the number one Dime is, or what Payton really has destroyed." I try to stress how Rickey's actions could have ruined our plan.

Rickey does not answer my question, so I get very nervous. I am even more nervous when I hear someone tug at our secret cabinet's handles. Rickey and I try to silence ourselves, hoping they will go away. I wish we could become invisible.

When the door opens, we see Mrs. Johns. She pretends to look for something. Then, she directs her chef to another cabinet.

I am so grateful that she believes we are gathering secret footage on her workers. I give her the thumbs up to make her think I am actually doing the secret hidden camera exposé Kitten told her I was here to do, but I don't dare breathe until she closes both of the cabinet doors.

CHAPTER 32
Ebony
Silent Movie

The video finally decides to play after I get out and play with the antenna on Tatyanna's grandmother's minivan. All of our work to tint the windows to avoid blowing our cover, and I have to get out anyway.

"No sound! You have got to be kidding me!" I scream.

Then I honk the horn three times as loud as I can, hoping Tyson is listening. He claims he knows the sound of his grandmother's horn. We will soon see, or at least I hope we will soon see and hear. Maybe he isn't even paying attention anymore.

We didn't plan on Tatyanna really being taken away by an ambulance, but hey now we know she really is the bomb actress. I hope I don't regret using that word. I meant to say that Tatyanna is the best actress.

I also hope Ciera and Darcy are as good as they claim to be, too. Tatyanna was an excellent distraction with her fake seizure, but we need audio and visual proof. We need evidence. We need a confession. Come on, AV girls.

*

"Do you know her?" Payton Payne says to Kitten and Charlotte. She is showing them a picture of me. Oh, now the sound and video want to work! I have to have the worst luck in the world. I swear I do.

"Yes!" Kitten and Charlotte say, as Kitten pulls on her ear.

Eris says the ear pull is my cue to save Kitten from her conversation with Payton Payne. I was really hoping not to see her touch her ears.

"Is she here? Is Ebony Robertson here?" Payton says as she gestures for her men to move around the restaurant to their "positions." I can only assume she is sending them to look for me.

Kitten and Charlotte do not speak. They do not move.

"So there I was using all of my resources to find your number one Dime, when I happen upon a copy of your video yearbook. Who do you think I saw eating lunch with you two? I will give you four guesses," Payton says to my friends, who are visibly afraid, as I watch and listen on the AV girls' very clear, high-definition video.

I have to go get Charlotte and Kitten out of there. Before I can exit the minivan, a man in a flannel shirt and khakis stands at my tinted window. I am instantly afraid that he is one of Payton Payne's henchmen, until I realize it is Mr. Thomas's FBI friend. I have seen him countless times at Mr. Thomas's condo. However, I don't know who to trust, so I let the window down cautiously.

He hands me a photograph of Philip Payne and a necklace. Then, he quickly walks away. Should I follow him? Will he lead me to Mr. Thomas? Where is the FBI? Where are the police?

At this point, I wouldn't even mind Kitten's security guard pal from school showing up here. She says he used to be a policeman in New Orleans. He owed Kitten's grandmother a favor, so he promised to look after Kitten for her when he moved to Chicago. He's a security guard by day and a policeman by night. I wish he were here right now.

What am I supposed to do to defend us with a necklace and a photo? Am I supposed to give Payton a paper cut or an allergic reaction to fake jewelry? This is useless.

After Mr. FBI man walks away, I look around for Mr. Thomas, but I do not see him anywhere. I shake the necklace, hoping it is a secret weapon. When I realize I will have to go into the restaurant alone and unarmed, I place the necklace around my neck and head across the street to Kyla's Kitchen, totally terrified.

"Check her!" Payton says, as I glance around the restaurant.

All of the blinds have been closed. Payton has all the customers sitting at a booth and each table in the restaurant is guarded by one of her men or women. I thought those were real customers in the restaurant, but most of them work for P.P.

Kitten's mom just established her restaurant and we are already ruining it. Mrs. Johns just received such rave reviews and has five-star ratings online, but now we are wrecking any chance she had to be successful. Payton Payne is here. Who will ever want to eat here again?

After Payton's first guard gives me a clearance, I am checked by a woman who also tells Payton I have no weapons.

"You wanted me and here I am! Have a seat, Ms. Robertson," Payton says as she asks Kitten and Charlotte to move from her table.

I look over at my sisters, Charlotte's parents, Kitten's mother, Kitten, Ciera, Darcy, Kylie, and Charlotte, who are all seated in guarded booths. I feel a sense of guilt that I didn't have a plan B. I usually have a plan B and a plan C.

"I'm a bit disappointed in you Robertson girls. You waited until the night before to finalize your plan. You only gave yourself two hours to set up all of your equipment. You hide in plain sight. You have the brother of your alleged enemy to come to my table. Who came up with this ridiculous plan?" Payton says as she looks at me.

"Me! I planned it alone. It is all my fault," I say as I squirm a bit in my seat.

"Liar!" Payton says as she slides me a file and a zip drive.

I do not ask any questions. I simply open the file and insert the zip drive into the red computer she gives to me.

"Wow! Number One."

"Actually, she prefers to be called Hera, like the Queen of the Gods, but only Zyanne Jeffries knew that. Poor Zyanne was so close, but even she didn't know Hera's real name. Did you already know her name? You already knew, didn't you, Ebony Ellen "Bunny" Robertson? Didn't you?" Payton says, as she asks me to answer her question. I don't think it is too fortunate if a mass murderer knows your name or you know her identity and one weakness.

I nervously respond, "Yes!"

"I thought you probably did when I figured it out. I know it is always hard to accept the answer that is right in your face. Reana Powers does seem so ideal. I could see how you could hope it was not her, but believe me, I've met Ms. Powers in person, and she is everything you do not want to believe about her and much more. She said she was a fan of mine. Can you believe that? I was insulted. I am her exact opposite, don't you think?" The notoriously evil Payton Payne asks me a question that I cannot possibly answer truthfully at this moment.

One of Payton's people hands her a piece of paper, and Payton begins to laugh a sinister laugh. Luckily, I do not need to answer.

My lips choose to betray me. "I would have thought you would like Reana. She and you are quite the same. You're both evil," I say with a shaky voice before biting my bottom lip a bit.

"You think I'm evil?"

"No, I know you are. " I say expecting to be shot on the spot.

"No, I met evil last night. Her name is Ms. Reana Ileana Powers, and she is nothing like me. I help those who need help. I listen to those who no one listens to. I make sure no one will ever forget them. Those kids who the world will leave beaten, bruised, and bullied are protected by me. Ms. R.I.P. is nothing like me," Payton says as she starts eating the mouth-watering food Kitten's mom has prepared. Somehow, my mouth remains dry, so I take a sip of water using both of my shaking hands to hold the glass. I barely get a sip.

"Did the world forget your son?" She continues to eat until I pull Philip Payne's picture from my pocket and place it on the table.

"Ms. Robertson, they killed my son. They bullied him every day since the moment he went to school. He was never cute enough, smart enough, rich enough, strong enough, or funny enough. Though he was all those things to me. For them, he tried to change himself, but it was never enough. They beat him and left him to die. No one saw anything or heard anything, so I have learned not to feel anything for people like that, people who do not see the little people. The only thing I hate worse than a bully is those spectators who sit silently, watching the weak be bullied, praying that they will never have to take a stand," Payton says before asking me where I got the photograph.

I am very afraid to answer, so I do not. She probably already knows the answer, anyway.

"Do you think Mr. Thomas was that kind of man? Is that why you killed him?" I ask a question that actually makes her stop eating this time.

I know Mr. Thomas is faking his death, but I test her to see if she does in fact know all.

"I've never tried to kill that man. I respected him. I only tried to hurt him a bit in order to slow him down. He handled the death of his son with such grace. It inspired me. He reminded me of the person I could have become, had they not tried to not only kill my son, but then murder his character. I didn't raise a gang member. He was beaten for being different. not for being in any gang!" Payton screams for her people to remove the necklace that is around my neck, and I instantly tense up.

Is this woman psychic? I need this necklace. She just sort of confessed to trying to hurt Mr. Thomas. Please let there be a camera in that necklace. Where are the sirens? Where are the heroes to come save me? Where is Mr. FBI? Am I wrong? Are we alone?

Eris stands behind me, having just kicked Payton's sinful soldier in a most precious male body part for touching her when she reached for me.

"You knew about the necklace the entire time!" Emani, who has been dragged out and separated from her boyfriend, says as Payton Payne's men and women tell her that the place is surrounded.

"Of course I knew! I own the patent on the technology hidden in that necklace. Well, I unofficially own the patent. You won't find my name on it, but it wouldn't exist without me. I designed it. I bet you Mr. Thomas's FBI friend would be upset if he knew that. I bet you Mr. Turner would be upset, too," Payton Payne says, as Mr. Thomas's men come in from the front and rear with their guns exposed. Payton Payne takes another bite of Mrs. Johns' famous po' boy sandwich.

When the FBI agent approaches our table, I tell him that I believe Payton Payne has more she needs to confess to. He looks puzzled.

Payton Payne smiles at me. Then, she asks me where I believe Reana Powers is right now and who is protecting her.

I ask, "You didn't hurt her did you, Ms. Payne? She is a bully, but she is also just a teenage girl."

She looks directly at the camera in the hidden camera necklace that was once around my neck and says that she did not touch Reana Ileana Powers.

"I sent a few messages to the people she admitted to hurting in her secret Bully Bragbook blog, but I did not personally hurt her," Payton Payne says as she raises her right hand.

"What Bully Bragbook blog?"

I can't believe the smartest girl in school was stupid enough to write down everything she has done. Reana Powers had to sit face to face with Payton Payne and admit to everything she wrote. That had to be terrifying.

"Oh, Reana has the same problem as me. She writes everything down. She wrote down every dirty detail she did to you and your schoolmates and shared it and a few videos with several other bullies around the world. She and the other bullies battle with one another. It is sort of a competition, and Reana Powers was one of the best. She was . . . is like their queen. I just sent her blog, name, and location via text message and email to all those people she mentioned in her blog. I believe I may have mentioned that she is the number one Dime at C.I.A. I didn't want to disrespect the queen," Payton says as she takes another sip of her sweet tea and hands her wrists to the officers to cuff her.

Mr. Thomas's FBI friend asks Payton for Reana Powers's location, but she does not say a word to him, even when he jerks her arms a bit as he pulls her toward the restaurant exit.

"Ms. Payne, Reana Powers has hurt everyone at C.I.A. in some way. They could kill her. You sent her location to them in text messages AND emails? You posted her secret Bully Bragbook for everyone to see?" I ask. My sisters look at me with widened eyes.

"Yeah, you know me, I believe in being thorough!" Payton Payne says as she asks Kitten's mother for a piece of caramel cake to go.

Kyla Johns doesn't know whether to listen to Payton or the FBI. She decides to cut a slice of cake.

Mr. Thomas's FBI friend screams that he doesn't want Payton to have any. He says the FBI is in charge.

"WHERE IS SHE? Where is Powers?" He asks.

"She is in Pain . . . I hope, What is your name?" Payton Payne asks him.

"Agent Johnson! And I'm not afraid of you, Payne."

"Agent Johnson, please do not raise your voice at me. I could just blow this place up," Payton says, as she instructs her colleagues to show their detonators to Agent Johnson and his men. I don't need Tatyanna TNT Tyson here to tell me that this situation is not good. If one detonator could destroy a stage at C.I.A. and ruin our Valentine's fashion show, I can only imagine what a dozen will do. I am staring at a dozen detonators.

Mr. FBI releases Payton's handcuffs and allows her to eat a sliver of her caramel cake.

"I'm sorry, Ms. Payne. Where is Reana Powers?" Agent Johnson says in a much lower tone.

Payton pats her mouth with an embroidered Kyla's Kitchen napkin and smiles at me.

"Oh, Reanna's at school. She loves C.I.A. Perfect attendance. Perfect grade point average. Reana "I'm Perfect" Powers is at Chicago International Academy right now," Payton Payne says before she looks in my direction.

I try not to let her see how very afraid I am, but I do look her in her eyes.

"Time is running out, so you can ask me only one question, Ebony. It will be your last question to me, so make it a good one. You can ask me why Reana Powers said she did what she did when I interrogated her last night. You can ask me how I have been able to hide for so long, or how I feel about my brother, my son's uncle being in jail for three life sentences just for being loyal to me. What do you want to ask me, Ms. Robertson?"

*

I have a million questions in my mind prepared for Ms. Payton Payne. I have been having nightmares about our meeting for years. She helped Johnny Turner to murder my innocent friends for no reason at all. Even the guilty ones did not deserve to die for bullying or being bystanders. She killed a lot of innocent people. I have a sister that will never be the same.

I could ask her was it worth it. I could ask her why she took away Zachary Thomas. Why she took away my sister's voice? I could ask her questions, but it wouldn't change anything. Her damage is already done. Once you ball up a piece of paper, once you tear up that same piece of paper, you can never ever get it back to the way it once was no matter how hard you try to straighten it out

"Ms. Payne, I will ask my question, but first I need to tell you that Mr. Thomas is alive. Dr. Thomas told us that they faked his death in your last explosion, but he is definitely alive. He's actually expecting babies any day now. For some reason, I think you need to hear that from me."

Payton Payne smiles a less sinister, more sincere smile.

I guess I'll never know if she chose to confess because of Mr. Thomas or not.

"Thank you. So what is your question, Ebony Robertson?"

Emani stands up and walks over to me. She whispers in my ear, as Payton Payne says Emani's full name aloud. Emani hates her middle name.

I ask Emani's question. "Can we leave?"

Payton smiles and asks her crew to permit everyone who is not an agent or a detective to exit the restaurant as if their life depends on it.

When people begin to run, I walk past Agent Johnson, expecting to see fear in his eyes, but there is no fear there. I guess he wouldn't be an agent if he weren't prepared to die for a cause. He came here today to save our lives.

We all run south when we exit, since that was the original plan. Even those who are not familiar with the plan follow us south. When the spectators and clueless city dwellers outside see us run, they too begin to run. Chicago is known as a city where movies are made, but the onlookers can tell that we are running from a real threat. Payton Payne isn't a movie villain. She is real.

I am at least ten blocks away before I turn around. The big boom was back at block seven or eight, but I couldn't look back. I have learned to hate the sound of explosives.

CHAPTER 33
Eris
The Power of Payne

"**L**et's go to the school!" I say once I realize my sisters and I are finally free from Payton's grasp. Maybe Reana is still okay. Maybe the students ignored Payton Payne's messages. Reana targeted so many people, but maybe they have chosen to forgive or forget. Maybe they do not want or need revenge.

Ebony looks around frantically for a car to hotwire, though Darcy and Ciera's cars are right in front of us. I run over to Ebony and hold her tightly, trying to get her to relax. I know Dad taught us to hotwire for emergencies, but we can't steal a car right now.

"I'll drive!" Kitten's mom says, as Ciera tosses her the keys.

"I'll drive!" Tyson says, as Darcy tosses him her keys.

Charlotte and her parents, Kylie, Ciera, and Darcy decide to stay here. I don't think any of them are prepared to face Reana Powers if she is alive. They say they are going to find a way to check on Tatyanna at the hospital.

I think of Tatyanna as I look through Reana's now-posted Bully Bragbook file with tears in my eyes. I read a blog Reana wrote about her.

Bully Bragbook

Okay, I must admit my number ten is my weakest link. The others were at least a challenge to control. She still believes in fairytales. If she were not useful, I would discard her like Tuesday's trash. You must remember to keep someone in your top ten who will do whatever you say, whenever you say it because they are merely afraid of what you might do. I know my number ten's every weakness, simply because she told them to me with her own mouth. Always listen. Always observe.

She is the type who never had a mother's love, so I knew to simply show concern for her. She confided her every secret to me without even a threat. Number ten believes I am her best friend, because she wants it to be true. She would never want to admit that she told her deepest, darkest secrets to a stranger. She doesn't know me. She only knows what I allow her to know, and I only tell her what I know she wants to hear. Always remember that you are a different person to each of your top ten. You may be their enemy, their best friend, or their protector. You may have to be all three.

Yours truly,

Hera

"Did she write about us?" Ebony asks.

"She wrote about everybody!" I say as I read one of Reana's earliest blogs.

Bully Bragbook,

I have never failed at anything I have done. This will be my greatest accomplishment. You all talk of the type of behaviors that remind me of a time long gone, when people stole lunch money and met after school for battles. You must learn to think outside of the box. How can you challenge yourself? I know that I am the smartest person at my school. I know that my family is the richest, but being smart and rich didn't keep me from being bullied in the past. The only way you can keep from being bullied is to become the biggest bully. The girls and boys at this school will fear me. I will never have to worry about being anything less than number one. If there is anyone who thinks they can battle me, I welcome the competition.

Prepared for battle,

Number One Hera

"I can't believe the bullies write what they do down and compare and contrast. They have videos and pictures in these comments. They give each other cruel, twisted advice. This is sick. I can't believe the bullies rank one another. This is just wrong," I say, as I watch Ebony closely. She is unusually quiet and distant. I cannot afford to have another sister break down.

CHAPTER 34

Emani
Cell Phones and C.I.A.

"Is that Alexis up there on the roof with Reana?" I ask Kitten as we pull up to C.I.A. We all look up through the crowd of people on the lawn at my sister and our biggest enemy on the roof.

"What's going on?" I ask a boy with a bat for a bit of information, but he is too filled with rage to answer me.

Kitten's mother begins asking people in the crowd if she can use their phone to call her husband.

"Your big sister asked the crowd to calm down, but that only angered them more. They want to see Reana fall," Tyra Jacobs says as she records the action with her phone.

I overhear someone say, "Alexis gave a great speech, but I think she should bring Reana down here and let us show her how it feels to get jumped!"

Reana Powers jumps off of the roof of C.I.A.

*

I do not look down at the ground. I watch my sister and Jeremy hold each other on the roof. The crowd is silent.

I hear many people begin to whisper that they see movement, so I walk toward where Reana fell.

Ebony and Eris stop me when the crowd begins to run away. They leave only because of the police sirens and the news helicopters.

"We have seen enough pain for a lifetime. Let's go home!" Ebony says as she turns me away from where Reana Powers' body most likely is laying.

As we are leaving, we are stopped by FBI Agent Johnson.

"How?"

"She let us go, too. Payton Payne gave us ten seconds to exit the building. I used a few of them trying to convince her not to push that button, not to push any of those detonators, but Payton Payne always finishes what she starts," Agent Johnson says as he hands me a piece of paper that he says is from Payton Payne.

"It was her last request, so I am giving it to you only because she is officially gone! She wants you to give it to Terrence," Mr. Thomas's FBI friend, Agent Johnson, says as he walks toward the suicide scene.

He tells me that he already read Payton's letter.

"Mr. Thomas is at the hospital with his wife and children by now. Let's just take a peek at that letter. It couldn't hurt," Eris says.

I consider opening the note from Payton, until I hear Alexis voice behind me. It is so wonderful to hear her voice.

"Reana refused to apologize. I still can't believe that it was her," Jeremy says as he hugs and kisses Alexis.

"So do we have to stay and make statements to the police, or can we leave?" I ask as I see the news reporters approaching.

They are a little late. The only news helicopter here to see the jump was Channel 3. I'm sure they will replay that footage over and over again. It is sad. Heroes don't make the news as much as those who choose to be criminals.

I hope they don't say her name. She doesn't deserve the fame. And it just may encourage someone else to do the same thing. It is the Philip Paynes of the world that need our attention.

* * *

We manage to maneuver our three vehicles through the heavy traffic. Tyson is actually a superb driver, but even he can barely keep up with Jeremy on that motorcycle.

"Is that Dad?" Eris says as she points toward what looks like our father's newest vehicle.

When the vehicle does a U-turn and begins to follow us, I am sure it is our parents. Uh oh! They were supposed to be at my Aunty Jay's house by now. She is supposed to host our monthly family dinner tonight. Dad speeds by us telling us to follow him. I watch him pass Kitten's mother and Jeremy.

No one in the car has a cell phone, but I wish we did, because I would like to know where we are going.

"Whose great idea was it for us not to carry our phones, anyway?" I ask before I remember that is was mine.

Payton had eyes everywhere. I didn't know if she controlled satellites, too. Plus, I didn't want to have any distractions, and I definitely did not want to have anything vibrating while I was hiding in that cabinet.

CHAPTER 35
Ebony
Room 3333

I cannot hide the truth from my mother any longer. I already know she can see that I am an emotional wreck right now. I could have had us all killed.

Mom squeezes me and my sisters after asking us if we are all right. Before we can all answer, she begins to scream at us for lying to her. One minute she is calling me her baby and the next minute she is yelling at me.

"If Doc Thomas hadn't called your Aunty Jay's, I would have never known. I can't believe you stole our cell phones. Which one of you has our phones?" Mom asks.

I point to my twin brothers' superhero book bags. I quickly admit that I put the phones in their bags as we were leaving the waffle house earlier. They rarely use them anyway, especially on family game night.

We are one of the only families alive with a house phone. My great-grandmother insists that we have it in case all of the world's cell phone towers fall and we need to make a call to the police. It takes my mother three years to send a text message and Dad really only uses his for car research. They both still ask me to post pictures for them. My poor parents are allergic to social media.

*

We all apologize to our parents.

"You could have been killed!" Dad says, just as a hospital security guard walks past us. We hug tightly.

"I taught you girls to be fearless. I taught you to do the right thing. I taught you to take risks, but I didn't know you would use those lessons against me for the rest of my life," Dad says, as we start walking toward the hospital.

He stops and turns to Alexis. "What did you just say? Did you say something, Alexis?"

"I said I am sorry, Daddy. I am the oldest. I should have been more responsible," Alexis says, as my father and mother just stand at the hospital entrance in complete shock to hear their oldest daughter's voice again.

The hospital doors are motion censored, so they stay open since there are too many of us standing here.

Aunty Jay and my mother do not speak, but they both have wet eyes.

"Say something else . . . anything else!" Aunty Jay says, as I admire the cute little sundress she is wearing. Even I would wear that dress. I usually love my blazers and skirts, but she looks great.

As Aunty Jay stands next to my mother, I can truly see the resemblance. They are both beautiful women with curves that would drive any man crazy. Uncle Joe stands behind her.

"Something else. Anything else!" Alexis says, and Aunty Jay giggles.

Mom, Dad, Aunty Jay, and Alexis start chatting, but the rest of us move inside after some visitors behind us impolitely ask us to stop blocking the entrance.

When I get to the desk, I ask to see Dr. Thomas. The lady at the desk looks at the crowd behind me and tells me that they only allow two visitors at a time at this hospital. She also asks me what Doctor Thomas's first name is so she can look up her room number. My sisters don't know her name either. We call her Doc, Dr. T. or Dr. Thomas. Mom even calls her Doc. The person who probably knows her name is outside catching up for two years of lost time.

"Her name is Dr. LaTara Thomas. She works at this hospital," Jeremy says as the receptionist suddenly remembers who Dr. T. is, and her room number.

She hands me two passes. Doesn't she see the army of people standing here? I begin to explain how ridiculous the hospital's policy is to her, but she gets on the phone.

"Who's going to go in?" Eris asks.

"You should go, Emani since you have the evil one's piece of paper. Mom can have the other pass," I say, as my mother finally walks up. I hand Mom a visitor pass and tell her that we will wait for her and Emani to return.

Mom makes a remark about Emani's almost normal, but obviously swollen face once she can really see it under the hospital's fluorescent light. Then, she asks why Emani's lips are swollen. After explaining about Emani's battle with her allergies earlier, I tell Mom about the visitor pass situation.

Mom smiles and walks over to the desk. I watch her fold her arms as the receptionist tells her something. Then, she says a few words to the receptionist.

"Okay, let's all go up to room 3333. The elevators are this way," Mom says a few minutes later.

Then, my mother hands me her visitor's pass. I do not ask any questions; I just follow my determined mother onto a very crowded elevator.

When we finally get to Dr. Thomas's floor, Mr. Thomas sits beside Dr. T.'s bed, holding her hand. I do not see the babies so I get a little nervous, but, like them, we came two weeks early and we are here and healthy as can be.

CHAPTER 36

Eris
Baby, Baby, Baby

"**W**hat are you doing out here?" Aunty Jay says when she notices that I am not in Dr. Thomas's room with the rest of our clan.

"Too nervous! I peeked in there and those babies are too tiny!" I say as I lean on the wall. Doc T. was so huge, I thought those babies would be ten pounds each, not five.

Stephan steps out again to check on me, and I just wave at him to leave me alone. I am never having any children, so he can quit smiling at me.

"So what are you going to do when my baby comes?" Aunty Jay says as she lifts up the crocheted shawl she is wearing over her sundress and rubs her small stomach.

"Your what?" I ask, as Aunty Jay puts her finger to her mouth and swears me to secrecy. Wow! I'm going to have another cousin or cousins.

"Sometimes babies come early. They come when they are ready to come. Babies are a lot like my nieces. They have their own little minds and they do things in their own time!" Aunty Jay says as she wraps her arm around me.

"Well, maybe I can hold the Thomas babies, but I will not kiss them. I don't want to hurt them," I say to my pretty and pregnant aunt. I never thought she would have children.

Emani comes out of the room smiling a one hundred-watt smile.

"You should come hold Elizabeth!" Emani says.

"She named the girl after you? That's not fair. Why not Ellen or Ella or Dieona? Look at how ugly you are. Is she sure she wants the baby to have your middle name?"

"Whatever! Dr. Thomas says she put all of our middle names into a hat and Mr. Thomas pulled my name. Her full name is Elizabeth Alexis Thomas. Doesn't that sound good?" Emani brags. Why can't life ever be fair?

We walk into Dr. Thomas's room and I congratulate her on her twin bundles of stress. Mr. Thomas's already wide smile widens as he kisses his wife on her forehead.

"Do you want to hold him?" Mr. Thomas says as he offers me his son.

I'm hoping this one is named after me. Maybe he will be a great athlete. I'll take Eric because it is close to the name Eris, or it could be Sire which is my name backwards. Please don't let Emani be the only one with a namesake. Alexis I understand, but Emani. Ugh!

"Don't I need to wash my hands or sanitize myself?" I say as I walk toward the soap dispenser instead of Mr. Thomas.

I think Mr. Thomas notices that I am taking a long time in the bathroom, because I hear him call my name with his deep tenor voice.

"Okay, so who am I holding? What do you think of the name Sire? That is my name backwards, Mr. Thomas," I ask as I look down into the warmest brown eyes I've seen in my entire life. The baby I hold smiles at me. It is a gummy smile that is filled with innocence and potential. I rub his faint ebony hair.

"You are holding Jonathan Phillip Thomas!" Doctor Thomas says as she looks at Mr. Thomas and smiles.

Mr. Thomas nods at her as if he, too, has heard the name for the first time from her mouth.

"I like the sound of that name, but let's give him a nickname. How about . . . Sire or, ummh, Smiley!"

CHAPTER 37
Emani
By Any Other Name

We triplets got our nicknames because Alexis could not say our names correctly, so I became Money instead of Emani, Ebony became Bunny and Eris was the only name she could say though she added an extra s at the end some times. There is sometimes a story behind a person's name.

I smile when Doctor Thomas agrees to fulfill Payton Payne's final wish of naming her son after Payton's son Phillip, but inside, I am a bit nervous for that baby boy. If I had known that Payton Payne was not only going to apologize for her deeds, but was also going to ask the Thomas's to name their unborn child after her deceased son, I may have accidentally lost that note because, like many people, I feel there is power in a name.

Dad says that some ancestors believed that when you name a child, you seal their destiny. I cannot help but wonder what the future for a child named after two deeply wounded people will be. Now I know that Dr. Thomas and Mr. Thomas are truly trying to honor the lives of Johnny Turner and Phillip Payne, but will their child be an honorable person? Both Johnny and Phillip were bullied to death. What is the destiny of Jonathan Philip Thomas?

AFTERWORD

Prom is postponed for a week after Reana Iliana Powers's failed suicide attempt to jump off the roof of the school building, despite Alexis's attempt to convince Reana to accept the consequences of her actions instead of taking her own life. When the junior-senior prom does occur, Jeremy Jackson Sparks and Alexis Robertson are given "Bravery Under Fire" medals for trying to save Reanna's life. Jeremy is then crowned prom king.

Jeremy Jackson's band EPITOME performs for a high-energy crowd at the prom. Emani Elizabeth "Money" Robertson and her date Rickey Thomas are caught sneaking into the prom by Principal Wells, but they are allowed to stay, despite Rickey being a college student with an expired high school ID. Katherine "Kitten" Johns and Timothy "Tiny" Armstrong are declared cutest couple at the prom.

Stephan Miles, Eris Robertson, Dylan Gibson, Charlotte Jericho, Emani Robertson, Rickey Thomas, Tony Tyson and Ebony Robertson lead a group line dance that Charlotte and Emani both created call the Rock and Roll. The rest of the prom dancers do the Rock and Roll, too. Principal Wells and Dean Norton get on the floor and rock their hips side to side, spin, roll to the front, back, left and right with the rest of C.I.A.'s faculty, staff, and students.

The Dimes are absent from prom.

Unlike the prom, C.I.A.'s graduation attracts a great deal of media attention when the newspapers discover that Reana Powers is not the only C.I.A. student who will not walk across the stage. News reporters ask graduation attendees for details on Reana Powers and the Dimes' organization. Though they do not mention Reana's name in the press for fear of copycat crimes and threats made on her life, they do continue to seek facts about her malicious deeds at C.I.A.

Though all of the Dimes officially graduate from high school, Reana Powers, Shiani Chan, Vita Rowe, and Kylie Calderone are not permitted to receive their diplomas on a C.I.A. stage. Their diplomas are sent in the mail to their parents.

After receiving Reana Powers's diploma in the mail, her parents receive the news that she has come out of her coma asking for them. They are told she has a concussion, injured her spinal cord, quite a few broken bones, and will require more stitches. Reana Powers is told that she will never walk again. Powers unsuccessfully attempts to mix cold medicine with her prescription medicine in order to create a fatal concoction for herself. After another attempt on her own life while under observation in the psychiatric hospital, Powers's parents have her involuntarily committed for her own safety. Eighteen-year-old Reana Powers's parents attempt to have her deemed unfit to testify, but are told that her Bully Bragbook blogs will be used in her trial, whether she chooses to evoke her Fifth Amendment rights or not.

All ten Dimes are investigated based on information discovered in Reana Powers's blogs. Of the ten, four face criminal charges for attempted murder, arson, conspiracy, and assault/battery. These four are Reana Powers, Zyanne Jeffries, Winter Gordon, and Vita Rowe. Brenda Agbayewa's theft charges are brought against her by outside sources and not C.I.A.

The Dimes await trial and sentencing for their crimes.

Further investigation brings up several offences against the Dimes that include graffiti, hate crimes, drug distribution, harassment, cybercrime, and bullying. Many witnesses from C.I.A. freely give statements to the investigators.

Because of testimony from anonymous sources, Kylie Calderone, Ciera Gonzalez, Darcy Egan, and Tatyanna Tyson are fined, placed under supervision, and required to do 365 service hours to the community.

Dimes-in-training Aesha King, Marisa Chu, Grace Vinson, and Teresa Peterson are given ten service hours to the community and are suspended for the first ten days of the school year for participating in Dime hazing rituals. Their attempts to restart the Dimes are extinguished before they can even host their first meeting.

Princeton Payne discovers the news about his sister Payton Payne through a letter she wrote to him prior to her suicide. His sources confirm the birth of Mr. Thomas and Dr. Thomas's son named after his nephew Philip. An imprisoned Princeton Payne anonymously donates a substantial amount of his family's fortune to Mr. Thomas's anti-bullying/peace, bravery, and love movement in honor of his sister and nephew. The money is used to continue Mr. Turner and Mr. Thomas's fight against bullying across the globe.

With help from an anonymous donation, Mrs. Johns's restaurant is rebuilt and attracts quite a crowd from tourists, due to its association with the notorious Payton Payne and its delicious New Orleans cuisine.

Mrs. Johns hires the girls to work for her to make some summer cash. The girls enjoy three summers of working together for Mrs. Johns. The money they earn is put into a savings account until the girls can decide what to do with it, despite Emani Robertson's desire to spend it all.

A week before the first day of the triplets' senior year in high school, Eric Robertson, father of Alexis, Ebony, Emani, Eris, Tevin, and Kevin Robertson receives a call from his frustrated sister-in-love, asking if he has room for one more person in his home. After their conversation, Eric Robertson decides to invite his nephew to move into the overcrowded Robertson household.

Robertson's nephew has earned himself a bad reputation in his hometown of Atlanta, Georgia, but Eric Robertson believes a change of environment just may keep him out of trouble. Tre' Robertson moves into Alexis Robertson's former bedroom on the third day in January during winter break. He is suspended for fighting a girl on the seventh day of school.

When Tre' becomes a student at C.I.A., he soon discovers that the Robertson sisters have formed an organization of their own called D.I.V.A.S. (Daughters Inspiring Values and Sisterhood.) The organization is open to females only.

The D.I.V.A.S organization attracts many girls at C.I.A because of its principles of tolerance, service, scholarship, respect, and purity. It also attracts the attention of many boys at C.I.A for the same reason.

Senior D.J. Morgan starts a secret society called M.A.D. (Men Against Divas). Tre' Robertson is one of the many boys to join.

Can the D.I.V.A.S. and M.A.D coexist on C.I.A's campus, or will another clash begin to disrupt the newfound harmony at C.I.A?

Now that the battle of the bullies has ended, will the battle of the sexes begin?

*Please be sure to read the final novel in the
Triplet Trilogy from Fenyx Blue entitled Royalty.*